THE CONUNDRUM OF A CLERK

LINDA RAE SANDE

This is a work of fiction. The events and characters described herein are imaginary and are not intended to refer to specific places or living persons. The opinions expressed in this manuscript are solely the opinions of the author and do not represent the opinions or thoughts of the publisher. The author has represented and warranted full ownership and/or legal right to publish all the materials in this book.

The Conundrum of a Clerk

Copyright © 2018 by Linda Rae Sande

V1.5

ISBN: 978-1-946271-14-3

All rights reserved.

Cover photograph © Period Images

Cover art by Justin Phillips, Yellowstone Graphics

All rights reserved - used with permission.

Edited by Katrina Teele Fair

This book may not be reproduced, transmitted, or stored in whole or in part by any means, including graphic, electronic, or mechanical without the express written consent of the publisher except in the case of brief quotations embodied in critical articles and reviews.

https://www.lindaraesande.com

*To a great team—Sara V., Kate O., Barbara R., Virginia S.,
and Jaylene S.—all my thanks!*

ALSO BY LINDA RAE SANDE

The Daughters of the Aristocracy

The Kiss of a Viscount

The Grace of a Duke

The Seduction of an Earl

The Sons of the Aristocracy

Tuesday Nights

The Widowed Countess

My Fair Groom

The Sisters of the Aristocracy

The Story of a Baron

The Passion of a Marquess

The Desire of a Lady

The Brothers of the Aristocracy

The Love of a Rake

The Caress of a Commander

The Epiphany of an Explorer

The Widows of the Aristocracy

The Gossip of an Earl

The Enigma of a Widow

The Secrets of a Viscount

The Widowers of the Aristocracy

The Dream of a Duchess

The Vision of a Viscountess

The Conundrum of a Clerk

CHAPTER 1

A VISITOR TO A VISCOUNT'S BEDCHAMBER

May 31, 1818, Bostwick House in Mayfair

The sounds of a dying fire and the faraway footfalls of servants pulled George from a blissful sleep. He didn't want to open his eyes. He was dreaming his wife was kissing him as his children played nearby. Their giggles had him grinning when the kiss ended. When he turned to discover just what had them making such happy sounds, he found several had lined up on the lawn and were peeking at him from between fingers held over their eyes.

Having been caught kissing their mother, Elizabeth, George turned in their direction and gave a deep bow, which resulted in another round of giggles before the children ran off and continued their play.

Despite their happiness, George frowned in his semi-conscious state. He had only fathered two babes—at least, so far—and his children were too young to be running about as these children were doing. His son, David, was only two, and his daughter, Christina, was barely a month old, so he knew he was dreaming. But the niggling feeling that something—or someone—was watching him finally had him opening his eyes.

A pair of round, blue eyes rimmed in dark gray and topped by long, curled lashes stared at him. The hair above the lashes was dark and curled in a haphazard fashion, and two chubby fists gripped the edge of the bed linens where they dropped over the edge of the bed. The eyes lit up in delight, and incomprehensible words came tumbling out of a mouth hidden from George's view.

"Well, good morning," George murmured, a smile lighting his own face before he realized two things at once.

His son, David, was in his bedchamber.

For his son to be *in* his bedchamber meant the toddler had learned to work a door handle. "You escaped from the nursery, didn't you?" George whispered. At any moment, he expected hurried footfalls to come from the hall as the nurse, Mrs. Foster, raced about in search of the heir to the Bostwick viscountcy.

From behind him, his wife, Elizabeth, stirred and was soon turned so her front was pressed against his back. "Who are you talking to?" she mumbled, before she had an elbow beneath her torso and could see over George's shoulder.

The toddler let out an excited shriek at the sight of his mother, and he let go his grip on the edge of the bed in favor of lifting his arms in the air in anticipation of being lifted onto the bed. George did the honors, snaking an arm beneath the gown-clad boy's bottom and pulling him up and onto his body. He rolled to lie on his back as Elizabeth backed up a bit to give him the space, her face betraying the humor she felt at seeing her son in their bedchamber.

"You know what this means?" she asked, as George settled the boy onto the front of his body.

"He knows how to open a door," he replied as he turned his attention to his wife of nearly three years. Her hair, dark auburn curls that matched those of their son, were sleep-tousled and surrounded a face he still found to be the most beautiful in all of England.

Or at least of those he had paid witness to during his four-and-thirty years.

Elizabeth blinked, her aquamarine eyes disappearing for a fraction of a second before she said, "It means he knows how to escape the nursery," she countered with a hint of concern.

David struggled a bit, his knees bending with his intention of crawling to his mother. George let out an "oof" before he moved to pass the tyke to Elizabeth. "Have a care, David. I haven't yet fathered my spare heir," he warned in mock annoyance. But David was already happily atop his mother's body, his mouth attached to a bare breast. "The little bugger!" George added in dismay. "He didn't even ask!"

Elizabeth let out a musical laugh, although its sound was nearly swallowed up by the velvet curtains that surrounded the bed on three sides. The open side faced the fireplace and the rest of the bedchamber. "Mrs. Foster is no doubt in a panic," she scolded her son. "You probably ran off whilst she changed Christina's nappy." At the mention of a nappy, she felt David's gown and was relieved to find it was dry. "Right after she changed yours."

At the sound of George clearing his throat, Elizabeth turned her attention on him. "What is it?"

"Christina is right here, my sweeting. You brought her to bed with us last night," he reminded her as he pulled the sleeping infant from the nest of pillows he had created for her when Elizabeth fell asleep nursing her.

"Oh, I remember now," Elizabeth replied, giving her daughter a quick glance. "I fed her a few hours ago, I think."

George glanced in the direction of the fireplace, stunned to find the hands on the mantle clock showing it was nearly eleven o'clock. "So much for attending church," he murmured. "I cannot believe I slept so late."

Well, he could, actually, given what he and his wife had been doing for most of the night. He had gladly abided the physician's recommendation that he abstain from sexual congress with his wife until his daughter was a month old, mostly because Elizabeth had exhausted him in that regard for the entire month leading up to Christina's birth.

With David, she had discovered frequent couplings helped alleviate the aches and pains of pregnancy, so George had happily accommodated her every request then as well as when she was expecting their latest.

The birth of Christina had almost been a relief, for he felt as if he needed as much time to recover as his wife. After a couple of weeks, though, he found his desire had returned along with a need to pleasure his wife.

Apparently she was of a similar mind a fortnight ago. Having pleasured her in ways not requiring intercourse, George now recalled how Elizabeth had moved atop him and captured his manhood between her engorged breasts. Rubbing him against the velvet-soft skin had him rock-hard and climaxing within a minute. In the blissful aftermath, she had kissed the tip of him and finally settled her head into the small of his shoulder.

He found her still there the following morning. The very thought of it now had the bed linens tenting halfway down his body. He rather hoped she wouldn't notice.

She noticed.

"George," Elizabeth said in voice meant to scold. She was grinning, though, when he rolled his eyes and sighed.

"I cannot help it, my love." He would have continued to ply her with words of adoration, but a knock sounded at the door.

Probably someone in search of David, he thought before he inhaled. "What is it?" he called out. Reluctantly, he sat up and reached for his dressing gown. The dark velvet robe had fallen from the bed and was now in a heap on the carpet below. He pulled it on, got up from the bed, and walked around the end of it to find his butler, Elkins, standing just inside the door. The butler's expression indicated puzzlement.

"There's a Mr. Streater calling for you, sir," Elkins replied, one brow furrowed as his eyes darted about the room.

George blinked. He expected the butler was helping in the search for David, so word that his friend, Theodore M. Streater, was paying a call came as a surprise. "Does he seem in good spirits?" he asked, wondering if something was amiss. The two fenced at least once a week at Angelo's Academy, so he figured something must have happened since their last match on the pisté.

"He does not, sir. 'Bereft' is how I would describe him on this day. He, in fact, didn't expect to find you at home but said he would be willing to wait until you returned. I believe he thinks you are attending church." The butler glanced around again. "Sir. When I arrived, your door was... open," he said carefully. "Is there any chance Master David has paid a call?"

Even though he was concerned at hearing Teddy Streater was "bereft," George couldn't help a slight chuckle. "He's with his mother," he said in a slightly loud voice, wanting Elizabeth to know her son's absence from the nursery had indeed been noticed. "Helping himself to an early luncheon. Pray tell, how long has it been since he went missing?"

Elkins eyes widened a bit. "Oh, no more than ten minutes, I should think. Mrs. Foster is beside herself with worry, though."

Ten minutes? "No doubt," George acknowledged. In that amount of time, the toddler could have visited every room on the first floor, bounced himself down the stairs on his bottom, run to the kitchens, and been back up the two flights of stairs to the nursery. "Please let her know Master David is safe before bringing Mr. Streater here. I should be dressed enough to receive him by then."

His eyes darting to one side, Elkins said, "I can return and assist you if you'd like, sir."

George shook his head. "That won't be necessary, but do

bring a tea tray, some coffee, and a cup of chocolate for Lady Bostwick." He gave a nod to Elkins' quick bow before the butler took his leave. He was on his way back to his bed when Elizabeth appeared from around the curtains.

"Do you think Mr. Streater has lost his position?" she asked, her face displaying concern. She lifted the sleeping David to her shoulder and settled him there before turning her attention back to George.

Her husband swallowed, his manhood reacting when her dressing gown briefly opened to reveal her nakedness. "I rather doubt it. When we fenced a few days ago, he said he had been promoted to Head of Clerks at the bank," George replied as he hurried to gather up some clothes.

Elizabeth was the reason Teddy had acquired his position as a clerk at the Bank of England. She had begun her charity, Lady E's 'Finding Work for the Wounded,' to assist returning soldiers in their quest for employment, and she had chosen him to be her first client.

Having lost his right arm during the war, Teddy was deemed unsuitable to return to his old position as a clerk— even though he wrote his numbers with his left hand and could perform all the duties required of the position.

When Elizabeth learned there was a clerking position open at the Bank of England—the very position he had held until he left for a second stint with the British army—she bribed the bank manager on Teddy's behalf. As a result of her intervention, Teddy was rehired. A few days later, she saw to it he had a wooden arm he could wear inside the sleeve of his topcoat.

"You're welcome to stay and greet Mr. Streater, of course," George said as he bussed her on the cheek. "Although I would suggest you wear something less... revealing, or I fear I shall require a quick tumble."

Elizabeth's eyes widened. "Oh!" she said as she used her free hand to grip the edges of her dressing gown together.

Then she realized he was teasing, gave him a quelling glance, and passed the sleeping toddler off to George. She hurried off to the dressing room. "Don't let Mr. Streater leave before I have a chance to see him," she called out. "Oh, and Christina is still sleeping. And although I rather like the little bed you made for her, I put her in the bassinet."

George glanced around and finally settled David onto the settee, positioning the boy so he couldn't roll off. Managing to pull on his breeches, stockings, a pair of boots, and a shirt before the expected knock at the door, George found a waistcoat at the same time he said, "Come!"

Pulling it on, he remembered Elkins' comment about his visitor seeming bereft. He schooled his features into a sober expression as he buttoned up the waistcoat and turned to face the opening door.

CHAPTER 2
A VISITOR TO A VISCOUNT'S APARTMENTS

A moment later

Elkins announced his visitor, and Teddy Streater gingerly stepped into the room. His attention was directed to the area where a settee and chairs were set up around the fireplace.

"Good morning," George said, not intending to startle his visitor. But Teddy jumped and immediately turned to regard him with surprise.

"Damn! I never knew you had such a large... salon?" he half-asked as his gaze swept the long room from left to right. He allowed a low whistle of appreciation before giving his head a shake. From the way he gripped his pocket watch in his good hand and dipped his head, he seemed anxious.

"Apartment," George finished for him. "It used to be three rooms before I had the townhouse refurbished," he explained. "The rooms were entirely too small, though." Indeed, the number of doors into and between each room— a study, a salon, and a bedchamber—chopped up a space made claustrophobic by dark wall coverings and even darker wood paneling. "Now it's where I spend time with my family," he explained as he waved an arm to the fireplace that had at one time heated the salon. "Have a seat. Tea is on the way," he added as he finished buttoning his waistcoat.

"I apologize. I hope I didn't wake you," Teddy said as he took one of the wingback chairs.

"You didn't, actually. My son managed that when he escaped the nursery this morning," he replied as he pointed over to the settee.

Teddy's eyes widened when he spotted the toddler on the settee. "That's him? I haven't seen the little bugger since his christening," he said as he gingerly moved toward the settee. "Got his mother's hair, he does."

George frowned, rather surprised at how much time had passed since the christening. *Two years!* "Elizabeth is in her bedchamber. She wishes to see you, so you have to stay until she's finished dressing," he warned, one eyebrow arching up. At Teddy's sudden look of alarm, George added, "You needn't look so worried. She'll be quick." He paused. "Is something amiss? Elkins said you looked—"

"My mother died yesterday," Teddy interrupted.

George blinked as he struggled to remember if he had ever met the woman. "Jesus, Teddy. I'm so sorry," he said in a whisper. "Where... where was she?"

"At the school," Teddy replied with a nod. "Well, in her apartment at Warwick's," he clarified, referring to Warwick's Grammar and Finishing School. Agnes Streater had been the headmistress of the boarding school for over thirty years. "She seems to have died in her sleep. She was... old," he added with a shrug. "One of the instructors found her and had a note sent to me right away. I was going to take her to church this morning," he added as his eyes suddenly brightened with unshed tears.

George took a breath. "I'd forgotten she was still working there," he said. Teddy rarely spoke of his mother, but then he was past thirty and long out of the family house. "Does your brother know?"

Teddy nodded. "He does, although..." He paused, not about to share how his older brother had reacted to learning of their mother's fate. "The two of them never got along. Michael was embarrassed by her position, I think," he added, *sotto voce*. But then, Baron Michael Streater didn't wish to have anything to do with Teddy, either, as if he thought his younger brother was waiting with bated breath for him to die so that he could inherit his title.

George winced, remembering how contrary the older brother could be. Although the man had finally married, it was possible that Teddy might one day be a baron and join George in Parliament. "Do you need... help? Do you need anything?"

Teddy shook his head. "I've just come from the solicitor's office."

Furrowing a brow, George was about to say he was surprised a solicitor would be working on a Sunday when he realized the man was probably Jewish. "So, you've already seen to her..."

"She was rich, George. Very rich."

George blinked again, his brows furrowing. "I thought she was the headmistress at Warwick's." *We are speaking of Mrs. Streater?* he almost asked, well aware that many young ladies, mostly daughters of London's wealthy cits, had at one time come under her strict thumb.

"She was," Teddy acknowledged with a nod. "And that's all I ever thought she was," he added as his breathing seemed to quicken.

"So, your father left her some blunt—"

"My father left us in *debt*," Teddy countered.

"So... she inherited something from an aunt or a—"

"She *owned* Warwick's," Teddy stated with a nod. "And she's left it all to me."

At this bit of news, George frowned before he was aware that Elizabeth had come into the room. He got to his feet as she nodded to Teddy's deep bow, amazed at how quickly she had managed to dress and pin up her hair—even if she did have a lady's maid to help. He wondered how much she had overheard.

"Oh, Mr. Streater, it's so good to see you again," Elizabeth gushed as she hurried forward. Instead of offering her hand, she stepped up and kissed him on the cheek.

The man's face reddened before he noticed George's smirk. "You as well, my lady," he managed to say. His gaze immediately went to the toddler. "He's already quite the strapping young lad," he added, wondering if Elizabeth could even carry the toddler.

"Two stone at two years," she replied proudly. "And he adores his little sister. She's sleeping at the moment or I would introduce you. I do hope they're treating you well at the bank?"

"Very," Teddy replied with a nod.

"He's just accepted a promotion as Head of Clerks," George added. "But he's actually here on another matter."

Elizabeth managed a happy, "Congratulations," before Elkins appeared at the door with the tea tray and her chocolate. A pot of coffee took the place of the usual teapot.

Teddy gave a nod as he retook his seat. "Thank you, my lady. I owe it all to you and your charity, of course," he said.

"I'll see to the serving," Elizabeth whispered as the butler set the tray on the low table in front of the settee. "Also, could you remind Mrs. Foster that both the babes are with me? I don't want her in any more of a panic than she probably already is," she added quietly.

"I will see to it, my lady," Elkins replied as he gave a bow.

After Elkins took his leave and shut the door, the lady of Bostwick House set about pouring coffee and adding milk and sugar. She gave a cup to Teddy.

"Now, what's this about the owner of Warwick's? I once attended that school, as did my friends, although they didn't board there," she explained as she gave a cup to George. "I had a governess, but I'm afraid I proved too challenging for her, so Father sent me there."

An involuntary shudder passed through her. Elizabeth couldn't claim her two years at the finishing school were her favorites. She attended because her parents had gone off to Italy to visit her mother's family, and because she had vexed her last governess to the point of distraction. Although she could already speak French and knew all the dances, she had learned how to draw and paint, appreciate the theatre for more than just a place to see and be seen, improve her sewing skills, and walk with a book on her head—even up and down stairs. Given the status of several of the girls at the school, security was of utmost concern, so burly men were posted outside of schoolrooms and provided protection when the students were out-of-doors.

Warwick's was also where she had met and befriended Beth Cunningham, who was now the Duchess of Somerset. Her best friends had also attended with her those two years. Charlotte Bingham, now the Duchess of Chichester, was living with her duke at Wisborough Oaks in Sussex, and Hannah Slater, now the Countess of Gisborn, was at Gisborn Hall near the village of Brampton, Oxfordshire. "Has something happened?" she asked.

Teddy dipped his head. "My mother, my lady. She died yesterday, you see, and I was just telling his lordship here that I'm in a bit of a quandary." He ignored George's look of dismay at being referred to as "his lordship" by his best friend. He set the cup and saucer on the table and lifted the cup with his only hand.

"Oh, please, do accept my condolences, Mr. Streater," Elizabeth said, her voice filled with concern. Then she frowned. "Mrs. Streater was your... she was your *mother?*" she asked, disbelief coloring her voice.

"Indeed."

Elizabeth did a mental calculation of how many times she had secretly cursed the headmistress of Warwick's Grammar and Finishing School, the ancient woman rather strict with her charges. It was difficult to imagine Mrs. Streater having at one time been married, let alone a mother to Theodore Streater and his older brother, Michael, a baron. "So, I rather imagine the owner of the school is searching for a new headmistress," she said as she gave a cup of coffee to her husband.

George cleared his throat. "I believe what Teddy is trying to say is that *he* is the new owner of Warwick's," he explained in a quiet voice.

Elizabeth's brows furrowed. "But..., but I thought Mrs. Worthington owned the school." Mrs. Streater always seemed so deferential in the presence of the woman who could claim that her son, Samuel, was one of the richest men in all of England. He had been responsible for the early steamships, his venture netting him vast wealth. His fortune was now in the hands of his widow, Adele, Countess of Torrington.

Teddy nodded. "As did I," he agreed. "For my whole life. I've always thought the most valuable item in her possession was my grandmother's garnet and diamond ring, but I've just come from the solicitor, and he claims my mother was indeed the owner of the school. As well as a..." He hissed at this point, a rather pained expression appearing on his face. "A fortune of some ten-thousand pounds."

George blinked.

Elizabeth blinked.

David blinked, waking up from his nap to display a huge grin directed at his mother.

"Ten-thousand pounds?" George repeated. "Bollocks, Teddy, you're... you're *rich!*" he said before turning to Elizabeth and giving his head a quick shake. "Forgive the curse, my lady."

"Oh, of course, darling. If you hadn't said it, I would

have," she claimed with an expression that matched his. She suddenly frowned. "You do know what this means?" she asked as she directed her attention to the bank clerk.

Teddy's eyes widened. "My two-hundred-and-eighty pounds a year at the bank is a pittance?"

Elizabeth grimaced, not entirely pleased he was earning less than three-hundred pounds a year. Given his years of experience and knowing the salaries of dozens of positions in London—she knew of such things because of her charity— she thought him worth more. Still, his salary would support a small family in modest accommodations. "You can afford to take a wife," she said, just as David giggled.

George and Teddy stared at one another. "She has a point, Teddy," George said. "It's been several years since Gertrude died. It is past time you took another wife."

But Teddy shook his head, ignoring the pang he felt at hearing his late wife's name. "What woman on God's green earth is going to want to marry a man with only one arm?" he countered in disgust. When he saw how Elizabeth and George both gave non-committal shrugs, he rolled his eyes. "I don't want to marry a woman who is merely after my fortune," he claimed.

"No one has to know you have a fortune," Elizabeth countered. "Who besides your solicitor knows?"

Teddy furrowed a brow. "Just you two. And him," he added as he glanced over at David. "My brother didn't show up for the reading of the will, and I haven't yet been to see him."

David was sitting up on the settee next to his mother, his face displaying the carefree happiness of extreme youth. He giggled, as if he knew Teddy had singled him out for acknowledgment.

"You could hire a matchmaker," George suggested.

"Oh, that would never do," Elizabeth said with a shake of her head. "Teddy requires a perfect match. A woman who will appreciate what he's been through. A woman who *values* him," she said, as if the man in question wasn't sitting just five feet away.

"Well, I rather doubt there's a matchmaker who specializes in finding wives for wounded soldiers," her husband said with a sigh.

Somehow, he knew even before the words were out of his mouth that Elizabeth would be struck with the very idea that suddenly came to him when he completed his comment. He stared at Elizabeth with the same intensity she stared at him, and they both said, "Finding Wives for the Wounded!" at exactly the same moment. Then they both grinned before turning their expectant gazes onto Teddy.

Teddy blinked, obviously rather startled. George was truly of the same mind as his viscountess! "What are you saying?" Teddy asked. "That you're going to bribe potential wives into marrying wounded men?"

Elizabeth allowed a look of offense. "Of course not, Mr. Streater. There are women out there—widows and... and those a bit on-the-shelf, or spinsters, even, who still harbor hope for a match. Hope for a husband and children," she explained softly. "We just have to find them, and interview them, and—"

"Elizabeth," George said in a hoarse whisper. "What are you suggesting?"

His wife sighed, well aware her son had turned his attention on her, as if he, too, wanted to know. "We're not as busy down at 'Finding Work for the Wounded' as we were in the beginning," she said. Indeed, for the first year after she had a shingle hung and opened the door to the establishment in Oxford Street, there had been a steady stream of returning soldiers bearing wounds that made it hard for them to secure employment. Now that the war had been over for a couple of years, fewer old fogeys sought their services. "Perhaps we could... repurpose one of the staff to matchmaking," she said.

"Or we could hire a matchmaker. Someone who has experience."

George regarded Teddy a moment, rather surprised to see a glimmer of hope appear in the man's eyes. "Perhaps," George agreed. "But, in the meantime, I believe Teddy has a more pressing matter."

Elizabeth turned to stare at their visitor. "What might that be?"

Teddy angled his head to one side. "I need a new headmistress for Warwick's," he said with a heavy sigh.

Rolling her eyes, Elizabeth said, "Well, that should be easy enough, Mr. Streater. Find out who among the current staff is interested in the position, and offer it to her."

Teddy exchanged a startled glance with George before he turned his attention back to Elizabeth. "That's brilliant, my lady," he said in awe. Then he sobered. He hadn't yet been to the school to discover who he was employing. "But will her interest alone qualify her to be headmistress?"

Considering the question a moment, Elizabeth realized the man had a point. "Perhaps not."

"You could post the position in the newspaper," George suggested. "Or..." He turned his attention to Elizabeth. "I don't suppose you've had any females apply for positions at 'Finding Work for the Wounded'?" he asked.

His wife's eyes widened. "But we have!" she countered. "A couple of nurses from the field hospitals, and..." She paused, as if in thought. "And a woman who claimed she couldn't tell us exactly why she was in Belgium, but that she was shot in service to king and country. Has a bit of a limp as I recall."

George and Teddy exchanged suspicious glances. "A spy, perhaps?" George asked, directing his question to their visitor.

"Or a courier," Teddy countered with a shrug. He had served as an officer in the army on three different occasions and was well aware of how women had served the war effort. "Or maybe she was there to follow the drum."

"I'll have Mr. Overby search the records," Elizabeth said as she lifted David onto her lap. "In the meantime, you already have a number of instructors to meet."

Teddy swallowed, realizing she had a point. "I suppose I should introduce myself to them, seeing as how I find I am their employer now."

George angled his head. "Aren't there servants as well? Cooks and housemaids?" he asked.

"I seem to remember a gardener," Elizabeth added. "And someone who saw to repairs."

Teddy seemed to wilt at each reminder of what he had inherited. "I can see to the accounting, at least," he muttered. "As for the rest... I fear I shall be at a loss."

Elizabeth waved the hand that wasn't holding onto David. "Just host a tea at the school and invite all the employees." When she noticed how uncomfortable Teddy seemed at the suggestion, she added, "I can help, if you'd like. Send out the invitations. Have the tea here, and I'll act as your hostess."

"Oh, would you?" Teddy replied, his countenance brightening.

"I will," Elizabeth promised. "But you must be the one to host. It will give you an opportunity to meet everyone. Assure them they still have positions. That is... if you intend to keep the school open?"

The query seemed to surprise the man. "Oh, I do," Teddy replied. Given how much he had inherited, owning the school had to have been lucrative for his mother. Where else would her fortune have come from if not from tuition fees?

Although he could sell Warwick's—and perhaps he still might if it turned out it was a venture beyond his ken—he thought it best to continue his mother's legacy. "With your help, I shall host a tea, and I shall meet each and every one of my employees. How does Saturday afternoon sound?"

"Saturday would be best," Elizabeth agreed. "Three o'clock in the afternoon. If you can send over a list, I'll see to the invitations, and have a footman deliver them."

When David giggled again, his attention on Teddy and his manner suggesting the new owner of Warwick's would fail, his mother regarded the boy with a frown. "Now, there will be none of that, young man," she said by way of warning. "Or you may find yourself betrothed to Lady Pettigrew's grandniece."

George had to suppress the urge to laugh when David's eyes suddenly widened in fear. "Do let us know how it goes, won't you?" he asked of his best friend. "And congratulations again on the promotion."

Teddy merely nodded before he said, "Thank you. I think." He stood up and gave a bow, kissing the back of Elizabeth's hand. "I'll go to the school now and find that list," he promised. He turned to George. "Tomorrow at Angelo's?" he asked.

George blinked. "If you're sure," he replied, realizing Teddy referred to their weekly sparring session. Given what had happened, he didn't expect Teddy to be available for their match.

"I am. I'll be in need of exercise," Teddy replied before he bowed and took his leave of Bostwick House.

CHAPTER 3
A SPY RETURNS TO LONDON

eanwhile, in the back of St. George's Church

Sure most of the parishioners attending that morning's service in St. George's had already taken their seats, Daisy Albright dared a quick glance around the nave before finding a seat in the back of the sanctuary—at the exact moment everyone stood up for the first hymn. Keeping her eyes straight ahead, she ignored the curious gaze of an older woman to her left. At just a bit over five-foot tall, she didn't stand out from those around her. The wig and hat she wore, along with cosmetics used to make her appear older than her eight-and-twenty years, ensured no one would recognize her.

Well, except for her father, perhaps. If he was in town, then she was quite sure he was seated somewhere close to the front. Probably in the first pew, given his status as a duke. But it had been a long time since they had seen one another. An occasional note sent to him assured him she was well and that she would pay a call when she was next in London.

This was her third trip to town since the sentiment had first been shared, and Daisy hadn't yet paid a call. The fact that her father had a wife and two small children shouldn't have given her pause, she supposed. But it did. Despite the life she had lived with her mother and sister and him—back before her mother's death—she had no place in his life these days.

She shouldn't even be in church, given her status as an illegitimate daughter. He would argue otherwise, though. *Rules be damned*, she remembered him saying when her mother insisted they abide Society's—and the church's—edicts. Her mother had done so because, she, too, was an illegitimate daughter and would never think to go against protocol.

Not when she was mistress to the heir of a dukedom.

Daisy wondered if she had made a mistake in coming to church. The London summer heat had perspiration dribbling down her back and between her breasts, moistening her stays. A twinge in her leg reminded her she needed to angle her heeled slipper just so, or she would have difficulty walking later that day. The edge of the lace ruffle at the end of her sleeve tickled the back of her hand, but she ignored it in favor of concentrating on what the bishop was saying. When that didn't work, she allowed her mind to wander, remembering where she had been three years ago—down in Dover —, two years ago—on the Continent, and a year ago...

York.

She resisted the urge to sigh aloud at how *that* assignment had played out. Nearly a year spent playing mistress to a marquess suspected of smuggling meant getting too close, becoming too attached. Then she had been forced to throw him over for a wealthy trader who proved to be the real target. A man who was responsible for arranging the shipments of liquor into York by way of a strip of beach owned by the marquess. At least their association had only lasted a few months before he was arrested.

She had never felt more soiled in all her life.

That return to London had her discovering she no longer

had a position with the Home Office. *Your limp gives you away, Miss Albright*, the secretary had said when she was dismissed with a small pension and the pay for her time in York. Her one assignment with the Foreign Office—the one in which she was sent to Belgium and was shot in the leg for her trouble—helped end her career, it seemed. Despite her offer to accept a position in an office as a clerk, she was told she was retired.

Trips to Bath and Brighton proved diverting but expensive. A brief stay in her childhood home had her experiencing melancholy before the first day ended. Every room held memories of her late mother. And the week spent alone at the Burrough's country estate in Derbyshire only reminded her there was a reason she stayed there in the past—she preferred the city.

Having come into her majority a few years ago, she knew there were funds in a bank should she need them. Her father had seen to it, assuring both her and her sister, Diana, there were dowries set aside for them. Now that her own funds were nearly depleted, she realized if she didn't land a position and soon, she would have to live off her inheritance.

The thought of becoming another rich man's mistress wasn't the least bit appealing.

"Pardon me, but are you going up?" the old woman to her right asked in a quiet voice.

Startled from her reverie, Daisy lifted her head to discover Communion was being served. She shook her head. "No. I'm..." She was about to say, "not allowed," but said, "I'm not." She turned a bit to allow the woman to pass, her gaze lifting in search of her father. Then she remembered he would have been one of the first to be served and decided it was too late to catch a glimpse of him.

When the service ended and the occupants of the first row filed out of the church, she pretended to read a hymnal when in fact she was watching James, Duke of Ariley, as he made his way down the aisle. *He won't recognize me*, she thought with some relief. *He won't even give a glance in my direction.*

What surprised her, though, was that his duchess, the former Lady Helen Harrington, sister to Stanley Harrington, Earl of Mayfield, wasn't by his side. She wondered if the duchess was ill, or if she was spending time away from London. If so, had the children gone with her? Or were they still in London?

It was odd to think she had a younger brother and sister. She had known for years she eventually would have other siblings besides Diana—her father required an heir, after all —but she hadn't imagined when she might meet them. What they might think of her.

Her thoughts wandered as she waited for the remaining rows of parishioners to exit before she finally stood and made her way toward the front door. Having sat too long, her leg bothered her a bit, and it was several steps before she could overcome the slight limp that the Home Office had claimed gave her away.

Concentrating on her gait, she was caught completely unawares when her father threaded an arm through her crooked elbow and pulled her off to the side in the vestibule.

Since she was in a church, she hadn't thought to be on guard, to tense her muscles and react by punching her assailant with a fist to his cheek followed by an uppercut to his chest and a knee in the groin.

Thank the gods.

For she was suddenly facing her father. Staring at his wide, blue eyes and expression of recognition.

"It *is* you," he breathed.

Daisy blinked. "Hello, Father," she replied with a quick curtsy.

"What the...?" He almost said, "devil," but caught

himself. They were still in the church. "I've been worried sick about you," he scolded.

Her eyes widening at his claim, Daisy gave a shake of her head. "You needn't have been. I am quite fine. Didn't you get my letters?"

James frowned. "Letters?" he repeated.

Daisy allowed a sigh of frustration. "I sent letters from Brighton, Bath, Cherrywood, and Scarborough."

The expression on the duke's face suggested he would be having a discussion with his man of business. "I may have," he hedged. "But why on earth are you wearing that hideous wig? And cosmetics? Daisy... that is a wig, is it not?" he asked in a quieter voice, his expression indicating his disgust.

Giving him a quelling glance, Daisy said, "Of course it is, Father. I didn't wish to be recognized." *By you*, she almost added, *in case your duchess was with you.*

The Duke of Ariley's' face screwed up. "Are you on a mission?" he asked in a whisper. Then he gave his head a quick shake. "Of course, you aren't."

Daisy angled her head to one side. "How do you know I am not?" she countered, a bit indignant. At one time, she had thought her work for the Home Office was a secret. And it would have been if her father wasn't a duke. If the Home Secretary hadn't admitted to Ariley that he had sent her on the mission to York. He had probably neglected to mention the Foreign Office had taken over that particular assignment before it was complete.

As to how James Burroughs, Duke of Ariley, even suspected her of working for King and country, she had no idea. He never said how he suspected her secret enough to ask in the first place.

And she hadn't asked.

"Never mind that," he said as he offered his arm. "I'm taking you home." He started to lead them to the front doors of St. George's. "See if we can't find you some proper clothes."

Daisy attempted to pull her arm from his. "I cannot be seen with you like this," she said in a hoarse whisper. "What will people say?"

Ariley turned and regarded her with a quizzical brow. "If I let you out of my sight, it might be another two or three *years* before I see you again, and, dash it Daisy, I cannot abide that."

A bit stunned by his response, Daisy regarded him for a moment. She had never for a moment doubted that he loved her and her sister, Diana. He had been a doting father, a doting lover to her mother. He had mourned Lily Albright for weeks after her death, and continued to be a good father well after the time she and Diana could look after themselves.

But he had an entirely new family now. A well-regarded duchess. Two children. The very last thing she wanted to do was embarrass the duchess by showing up on her doorstep. She was the duke's illegitimate daughter!

"My Helen wishes to meet you," he said then. At Daisy's continued look of surprise—she was quite sure no wife of an aristocrat wanted to have anything to do with by-blows or bastard children—he added, "She married me knowing I already had a late mistress and two daughters. I made it clear you and your sister were important to me."

Although his words merely reinforced her memory of his devotion, she still wasn't convinced meeting his duchess was the best idea just then. "Did you tell her what I was doing for employment?" she asked, thinking if Helen shared the *on-dit* with those who visited her parlor, then it was no wonder she had lost her position in the Home Office.

"No. Of course not," James replied. "I didn't even *know* for the longest time."

"May I enquire as to who told you?"

He inhaled sharply, his eyes darting to one side—clear

signs he was about to either change the subject or claim he didn't remember. So Daisy was shocked again when he said, "Chamberlain," referring to Matthew Fitzsimmons, Viscount Chamberlain. "And only because he thought I already knew. I pretended I did, and he said a bit more than he should have over drinks at White's."

Daisy arched an eyebrow. "Chamberlain knows better than that," she said. Chamberlain had been running the Foreign Office for years, and he only knew about Daisy because of her assignment in Belgium. And because there had been that bit of interoffice cooperation at the end of the York assignment. Smuggled liquor from another country fell under the Foreign Office's purview.

Oh, and because Chamberlain's niece had ended up stranded on a deserted island with the marquess for whom Daisy had been a mistress for nearly a year.

She gave her head a quick shake, her regret over that particular assignment still too painful.

The first rule of being a mistress was to never get too close. Never fall in love or believe an offer of *carte blanche* would be extended for longer than the time on the original contract.

She had come to care for Ethan Range, Marquess of Plymouth, during their year together. *I probably didn't love him, exactly,* she decided. But the pain she had felt at telling him she had accepted the offer of another protector had her cringing. Had her wishing she could tell the Home Office she was done trying to discover the true culprit.

The Duke of Ariley looked suitably chagrined. "All right, then. I forced it out of him."

Daisy blinked, once again pulled from her reverie. "What?"

Her father shrugged. "I threatened to have Chamberlain fired from his position if he didn't tell me what he knew about you."

Rolling her eyes—she nearly laughed at hearing her father's claim—Daisy sighed. "Well, I can no longer claim to be in service to King and country," she murmured. She was about to add, "Because of you," but the duke surprised her.

"Because of me," he said in a whisper. "At the time I threatened him, you were in Belgium. I was... beside myself with worry. You could have been *shot*..."

"I was shot," Daisy said, matter-of-factly.

"You could have been kill... wait. You were *shot?*" he asked, his voice rising so anyone left in the church could have heard him.

Closing her eyes a moment, Daisy waited for him to calm down before she said, "Flesh wound. In the leg. I am fine," she said before he could quiz her further.

"Were you the agent who got the missive to Wellingham?" he asked in a hoarse whisper.

Daisy blinked before giving her head a shake. No one was supposed to know about that mission. Four agents, all given what was supposed to be the same note and dispatched from various locations, were to rendezvous with Wellingham just before what became the Battle of Ligny.

But she didn't make it. At least, not in time. Not quite.

Someone did, though. For the message did make it, and eventually Napoleon was defeated.

Just not that day.

"I was shot just before I got there," she whispered.

"Jesus, pet, you could have been killed," he replied in a frantic whisper.

"But I wasn't."

He was suddenly pulling her out of the church and down the front steps to his town coach, a gold ducal crest emblazoned on a door that a footman was seeing to opening the moment he appeared from inside the church.

Daisy thought about attempting to escape. Thought for a fraction of a second about stamping a half-booted foot onto the duke's Hoby-clad foot. But the image of his valet attempting to repair the damage to the top of his boot had her deciding to simply allow him whatever he wanted. "You really intend to introduce me to your duchess when I look like this?" she asked once they were both in the town coach.

"Of course not. I'll have Jarvis escort you to your bedchamber where you can wash off those cosmetics and change into one of your gowns."

Daisy stared at her father. "My gowns?" she countered.

James gave a shrug. "Yes, your gowns. You have a bedchamber at Ariley Place. I saw to it anything you left behind in Kent was moved into it after your visit there last year," he explained. "Figured if you went there again, you would find my note and understand how badly I wished to see you again."

Daisy inhaled, holding the breath a moment. "You're certainly full of surprises," she murmured, a wan grin appearing. She wondered what he might have written in the note. "Too bad you didn't read the ones I sent to you," she said in a whisper.

He angled his head. "Daisy," he said on a sigh. "What ever happened to have you going off to... *work*... when you could have stayed under my protection? Made a good match and been married? Had children?" he asked in exasperation. "My grandchildren might have been playmates for my new children." He managed to avoid a wince when he realized how the last might have sounded to his oldest daughter.

Angling her head to match his, Daisy pulled first the awful hat and then the hideous wig from her head. The brunette hair beneath fell in curly waves around her face, youthening her appearance by at least ten years. She then unbuttoned and pulled the ragged pelisse from her shoulders, revealing a sky-blue gown of fine lawn embroidered with tiny flowers and leaves. Digging into her reticule, she pulled out a linen handkerchief and wiped her lips before folding it and then giving her face a quick wipe.

James watched in fascination as she transformed into the daughter he remembered. "It's not too late," he whispered in awe.

Daisy gave a shrug. "I never wanted that life, Father. I am too much my mother's daughter, I fear. Although I promise I shall never accept an offer of *carte blanche*, I cannot be content doing embroidery all day long—"

"Your sister was a dance instructor," he interrupted. "At Warwick's. Now she's a viscountess. Runs her own household. Or, at least, she will when she returns from her wedding trip."

Her lower lip caught with a tooth, Daisy considered how to respond. She knew very well her younger sister would one day be a countess—The Countess of Aimsely—for Diana had married the oldest son of Mark and Patience Comber, Earl and Countess of Aimsely. Adam Comber, Viscount Breckinridge, might have been a ne'er do well in his younger years, but before the eve of his thirtieth birthday, he had quite suddenly decided to marry Diana Albright. "I sent her my congratulations when I learned of it," Daisy said with a grin. "She is far better suited to the role of an aristocrat's wife than I would ever be."

For just a moment upon learning of her sister's marriage, she wondered who might take Diana's place at Warwick's Grammar and Finishing School. The thought of teaching arithmetic and dancing to daughters of wealthy cits didn't hold much appeal, though. "Poor Mrs. Streater must have been beside herself on attempting to fill that position," Daisy commented.

For just a moment, James appeared interested in what she had said, but at her quick head shake, he realized she wasn't about to apply for a position at the finishing school. "If you cannot see yourself teaching young ladies or running your own household, perhaps... perhaps you would be willing to run one of my estates. As an estate manager. Or..." He faltered, not sure if she had the skills to run what was essentially a business.

What practical skills did former spies possess?

"Careful, or I may require you make me an estate manager," she warned with a grin. "Actually, I have an application pending at Lady Bostwick's charity," Daisy finally admitted. "Finding Work for the Wounded. She has been successful at placing old fogeys in positions all over London. Good positions."

James couldn't help the wince that appeared at her mention of "old fogeys." "I'm aware of her success," he replied, his words sounding sharp even to his ears. "Faith, Daisy. You're the daughter of a duke. *My* daughter. The least you could do is take your inheritance—"

"I started to, Father. Last year," she interrupted. "The interest, at least." She knew she would be in need of the funds whilst on her travels. Her salary had been enough when she was on assignments, but when the Home Office let her go, there was no pension. No hope for a future position.

Furrowing his brows, James gave her a sideways glance. "You didn't take any of the principal," he countered.

He had her there. She had felt like a thief just taking the interest that had accrued. She knew he intended it for a dowry. "It's true. I... I thought it best I leave it in case—"

"Take the money," James said in a hoarse whisper. "Use it as you see fit. But please, don't live in squalor—"

"Oh, I do not live in squalor, Father. I only dress as if I do when... when it suits my needs," she countered. *Like when I don't wish to be recognized because I feared you would have your duchess with you.*

So much for her disguise.

"Pray tell, how long did it take for you to recognize me?" she asked.

Her father allowed a broad grin. "Not even a second. I know those eyes..." His voice broke, his own eyes brightening with tears. Struggling to maintain his composure, he finally managed to add, "You have your mother's eyes, as does Diana," he whispered softly.

"Oh, Father," Daisy said as she sighed. She half-stood, turned around, and sat down next to him in the velvet squabs. Her head angled to rest on his shoulder. "Even after all this time." Her mother had died when she was eighteen. Now Daisy was nearly nine-and-twenty.

One of his arms wrapped around her back. "I love Helen. I do. But there are times I miss your mother very much," he said, his words so quiet she almost couldn't hear them over the noise of the coach wheels.

"Me, too," she replied, just as the coach came to a halt in front of Ariley Place.

When she stepped down from the coach, her hideous wig and hat hidden beneath the pelisse draped over her arm, she allowed her father to escort her up to the white painted door. Ariley Place would be her home for a few days, it seemed. But just a few.

She had no intention of living under her father's roof. Although she adored him, she feared if she did live with him, she would end up married to a fat, balding viscount.

CHAPTER 4
A MEDDLING OWNER ON A MISSION

eanwhile, at Bostwick Place
Elizabeth finished her chocolate about the time George returned from escorting Teddy to the vestibule. "How is it Mr. Streater never knew his mother owned Warwick's?" she asked, suspicion evident in her voice.

George shook his head. "Probably for the same reason I never knew my uncle owned gypsum mines and was in possession of a fortune when he died," he replied with a shrug. He had inherited all of it upon Joseph Bennett-Jones' death in January of 1815, but it wasn't until the will was read that he learned the details. Learned he not only owned the Sussex estate at which he spent some summers with his uncle, but also a townhouse in London and three mines in Sussex. "My uncle was a miser, and I rather imagine Mrs. Streater was as well, especially after having been left in debt by her late husband."

Elizabeth frowned at his description. "Did your uncle have any other business concerns?"

Angling his head to one side, George said, "Not that I'm aware of, but that's not to say I would be surprised should some solicitor approach me with news that I own a mill, and, oh, by the way, I'm several years in arrears on the taxes," he said in a quiet voice. He had often wondered if there was a mill somewhere near the manor home in Sussex.

"I'm going into the office today," Elizabeth stated as she stood up and turned to lift David into her arms.

"It's Sunday," George said, moving to take the heavy toddler from her.

"Which is exactly why I wish to go. No one will be there, and it will give me a chance to look for that woman's application," she replied as she gave up her hold on David. "I don't know why, but I can't seem to get the thought of her out of my head. I only caught a glimpse of her that day, but for some reason, I think I should have..." She paused and sighed. "Recognized her."

Frowning at the odd comment, George asked, "Because you've met her before?"

"I'm sure I have not," Elizabeth countered. "But... she was so familiar, I'm thinking she may be related to someone I do know."

George angled his head to one side. "May I escort you?"

Elizabeth's eyes widened. "I would like that," she replied. "Are you sure, though? I would hate for you—"

"I am sure. Besides, I haven't been to your office in an age. And I admit to a bit of curiosity about your recent applicants."

Allowing a shrug and deftly capturing David's chubby fist as he was about to grab an earbob, Elizabeth said, "Let's go directly after breakfast."

George lifted David into the air, which had the toddler giggling in delight. "I think you mean luncheon, my sweeting. It's well after one," he chided.

Her eyes widening in surprise, Elizabeth dared a glance at the clock on the mantle. "Poor Christina must be starving again," she said as she hurried to the bassinet. "I'm taking her to the nursery right now," she replied, disappearing through the door to the dressing room with the swaddled infant.

George tossed David into the air. The boy giggled in delight as he landed in his father's arms. Then George gave the boy a frown. "You wet your nappy," he accused, suddenly aware his sleeve was damp where the boy's bottom landed.

David continued to giggle as George raced to the nursery, arriving just ahead of his wife.

"Your son peed on me," he said as he passed the toddler to the startled nurse.

"That will teach you to toss him about like a rag doll," Elizabeth countered, her grin wide as she held Christina in her arms. The infant appeared to be sound asleep.

George kissed his daughter on the forehead and kissed his wife on the lips, ignoring the nurse's gasp of embarrassment. "Join me in the breakfast parlor, won't you? You can bring Christina, of course," he added when he noticed her conflicted expression. "She doesn't appear to be starving."

"I'll come with you," she finally replied, bussing David on the cheek. "But I'll leave Christina here." She gave up her hold on the infant as the nurse took the babe. Rather stunned when one of George's arms snaked behind her waist, Elizabeth asked, "What's this about?" when he had closed the nursery door behind them.

"Your idea," George replied. "For matchmaking. Were you sincere?"

Elizabeth blinked. "But, of course. I cannot imagine Mr. Streater finding a wife on his own," she replied.

"Neither can I," her husband agreed. "But Teddy..." He paused and sucked in a breath, which had Elizabeth pausing on the landing of the stairs.

She stared at George. "What is it?" she asked, worry evident on her features.

"Remember, he has been married before," George replied carefully.

Elizabeth's eyes widened. "What happened?" she asked in a whisper filled with alarm. In all her dealings with the clerk, he had never mentioned having been married.

"Widowed," George countered right away, his head shaking. "He wasn't married long before he went off to war the second time. His childhood sweetheart, I think she was. Anyway, he went off to the Continent, came back, got the position at the bank, we resumed our weekly fencing matches, and then..." He sighed again.

"What?" she asked, becoming more alarmed.

"When the wars on the Continent started again, Teddy resigned his position and returned to the army for a third stint. He is a soldier, first and foremost. An officer, of course. While he was off losing his arm, Gertrude died of influenza. Even with this windfall inheritance and a new venture to keep him occupied, I fear he may be a difficult match for just any woman."

Elizabeth entered the breakfast parlor and waited for a footman to pull out her chair. "He seems agreeable, though," she argued.

"He is. I just... I'm not sure life with an English miss is going to suit him," George countered as he took a seat.

"You're saying he needs a woman who can... *challenge* him?" she queried.

George winced. "I'm not sure what I'm saying," he finally admitted as he acknowledged the footman who set a plate of breakfast foods before him. "Perhaps if women were allowed in the army, that's the type we would be seeking on his behalf."

At first, Elizabeth frowned. Despite having read novels featuring females in the oddest of situations, she couldn't imagine a woman dressing in a uniform and shooting a gun, let alone stabbing someone with a bayonet. But then she considered the other positions a woman might hold if they were attached to an army regiment.

Or not attached to a regiment at all, but sent to war for other reasons.

Elizabeth held her fork over her plate and stared at her husband. "That's *brilliant*, George," she said, her aquamarine eyes wide. "Perhaps I'll find just such a woman when I search the applications this afternoon."

About to tuck into his meal, George gave her a curious expression before allowing a nod of acknowledgement. One thing he knew for certain—when his wife put her mind to something, she wouldn't let go until it was sorted.

And she wanted Teddy sorted.

CHAPTER 5

AN APPLICATION IS DISCOVERED

An hour later

As George held open the door to *Finding Work for the Wounded*, he glanced up and down Oxford Street. He had thought traffic would be slight on a Sunday, but a parade of horses and equipage passed by, apparently on their way to the country.

Elizabeth stepped into the offices, removing her gloves as she made her way to a desk in the back corner. "You should probably throw the bolt," she said when her husband closed the door.

Not about to argue, George did so and then turned to survey the small office. On a busy day, three people would be at the desks, and a line of former soldiers and sailors—and those claiming to have served as such—would be in the vestibule awaiting their turn at telling their tale of woe and listing their qualifications. At one time, the stacks of paper on each desk might measure a foot in height, but these days, they were barely an inch high.

"May I help?" George asked, noting how Elizabeth was perusing a stack of notes left by the two employees, Mr. Augustus Overby and Mr. Nicholas Barnaby. The two "By's" were also her first employees, hired the day after she had first opened the doors to her charity.

Elizabeth lifted her head and nodded at one of the desks. "Are you quite sure you wish to do this?"

George wondered at her hesitance. "Why wouldn't I?" he hedged.

She sighed. "I'm afraid you'll feel sorry for every applicant and hire them on the spot, regardless of their qualifications or your needs," she claimed.

George blinked, realizing she had a point. "May I at least help you find the woman you're looking for?"

Elizabeth allowed a grin. "Yes," she said as she glanced toward a stack of paper on a small table at the very back of the office, opposite her desk. "Those are applicants we haven't yet been able to match with positions. I'm afraid that's where we'll find the woman I am remembering."

"Why do you say it like that?" he asked, noting her tone of sorrow.

Sighing, Elizabeth replied, "I've not placed but five women in any positions for the past two years. Two were nurses. They work at St. Bart's now. Two more were placed as seamstresses. Not exactly jobs that pay very well."

"Neither are jobs making hats, but what else is there?" he countered.

Elizabeth straightened, a note held in one hand and an expression of disbelief on her face. "Governess, housekeeper, companion, chaperone... factory worker." This last was said as she gave an involuntary shiver. "I would never consider sending a woman to work in the mines, but I understand some do."

"They push carts in the coal mines," George commented as he picked up the stack of applications. He settled in at one of the desks.

"Do you employ any women in your gypsum mines?" Elizabeth asked.

George started to shake his head and then frowned. "I've absolutely no idea. Each mine has a foreman that sees to the hiring." He received regular reports from each mine—yields, costs of operation, auction results—but nothing specific about employees other than a total number. "I shall have to write and ask," he murmured.

He started to thumb through the applications, turning each over onto the desktop so as not to mix them up. It was possible that whoever stacked them did so in some kind of logical fashion. He soon realized there was no rhyme or reason to their order. Every applicant listed some sort of ailment or malady, any one of which might preclude them from employment.

Except for one.

Slight limp.

The reason for the limp was listed as "shot in the leg".

George blinked and set aside the other applications, his attention fixed on Mr. Barnaby's less-than-stellar handwriting. *D. Albright* was the name written at the top of the form he held. The other attributes—age, eight-and-twenty; height, five-foot; languages, French and Italian; and education, governess and tutors—could have been any sort of soldier of middle class background.

Except for the reference to an office in Whitehall, and a note that a character would be provided upon request.

"How many five-foot tall soldiers do you suppose were shot in the leg?" George asked as he straightened in the chair.

In the middle of penning a note for Mr. Overby, Elizabeth considered the question. "Deliberately?"

George furrowed a brow. "How else would one be shot in the leg?" Then he frowned. "If they were running, I suppose, or—"

"If they were a courier," Elizabeth offered. "I overheard Mr. Comber telling someone that the courier in his unit in the Kingdom of the Netherlands barely came to his chest. Thought the man was merely a boy at first."

Thinking most men were shorter than Alistair Comber, the second son of the Earl of Aimsley, George wasn't about to argue. However, it had him wondering about this particular applicant. The mention of the office in Whitehall had him imagining all sorts of scenarios. "What about a spy?" he asked, holding up the form he held.

Elizabeth looked up from the missive she was writing and angled her head. "A five-foot tall *spy?* Why, I can't imagine..." She inhaled sharply. "That's her," she said, getting up from the desk to join her husband.

He offered her the form before she could reach for it, noting her impatience. "You think *D. Albright* is your man?" he asked with a grin. Then he sobered and seemed in deep thought for a moment. "Albright," he repeated.

"What is it?" Elizabeth asked as she quickly read the application, becoming more and more excited as she realized it had to be the woman she remembered.

"Well, he's been happily married for a few years, but Ariley used to have a mistress with that name. Lily Albright, I think her name was. A courtesan of some renown. Her father was Sir Ronald—a baronet—but he never acknowledged her as his own, even though everyone knew she was his daughter. Ariley had two daughters with her, although they always stayed in Kent."

Elizabeth's eyes widened. "Diana Albright. She was the youngest." She almost immediately let out a sound of disappointment. "It can't be her. She just married Alistair's brother, Viscount Breckenridge."

Angling his head to one side, George asked, "Didn't Miss Albright teach at Warwick's? Arithmetic or some such?" Although he had never stepped foot in any of the buildings associated with Warwick's Grammar and Finishing School, Teddy had done so a number of times simply because his mother's office was there, as was her apartment. The late headmistress had worked at the school for over thirty years. *Owned it*, George corrected himself.

Which had George realizing why it might be a baroness had become a headmistress of a finishing school—*necessity*. Teddy had said his father had left them in debt. His mother had probably been forced to seek a means to keep the family out of debtors' prison. And what baroness wanted her meager title associated with the work she performed?

"And she taught the dance classes," Elizabeth put in, her thoughts still on the Viscountess Breckinridge. "Which means she's definitely not this *D. Albright*."

George furrowed a brow and then realized his wife had a good point. Besides, a limp would probably have prevented Diana from teaching dance at the finishing school.

"But this is the woman I was thinking about, I'm sure of it," Elizabeth said, looking in vain for a means to contact the woman. "The older sister. I'm trying to remember her name. There's no address," she said with a sigh of frustration. "How are we to find her?"

Frowning, George gently took the paper from her and re-read the entire page. "Ah, here at the bottom. Says she will return to the office to learn if anything has come available."

Elizabeth sighed, obviously disappointed. "That's no help. What if she never comes back?"

George hesitated to suggest the woman's failure to return would be an indication that D. Albright had managed to secure a position somewhere else. Besides, if she really was Ariley's daughter, why would she be in search of a position at all? "May I ask why it is you think a former spy would make a good headmistress for Warwick's?"

Blinking, Elizabeth gave him a quelling glance. "I wasn't thinking of her for *that* position," she countered. "Although, now that you mention it, she might be a good candidate."

"Well, if not Warwick's, what did you have in mind?"

Elizabeth sighed. "Matchmaking," she replied. "I was thinking of her to be in charge of *Finding Wives for the Wounded*."

His wife's logic having escaped his reasoning, George gave a shake of his head. "My sweeting, I love you dearly. You know I do. But there are times you leave me perplexed. Addled." He reached out and pulled her onto his lap. "Truly vexed. *Now* is one of those times." He kissed her cheek.

Dimpling, Elizabeth arched an elegant eyebrow before she settled her head against his shoulder. "Perhaps 'matchmaking' isn't one of her skills, but I should think she can run an operation."

"An operation?" George repeated.

"Yes. If she truly was a spy, I should think she had to have her wits about her. Be able to think on her feet. Investigate. Improvise when necessary. Finish the job at hand," she reasoned.

"Isn't that what a headmistress has to do?" he teased. "You make her sound like a Bow Street Runner," George murmured.

"Oh, is that what they do?" she asked with a teasing grin.

"You read too many novels," he accused, before he captured her lips with his own. He kissed her thoroughly, rather glad to know there wasn't a chance they would be interrupted by a curious toddler or a crying babe.

They were interrupted, however, by a loud knock at the door.

CHAPTER 6
INTERRUPTED

*E*lizabeth scrambled to get up from her husband's lap, as if she was embarrassed at being discovered sitting on it.

George gave her a look of surprise before he, too, stood up. "I don't think I've seen you move away from me so quickly," he said, a bit disappointed. He was quite sure their *tête-à-tête* was about to become an assignation of the carnal sort.

Straightening his topcoat, he moved to the front door.

"I was just surprised, is all," Elizabeth countered, wondering who would attempt to gain entry to her charity's office on a Sunday afternoon. Although she had considered coming to the office without her husband, she knew a groom and a tiger would be minding the coach at the curb just outside the door.

Unbolting the door, George held one of his booted feet against the base of the door and turned the handle. He opened it a few inches, making sure to keep his boot firmly in place to prevent someone from shoving the door open from the other side.

His tiger stood beyond the door, giving a bow when part

of George's face appeared in the opening. "Pardon, my lord, but there's a gentleman here who says he needs to speak with you."

At first wondering how someone would even know he was in the charity's office, George remembered the gold Bostwick crest painted on the door of town coach. For the longest time, he had favored leaving the glossy black Tillbury unmarked, but his father-in-law, David, Marquess of Morganfield, insisted his daughter ride in a town coach decorated in accordance with her title.

George had resisted if only because he feared a highwayman or other thief would recognize an opportunity when it presented itself.

"Who is it?" George asked, opening the door a bit wider.

"It's just me, George," Teddy said from where he stood behind the tiger.

"Is everything all right?" George asked in alarm, removing his foot from his side of the door and waving his friend into the office.

"Yes, yes. I was just passing by on my way to Warwick's and saw your coach. Remembered another reason why I paid the call earlier," he said, just then noticing Elizabeth standing next to one of the desks. "Your ladyship," he said as he gave a bow. "Pardon the interruption."

Elizabeth gave a nod. "Of course, Mr. Streater." She glanced around. "Do take a seat, won't you?" she said as she waved to the chair George had been using. "I apologize, but I don't have the means to make tea at the moment."

"I wouldn't expect you to," Teddy replied as he stood next to the chair, obviously waiting for Elizabeth to be seated. Given the limited number of chairs, she returned to her desk as George sat on the edge of it.

"What's this about?" George asked when he noticed how Teddy seemed to be struggling with what to say.

"Warwick's, of course. In all the confusion of the last two

days, I had forgotten mother was in search of a new instructor."

George exchanged a quick glance with Elizabeth. "Dance and arithmetic, perhaps?" he offered.

Teddy's eyes widened as his brows furrowed. "How did you know?"

Elizabeth replied, "We were just discussing Miss Albright's recent marriage to Viscount Breckinridge."

Teddy took a deep breath, heartened he didn't have to explain what had happened to have Miss Diana Albright resign her position so unexpectedly. He had been afraid he would have to deal with a possible scandal. The only usual reason for such quick weddings was because a young lady found herself with child. Or an angry father was threatening to withhold a dowry. "What am I to do?" Teddy asked. "One of the instructors has taken on the dancing—for now—but I've no one to teach the arithmetic. I don't even know where to go—"

"Why, you've come to the right place, if you're of a mind to hire someone who might have been wounded in the wars," Elizabeth said happily, glancing over at the stack of applications that George had left on the very desk at which Teddy was sitting.

Blinking, as if he had completely forgotten he had come to the offices of a charity whose sole purpose was to place veterans into jobs, Teddy allowed a sigh of relief. "Are you saying you might actually have someone?" he asked.

"Where would you like me to send the candidates?"

Sitting back in his chair, Teddy thought a moment. "Warwick's, I suppose. The headmistress' office. I plan to be there tomorrow and possibly Tuesday, of course," he finally replied. "The bank has given me two days to see to my mother's arrangements, but I expect I'll be using the time to be sure affairs are in order at the school."

Elizabeth furrowed a brow, rather surprised a man who

had just inherited ten-thousand pounds still intended to continue his position at the Bank of England, especially when he had such a lucrative enterprise to oversee. "Very good. I'll send a courier with characters as I find them—"

"Oh, just send the candidates," Teddy interrupted.

It was Elizabeth's turn to blink, but before she could respond, George said, "Is haste really necessary? I shouldn't want you hiring the first person that crosses your threshold," he warned.

Teddy gave a shake of his head. "I would do it myself, but the thought of speaking in front of a room full of schoolgirls has me quite vexed."

A 'tsk' sounded from Elizabeth's corner. "A few days without arithmetic isn't going to hurt anything," she chimed in. "Why, you'll quickly become a favorite headmaster should you give those girls a week or two without numbers."

Squirming in his seat, Teddy said, "Could I prevail upon you to never call me that, my lady? My intention is to have someone in place of my mother as soon as possible so I can get back to my true calling." He almost added the word, 'numbers', but thought better of it given Elizabeth's obvious dislike of arithmetic.

"Of course. I apologize, Mr. Streater. But do know I shan't be offering you a bribe to hire anyone for the school," she warned, dimpling when she saw his look of alarm.

Teddy shook his head as he said, "Of course not." He gave a long sigh. "I believe I will go to the school now. Spend some time in my mother's old office to determine what must be done immediately."

When their visitor took his leave, George turned his attention to Elizabeth, thinking they could simply pick up where they had left off in their *tête-à-tête* before Teddy's arrival. But he watched as she hurriedly pulled on her pelisse and hat and retrieved the application for D. Albright from the desk where he had been sitting.

"Where... where are we going?" he asked as she moved to the door.

"Ariley Place. Surely the duke knows where his daughter is," she replied. "Where we might find her."

"What makes you think she's Ariley's daughter?"

Elizabeth allowed an audible sigh. "Remember when I said she looked familiar?"

"Yes," he finally admitted.

"She looked like Diana Albright. She's Diana's older sister. She has to be. So we're going to Ariley Place."

"On a Sunday?"

Elizabeth paused, realizing just then that paying a call this late in the day was reserved for close family and friends. "Well, aren't you a close friend of Ariley's?" she asked. "I know his duchess, of course, but she's much older than me."

George couldn't decide if he should gently chide his wife or merely go along with her scheme. "I know the duke, yes, but I can't say we've ever so much as shared a drink at the club. But we can at least leave a calling card, I suppose," he offered when he saw her look of disappointment.

"That will have to do then," she agreed, as the two took their leave of the office. Elizabeth turned to lock the door before allowing George to help her into the town coach for the quick trip to Park Lane.

Truth be told, she had no intention of simply leaving a card, but she thought it best not to inform her husband.

There was a job to fill, and she was sure D. Albright was the perfect candidate.

CHAPTER 7
MEETING A STEPMOTHER
FOR THE VERY FIRST TIME

eanwhile, at Ariley Place
Daisy's father hadn't been fibbing when he said there was already a bedchamber for her on the first floor of Ariley Place. Two walls were covered in peach silk, and her carved mahogany furniture, made by Chippendale and moved from the house in Kent, sat on thick Turkish carpeting that swallowed up her footfalls as she gingerly stepped into the room. The peach-covered bed, topped by a dark peach satin canopy that swept up to the high ceiling at its middle, was the largest she had ever seen. Green tassels hung from the edges between the bedposts. Her green and white japanned dressing table had been positioned between the room's two windows.

When Daisy peeked into the next bedchamber down the hall, she recognized from some of the items on the dresser that it had been set up for her sister, Diana. Despite it being a Sunday, a maid was in the room, unpacking a trunk. When Daisy asked what she was about, the maid said she had been given instructions to prepare an apartment in the event Diana and her new husband, Adam Comber, Viscount Breckinridge, might stay at Ariley Place whilst in London.

"These are her ladyship's things from Warwick's," the maid explained. "Furniture, too. His lordship made sure she had the very best whilst she taught at that school. Thought I should see to it today since it's possible Lady Breckinridge will pay a call soon."

Daisy wondered if Jarvis had been instructed to send a footman with word to Diana that Daisy was in residence at Ariley Place. But she shook her head when she remembered the new viscountess had only recently married. Adam surely would have taken her on a wedding trip somewhere away from London.

My sister is a viscountess, Daisy thought with a hint of pride. Their mother had always thought they might end up in advantageous marriages, which was probably why the former courtesan hadn't trained them for the same life she had led prior to meeting their father.

Well, that and their father was a duke who wouldn't have allowed it.

Returning to her bedchamber, Daisy opened the wardrobe to find all her gowns from Kent lined up on hooks, several pairs of slippers neatly arranged below. The chest of drawers contained all manner of petticoats and chemises, garters and stockings, fobs and fripperies, each one carefully folded and arranged.

Had all of this been in her bedchamber in Kent?

Having shed the blue gown she had worn to church, she found a primrose sprigged muslin gown with a thin edge of lace around the neckline and a huge, lace-trimmed flounce at the hem. Adorned with an orange grosgrain ribbon below her breasts, the dress had her wondering if she might be trying too hard to live up to her name.

She remembered the day the modiste had delivered it, the protest she had put voice to over how much it made her look like a proper English miss—too much like a young woman still in the schoolroom. But her father complimented her whenever she wore it, claiming it made her look like one of her aunts when she had been the same age.

Aunt Elise, no doubt. Her youngest aunt. Elise was a viscountess, too. Widowed for two years, she had just married Godfrey Thorncastle, Viscount Thorncastle, the very same day Diana had married her viscount.

Thinking her father would assume she was deliberately hiding if she didn't make her way to the ground floor salon—and soon—she decided not to change. A quick repair of her top knot was required, though. She had flattened it so the wig would fit over it. About to remove the pins, a quiet knock at the door had her freezing in place.

You're not on a mission, you silly goose, she chided herself as she relaxed and said, "Come."

A maid then ducked her head in before she dipped a curtsy. "His grace has asked that I be your lady's maid whilst you're in residence, my lady. May I be of help? Name's Cady."

"You don't have Sundays off?" Daisy countered, rather surprised at Cady's short stature. She almost remarked on it, and then thought perhaps Cady's assignment had been deliberate on her father's part.

The maid was shorter even than she was!

Cady angled her head to one side. "Usually. But I'm happy to help, milady." She stepped forward and held out the chair in front of the dressing table.

Sighing, Daisy said, "Very well, Cady. I am Daisy... Burroughs." She almost said. "Albright." Years of practice did that, but she knew her father would be hurt if she continued to use her mother's name whilst in his household. "The duke's oldest daughter."

She added the last knowing if she didn't offer it, there would be speculation amongst the servants as to her relationship to the duke. "And I am in need of a repair to my hair."

Taking the proffered chair, Daisy watched in the looking glass as Cady plucked the pins from her messy bun. The maid then helped herself to a brush on the dressing table and got to work. Within minutes, she had Daisy's mane brushed out, wound up, and pinned into place while managing to leave a few curls at her temples. "Would you like me to do anything else, my lady?" Cady asked as she surveyed Daisy's hair.

"Thank you for offering, but no. I should be getting down to the salon," Daisy replied. She paused a moment. "Where exactly might that be?"

"Ground floor, front of the house, opposite the dining room, my lady," Cady said as she dipped a curtsy. "I can see to helping you undress later tonight." The maid then took her leave of the bedchamber while Daisy regarded her own reflection in the looking glass.

Having removed the remaining cosmetics from her face, and with the soft curls hanging from her temples, she was stunned to see how much younger she looked than she had that morning when she had left her hotel room for Hanover Square. Younger and... fresher, perhaps.

Had she really been dreading meeting her stepmother so much that she had allowed the prospect to age her? Or was the relief at having cleared the air with her father the true reason she looked as young as she did?

Daisy made her way downstairs and found the salon at the front of the house. Having passed the parlor on the first floor, she could understand why her father said he would introduce her to his duchess in the salon—the parlor was huge and included enough seating so twenty or more could be hosted at one time.

The salon, on the other hand, was small. Intimate. Perfect for three people to enjoy a cup of tea. It also featured a window looking onto Park Lane.

After studying every piece of furniture and all the knick knacks in the room, Daisy thought she had a clear picture of the woman who could be called her stepmother. She was sure from the decor that Helen, Duchess of Ariley, was proper to a fault, mired in the mid-eighteenth century when it came to tastes, and probably stiff as a board when it came to everything else.

She hates me, she thought, not for the first time. What wife ever wanted the evidence of their husband's former liaisons to appear on their doorstep? Live under their roof? Especially when said husband had declared fidelity as part of his wedding vows, as her father had claimed to have done?

As much as I love her... he had said earlier, when they were still in St. George's.

That her father claimed to feel love for the woman and for the two children Helen had birthed since their wedding was simply a testament to how agreeable Helen Harrington could be whilst in his presence. Daisy rather doubted the duchess was agreeable otherwise, judging from her salon.

So it was a bit of a surprise when her father appeared on the threshold, Helen at his side. A surprise because the duchess was positively beaming in delight. At first, Daisy thought perhaps she was forcing the smile, but having spent years learning the tells of those she dealt with in her position as an operative for the Home Office, and later, for the Foreign Office, Daisy soon determined the woman's smile was genuine. She could see it in her eyes.

"Oh, *finally*," Helen said as she hurried into the room, her hands outstretched in front of her.

Daisy had barely straightened from her deep curtsy, stunned as the duchess took her hands and gave them a gentle shake. "It's an honor to meet you, Your Grace," she said with a nod.

"Now, there will be none of that," Helen said as she gave Daisy's hands another shake. "I've been discussing this with your father for over eight years. I told him you should refer to me as 'mother,' but he claims you would never do so. Can you at least see to calling me 'Helen,' do you suppose?"

Daisy blinked, doing her best to hide her surprise at how welcoming her stepmother seemed to be. She had never imagined her father's wife would be like this. Given how he regarded her mother, though,—how formality and fussiness wasn't to be abided in their home and among close friends— she realized she shouldn't have been so surprised. "I can and will, of course," Daisy agreed. "I must apologize for not having paid a call before now. My... employment situation wouldn't allow it."

Helen's eyes widened. "Is what your father said true then? That you were some sort of *spy* for the king?"

Daring a glance at her father, Daisy watched as he rolled his eyes and gave a slight shake of his head. "Not exactly," she hedged. "I was more of an... an operative. For the Home Office," she finally admitted. She supposed it didn't matter if the woman shared this bit of *on-dit* with the women who visited her large parlor during their morning calls. She no longer worked in Whitehall and was no longer privy to the secrets they were harboring.

James, Duke of Ariley, stepped up next to his wife and took one of her hands in his. "Sweeting, I'm not really sure Daisy can tell us very much of her former life," he said gently, noting Daisy's slight grin at hearing his words.

Her stepmother's delight dimmed a bit, but her smile didn't falter. "Well, my next guess would have been Lord Chamberlain. He's my brother by marriage—Caroline is his wife. I hear he has spies working for him in the Foreign Office," she said as an elegant eyebrow arched up. "Oh, where are my manners? Do have a seat," she said as she motioned to the settee.

Daisy dipped her head. "Thank you, Helen," she managed, barely hesitating with the name as she gave her father a quick glance. The man was regarding her with the slightest of grins, his eyes bright, and she wondered if he was on the verge of tears.

She took a seat on the velveteen settee at the same moment Helen sat across from her, relieved when Jarvis, the butler, appeared at the door with a silver tea set followed by a maid who carried a silver tray laden with cakes and biscuits.

From where she sat, Daisy had a view through the salon window. She glanced out to see that a glossy black coach had pulled up in front of the house. She couldn't make out the crest painted on the door from her vantage, but the matched greys suggested someone of wealth. "Were you expecting more guests this afternoon?" Daisy asked as she watched the maid set the tray on the low table in front of the settee. There were enough cakes to feed the entire staff of Ariley Place.

"We rarely host guests on Sundays," Helen replied sadly as she allowed the maid to pour the tea. "But if you're referring to the number of cakes on that tray, it's only because Jarvis knows all too well how much James likes them. Why, he'll eat every one of them if I don't keep count," she claimed with a teasing grin aimed in the duke's direction.

"She has the right of it, but then you already know what a sweet tooth I possess," her father said as he accepted his cup of tea.

For the first time since arriving at Ariley Place earlier that afternoon, Daisy smiled. "Oh, Father, I do," she replied, finally relaxing a bit.

She sipped her tea and answered Helen's gentle questions, countering with her own about the children. *My half-brother and sister*, she remembered, wondering why she thought it odd that she would have younger siblings. She had always known her father would have to marry and sire an heir. That he had waited so long to do so had just delayed the inevitable.

Daisy was about to help herself to a biscuit when Jarvis once again appeared on the salon's threshold. When the duke looked his way, the butler hurried over and whispered something. Then she clearly heard the butler's murmur of, "Miss Albright," and an apology.

Straightening on the settee, Daisy dared another glance out the window before turning her gaze back to the duchess and then onto her father. She was about to ask him what had him glancing her way when he announced, "Pardon me. I'll be but a moment." Then he bowed and took his leave of the parlor.

Noting how her... *stepmother*—it was hard to think of Helen in that context—gave her husband an uncertain grin, Daisy turned her attention on the duchess and continued asking questions about the children.

Someone had paid a call, but she would have to wait until her father returned to discover just who, and she may as well learn more about William and Rose in the meantime.

At least a little bit.

For if the duke didn't return in exactly one minute, she was going to be joining him.

CHAPTER 8
VISITORS BRING
GOOD NEWS

A few minutes ago

Elizabeth watched as George stepped down from the coach, ready to follow him when he turned to hold out his hand. But instead he said, "Let me make the inquiry. With any luck, the butler knows something, and if not, I can leave my card with a note for the duke."

About to put voice to a protest, Elizabeth found she couldn't when he shut the door. Opening the curtains of the coach window, she grew impatient as her husband made his way to the front door, finally lifting the brass knocker when the door didn't immediately open. What she did see was someone watching from one of the front windows. Not someone who was standing in the window, openly curious, but someone who was glancing out from where they sat inside the room beyond.

A woman. A brunette woman who definitely wasn't Helen, Duchess of Ariley.

Elizabeth let herself out of the coach and hurried up to join George just as the butler opened the door. George already had his calling card out and was about to offer it to Jarvis, but Elizabeth slipped her own, larger card, into the butler's gloved hand before he could reach for her husband's. "Might Miss Albright be in residence?" she asked. "It's very important I speak with her as soon as possible."

George angled his head toward her. "Sweeting," he started to say when he noted the look of confusion on the butler's face. "Lady Bostwick meant to ask for *Lady D...*," he paused when he realized he didn't know the young woman's first name.

He couldn't help but note how Jarvis' eyes widened just a bit before his face returned to its normally staid expression of boredom. "I'll see if Lady Daisy is in residence," he said as he took both cards. He opened the door wider and indicated they should step into the vestibule.

Having been invited to call on the duchess on more than one occasion, Elizabeth already knew the lobby of the Ariley Place mansion was larger than most. Instead of a small vestibule with only an umbrella urn and hooks for coats and a shelf for hats, this entry included a settee and a side table, paintings hung on the silk-covered walls, and a statue of a Roman general in one corner.

She was sure it was placed there to intimidate callers. Either that, or it made for a suitable hat rack.

Moving to take a seat, she watched as Jarvis exited the entry and made his way to the adjacent room.

"Why didn't you wait in the coach?" George asked as he joined her on the settee.

"She's here. I saw her in the window of the ground floor parlor. Right next door," Elizabeth whispered.

George frowned. "Ground floor parlor?" he repeated. Most parlors in townhouses were located on the first floor.

"More of a salon, really. It's small, but looks out onto Park Lane, whilst the larger parlor upstairs has a vantage over the side gardens," Elizabeth explained. "I apologize. I just... I am positive she's here, and I wanted to save you the trip of having to come back to get me."

George held her gaze for a moment before he lowered his lips to hers and gave her a quick kiss. "It wouldn't have been any trouble, my sweet," he murmured. He was about to kiss his wife again when he realized they weren't alone.

Elizabeth managed to stand before he did, dropping into a deep curtsy in front of James, Duke of Ariley. "Your Grace," she said, offering her gloved hand when the man held out his.

"This is a pleasant surprise, Lady Bostwick," James said before brushing his lips over her gloved knuckles. "Bostwick," he added as he nodded to George.

"Please excuse the interruption, Your Grace. Especially on the Lord's day," George said after he bowed.

"It's no trouble," James replied with a shake of his head. "But I have to admit to a fair bit of surprise that my oldest daughter would have a caller when she has only been in residence a couple of hours. However did you know to find her here?"

Elizabeth and George exchanged quick glances. "I didn't," Elizabeth admitted. "I merely thought you might know where we could find her. It's about a position, you see. One of some import that requires someone of her abilities to fill it just as soon as possible."

"Position?" the duke repeated. He glanced down at the larger card he held. Engraved in black lettering was the name of Elizabeth's charity, *Finding Work for the Wounded*, followed by her name and the address of the charity's office in Oxford Street. "She applied there?" he asked with some concern.

Or had he taken offense at hearing her words?

Elizabeth took a careful breath. "She did. I have a client in need of someone with her... skills."

James, standing just on the other side of the threshold, dared a look in the direction of the adjacent parlor and wasn't surprised to find Daisy watching him from where she stood just outside it. He sighed, sadness evident on his face. "Is the position in London at least?" he asked, a bit of hope sounding in his voice.

"Yes. Yes, of course," George answered.

The duke seemed torn for a moment, before he finally allowed a nod. "Very well. Come. You'll be more comfortable in the salon," he said as he led them to where Daisy stood. "I suppose you've already met," he commented.

"We haven't, actually," Elizabeth replied. "It's very good to make your acquaintance," she said as she took Daisy's hand and gave it a shake.

"Lady Bostwick," Daisy said as she dipped a curtsy. "You must know my stepmother—"

"Oh, Elizabeth, do come in for some tea and cakes," Helen interrupted as she motioned for them to come into the salon. "And George. Why fatherhood seems to agree with you," the duchess said as her smile reached her eyes. "You look younger than I have ever seen you. Oh, forgive me. *Bostwick*. It's so hard for me to think of you in that way," she added, as George kissed the back of her hand.

He angled his head to one side. "You are too kind, Your Grace. I was sure Master David was having the opposite effect on me. He has sorted door handles, you see."

"Master William is just as vexing for Ariley," Helen replied in some delight. "First boys, I suppose." She sighed. "But you're not here on a social call, are you?" she asked when she noted they still wore their coats.

"We're here to speak with Lady Daisy."

"Which is perfect timing, given I was about to join my duchess on a visit to the nursery," the duke said. "Will you excuse us both?" he asked as he gave a nod.

Helen was quick to step up next to him and give a nod of her own. "Do come again this week, won't you, Elizabeth?" she said, before she gave a nod. Arm-in-arm, she and the duke made their way to the main stairs leading to the first floor.

George watched them go, wondering if Ariley would give him the cut indirect the next time they saw one another. Elizabeth's insistence on meeting with Daisy Albright had her behaving as she would when at her charity's office. But now they were in Ariley Place. A duke's Mayfair mansion. At least the duchess had invited Elizabeth to pay a call later in the week, so perhaps all would be well for her.

"How do you take your tea, Lady Bostwick?" Daisy asked once Elizabeth had settled into the chair opposite the settee. Tempted to simply stand by the fireplace, George finally took the chair next to it.

"Milk and sugar, please. Oh, I do hope my visit isn't an inconvenience."

Daisy shook her head as she handed a cup and saucer to the viscountess, just then noting that Elizabeth was several years younger than she was. "Not at all. You may have arrived at the perfect time, in fact. I wasn't sure if her grace should learn what it was I had been doing the past few years."

"But his grace knows?" George half-asked, one eyebrow cocked up in query.

Allowing a wan grin, Daisy allowed a nod. "I think I've told him enough to compliment what he already knew," she hedged. She took a cup of tea for herself, rather relieved to have something to hold onto as they conversed.

"Have you ever played matchmaker?" Elizabeth asked before she took a sip of tea.

Daisy blinked. "Not that I recall," she answered, a grin brightening her face. "At least, not deliberately."

"In your... *prior* work, did you ever have to oversee an operation, or a business concern of any kind?" the viscountess asked. "An office or a—?"

"If you're asking if I have the administrative skills necessary to manage an office, I can assure you I do," Daisy replied quickly. "And I can do so with the utmost discretion." She hoped she didn't sound desperate. The Bostwicks were obviously considering her for something important. Why else would they seek her out on a Sunday afternoon? And however had they sorted she was Ariley's daughter? She knew she hadn't included the information on her application.

Elizabeth and George exchanged glances. "You may be aware that until your sister's recent marriage, she was an instructor at Warwick's Grammar and Finishing School," George said by way of a preamble. He couldn't help but notice how the air seemed to leave Daisy Albright all at once. "The headmistress of that school died recently, and her son finds himself in need of replacement."

"As well as a dance instructor and someone who can teach arithmetic," Elizabeth added, wondering at Daisy's odd reaction.

Daisy's gaze went from Elizabeth to George and back again to Elizabeth. "So... you're looking for a headmistress who has skills as a matchmaker and who can teach dance and arithmetic?" she guessed.

Elizabeth blinked before her eyes widened. "Oh, those would be impossible skills to find all in one woman, I should think," she replied. "Mr. Streater's hope is simply to find a headmistress to replace his late mother. I was merely asking about matchmaking skills as I am considering another charitable concern. Finding wives for the wounded. I'm simply not qualified for such an endeavor, you see."

Grinning, in part because she found the viscountess' enthusiasm infectious and partly because she couldn't believe the woman would consider her to be the headmistress of a finishing school, Daisy sighed. "May I ask why you even thought of *me?*"

George leaned forward. "My wife's charity doesn't have many applicants of your sex. Although she has placed a few, she remembered you and thought you might be suitable to the task."

Daisy angled her head. "But, you don't even know me—"

"No, but your application suggested you have skills in a number of areas," George replied. "As a duke's daughter, you no doubt possess a level of education surpassing those who are employed at Warwick's. Discretion, of course, is important, as is management of the people who would report to you. Teachers and servants."

"Students and their parents," Elizabeth put in, an elegant eyebrow arching.

Frowning at this last bit, Daisy allowed a sigh. "This... Mr. Streater. Is he... *familiar* with Warwick's? Will he be present at the school?"

"Not if he can help it," George answered with a shake of his head. "He is in charge of the clerks at the Bank of England." He dared a glance at his wife before he added, "He's my very best friend, and I know he is quite out of his element and desperate to find someone to fill his mother's shoes. Someone whom the existing staff can be assured is not the dragon that Mrs. Streater has been for the past two decades."

"George!" Elizabeth scolded, before she leaned forward and added, "He has the right of it, of course. I couldn't abide Mrs. Streater when I was a student there, but her son is a charming man. He was my very first client at *Finding Work for the Wounded*, in fact."

She didn't add that she had been the one to seek him out. She remembered Mr. Streater from a *musical* soirée, and despite having asked for an introduction, she had been denied the chance to meet the second son of a baron by Lady Pettigrew, a cranky old viscountess.

Her brows furrowing, Daisy leaned forward. "Was he your matchmaker, too?" she guessed, her gaze darting between the viscount and viscountess.

George and Elizabeth once again exchanged glances. "Not exactly," Elizabeth hedged at the same time George said, "He was instrumental." When his wife gave him a look of surprise, he added, "He said I would like you."

Elizabeth blinked and blushed when she remembered what George had said to her the night they had shared their first meal together. The first time they had been intimate.

You helped my friend get his job back at the bank.

Had she never started her charity, she might never have met George Bennett-Jones.

Daisy suppressed a grin while she watched the couple interact, reminded of how her father once behaved with her late mother. "May I ask as to Mr. Streater's... infirmity?" If the man had been Lady Bostwick's first client, it stood to reason he had been wounded in a war.

"He lost most of his right arm at Quatros Bras," George replied in a hushed tone, well aware of his wife's look of disbelief. The woman who sat before them was perceptive. And clever.

Daisy gave a slow nod. "And yet he is the head of clerks at a bank," she whispered.

"Because my sweeting saw to it he was rehired there," George stated, unaware he used his private name for Elizabeth.

Daisy straightened and considered the viscount's words. When had she ever heard an aristocrat refer to his wife using a term of endearment usually saved for the privacy of their home? Or their bedchamber?

Father, she remembered then.

The duke never seemed embarrassed at how he addressed her mother in public. Or in front of his daughters.

My sweeting.

The reminder almost had tears collecting in the corners of her eyes. "So... I would not be sharing the responsibilities of running Warwick's with another?" she asked then, her eyes darting between the two who sat across from her.

"You will be on your own, I fear," Elizabeth said in a

quiet voice. She exhaled. "Oh, dear. We're not exactly presenting this opportunity in the best possible light, are we?" she murmured.

"And yet, I find I am intrigued," Daisy said before allowing a nod. "How might I apply for the position?"

Elizabeth brightened. "I can send a note to Mr. Streater when I return to Bostwick Place," she said with some excitement. "I know he will be at Warwick's on the morrow. Perhaps you could meet him there? In his late mother's office?"

Daisy allowed a shrug. "I find I have nothing scheduled for the early morning, although I have to believe my... stepmother might have some calls in mind."

"Calls you would rather not make?" George guessed.

Her eyes widening, Daisy asked, "Is it that obvious?"

Elizabeth giggled. "Feel free to blame my husband. He already believes the duke will shun him at every event for the rest of the Season for having paid this call," she said as she dimpled.

"Sweeting," George said with a sigh.

Daisy understood his meaning immediately. They had interrupted her father's attempt at introducing her into the life at Ariley Place. "Do not be concerned. I shall see to it you are held in his grace's highest esteem," she said as she regarded him. "I do have some influence in that regard."

George blinked. "You would do that?" he asked in a whisper, as if he thought the Duke of Ariley might be standing just outside the door to the salon, listening to their every word.

"Of course. Why just today, I have discovered that as his oldest daughter, I have him wrapped quite tightly around my pinky," she said as she held up her smallest finger.

"Surely you knew it before today," Elizabeth replied with a grin.

Daisy allowed a wan smile, deciding it was better not to admit she hadn't known it until that morning.

What a fool I have been, she thought with a sigh before saying, "I will pay a call on Mr. Streater in the morning." Then she offered them more tea.

Thanking her for the hospitality but reminded of the time by the chiming clock on the mantle, Elizabeth shook her head. "I've a babe at home in need of her dinner. I do hope you and Mr. Streater get on with one another."

"As do I," George said, standing when his wife did. "If you could give our regards to the duke and duchess?"

Daisy grinned. "I shall," she promised as she led them to the vestibule, her limp more evident now that she had been sitting too long. "However can I thank you for considering me?" she asked as George kissed the back of her hand.

"Accept the position when Mr. Streater offers it," George replied. Despite his warning to Teddy, he had a feeling his friend would offer the position to the first applicant who appeared at Warwick's.

Elizabeth rolled her eyes. "And should you think of someone in search of a husband..." she added before she stepped out the front door.

"Now, sweeting," George scolded as he followed her out.

Daisy stood and regarded the closed door for a very long time before she turned and made her way up to the nursery.

She needed to plead for clemency for Lord Bostwick. And it was past time she meet her new siblings.

CHAPTER 9
A SURPRISE IS REVEALED

The next morning

"You're going where?" James, Duke of Ariley, asked as a footman set a plate of eggs and a rasher of bacon in front of him. He had already finished a cup of coffee and was about to start another when Daisy brought up her plans for the day.

"Warwick's Grammar and Finishing School," Daisy replied, wondering if her stepmother ever ate breakfast with her father. A copy of *The Times*, newly ironed and half-open before the duke, had held his attention until Daisy entered the breakfast parlor.

"You *are* aware your sister no longer holds her position there," he half-asked, his gaze taking in her smart hairstyle and carriage gown. Seeing her like this had him understanding just how she could pass as a spy for the Home Office—no one would guess she wasn't anything other than a prim and proper daughter of the *ton*, albeit an older one.

"I am. But I should have liked to have been a visitor to her classroom when she taught arithmetic." Daisy paused, knowing he would eventually ask as to her reason for visiting the school. Instead of waiting for the inevitable question, she relented and simply admitted why she had requested a conveyance for the morning. "Lady Bostwick believes I could be headmistress of the finishing school."

James set down his coffee cup in its saucer, the fine china clattering a bit as his brows furrowed. He had wondered why the Bostwicks had paid the call the day before. He had intended to ask Daisy when she appeared in the nursery, but the delight in her eyes at meeting her younger brother had him thinking instead of how happy he was the two had finally met.

And then, when Helen had given up her hold on Rose so that Daisy could hold the babe, he had fought back tears. The expression of joy on his eldest daughter's face as Rose opened her eyes and smiled would stay in his memory for the rest of his days. Surely some sense of maternal longing would settle in her breast. Some desire to marry and have one of her own.

He need only find a man worthy of her. He rather doubted she would manage it on her own.

About to follow that line of thought, he remembered what Daisy had just said and frowned. "Has Mrs. Streater finally been fired?"

Daisy blinked. Apparently word of the old woman's death hadn't yet reached Ariley Place. "*Retired*, is more the thing. She died, and her son has inherited the school. According to Lady Bostwick, Mr. Streater is desperate to find a replacement."

His copy of *The Times* forgotten, James stared at his daughter. "This is a surprise. She's been running that school for... *forever* as far as I can remember," he remarked. "Have you... *experience* working in finishing schools that I'm not aware of?" he asked. Despite having tried to discover exactly what Daisy might have done in her various guises as an operative, she had never come out and admitted anything to him.

What little he knew had come from Lord Chamberlain, and he only knew of her assignments for the Foreign Office.

"None," Daisy replied before she lifted a forkful of eggs to her lips. "But it's an administrative position with a few employees to manage, so I believe I can do it."

"Do what?" Helen asked from where she had paused on the threshold of the breakfast parlor.

Daisy exchanged a quick glance and a shake of her head with her father, who seemed to understand her meaning immediately.

"Ride a horse. My daughter hasn't been on a mount since her mother died," James stated, already standing. He moved around the table to join his wife, taking one of her hands in his and kissing the back of it. "I hope I didn't wake you when I took my leave of you this morning," he whispered, before he kissed her cheek.

"You know I cannot sleep if you're not next to me," Helen replied, her whisper matching his. In a louder voice, she added, "Daisy is welcome to try Adonis. He's in need of exercise and is ever so gentle."

"Adonis?" Daisy repeated, a grin coming to her face. "Father," she scolded.

"*I* didn't name him," James said as he led Helen to her place at the table. "Seems he already had the moniker when Mr. Comber trained him."

"Mr. Comber?" Daisy repeated, straightening in her chair.

"Alistair. The second son of Aimsley. Oh, and your sister's newest brother, I suppose," James added. "The man is a crack with horses. When you're ready to choose a mount of your own, I'll be sure to enlist his services."

Although she had loved riding horses when she was younger, Daisy found she didn't miss the pastime. The idea of parading in the park amidst other members of the *ton* at five o'clock in the afternoon held little appeal. "Thank you, Father," she said with a nod.

"Will you join me on morning calls today?" Helen asked as she regarded the plate of breakfast foods the footman had set before her. "I thought to leave about one o'clock." Although she would have been fine with the eggs, sausages and unbuttered toast, the kippers had her struggling to maintain her composure.

Daisy noticed, and quickly reached over to remove the plate from in front of her stepmother. She turned to the footman. "Remove the kippers from the sideboard. Immediately," she ordered. "Take this, as well," she said as she shoved the plate at him.

Blinking, the footman quickly bowed and whisked the offending dish from the room. Even before he had taken his leave, Daisy had rushed to the window and opened it.

"What...?" James started to say as he watched Daisy and then turned his attention onto his wife.

Daisy remained by the window and regarded the duchess, who merely angled her head and gave it a small shake. Daisy's eyes widened in response, a clear sign she thought it was past time the duchess inform his grace she was expecting another baby. Helen had to be at least two months pregnant.

After four children, how could her father not have noticed his wife's condition?

Although she would have liked to finish her breakfast, Daisy said, "If you'll excuse me, I have an appointment in Glasshouse Street. Forgive me, but I rather doubt I shall be back in time to join you." With that, she hurried out of the breakfast parlor, took her pelisse from Jarvis, and left through the front door. Half-expecting to have to hail a hackney, she rolled her eyes when she saw her request for a conveyance had been filled by way of a barouche.

"How long have you been waiting for me?" she asked of the driver.

The man gave a shrug. "I only just pulled up to the curb this very minute, my lady," he replied in alarm. "I feared I had kept you waiting."

Daisy was reminded once again she was the daughter of a duke. "You have not. Warwick's, in Glasshouse Street," she stated as she allowed a tiger to help her into the equipage.

"Yes, my lady." And with that, the driver had the horses in motion.

CHAPTER 10
CONFESSION IS SUCH A RELIEF

*M*eanwhile, back in the breakfast parlor
"May I inquire as to what that was all about?" James asked, his attention having returned to his duchess. Although her complexion had appeared a pasty white only a moment ago, color had begun to return to her cheeks.

She sighed and allowed a shrug. "I wasn't sure, so I haven't said anything. I may just have a stomach flu—"

"Or you could be expecting my spare heir," James interrupted, a grin slowly widening to lift his cheeks. Crinkles formed on either side of his eyes. "I was going to ask you last week—"

"Last week?" she countered, her eyes wide. "But... *how?* I didn't suspect until..." She sighed. Since she was still nursing her daughter on occasion, her monthly courses hadn't yet resumed.

Now it seemed they wouldn't.

James broke out into laughter. "I have fathered four children. I'm well aware of morning sickness, my love." He shook his head. "You poor thing," he said with a good deal of sympathy as he leaned over and bussed her on the top of her hair. He turned his head to the side. "Bring some toast, please," he called out.

A footman was through the door in only a moment, a plate of unbuttered toast held out.

"I do hope it is a boy," Helen murmured.

"I wouldn't mind another girl," James countered, despite how vexed he felt by his eldest.

"But you need a spare," she argued.

James allowed a wan grin. "There will be other opportunities." He sobered. "I hope?" he added as his brows furrowed. "You weren't thinking to... to take a lov...lover after another boy is born. Were you?"

Helen gave him a quelling glance. "James," she scolded. "I wouldn't do such a thing." She stared at him a moment, her long lashes widening in alarm. "Were you... thinking of taking a m...mistress?" she asked, barely able to get the word out.

His eyebrows reaching nearly into his hairline, James gave a shake of his head. "Never!" he replied. "I pledged fidelity, remember?"

"As did I," she replied defensively. Her sigh of relief rather loud, Helen allowed a wan grin. "Well, then," she managed as she helped herself to a piece of toast. "If you're not doing anything important during the next hour, perhaps you... you could help me take my mind off how your daughter seemed to know about my condition," she suggested, one of her brows furrowing.

Angling his head, James remembered just then that it had been Daisy who had noticed Helen's distress, effectively taking matters into her own hands and ordering the servants about as if she were the lady of the house. As if she knew first-hand the symptoms of morning sickness. "What are you suggesting?"

Dipping her head a bit, Helen finally replied. "Has she given you a grandchild?"

James straightened so suddenly, Helen blinked. "Of course not," he answered, perhaps a bit too quickly. It was possible Daisy had had a baby. She was old enough. She had been away from London for a long time. But he was sure her former employer would have informed him if she had ever shown signs of carrying a child.

She wouldn't have been able to remain in her position if she were pregnant.

Would she?

Left unsettled by his wife's query, James returned his attention to *The Times* and pretended to read while he plotted how he was going to discover if there was a grandchild out there. Somewhere.

CHAPTER 11
AN INTERVIEW GOES FROM
AWRY TO ALL RIGHT

half-hour later, at Warwick's

Theodore Streater regarded the ledger spread out before him, his brows furrowing as he attempted to make out the column of numbers followed by another column of two or three letters that filled the page. As an accomptant, he spent hours and hours every day working with ledgers, entering numbers and adding and subtracting, his only issue the occasional errant drop of ink obliterating his carefully formed numbers.

Fairly sure these numbers were written in his mother's hand, he wondered at their meaning. He glanced over at another ledger. That one had been easy to decipher—the salaries for the instructors and servants were entered at the end of each month right next to each name, although an occasional deduction showed his mother charged the live-in instructors for their rooms.

A second ledger was made up entirely of incomes and expenses for the school—tuition fees vs. gas, coal, candles, oil, food, ink—all neatly entered for every month going back to who-knew-when.

This third ledger, though, had him flummoxed. The

numbers were larger, and listed in one long column with only initials or single letters noted next to each entry. His concentration was such that he didn't hear the knock at the office door, nor look up when it opened.

"Pardon me, sir, but are you Mr. Streater?"

Teddy gave a start, his head jerking up to discover a rather lovely woman regarding him from the doorway. She had her head through a slight opening, as if she didn't dare open it enough to reveal the rest of her.

At the moment, Teddy rather wished she had not just interrupted him, but had come all the way into the office, removed the ledger from the desk, and seated herself on his lap.

She was that beautiful. And it had been that long since he was in the company of a young woman and no one else.

"Hullo," he managed to say, setting aside the ledger in favor of staring at his visitor.

"Good morning," Daisy replied. She stepped all the way into the office and dipped a curtsy, which had Teddy remembering he wasn't standing.

He got to his feet, his wooden arm banging against the mahogany desk before he managed to get it down by his side. He gave a bow. "Theodore Streater, at your service, Miss...?"

He rather wished he *was* in her service. Doing anything she wanted him to do. Whenever she wanted him to do it.

He almost said something to that effect when she said, "Miss Daisy Albright. Lady Bostwick sent me. Said... she said you were in need of me."

Teddy blinked before he silently blessed Elizabeth Bennett-Jones.

Again.

The woman had been responsible for him regaining his position as a clerk at the Bank of England. She saw to paying the bribe that had the manager re-hiring him despite the fact that he was missing his right arm.

And, apparently, she had already arranged for a match-maker to send him a beautiful wife. "This is a pleasant surprise," he managed. "And so soon."

"Oh?" Daisy replied, moving to stand before the massive desk she knew was meant to intimidate anyone who stepped into the office. Either Mrs. Streater had inherited it from a male relative, or she had purchased it with the intention of frightening anyone who came into the office. The thought that *she* might be the one to sit behind it should she be hired in the position of headmistress had Daisy fighting a frown. And then she thought perhaps it would be possible to replace the monstrosity with a small escritoire. Something more suitable for a woman.

She didn't want any of the instructors to fear her.

Daisy held out her left hand, intending to shake his. Although his right sleeve appeared as if an arm filled it—a gloved hand extended beyond the hem of the sleeve—she remembered the mention of him having lost his right arm during the war. "Lady Bostwick was quite insistent I needed to see you as soon as possible. In the event you had others under consideration for the position."

Teddy blinked. "Well, she needn't have worried," he replied as he reached out with his left hand. Instead of shaking hers, he lifted her hand to his lips. He had to bend over the desk in order to bestow the kiss on her kid-gloved knuckles, but he managed rather well before he motioned for her to sit down. "She didn't even know I was in want of someone until yesterday morning." He almost added, *But then, I didn't either*, but decided against it.

Odd, wasn't it, that the very suggestion of a wife would have him considering marriage again?

"Then I am doubly honored she sought me out," Daisy replied as she settled onto the hard wooden chair in front of the desk. She had a thought she would replace it with a tufted chair should she be hired. No need to have visitors to her office feeling uncomfortable.

Teddy was at a loss as to what to say. How did one propose to court someone? He had befriended his first wife back when they were still in the schoolroom. Gertrude had been the only sister of one of his friends. He found her amiable and willing. Theirs was not a love match, *per se*, but he had grown more fond of her as they aged.

That war had interrupted their union—twice—was all his fault. He had been the one to answer the call, the soldier side of him determined to help defeat Napoleon—again—no matter the cost. That Gertrude had succumbed to pneumonia was merely fate. That she had died whilst he was on the Continent, losing his arm and almost his life, was the worst blow.

"I should tell you that I am a widower," Teddy said as he took his seat, making sure his wooden arm was left resting on the desk.

"I don't see as how that's relevant," Daisy replied, one brow furrowing in question.

Teddy blinked. "Well, then you should at least know that I was devoted to my late wife. I never took a mistress, nor did I seek comfort in the arms of a..." It was at this point he realized he was being entirely inappropriate. These were the traits he could mention when he was actually courting her. Perhaps when they were in a barouche or a phaeton, on their way to the British Museum or to Hyde Park for a ride in Rotten Row.

Or, on second thought, perhaps he shouldn't be mentioning them at all.

"Of a...?" Daisy prompted, wondering what he was about to say. She was rather curious as to how he might refer to a prostitute. Had George Bennett-Jones sent word ahead about her former position? Assumed she had filled the role of mistress in one of her guises as an operative for the Home

Office, or later, for the Foreign Office, and was therefore tainted? Ruined?

She *was* ruined by all definitions of the word. Besides the Home Office Secretary and Lord Chamberlain and those who worked for them, though, who in London even knew anything about her missions? Her former liaisons should hardly matter when it came to filling a position as a headmistress.

Teddy shook is head. "No one. I'm just... I am in search of someone with whom I can spend the rest of my days —*nights*, rather, since I intend to keep my position at the Bank of England."

Daisy blinked, a bit shocked at hearing his words. At least the man was honest. Upfront about his expectations. She rather wished Lord Bostwick might have mentioned something the afternoon prior, so that she could explain she had no intention of practicing her late mother's occupation.

"So... you're in search of a mistress who can also act as headmistress for Warwick's?" Daisy asked in a measured voice. She was about to stand up, curtsy, and take her leave of the office when she saw the matching look of confusion cross Mr. Streater's face.

The look of alarm and realization.

He was halfway up from his chair, his one hand waving in the air. "Oh, please, forgive me, Miss Albright," he nearly shouted. He sat down—hard—and allowed a sound that could have been disgust or defeat, or perhaps a frog on the verge of dying. "I think there's been a misunderstanding, and it's been entirely on my part." The word "dammit" was added in a whisper.

Angling her head to one side, Daisy gave him the benefit of the doubt. "You thought I was here at the behest of a matchmaker, when in fact, I am here to apply for the position of headmistress of Warwick's," she stated.

"Exactly," he murmured, his shoulders slumping.

Daisy wondered how the man before her, who had seemed so confident and self-assured only a moment ago, could become the epitome of a broken soul in mere seconds. "Are you still in need of a headmistress?" she asked in a quiet voice.

Teddy nodded. "I am. I cannot... I cannot do this. I cannot run a finishing school, or teach the classes lacking an instructor. I've no idea how. I have a position at the bank—a good position," he replied.

Daisy allowed a nod. "May I inquire as to if there are others seeking the position? Others you may have under consideration?" she asked, her voice gentle. She didn't want him believing she was still about to bolt from the office.

Teddy allowed a one-shouldered shrug. "I thought perhaps one of the instructors could fill the position, but after reviewing their characters and reading my mother's notes on their employment, there's not a one I would trust with my mother's legacy," he explained. "Well, except for perhaps Miss Albright, but I discovered she has recently married a viscount and resigned her position." He suddenly straightened, his brows rising to new heights on his forehead. "Is she a relation of yours, perhaps?" he asked, with almost too much hope.

Heartened by the renewed interest he showed, Daisy allowed a grin. "The Viscountess Breckinridge is my sister. As for my qualifications, I know everything she knew upon being hired by Mrs. Streater. We had the same governesses and the same tutors," she replied, straightening so she sat on the front edge of the hard chair.

"You're hired," Teddy said.

Daisy blinked again. "But... but you haven't even asked me about my administrative skills," she argued.

"The fact that you even know the word is proof enough you are qualified," Teddy countered. He frowned. "But do tell," he encouraged.

Taking a deep breath—Daisy understood the job was hers as long as she didn't say something stupid—she decided truth would be best when it came to her past employment. "For the past several years, I have been employed by an office which exists to serve King and country, engaged in missions to expose traitors and those who would see us defeated by the French," she said quickly, pleased when Mr. Streater suddenly leaned forward, his eyes wide with interest. "I can provide references, of course."

"Of course," Teddy replied with a nod, half-tempted to ask for names. He didn't want to appear ignorant if he didn't recognize them, though. Although his first thought was to inquire about her work to expose traitors, it dawned on him by which office she might have been employed.

One in Whitehall, no doubt.

He had a suspicion she wouldn't be able to provide any particulars even if he asked. "Go on."

Daisy angled her head, a bit concerned when her would-be employer didn't ask for names. "I was raised in an aristocrat's household, and I understand the importance of propriety and virtue." Even if she was no longer a virgin, she thought it important to bring up the fact that it was a valuable asset for young ladies. "I am not adverse to doing the paperwork required of the position, nor am I intimidated by younger daughters of the wealthy or cits who think they have London in the palms of their hands. I am fair, but I can be judgmental when circumstances require it. I will not tolerate misbehavior, nor will I show favoritism." At this point, she wasn't sure what else to say, so she merely sighed and went silent.

"Can you teach arithmetic?"

Daisy stared at Theodore Streater a moment before she finally allowed a nod. "If I must, I can," she admitted.

"You're hired."

"But, what about a dance instructor?" she countered, remembering her sister had done that, too.

"Can you teach dance, too?" Teddy asked, his voice filled with such hope—such awe—that Daisy found she wanted to please him anyway she could.

"If I must," she replied, a bit more hesitant. If dance classes were later in the day, her limp would be evident. She was about mention it, but the look on his face reminded her of how Ethan Range, Marquess of Plymouth, appeared when he was in ecstasy. Of how his face lit with such joy. Of how his features seemed strained but youthened at the moment of his release.

How she missed having a lover who appreciated her skills, even if they were a bit limited.

For a moment, she almost wished she was applying to be Theodore Streater's mistress.

"I will teach the dance class, of course. Until I can find someone better qualified to fill the position," Daisy finally said with a shrug. When he regarded her with an expression of—*was that devotion? Gratitude?* Relief, certainly—she allowed a grin.

Until he asked the next question.

"Can you... can you teach grammar?"

On the verge of replying in the negative, Daisy realized this was her opportunity to mold young ladies into women who would might actually use the knowledge they learned at the school. Just because daughters of aristocrats were usually taught at home by governesses and tutors and then rarely used anything they learned once they married, daughters of the middle class and the wealthy of London might actually benefit from what they learned. "I can," she finally said with a nod. "When do I start?"

Glancing about the office, as if he was seeking answers from the walls, Teddy said, "Tomorrow? Or the next day, if you find tomorrow too soon. Or the day after, perhaps? It has to be before Saturday, though. I'm hosting a tea—or rather, Lady Bostwick will be hosting the tea—for all the instructors. That is where I plan to introduce myself as the new owner. I wish to use that occasion to formally introduce the new headmistress, you see."

Daisy had to suppress the urge to chuckle. Apparently, Mr. Streater wasn't expecting to inherit a finishing school. But wouldn't his mother have mentioned the inevitable at some point? Apparently, the woman had been ancient back when Lady Bostwick attended the school. "Tomorrow will be fine," she said, once again amused by his look of relief. She hesitated with her next question, but given she had no intention of dipping into the funds her father had bestowed in the form of her inheritance, she asked, "And what of compensation?"

Other than having learned all the salaries of those who worked at the school, Teddy hadn't actually given the matter of salary for a headmistress a moment's thought. "I can pay you one hundred pounds a year," he offered. The number matched the amount his mother had been taking by way of pay, at least according to the ledger still before him on the desk.

"One-hundred-and-fifty," Daisy countered. She had made more than that working for the Home Office, but her position as an operative required she inhabit the role continuously until a mission was complete. She imagined a role as headmistress of a boarding school would be similar.

"Two-hundred, and that's my final offer," Teddy stated.

Daisy blinked.

Well, there was definitely a reason he needed *her* to teach the arithmetic class, it seemed, but what did that say about his skills as an accomptant for the Bank of England? "Done," she replied, wondering if he was a bit addled by her presence, or if he was playing with her. No matter. At least he was a charming man.

Charming and obviously besotted.

She wondered if he had an apartment on site and what it might be like to bed him. She had never been with a man who was missing a limb, but surely the loss of an arm wouldn't prevent him from being able to make love.

She could just imagine that conversation.

Now that we have the particulars out of the way, may I inquire as to your availability as a lover? she might ask. *Given my service to King and country, and yours, I am thinking we might suit one another in that regard. That is, if you don't have a young lady in mind for the position of your wife?*

She thought of how he might blink before asking, *Are you quite serious?* Then, even before she could answer, he would add, *You're... you're propositioning me?* and behave as if he were scandalized.

She supposed he would be.

Anyone would be!

And she would smile demurely, of course, amused by his question. *When I arrived, you thought I was here so you might consider courting me,* she would remind him. *Has your interest in me waned since then?*

And Mr. Streater would blink again. *No,* he would manage to respond, although she was sure the word would come out sounding more like the croak of a frog in heat.

*D*aisy gave her head a bit of a shake, stunned she had allowed the momentary reverie.

Whatever was she imagining? And why? Did she really miss the company of a man so much? The thought of Mr. Streater as a bedmate was completely incongruous to her desire to work for the man. Especially as a headmistress of a finishing school.

Then she remembered her father and how he behaved with his duchess. So beholden. So... *in love.* Her heart clenched a bit, and she found she had to swallow away the sudden tightness in her throat.

She placed a calling card on the edge of the desk. "I will arrive tomorrow at precisely eight o'clock in the morning. I shall see to it the classes are all taught by those who should teach them, all at their regularly scheduled times." She paused and took a breath. "Now, is there a room I'm expected to occupy when I'm not here in the office?"

Obviously relieved at learning she would be there on the morrow, Teddy allowed a sigh. "It's a bit more than just one room," the new owner of Warwick's replied, sounding a bit defensive as he stood up. "Let me show you to your apartment," he added as he moved to open the office door. "One of the maids saw to it my mother's effects were removed yesterday—not that there were many," he explained as he led her down the hallway to an adjacent door.

"Pray tell, why ever not?" she asked. Daisy imagined an older woman would have acquired all manner of *objets d'art* over the course of her lifetime, as well as keepsakes and jewelry, clothing and shoes.

"I discovered she lived the life of a pauper when she could afford far better," Teddy answered as he reached for the door handle. Although he hadn't had a chance to check on the maid's progress, he was surprised to find the four rooms nearly empty. Only a few sticks of furniture occupied the parlor, the bedroom, and a small bathing chamber. The kitchen didn't even have a table at which to eat a meal. "Oh, my, it's worse than I thought," he murmured, daring a glance at Daisy. Sure she would be appalled at the sparse accommodations, he was relieved to see she wasn't openly dismayed.

"It will do just fine, Mr. Streater," Daisy said as she ducked her head into the bathing chamber. "Might I arrange to have some things brought in this afternoon? I think I should like to spend the night here."

Teddy stared at her, his gaze darting to a door in the

bedchamber. "Of course," he replied, the sound of his swallow nearly audible.

Curious as to what had him reacting with such nervousness, Daisy hurried over to the door and opened it, only to discover it led straight into the office. "This is convenient," she said as she turned to regard him. She was tempted to add, *Should you wish to pursue me for a position other than that of headmistress, know that I can be found here after my workday is complete. Nine o'clock, shall we say?* but good sense had her holding her tongue. The poor man would probably be so tongue-tied, and he might actually think she was serious.

Apparently having trouble finding his voice, Teddy finally managed an, "Indeed," before he straightened. He reached into a waistcoat pocket and held out the key to the apartment. "In the event I'm not here later, please know that there shouldn't be anyone in this building but you and the servants. Their rooms are upstairs. I'll inform the housekeeper she's to expect you."

Daisy dared a glance out the apartment door. There were two other closed doors across the hall, and a set of stairs at the end of the hallway. "No one else lives on this floor?" she queried.

"I should hope not. The rooms across the hall appear to be for storage." He had taken a look in both, a bit surprised to find costumes hung from pegs around one of the rooms and trunks filled with what could have been a theatre troupe's props in the other. He had been about to seek out one of the instructors to ask if the costumes belonged to the school when he discovered an inventory sheet for the theatre appreciation class. Apparently, students not only attended the theatre and read plays, but they put them on, too.

"Do all the instructors board here as well?" Daisy asked, remembering that Diana shared one of the adjacent houses with a number of other teachers.

Teddy sighed. "I think most of them do. Truth be told,

I'm not really sure. By now, I expect they all know what's happened, but it's not because I have… informed them," he stammered. "I haven't met them. But the tea is this Saturday," he said again.

A look of sorrow crossed Daisy's face. "I am sorry for your loss, Mr. Streater. Your mother managed a rather successful school for a very long time. I do hope I can meet your expectations." She sighed and gave one more glance around the small apartment. "If there's nothing else, then I shall take my leave and pay a call on Bostwick Place to let her ladyship know I have accepted the position." With that, she gave a curtsy.

Teddy bowed and watched her go, settling onto the threadbare settee and wincing as he did so. The stuffing had long since lost its cushioning effect.

Whatever had been going through the beautiful head of Miss Daisy Albright when we were in the office? he wondered.

He knew what had been going through his head.

Both of them.

Why, he had almost propositioned her! Almost asked if she might consider joining him in his bedchamber in Bruton Street. And every other room of the townhouse he had occupied since gaining his position at the bank. The only reason he hadn't was the thought that his words would come out sounding like a frog in heat.

For some reason he couldn't quite put his finger on, Daisy Albright didn't come across as the type of woman who would make an agreeable wife—at least, not in the traditional sense. Perhaps because she would be far too *managing*. Far too controlling. She would probably henpeck him to death.

And he would love every minute of it.

For he was quite sure she was a completely different type of woman when it came to matters of a carnal nature.

The thought of waking up to find her in his bed had his

heart beating a bit faster, had his breaths quickening, had his breeches suddenly feeling far too tight.

He glanced down, rather stunned to discover just why. After so long without a woman, it was becoming apparent he needed one.

He wondered if he should hire a mistress.

The thought surprised him.

What would he look for in a lover? Brunette, blonde, or red-headed? Short or tall? Voluptuous or slender?

Every time he tried to imagine who he wished to discover lying next to him in bed, a vision of Miss Albright filled his mind's eye.

When his wooden arm bumped against the side of the settee, he winced. *What woman would want to wake up next to me?* he wondered. *To this?*

He thought of the fairy tales that featured frogs, but found he couldn't imagine being kissed by a princess.

Perhaps a mistress could abide him and his missing arm —if she were paid enough. He could certainly afford to hire one now that he was rich.

The idea had him straightening on the settee. Surely George could provide some guidance. He'd had a mistress for eight years before he married Lady Elizabeth.

Reminded that he had an appointment at Angelo's Fencing Academy to spar with the viscount later that afternoon, Teddy made his way back to the office to finish the review of his mother's ledgers.

For the second time in two days, he would have a chance to speak with his best friend.

CHAPTER 12
A NEWLY RICH MAN

*M*onday afternoon

The walk down Jermyn Street had Theodore Streater wondering why he had never visited the shops along the venerable street before. With windowed storefronts displaying all manner of goods, he could easily spend the entire allowance he had granted himself for the month.

Having left the school the hour before, he had thought to simply head straight for Angelo's Fencing Academy and wait there for his appointed time on the pisté with George. The reminder that he had funds he could spend—funds that would purchase anything from a new townhouse down to a new toothbrush—had him deciding it was instead time to shop. His townhouse might be modest, but that didn't mean the furnishings inside had to remain so.

I can use a new bed, he thought, trying with all his might not to imagine Miss Albright, naked, in the middle of it. *Or all new furniture.* An image of his new headmistress sitting primly and fully clothed on a velvet settee flashed through his mind.

That was more like it.

Prim and proper. Miss Albright had to be proper given her new position.

His mind made up, he decided he could afford to pay a call in St. Martin's Lane and place an order at Chippendale's. From there, he would simply hail a hackney to take him to the Opera House in Haymarket where the academy was located.

When he passed a tailor's shop, he thought of what it would be like to have a different suit of clothing for every day of the week instead of the two he owned now. He could afford a pair of Hobys and a pair of Hessians. Another pair of shoes. Two of each, even. A thought of employing Stultz of Clifford Street to make his suits made him grin. He was smiling when he thought of ordering a new coat at Schweitzer & Davidson of Cork Street. Why, he could afford to be as well-dressed as any aristocrat!

He stared at his reflection in the window at Floris, the purveyor of colognes, perfumes, brushes and combs a reminder he could use a new toothbrush. Although he had rarely used cologne, he was suddenly interested in the idea of it, which had him entering the fragrant shop.

The scents of lime, flowers, and exotic spice filled his nostrils as he made his way to a display of bottles. He was about to lift a bottle of "Limes" from a display when the shopkeeper approached and offered to help.

"It's our most popular scent for the summer," the man said as he regarded Teddy. "Would you like to try it?"

Teddy gave a non-commital shrug. "I suppose. But I was interested in something more... suited to me."

The shopkeeper's brows elevated. "A custom fragrance, perhaps?" he asked in surprise.

Remembering how Mr. Whittaker at the bank made comments as to the fact that he only wore custom colognes, Teddy angled his head. "Perhaps," he replied. "What might that... be like?" He knew he didn't want to smell like Mr.

Whittaker. The bank official could be mistaken for a molly given he exuded an odor akin to most of the women who attended the opera.

"One of our chemists can assist in that regard," the shop-keeper said. He turned and led Teddy to a back counter where a very young man was sniffing the contents of several different bottles, his face displaying various expressions ranging from disgust to approval. "Mr. Tennison has the best nose in the business, Mister...?"

"Streater," Teddy offered, giving a nod to the young man who held out his hand.

"It's good to meet you. Might I ask what it is you do?"

Teddy frowned. "Do?" he repeated.

"Yes. Do. Even men of leisure do something. Drink? Hunt? Play cards? Gamble? Archery? Attend the theatre?"

"I fence," Teddy offered, deciding he wouldn't mention his occupation just yet. He wondered what the man might come up with for a working man.

"Ah," Mr. Tennison replied. "A sporting man."

It was at that moment that Teddy realized just how lucky he had been to have come to the attention of the former Lady Elizabeth whilst they both attended the same *musicale* at Lady Worthington's house in Park Lane three years prior. How lucky he was that Lady Elizabeth had decided she would do what she must to see to it he was rehired in his old position at the bank. How lucky he was to be fitted with a prosthetic arm—a carved wooden arm on which he could pull on a glove and fool most people into believing he had two. For with his comment that he fenced, Mr. Tennison's visage displayed a look of admiration and respect. "And I am the head of clerks at the Bank of England," Teddy added, just to reinforce his claim.

The man's face fell. "Well, I suppose I can come up with something appropriate for both," he said, without a lot of enthusiasm.

Teddy blinked, realizing he shouldn't have admitted to having a position at all. "I understand it will be a challenge, but I was told only you could rise to it," he said with an arched brow, deciding that by daring the young man, he might regain the chemist's interest.

"Indeed. Your informant is most correct."

Teddy had to suppress his look of admiration as the young man was spurred into action. He watched as Mr. Tennison moved to a leather case of small bottles and began opening several, one after another. For the next five minutes, he used the eyedroppers in the bottles to create a mixture in a small, clear bottle, finally filling it from a large bottle of what Teddy realized was alcohol.

"Hold out your wrist," Mr. Tennison demanded, an eyedropper poised over the top of the bottle he had just mixed. "I've held off on including too much citrus, but I can always add more if need be."

Teddy did as he was told, extending his gloved hand. His sleeve didn't retreat enough to expose his wrist though, and despite his attempt to bend his arm more so it would, Teddy thought his ruse would be discovered when he didn't raise his other hand to help push back his sleeve.

He was about to raise his hand to his lips and use his teeth to remove his glove when Mr. Tennison simply pushed back his sleeve and aimed a drop of his newly mixed cologne so it dropped onto Teddy's bare wrist.

"What's it made of?" Teddy asked, before lifting his wrist to his nose, rather surprised when the scent proved rather pleasant.

"Spices, citrus, the barest hint of a floral, and some amber," Mr. Tennison replied. "Do wear it for a few more minutes before you decide, though." And with that, he disappeared behind a curtain.

Teddy gave a nod to the shopkeeper, who had been

watching with some interest. "I'm in the market for a toothbrush, as well."

"Right this way, sir."

Before Teddy took his leave of the shop, he had a new cologne Mr. Tennison had dubbed "Head of Clerks," a toothbrush, and a tortoise shell comb. He might have been talked into the matching brush, but he knew he had a perfectly good brush back at his townhouse.

By the time he needed to be on his way to Angelo's, he had visited nearly a dozen shops along the street and had orders in for suits of clothes, boots, shoes, stockings, and cologne.

It wasn't until the hackney was nearly at the fencing academy when he realized he had spent more money in two blocks than he had spent in his entire life. "Being wealthy is hard work," he informed his valet later that day, when he finally stepped into his townhouse.

Augustus Myers stared at his master for a moment before saying, "Of course it is, sir."

CHAPTER 13
SHARING GOOD NEWS

A half-hour later
Elizabeth looked up from writing the third invitation to Mr. Streater's Saturday afternoon tea and found Bates regarding her with a look of expectation. He stood on the threshold of her salon. "Yes?" she prompted.

"As I said, there is a Miss Albright to see you, my lady," he said with a nod.

Furrowing a brow, Elizabeth wondered how she could have been so engrossed in her project for Mr. Streater's introductory tea that she wouldn't have heard the butler's knock. "Miss Albright?" she repeated, her voice betraying her confusion. "Already?" She glanced at the tiny clock on the edge of the escritoire to confirm it was still well before noon.

"Shall I tell her you are not at home?" Bates asked, his hands going behind his back.

"No. I've been expecting her," Elizabeth replied, her gaze sweeping the salon to be sure her son hadn't run pall-mall through it. At some point the night before, just before she and George had retired to their apartments, David had escaped the nursery and gained entry into the first floor parlor. Somehow, the two-foot tyke had managed to arrange every vase, including one from the Ming Dynasty, into a circle on the floor. He was seated in the middle, surrounded by small rubber balls and practicing his ball toss when George discovered him.

Elizabeth was sure they would be finding small rubber balls in the bottom of vases for years to come.

"Have a tea tray brought up, would you?"

"Very good, my lady." He bowed and left the salon as Elizabeth turned to finish the invitation she had been writing. Once it was complete, she set it aside with the other two just as Daisy Albright appeared on the threshold.

"Do come in, Miss Albright. Are you on your way to Warwick's? I do hope you haven't changed your mind about the position," Elizabeth said as she returned her visitor's curtsy.

Daisy shook her head. "I've just come from there, in fact, my lady."

The viscountess' eyes widened. "Already?" She led the young woman to an overstuffed chair and indicated she should be seated. "Mr. Streater has already interviewed you? Did he say when he might have an answer for you?"

Daisy settled into the comfortable chair, her grin of satisfaction as much from the furnishing as from Elizabeth's query. "He did. He hired me on the spot. I can move into the apartment in Glasshouse Street today." She paused before she sighed. "Besides acting as headmistress, it seems I will also be teaching grammar as well as my sister's classes, at least for a time."

Elizabeth blinked. "Well, this is a bit... unexpected," she replied. "Or not," she whispered, remembering how desperate the bank clerk had sounded the day before. "Tell me. How did you find Mr. Streater?"

The former operative allowed a shrug. "A bit overwhelmed, I thought. Not as bereft as I would have expected, seeing as how his mother has just died. Eager to please.

Scared to death. Generous." She gave the question another thought before her eyes widened. "Oh, and charming," she added with a wan grin.

Angling her head, Elizabeth regarded her client with new-found appreciation. "Do you really think so? I only ask because..." Here, she paused, not sure if she should tell Daisy about her intention to find a wife for the young woman's new employer. "Well, he is in need of a wife."

Daisy frowned. "Eventually, perhaps," she replied. "I wouldn't have him courting anyone just yet, though. He seems a bit... overwhelmed, what with his mother's death and all."

Returning the frown, Elizabeth was about to argue the point, but a maid appeared at the door with the tea tray. "I do hope you'll join me for a dish of tea," she said, noting Daisy's look of surprise.

"Yes. Yes, of course," her visitor said, watching as the maid set a tray of warm biscuits before her. She hadn't expected such hospitality, especially since she was paying a call well before noon.

A curl of steam rose from several of the biscuits, a testament to how recently they had been removed from the oven. The salon was soon filled with the delightful scents of gingerbread and spices.

Elizabeth leaned forward and said, "I've learned the exact moment to request a tea tray," she said in a whisper. "Cook makes biscuits most mornings."

Daisy shared her grin. "A different flavor every day?" she guessed in a whisper.

The viscountess' eyes widened. "Indeed." She sobered then. "May I inquire as to why you think Mr. Streater isn't yet ready to take a wife? Besides because of his mother's death, of course."

Angling her head to one side, Daisy gave her response a good deal of thought before she put words to it. "In my prior... position,"—she said the word carefully, even though she was fairly sure the viscountess knew she had been a spy up until just a year ago—"I find that men who have undergone a series of life-altering events in quick succession tend to be a... a bit *addled*. They are so overwhelmed, they are no longer capable of critical thought, or of making rational decisions. Unlike us," she said as she indicated Elizabeth and herself with a quick wave of her hand, "We can handle any number of tragedies on any given day, while they simply cannot."

Rather startled by Daisy's words, Elizabeth blinked. Her guest had the right of it, although when Elizabeth considered her husband, she thought he would be quite capable should life deliver a series of unexpected events his way. The man had helped deliver David when the babe wouldn't wait for the midwife, after all, his manner so calm, Elizabeth remembered yelling at him to at least pretend to be in a panic.

Although, come to think of it, she had done enough of it for the both of them.

But then she wondered how George had dealt with his uncle's death and his inheritance of the Bostwick viscountcy. In a matter of minutes, he went from a life of fencing and riding and other gentlemanly pursuits, including twice-weekly liaisons with his mistress, to that of an aristocrat with responsibility over property, tenants, gypsum mines, dilapidated cottages, a run-down townhouse, and the need to give up his mistress and find a wife.

Her thoughts turned to Theodore Streater. Perhaps Daisy was right. With the recent death of his mother, Teddy would want time to mourn. Time to ensure the estate was settled. Time in his new position at the bank. Time to meet his new employees and to take stock of his mother's legacy. "You're right, of course," she finally agreed, her head nodding. "But I do think I may be onto something with regard to finding wives for the wounded."

Daisy straightened. "Because you don't believe they can find them on their own?"

The viscountess gave a slight shrug. "How likely is a man who is missing an arm, or a leg, or an eye, or any number of... *parts* to find a woman willing to marry them?" she countered, an elegant eyebrow arching with her query.

Frowning, Daisy realized her hostess had a point.

To a point.

"There are any number of women who are in the same situation," she said softly, remembering a neighbor in Kent whose right arm had always been twisted. The woman was a spinster, and behaved as if she had never considered herself biddable.

She thought of her own situation. Her limp, when she couldn't hide it late in the day, made her appear almost a cripple. Although the Marquess of Plymouth had claimed he rather liked how it caused her hips to sway provocatively, he never appeared in public with her.

Well, he rarely appeared in public the entire time she had been in his employ in her guise as his mistress.

"There are any number of seamstresses, or milliners, or costermongers who would choose marriage to an old fogey over a life of loneliness," Elizabeth said, "Or the opportunity to live in better accommodations," she added, remembering that her modiste employed seamstresses who lived in squalor because they were paid so little. George always saw to it she had coins to surreptitiously slip to the girls who hemmed her gowns as she stood on a box. She always made sure the modiste didn't pay witness to the secret tips lest she dock their pay.

Daisy regarded Elizabeth for a moment, deciding not to mention that not all marriages made life for a woman better. Some men were despicable. Violent in nature. Selfish, or rude.

At the thought of Theodore Streater, she furrowed her

brows. She couldn't imagine him as a violent man. He didn't seem selfish or rude. "May I ask your opinion of Mr. Streater?" Daisy queried, realizing too late the question wasn't in line with Elizabeth's last comment.

The viscountess regarded her guest for a moment, a secret grin causing a dimple to appear. "Mr. Streater's father was a baron, but his older brother holds the title now," she replied, deciding a bit of background was required before she answered the question.

"Then how did the finishing school end up in Mr. Streater's possession and not the baron's?" Daisy asked, one brow furrowing in confusion. The usual inheritance rules would have the baron inheriting the school.

"Mrs. Streater—Baroness Streater, I should say—didn't hold her oldest son in high regard, it seems," Elizabeth replied. "She apparently decided that her second born was a better choice when it came to running the school, so she bequeathed it—and her fortune—to Theodore."

Fortune? Daisy had to bite her tongue, about to repeat the word in disbelief. How could the baroness have amassed any kind of fortune? Warwick's Grammar and Finishing School couldn't be that lucrative!

Could it?

Then she remembered Mr. Streater's less than complimentary comment about his mother. *She lived the life of a pauper.* If she died with some fortune, that meant she was really a miser.

Elizabeth noted her guest's concentration, and then she leaned over the low table that separated them. "When you discover how she managed it, would you tell me? I admit I am beyond curious, especially since her husband apparently left the family deeply in debt."

Allowing a wan grin, Daisy replied, "If Mrs. Streater died having a fortune, then she was probably a miser. She lived in near squalor in an apartment next to her office at the school. The same apartment I'll be moving into later today."

Frowning, Elizabeth tore her gaze from Daisy and lowered it to the tea tray. For the two years she had attended the boarding school—a large Carlington House footman had been assigned to act as her protector whilst she was in residence—Elizabeth had despised the headmistress. To learn that Mrs. Streater lived on the premises in less than comfortable surroundings was a shock. To learn she was Theodore's mother—and a baroness—was even more so. "I never would have guessed," she murmured.

Daisy sighed. "I don't believe her son was aware of her circumstances, either. He seems... a bit overwhelmed at what he's discovered."

Allowing a nod, Elizabeth said, "My husband knows him far better than I do. Seeing as how they've been friends for years. They fence, you see—"

"You mean, they used to?" Daisy interrupted.

Elizabeth helped herself to another biscuit. "Oh, no. They are still fencing partners. They spar with one another at Angelo's Fencing Academy. Mr. Streater is quite adept with a foil, you see."

Blinking, Daisy considered the comment. However could a man with only one arm participate in the sport of fencing? "I should like to pay witness to that," she murmured, the thought of her new employer employing a foil to fend off an intruder causing a frisson to pass through her body.

The viscountess frowned. "I don't know if they allow ladies into Angelo's," she said with a shake of her head.

Daisy allowed a slow smile. "Then a disguise may be called for," she replied with a wicked grin.

Her eyes widening in delight, Elizabeth was about to ask if she might join the duke's daughter when there was a knock at the door.

"I should take my leave," Daisy said as she moved to

stand up. "I've movers to arrange and a household to set up this evening," she added, when she noticed Elizabeth's expression of disappointment.

"Well, thank you for coming," her hostess replied. "I should like us to do this often, if possible. If only because we have ... common goals."

Daisy furrowed a brow, wondering to what Lady Bostwick referred. "Common goals?"

"Why, to keep Mr. Streater happy, of course," the viscountess replied.

The door opened and George stuck his head through the opening. "Oh, pardon me," he managed, about to step back and shut the door. "I didn't realize you had a guest."

"Oh, George, do come in. Miss Albright has paid a call to let me know that she is Warwick's new headmistress," Elizabeth said as she stood up and hurried over to him.

"Already?" he replied, managing to bow in Daisy's direction and kiss the back of his wife's ink-stained fingers all while Elizabeth attempted to kiss his cheek. "Congratulations are in order then, Miss Albright," he said.

Daisy stood and nodded. "Thank you. I have both of you to thank, in fact, for I wouldn't have learned of the position if you hadn't found me yesterday."

George turned his attention back to his wife. "I just wanted to let you know I'm off to the tailor's shop for a fitting. We have the theatre Saturday evening, and I fear my best waistcoat has seen better days. Then I've a sparring match scheduled with Teddy," he added, his brows waggling.

"Well, do be careful. He left you with an awful bruise the last time you two fought," Elizabeth complained, one of her hands going to his midsection.

"We don't fight, darling," he replied, his voice kept low in an effort to placate her. "We spar."

Elizabeth gave him a quelling glance. "Well, perhaps you could spar a bit less *violently*," she suggested, just before she kissed him again on the cheek. "You needn't allow him to poke you so hard."

Daisy averted her eyes, rather stunned at how affectionate the viscountess could be with her husband. She was sure Viscount Bostwick's ears were bright red with embarrassment.

"I'll implore Teddy to go easy on me," George whispered before he gave her a quick kiss, stepped back and closed the door.

Sighing, Elizabeth returned to her chair just as Daisy took a step toward the door. "Oh, must you leave already?"

Daisy nodded. "I've some packing and moving to do," she reminded the viscountess. "I intend to spend the night at the apartment in Glasshouse Street," she added.

At the thought of watching Lord Bostwick spar with Mr. Streater, though, Daisy wondered if she might just have time to pay a visit to Angelo's later that afternoon.

She could always finish moving in later that night.

CHAPTER 14
ASKING FOR ADVICE

*L*ater *that afternoon*
"You want me to do *what?*" George asked in alarm. He stared at his best friend from where he stood in the changing room at Angelo's Fencing Academy, nearly ready to take on Teddy in a match on the pisté. Due to Teddy's position at the bank, he was rarely available for a match on a Monday, but the death of his mother had him taking a couple of days off "to settle her affairs," he had explained to his superior.

"Help me find a mistress," Teddy said in a hushed tone. He glanced around, lowering his head before he added, "After today's interview with Miss Albright, I find I am... frustrated," he added with a sigh.

George glanced around the room, wishing the other two fencers would finish dressing and take their leave. He knew Daisy Albright had already paid a visit to the finishing school and secured the position of headmistress. She had paid a call on Elizabeth earlier that morning with her good news.

Meanwhile, Teddy mentioned he had spent the afternoon shopping before making his way to Angelo's. "What exactly happened with Miss Albright?" George asked. *Good*

God. Had the duke's daughter said something? Done something? Whatever she did seemed to have Teddy rethinking what they had discussed just the day before. He thought Teddy would be in search of a *wife*—not a mistress.

"Nothing," Teddy replied, his head shaking as he pulled a loose shirt over his head. "Nothing, except that I hired her, and for the fact that my cock decided it rather liked the woman." He sighed. "Still does," he added in a hoarse whisper.

Blinking in attempt to keep from grinning, George finished preparing for their match and sat down on the bench next to where his clothes lay folded. "I take it you found her... attractive?"

Teddy sat down on an adjacent bench—hard. "I would have to be *dead* not to," he countered.

"Did you... interview her?" he asked. "Or just offer...?"

"Of course, I spoke with her. I hired her. Showed her my mother's old apartment. She's moving in this afternoon," Teddy said, acting almost as if he was regretting having met with Miss Albright. "She starts tomorrow morning."

This last comment was a bit of a surprise. George hadn't given a thought as to Miss Albright's availability. "That's marvelous news," he replied, thinking Elizabeth was probably feeling a great deal of pride at having remembered Miss Albright's application and for arranging the interview. That meant she would be especially happy when he returned home. Perhaps they could steal a few moments alone before dinner and repeat what they had done the night before.

He had to erase that memory almost as soon as it appeared in his mind's eye, lest his own cock begin behaving as Teddy claimed his was doing.

"I'm beginning to think it's not," Teddy countered. He thought of what it would be like should he ever find himself in the office, knowing the comely Miss Albright was living just beyond the connecting door.

He would have to avoid visits to Warwick's as much as possible.

George furrowed a brow. "But, you were desperate to find a headmistress, and now you have one," he argued.

"I would rather have hired her to be my *mistress*," Teddy replied in a whisper. "Which is odd, because... I can't say I'm usually attracted to the prim and proper ones," he murmured as he changed clothes, wondering if his reaction to Daisy Albright was because he hadn't been with a woman—any woman—for so long.

George frowned, wondering if they were talking about the same young lady.

"You are still speaking of Miss Albright?"

"Yes," Teddy agreed. "She was sporting a pair of wire spectacles perched on the end of her nose, and she was wearing one of those despicable... fichus, I think they're called, that covered everything up to her neck." He lifted his head as his one hand went up to his own neck, as if to illustrate his meaning.

His brows furrowing deeper, George was about to ask if maybe a different woman than Daisy Albright had appeared at Warwick's that morning. Then he remembered what he was fairly sure she had been doing for King and country not so long ago. "She's merely playing the part, Teddy," he replied, a sly grin replacing his frown. Perhaps the fichu was also meant to hide the evidence of her collarbones. Although she wasn't terribly thin, she wasn't well-fed, either. No one would mistake her for an aristocrat's daughter.

He could imagine Miss Albright having her way with just about any man if she chose to do so. He could also imagine her acting deferential. "It's possible she's a passionate firebrand just waiting for a man like you to take on as her cause," he teased.

Teddy's eyes widened before they rolled in mock disgust. "Ha ha," he replied.

All the air went out of George in a *whoosh*. He had been about to add something more teasing like, *Why didn't you ask her to be your mistress?* when he remembered to whom the young lady was related. It would have been a disaster had Teddy offered *carte blanche* to the daughter of a duke. "Are you aware of Miss Albright's relation to a member of the aristocracy?" he asked instead.

"Her sister?" Teddy countered. "Yes, of course. Diana is the one who accepted a position of another kind just a few weeks ago," he said, referring to Diana Albright and her new title of viscountess. "Which is why Miss *Daisy* Albright will be teaching arithmetic and dancing until another instructor can be found," he added.

George was about to mention the Duke of Ariley, but a footman entered the changing room and gave him a nod.

"Our pisté calls," he said as he moved to stand up.

"About time," Teddy said as he regarded his chronometer. "I have never needed a good, hard match as much as I do right now, but I do have to pay a call on the coroner when we're finished. I still have to make arrangements for mother's burial," Teddy replied. "Don't go easy on me, George."

"I never do," the viscount replied, leading the way to the pisté. The two saluted one another with their raised foils and then took up positions opposite one another.

From where she stood off to the side, Daisy crossed her arms and pretended boredom. Garbed in men's breeches, an elaborately embroidered waistcoat, a puce topcoat and shoes featuring two-inch heels, she wondered how foppish men managed to keep their high wigs from tipping off their heads. She had powdered this one until it was nearly white, cringing at the thought of how difficult it would be to get the powder out should she ever decide to use the wig again.

Large gems made of paste decorated several fingers, although she had begun to regret having worn them. Her hands were far too small and feminine to be mistaken for a man's. Better to have worn a pair of leather gloves.

Her disguise had come straight from the valise she had retrieved from the hotel after leaving Warwick's that morning. She had checked out and then arranged for her trunks and furnishings to be delivered to the school, rather dismayed when she spent most of her available coins on the drayage.

A glance in a cheval mirror in her room at Ariley Place confirmed she could pull off the look of an effeminate man with ease—as long as she didn't speak. Even the beauty mark high on her cheek matched one she had seen on a dandy she had passed while on her way to the fencing academy.

The others who stood watching the match paid her no attention. A few engaged in placing bets, despite the fact that Viscount Bostwick was merely sparring with her new employer.

She'd had to suppress the urge to gasp upon seeing Theodore Streater on his way to the pisté. Minimally dressed for the match, he wore breeches that were a bit loose about the thigh but were cuffed just below it. His stockings outlined muscled calves. His snow-white shirt might have been ready made, but the right arm had been shortened and sewn closed just beyond where his upper arm ended. The left sleeve billowed a bit as he dropped into his first stance.

And that stance is what had Daisy most impressed. Despite missing most of his right arm, Mr. Streater was able to balance on a center of gravity far different from a usual fencer. His bent front leg, not extended as far as his opponent's, seemed to strain against the fabric of his breeches just before he danced backwards, parrying an opening attack from the viscount.

The scrape of metal on metal echoed off the walls as the

two finally engaged for several parries and thrusts before Lord Bostwick retreated. Daisy knew he said something to his opponent, but from where she stood, she couldn't hear it. It must have been a compliment, though, for Mr. Streater gave a slight bow and returned to the middle of the pisté.

For the next twenty minutes, she continued to watch as the two advanced, Mr. Streater employing the *balestra*—short, sharp jumps that carried him into a lunge when attacking—while Bostwick made his advances with larger, smoother moves. Given the quiet that surrounded her, Daisy realized many watched as if they thought this a true bout. They had been conversing during the last sparring match, barely paying it any mind.

By the time the two had engaged, parried, and disengaged at least a dozen times, Daisy realized the lack of a right arm did little to hamper Mr. Streater's abilities. His lean but muscled frame was a study in contrast with Viscount Bostwick's larger shoulders and thicker legs. While the viscount excelled at power and longer strides, Mr. Streater was quick, his moves economical. Had the two been engaged in a bout, she was quite sure her employer would have been the winner.

At one particularly clever series of moves, Mr. Streater had his opponent all the way to the end of the pisté and completely off-balance. The attack had her holding her breath, the excitement sending frissons through her lower body. She was imagining what her new employer might look like stripped of his clothing. How his lean, sculpted body might look with a sheen of perspiration covering it. How he might cover her body with his own, his manhood seeking the heated space between her thighs...

Daisy was jerked from her reverie when the crowd suddenly gave a collective shout. An "oomph" erupted from Bostwick as his opponent's button-tipped foil poked him between two ribs, and applause broke out from the gallery of onlookers. Money surreptitiously changed hands as Bostwick could be heard saying something about another bruise, his voice betraying his annoyance.

So provoked was he by the poke, Bostwick lunged and set about attacking Mr. Streater, who managed to retreat until he was nearly off the pisté. "Enough!" he shouted, just as Bostwick's foil caught his right shirt sleeve—or what was left of it—and nearly tore it from his body.

Bostwick's eyes widened at the same time Mr. Streater said a mild curse followed by, "Not again."

"My apologies. I'll see to having it repaired," Bostwick offered as he stepped up and saluted the one-armed man. "And laundered, of course."

Reluctantly, Mr. Streater followed suit with his foil and, at the smattering of applause from those who watched from the sidelines, they both gave exaggerated bows before heading for the changing room.

With the show over, several took their leave of Angelo's, while others wandered off to another pisté to watch a different pair of gentlemen complete their sparring.

Before she took her leave, Daisy made her way in the direction of the changing room, thinking she might simply walk in. Curiosity had her wondering if Mr. Streater might change into a different shirt, given Bostwick's offer. She thought of seeing just how injured the clerk had been during the war. Did he sport wounds beyond the missing arm? Had he taken a bullet? Or been stabbed by a bayonet?

She was nearly to the door when a footman stepped in front of it. More like a bouncer, the barrel-chested man said, "Apologies, sir, but only those scheduled to spar are allowed."

Daisy angled her head. "Of course," she said, pitching her voice to a low timber. "I'll speak with Lord Bostwick at White's." With that, she took one last look about the academy and made her way out the front doors.

She was nearly to a hackney when an arm hooked into one of hers. The familiar scent of her father's cologne gave him away before his whispered, "Whatever do you think you're doing?" sounded in her ear.

Shaking his arm from hers, Daisy continued toward the hackney. "How did you know it was me?" she whispered, obviously annoyed he had once again seen through one of her disguises.

And just where had he been during the match? Had her attention been so focused on Mr. Streater that she completely missed his presence among the onlookers?

I've lost my edge, she thought with some dismay.

"We've been through this," James, Duke of Ariley, replied, directing her to his coach, which was parked behind the hackney. "And why, pray tell, is there a drayage cart in front of my house?"

Daisy climbed into the duke's town coach and took a seat in the velvet squabs, facing against the flow of traffic. Her father followed her in, and gave a grunt when he realized she had left the other side for him. "Truth be told, I wasn't positive it was you," he said as he took a seat, his hands moving to grip his knees as a groom shut the door. "You look like a damned dandy," he complained.

"Which was the point," Daisy replied, pulling the wig from her hair. Her dark locks fell well past her shoulders, a sight that had her father's eyes widening. "And the drayage cart is there because I am moving into an apartment in Glasshouse Street. At Warwick's," she added. "I was hired by Mr. Streater this morning." She paused as she stripped the rings from her fingers. "Thank you for seeing to it my things were brought here to London from the house in Kent."

A combination of shock and sadness fell over the duke just then. "You're already moving out?" he asked in a quiet voice. "I thought... I thought you would—"

"Although I do appreciate the hospitality—my bedchamber is the most beautiful I've ever had the pleasure of sleeping in—I cannot very well be the headmistress of

Warwick's and live in your house. I must live on the premises of the school," she explained.

"Today?" he countered, his voice a bit louder.

Daisy sighed as she undid the buttons of her topcoat and waistcoat. "I begin my position in the morning," she argued, before removing the garments. "I don't wish to be late on my first day." She pulled the large, white shirt from her body, eliciting a look of shock from the duke. "Daisy!" he scolded, one hand moving to cover his eyes.

But underneath the shirt was the bodice of a day gown covered by a spencer. And in the next move, she had the breeches unbuttoned and pushed down her legs as the rest of the gown's skirts followed, covering her legs at the same rate the breeches fell to her feet. She kicked off the breeches, then slipped her feet back into the dance slippers.

Regarding her father with a sigh, she said, "I can't exactly be seen in your company looking like a dandy when we get to Park Lane," she replied. "Whatever would the neighbors think?"

The duke blinked before giving a shake of his head. "I am impressed," he finally admitted. He lifted a finger to her face, plucking the velvet beauty mark from her cheek. "That's better," he murmured, just before he flicked the black *mouche* from his finger, sending it sailing out one of the coach windows

"Father!" Daisy protested as she watched the beauty mark disappear. "Do you have any idea how much those cost?" she asked with a sigh.

"Your inheritance is at your disposal," he replied, angling his head in defiance. "Not that I've completely given up on an advantageous marriage for you."

Daisy blinked before allowing a sigh of frustration. "I was shot in the leg. I have an awful limp in the afternoons. Do you really think there is a man out there who will—?"

"Yes, yes, I do," James interrupted. "You'd be a catch for any aristocrat—"

"I'm illegitimate!" she argued.

"You're the daughter of a duke, for God's sake!"

Daisy recoiled at the comment. And the curse. Her father rarely raised his voice, but it was apparent she had offended him. "I apologize," she murmured, her eyes downcast. "I meant no offense. Truly."

"Just for once, can't you forget that I am a duke and remember that I will always be your father?" he asked, exasperated.

Shrinking at his forceful words, Daisy settled into the squabs and silently cursed the tears that pricked the corners of her eyes. "I cannot. For mother always warned us that you were to be a duke. That you would one day have to do your duty. That you would have to marry, and sire an heir, and forget we existed."

Recoiling as if he had been punched in the face, James regarded his daughter in horror. "Lily would *never* have said such a thing," he countered in a quiet voice. "I acknowledged you and Diana as my daughters from the day you were born," he added. "It's on your birth record. I gave you my *name*, which you... you have apparently decided is not worthy of you—"

"I could not have been a spy if I'd used the Burroughs name," she countered, her voice kept low but sounding ever so impatient. "And it is *I* who is not worthy of the name."

They had been through this. She was sure Diana had given him the same argument when she was hired at Warwick's four years ago. At least her marriage to a viscount would have appeased their father, even if Adam Comber had no idea he was marrying the daughter of a duke until the day of their wedding.

James took a deep breath and held it a moment, as if he were counting to ten.

Sighing, Daisy was about to add to her argument—she couldn't be headmistress of Warwick's using the Burroughs name—but instead directed her gaze out the coach window.

"Why were you at Angelo's?" James asked, his voice no longer sounding strained.

Daisy allowed another sigh. "My new employer was sparring with Lord Bostwick," she said. "I was curious as to how a man with only one arm could fence."

James blinked. "Curious?" he repeated. "What if you'd been discovered?"

"I wouldn't have been..." *Except by you.* "Had anyone said anything to me, I would have feigned offense and stalked out the door," she added as she gave her skirts a shake. She pulled a pair of gloves from one of the gown's pockets and slipped them on. When she finished, she took a deep breath and was about to settle back into the squabs when she remembered her hair. She quickly gathered it into a bun atop her head, pulled a few pins from her other pocket, and secured it in place, all while her father watched in fascination.

"Why is it you're able to dress your hair in a matter of seconds, and it takes my wife's lady's maid an hour to do it?" he asked as he watched her pull an eyelet bonnet from another pocket. She pulled it on and was tying the ribbons when the town coach came to a halt in front of Ariley Place.

"Necessity?" she replied with an arched brow. "I can dress myself, too," she added with a smirk, just as a groom opened the door and set down the steps. She gathered up her disguise into the crook of one elbow and stood up.

When she appeared in the doorway, ready to take her leave of the conveyance, Daisy made sure to glance at the servant, whose expression of boredom turned to shock in a matter of seconds. "My lady?" he whispered, quickly offering her a hand.

Daisy gave a nod, descended the two stairs, and then stepped aside. Once the duke was out of the coach, Daisy watched with a bemused expression as the groom stuck his head into the coach. He glanced around, as if he were looking for someone.

Placing her arm on the duke's proffered arm, she said, "You'll have the neighbors all in a twitter about this," she warned.

"About what?" he countered.

She was about to say, "Two days in a row, escorting a woman other than your wife to your front door," but thought better of it. A sideways glance was instead her only response as they made their way to the front door. Just as they stepped into the house, the butler was quick to inform her that the drayage cart with her furnishings had just departed.

Daisy turned to her father and angled her head. "I must visit your cook, and then I must go," she said, giving him an apologetic glance.

He sighed. "Then go in the coach, and be sure to return tonight and join us for dinner," he said, not making it an invitation she could turn down. "I'll send the coach for you at six o'—"

"Seven," she interrupted. She needed as much time as she could manage setting up her new household, although the thought of playing with her siblings for a few minutes nearly had her changing her mind.

"Half-past-six," he countered, his manner suggesting he was done with negotiating.

Daisy sighed. She rather doubted the small kitchen at the apartment would have anything edible left in it. "Very well." She leaned up on tiptoes and kissed his cheek. "I would tell you not to worry for me, but I suspect it would do no good." She dipped a curtsy. "I'll take the rest of my things when I go back tonight," she added before she hurried to the kitchens.

Once the cook had supplied her with two tins of biscuits

and enough food to last her a few days, she headed to the coach.

She wanted to arrive at her apartment while the movers delivered her furniture. Although they could simply leave the items out front, she needed them to put the furniture in place, and she knew they wouldn't leave without her—they were expecting a tip.

CHAPTER 15
A MEETING OF THE MINDS

Tuesday morning

As she regarded Alpha House from her vantage on the other side of Glasshouse Street, Daisy wondered if it was too soon to introduce herself to the instructors who lived within. According to the information she could find in Mrs. Streater's desk, only one of the teachers didn't live at the school. Mrs. Pendergast, famous for her penmanship and comportment classes, lived in a townhouse in Kingly Street.

Daisy had learned two of the instructors were past thirty. Both had been governesses before being hired by Mrs. Streater more than a decade ago. Miss Betterman taught the art and music classes while Miss Anders taught French. A third, Mrs. Fitzgerald, fancied herself an expert in Shakespeare, her theatre appreciation class rarely touching on a play written by anyone else but the Bard. From the notes Daisy could find in Mrs. Streater's old desk, Mrs. Fitzgerald also taught a literature class for the older girls.

That left Miss Crofter, a younger woman who wore a pair of spectacles perched on the end of her nose and who possessed the skill of unlimited patience. She taught the needlework classes. And, from what Daisy had heard from her stepmother the night before, Miss Crofter made her distrust of members of the opposite sex known at every opportunity.

Daisy secretly wondered if the woman had been courted and then ruined by a rake, or if one of her sisters might have suffered that fate. Young ladies didn't hold such poor views of men without a reason.

Having studied the daily schedule—Mrs. Streater had been thorough in her documentation of everything that happened at Warwick's—Daisy knew to report to the small ballroom to teach dance at eleven o'clock and then return to the same building to teach arithmetic at two o'clock in the afternoon. Grammar followed, although she found notes mentioning a morning class when necessary.

Unfortunately, Mrs. Streater's notes didn't indicate the progress of any of the classes. If ever there was a time she wished her sister was in town, this was one of those times.

As she approached the front door of Alpha House, the hairs on the back of her neck had her slowing her steps. The feeling of being watched had her slowly turning around, her gaze taking in the morning traffic. Dray carts and carriages, coaches and a few men on horseback made the most noise while a few men walked the pavement. One rather tall, dark-haired gentleman stood across the street, apparently in wait of a hackney. Given the distance, she couldn't make out his facial features.

When she was sure no one was watching her in particular, Daisy returned her attention to Alpha House. She wondered if she had erred in choosing a drab round gown for her first day. The brownish-orange color did nothing for her complexion, but it had allowed her to blend in, back when she was an operative. Despite her brunette hair, currently pulled back and wound into a tight bun on the back of her head, she wouldn't be noticed in a crowd.

Daisy paused when the front door of the house suddenly

opened. Two women chatted with one another as one turned and used a key to lock the door.

"Good morning," Daisy said as she curtsied.

The two women exchanged quick glances. "Good morning," they responded in unison, both bobbing curtsies.

Introducing herself as the new headmistress, Daisy watched carefully for their reactions. Miss Betterman was quick to offer a hand and a welcome. "Miss Albright? Why you must be related to Diana," she said with a warm smile.

"I am her older sister," Daisy acknowledged as she took the proffered hand and gave it a shake. Although she hadn't seen her sister in quite some time, she decided she must still bear some resemblance to Diana given the woman's comment.

"Miss Jane Betterman. I teach the art and music classes, and this is Miss Annabelle Anders," she said as she turned to indicate the slight woman who stood next to her. Despite wearing a gown nearly the same color as Daisy's, Annabelle looked resplendent in hers. Given her chestnut hair and slight freckles, it stood to reason she would.

"Why, I must admit I am surprised," Annabelle said as she shook Daisy's hand. "If I may be so bold, I wouldn't have expected our new owner to hire a headmistress for at least a week. I half-expected he would ask one of us if we were interested in the position." This last came with a roll of eyes that suggested the idea was ludicrous.

Daisy had at first wondered if Miss Anders expected to accept such an offer, but from the way she made the comment—almost disparagingly—she rather doubted it. "He may still," Daisy replied carefully. "He's hosting a tea Saturday afternoon to introduce himself to everyone."

The two teachers exchanged quick glances and nods. "We were just on our way to our classrooms," Jane said. "With all the rain last night, I expect I'll have a bit of clean-up to do."

"Me, as well," Annabelle agreed with a sigh.

Daisy frowned. The mention of rain and a clean-up suggested a leaky roof. "How long has the roof leaked in your classroom?" she asked as the three of them turned and made their way toward one of the classroom buildings.

Jane and Annabelle both giggled. "We've never known it not to," Jane said with a wave of her hand. "But there's a bucket that catches most of the water. I just have to see to emptying it if Mr. Jenkins doesn't get to it first."

"Mr. Jenkins?" Daisy repeated. "Isn't he the gardener?"

Annabelle gave a shrug. "He is, but he's sweet on Jane."

Jane colored up and gave her colleague a look of shock. "Annabelle!" she scolded, before daring a worried glance at their new headmistress.

Trying with all her might to suppress a grin, Daisy changed the subject. "I shall inform Mr. Streater and see if we can't arrange for a repair."

The two instructors exchanged glances again, although neither offered a response just then.

"I'll be sure to mention it at the tea on Saturday," Daisy offered. "I do hope you can both attend. You should be receiving invitations any day now. Lady Bostwick is seeing to them."

The mention of an aristocrat's wife had the two exchanging quick glances again. At least this time, they seemed impressed.

"How do you find him?" Annabelle asked, her voice kept low. They had just entered the building that held four class-rooms, two of which featured buckets near to brimming with water in the middle of their floors.

Daisy tore her gaze from the evidence of roof leaks and replied, "Oh, Mr. Streater is quite agreeable. Since he is the head of clerks at a bank, I rather doubt we'll see much of him, though."

"Or his money," Jane said under her breath.

"Jane!" It was Annabelle's turn to scold.

"Oh, I have reason to believe Mr. Streater will see to the maintenance of Warwick's," Daisy offered, remembering the reference to him having inherited a fortune. "And if he does not, then I shall."

All she had to do was see to it that part of his fortune was spent fixing the roof.

And who knew what else.

"Mrs. Fitzgerald has arrived rather early," Annabelle remarked, noting the older woman was already in one of the classrooms. A platform was situated at one end of the room, apparently for use as a stage, and a pile of costumes covered a table. "But then I believe dress rehearsals are beginning for her next production."

Daisy paused by the door, deciding it better she not ask what play that might be. "Thank you for walking with me this morning. And for sharing your insights," she said as she gave a wave to the other teachers.

"Just so you're aware, I am not... *cavorting* with Mr. Jenkins," Jane said in a whisper.

Angling her head to one side, Daisy furrowed her brows. "Do you wish to?" she asked in all seriousness.

Jane blinked. She started to say something, but closed her mouth before she could utter a sound.

Annabelle rolled her eyes. "Of course, she wishes to, but—"

"Then you should make your wishes known to Mr. Jenkins," Daisy said in a whisper. "Or you will always wonder what might have been." She, more than anyone, knew what it was like to wonder about the might-have-beens. Regret did that. Jane Betterman was of an age where any interest from a man should be taken seriously. Acted upon. "Just... use *discretion*," she added with an arched brow.

Staring at the headmistress, as if Daisy might have sprouted three heads, Jane gave a quick shake of her head. "Of course," she replied in a hoarse whisper. For a moment, she seemed almost lost in thought. "Pardon me, but my first class is due to start in a few moments."

"Don't let me keep you from it," Daisy replied, just as a middle-aged man passed them, tipping his chapeau before he entered the classroom where Jane was about to teach a drawing class. "Mr. Jenkins, I presume?" Daisy asked as she crossed her arms and straightened.

"Indeed," Annabelle replied with an arched brow. "Widowed two years now. Has a daughter who attends here, although I don't believe she pays the same tuition as all the other girls."

"Well, I should hope not," Daisy replied. The comment earned her a look of surprise from the younger woman. "Employees of the school should benefit from some consideration."

"May I say, I find your position rather enlightened?" Annabelle said then. She glanced toward another open door, where several young ladies were regarding them from where they sat at wooden desks. "I must go. Although most of our students have learned some French from the their mothers, they have not learned *proper* French," she said as she gave a slight curtsy.

"Good day," Daisy said in perfect French, returning the curtsy. She took a deep breath and then was about to take her leave of the building when Mr. Jenkins walked by with a bucket full of water. "Pardon me, but are you Mr. Jenkins?" Daisy asked as she moved to walk by his side. When he seemed about to stop and bow, she added, "Please, don't stop what you're doing on my account. That pail looks rather heavy. I just wanted to introduce myself," Daisy said.

"Miss Albright, aren't you?"

Daisy blinked, rather surprised he already knew. "Why, yes." Try as she might, she could not remember having met the man before. His skin was bronzed from too much time in the sun, and he sported a body with broad shoulders and legs that suggested he rode a horse. His clothing, a rough muslin shirt, dark wool waistcoat, and breeches stained green at the knees, gave away his profession. Although his blue eyes and broad face were anything but aristocratic, Daisy could understand why Jane would be attracted to the man. "How did you know?" she asked, her curiosity piqued.

"You look just like the other Miss Albright. Or Lady Breckinridge, I suppose I should say," he replied as he opened the exterior door and allowed her to step through before he joined her again. "I'm guessing older sister, but please don't take offense. She once told me she had an older sister," he explained. He paused to empty the bucket onto a carefully tended flowerbed that rimmed the classroom building. When half the bucket was empty, he moved to the other side of the crushed granite path and poured the rest onto a spiraled topiary tree.

Not having seen Diana in several years, Daisy wondered at how they might be taken for sisters. There were similarities, of course. They shared the same parents. But beyond height, hair color, and eyes, she couldn't remember any other similarities. "No offense taken. My sister is a lovely woman," Daisy replied with a wan grin. "Before you start your day—"

"Already two hours into my day, my lady," Mr. Jenkins interrupted. "I'm the first one here. Up with the sun."

"Of course," Daisy replied. She glanced about the grounds, realizing that with all the boarding houses, two classroom buildings and the building that held her office and the servants quarters, the gardener had a good deal of work.

"If you're planning to raise the tuition I'm paying on behalf of Emily, I'd appreciate knowing right now," he stated, rising to his full five-foot-ten-inch height.

Daisy regarded the gardener for a moment. "If you're referring to your daughter, then please know that I shall be petitioning Mr. Streater to *reduce* Emily's tuition to a more appropriate amount. Shall we say... one shilling per term?"

Mr. Jenkins frowned as he stared at Daisy. Then he blinked. "Emily *is* my daughter," he acknowledged with a nod. "Why... why would you do that?" he asked, the cant of his head suggesting he was suspicious of her motives.

Daisy crossed her arms over her chest. "How long have you worked here, Mr. Jenkins?" she countered.

The gardener took a deep breath and seemed to think on the question for a moment. "Sixteen years," he finally said. "I started the year before Emily was born."

Eighteen-oh-two? Daisy thought then. His loyalty should be worth something. "I should think sixteen years in service to Warwick's would be worth a greatly reduced tuition for your daughter," she said with a nod.

Mr. Jenkins' look of confusion finally turned to one of relief. "Thank you, Miss Albright," he murmured. "It *is* Miss Albright, isn't it?" he added, his brows suggesting he was suddenly wondering if he had guessed right as to her identity.

"It is," she admitted. Daisy was about to take her leave and see to returning to Mrs. Fitzgerald's classroom when she remembered her earlier conversation with Jane and Annabelle. "It's really none of my business, but I was wondering if you might hold a candle for one of the instructors here? Miss Betterman, perhaps?" she queried. Despite the gardener's attempt to rein in his surprise, she noted how he struggled to keep an impassive expression, how his eyes darted to one side, a clear sign he was nervous. "I only ask because, well, I think you should know that what you and Miss Betterman do after you have completed your duties here at Warwick's is between the two of you."

Mr. Jenkins blinked. "It is?" he murmured.

Daisy allowed a brilliant smile. "It is. I want the people who are employed here to be happy, Mr. Jenkins," she said then.

The gardener finally allowed a nod, as if he once again

suspected some sort of trap. "The former headmistress certainly wasn't of that opinion," he replied.

"I'm sure she wasn't," Daisy replied. "Which reminds me. Was Mrs. Streater aware of the leaky roofs in the classrooms?"

Mr. Jenkins nodded. "Well aware. She had a roofer here a few months ago. Mr. Thatcher. So that he could assess how much it might cost to do the repairs. I believe she told him to replace the roofs whenever he could get to it."

Well, that was a relief. Daisy wondered how she might contact Mr. Thatcher to confirm he had been hired. "Do you know how much he quoted her to do the work?" she asked, one eyebrow arched in query.

The gardener sighed. "He told her the entire roof needed to be replaced. Which it does. And not just on this building, but on *all* of them. They all leak," he said as he waved to the line of houses along Glasshouse Street.

"All of them?" Daisy repeated.

"Indeed. Mr. Thatcher gave her the numbers. I know because I watched as she wrote them all down in her ledger. I was in her office at the time. To pay Emily's tuition," he added, as if he thought it necessary to justify his reason for being in the headmistress' office.

Ledger? Well, if Mrs. Streater did indeed record the amounts, they would be in one of the ledgers Daisy had pulled from the drawers in the massive mahogany desk. Surely she could determine which one was intended for necessary maintenance.

"Thank you, Mr. Jenkins. I'll be sure to discuss the issue with Mr. Streater when he next pays a call," she said as she held out her hand. "Oh, and if you can, please plan to attend the tea Mr. Streater is hosting on Saturday afternoon. That's where he'll introduce himself to all the employees," she explained.

Rather surprised at the offer of a handshake, Mr. Jenkins

took her hand and gave it a gentle shake. "Thank you, Miss Albright," he replied. "If there's anything I can do—"

"Roses," Daisy replied. "I look forward to seeing roses outside my office," she said with a wink. And then she turned and made her way back toward the building that housed her apartment and her office.

Given their classes were about to start, introductions to Mrs. Fitzgerald and Miss Crofter would have to wait.

A quick glance to where the tall man had been standing earlier that morning showed he had left the premises. Probably into a hackney, she thought. And never to be seen again.

CHAPTER 16
TEA WITH A SIDE OF ART

ater that morning

At precisely eleven o'clock, Daisy entered the classroom building which housed a poor excuse for a ballroom. Although the floor was a proper wood floor, its boards at one time sanded and varnished to a high sheen, it was worn in spots. The walls had been painted a sickly shade of yellow, or perhaps the years had merely allowed the paint to discolor. Daisy thought a colorman could restore it as well as the other classrooms. They all needed a new coat of paint.

She was heartened to see a piano-forté in one corner and was about to ask if there was someone to play it for the class when Miss Betterman appeared at the door. She carried an armful of sheet music.

"I wondered who might play for this class," Daisy murmured as she accompanied Jane to the instrument.

"I'm happy to do it on the days you need me to," Jane replied. "And although I've been filling in as the instructor, I just haven't known what music to practice these past two weeks."

Diana had been gone from the school for at least a fort-night, which meant this class and the arithmetic class hadn't had a regular instructor. "What dance are they learning?" Daisy asked, hoping she wouldn't make a fool of herself. It had been years since she had done any dancing.

"The cotillion. And if they behave, then the waltz," Jane whispered. "Only because I know how to do the cotillion, and I wanted to learn to waltz. The other Miss Albright had only just started teaching it when she announced she was leaving us."

Daisy had to suppress a grin. Of course Diana would teach the waltz, probably to spite the patronesses of Almack's. Most of the girls who were lined up on the far wall were of an age to secure a voucher to perform the dance during the Wednesday night subscription dances at Almack's, but Daisy doubted any of them actually held such a voucher.

She clapped her hands together, and the murmuring among the young ladies ceased. "Good morning," she said, relieved when a chorus of "Good mornings" sounded in return. "My name is Miss Albright, and I shall be your instructor until such time that a new teacher can be hired." She wasn't surprised when a few inhalations of breath could be heard. Her name no doubt had them guessing she was a relation to their former teacher. "We'll spend half our time on the cotillion and the rest of the hour on the waltz, which is just about the amount of time these dances require during a regular ball."

One young lady raised a hand. When Daisy gave her a nod, she curtsied and asked, "My name is Miss Hornby, ma'am. How do we decide who will take the positions of the men?"

Daisy dared a glance at Jane, but the art teacher was busy arranging her sheet music on the piano-forté. "How did you do it when my sister taught you?"

Several girls exchanged quick glances before the same young lady said. "We had to count off. Evens played the men, and odds played the women."

Deciding that seemed fair enough, Daisy said, "Then we shall do it like that for the cotillion..." A chorus of disappointed sighs greeted her. "But evens will play the women, and odds will play the men. Then you will switch for the waltz."

The mood in the room changed entirely.

"Count off," she called out. "And then form up. Three couples to a set." She hoped she had that right. She hadn't danced a cotillion in an age. "Then decide whom among you is to be the first, second, and third couples."

With four-and-twenty girls in the class, the three sets of six girls hurried into position. All Daisy could think about was how ridiculous they looked once the music started and they addressed their partners and then the center of the set. The first couple performed the *Balance*, or the waltz steps, promenading forward between the other two couples before separating and then moving off behind them. They honored the other couples with a bow.

Surely she could find some young men who could use the dance practice. But what could she use as an incentive to get them into the classroom at eleven o'clock in the morning? She made a mental note to discover if there might be a boy's school somewhere nearby.

In the next measure, she watched as the odd partner was discarded and hands were joined for the circle to the left. Everyone seemed to know what to do, although there were some stutter steps before the odd one ended up in the center. The new center couple then waltzed to the other side from the original first couple, and the whole routine repeated until the third couple completed their turn as a center couple.

Daisy found she enjoyed watching the proceedings. For the most part, everyone seemed to know their left foot from their right.

When the introductory music for the second figure began,

she noted the couples didn't address one another, but they did the *Contretems*—the 'all forward and the all back' move—she remembered from the last time she had done the dance. It was during the next count of eight when the chaos began. Those who were playing the parts of the men seemed to forget about changing partners after the ladies waltzed to the right.

Daisy clapped her hands. "Let's try that again from the beginning of the second figure," she called out, realizing that with three more figures to go, they might spend the entire hour doing nothing but the cotillion.

When her chronometer showed it was half-past the hour, the young ladies had barely made it through the third figure. Daisy clapped her hands twice and allowed a sigh. "How many times have you practiced this dance?" she asked of the girl who stood nearest to her.

"This is our third time, Miss Albright. But the other Miss Albright's been gone for a fortnight, so we've been attempting to learn it on our own."

Daisy blinked. "Well, you've managed rather well then," she commented. "In reward for your initiative, let us now take up the positions for the waltz. Switch your sexes, couple up, and form a large circle."

She couldn't miss the round of titters that followed her instructions, and Daisy nearly joined them in their merriment. As for the waltz, she discovered they had been practicing it, probably to the exclusion of all the other dances, for some time. Their execution was flawless. Even the youngest girl held her head correctly, the box formed by her and her partner's arms perfectly positioned throughout the first rotation.

When the music ended, Daisy applauded. "Very nicely done," she said, daring a glance at her chronometer. Although it was still a few minutes before noon, she dismissed the class and hurried over to thank Jane. "I don't know how I could have done this without you," she murmured.

"It's no trouble. I always did it for Diana," Jane replied. "But it means I only have time to teach three art classes."

Daisy nodded her understanding. "And the other instructors?"

"At least four classes, except for Annabelle. She does two and then tutors French over at St. Martin's."

"St. Martin's?" Daisy repeated, not familiar with such a place.

"The boys' school?" Jane clarified.

Daisy's eyes widened. "How far is it from here?"

Jane blinked at the headmistress' reaction. "Perhaps a mile from here," she replied. "Maybe a bit less."

"How does she get there?"

"She walks, of course. Miss Knox goes with her." At Daisy's look of expectation, she added, "The housemaid from Gamma House. Says she doesn't mind since it means she isn't at the house when the girls who live there return from classes." This last was accompanied by an arched eyebrow, as if the girls of Gamma House might be a bit troublesome.

"Anything I should know about?" Daisy asked, one of her eyebrows matching Jane's in height.

"Oh, it's nothing. Sometimes the girls can become a bit argumentative with one another. There's some jealousy, too, since the daughters of the aristocracy sometimes attend *ton* balls while the daughters of cits are only invited to private routs or balls hosted by family friends."

Daisy considered the comment a moment. "Aren't barons the only aristocrats who allow their daughters to attend here?" she asked, turning to walk back to her office. Most higher members of the peerage wouldn't allow their daughters to attend school outside of their homes, preferring to employ governesses and tutors for safety reasons.

Jane leaned in closer. "Officially, but we have several illegitimate daughters here," she said, her eyebrow once again arching up. "And at least one viscount's daughter. Miss Batey. You probably noticed the burly man hanging about the classrooms? He's her protection whilst she's here. She doesn't board here, though. A town coach picks them up every afternoon at precisely four o'clock."

Daisy considered this bit of information. Fifteen years ago, a number of aristocrats' daughters attended—boarded, even—and their hired protectors had been rumored to spend their idle time playing dice outside the classroom buildings. "Is her father a widower?" she asked.

"Indeed. Viscount Lancaster. His viscountess died in the childbed a couple of years ago. He couldn't abide sending Analise to the country to live with his sister, but he didn't want a governess living in his home, either. Too much risk of a scandal."

Making a mental note to ask Helen about the viscount, Daisy nodded her understanding. "And how are the... illegitimate ones treated by the others?" she queried, half expecting to hear they were chastised by the others.

Jane allowed a chuckle. "Like queens, of course. Most have dowries larger than legitimate daughters and will marry well. Two already have this Season."

Daisy resisted the urge to stare at Jane. This was good news. Even so, she was rather glad she had never had a Season in London, her mother insisting they stay in Kent while her father made the short trek to London when he needed to be in town. Back then, he hadn't yet inherited the dukedom, and so he didn't have to attend Parliament, but his father expected him a few days a week so he could teach him what he would need to know once he inherited the Ariley dukedom.

Jane took a breath. "May I ask you something? I don't mean to pry—"

"Of course," Daisy replied, her gaze taking in the front of

the building in which her office was located.

"We call it Omega House," Jane offered, noting the object of Daisy's attention. "Only the servants board there."

"And me," Daisy said.

"Are you here because Diana married and left us?"

Daisy considered how to respond. "I'm here because I applied for the position. Mr. Streater hired me. The fact that Diana was a teacher here may have helped my cause in that regard, but truth be told, I cannot say exactly why Mr. Streater hired me."

"So... you're not his mistress, doing him a favor?" Jane asked, the mirth in her eyes a clear indication she was teasing the headmistress. "I am teasing," she said then, just before she suddenly sobered. "Oh, dear. You're going to let me go, aren't you?"

Daisy giggled, the musical sound surprising the art teacher. "No. I didn't even know there was a 'Mr. Streater' until this past Sunday. An acquaintance informed me Mr. Streater was in need of a headmistress and thought I could manage the position," she explained. "Tell me. Is there an instructor who thought she might apply for the position? I would hate to learn I am considered an usurper."

Jane shook her head. "I can't imagine anyone wanting the position. I'm sure Miss Crofter thinks she could do a better job than Mrs. Streater, though. She was quite vocal with her displeasure at how we 'pandered to this patriarchal society'," Jane said in an exaggerated manner. "But Miss Crofter would never make a suitable headmistress. She's on the young side and beyond a bluestocking in her beliefs."

A bit worried at hearing this assessment of the sewing teacher, Daisy said, "I suppose I shall meet her at dinner or before class on the morrow. Which reminds me. Where should I eat dinner this evening?"

Jane sighed. "We switch off every night except Sunday. One of us eats in Beta, one in Gamma, one in Delta..." She allowed the sentence to trail off. "Sunday, the instructors eat together in Beta House, since all those girls spend Sundays with their families." She paused a moment. "And we do dress, of course, although I wear the same gown nearly every night."

Daisy rather liked the sound of the dinner arrangements. They seemed so civilized. "Which house should I go to tonight?" she asked. With five instructors and her and only five boarding houses, it meant there would be some doubling-up.

"Your choice, I believe," Jane replied. "Mrs. Streater wasn't much for socializing, but I rather think it was because she was embarrassed."

"Embarrassed?" Daisy repeated.

"She didn't have a variety of dinner gowns."

Daisy wasn't about to admit dinner gowns were in abundance in her wardrobe. She was quite sure she had never worn some of the frocks she found in her wardrobe at Ariley Place, wondering if perhaps her father had a modiste make them by taking the measurements off one of her old gowns. The joke would have been on him had she gained a stone or two since her time in Kent. Instead, she had lost some weight, given how the outline of her collarbones appeared whilst she dressed the morning of her interview with Mr. Streater. She hoped her elaborate fichu hid the evidence of living on meager funds this past year.

The reminder of those few months when she had gained a bit of weight came back, and she found she had to redirect her thoughts or she would have trouble breathing.

"Do any of the instructors have a home—a husband—to go home to at night?" she asked as they entered Omega House. She used her key to access her apartment and opened the door.

"Only Mrs. Pendergast. She's quite private. Comes to teach her two classes and leaves when they're done. None of the rest of us is married," Jane explained, her gaze going to what she could see of Daisy's apartment. "Mrs. Fitzgerald has been a widow as long as I've known her. We have rooms here at Warwick's. In Alpha House. But none are quite like this," she added, her look of surprise coupled with admiration.

"Will you join me for tea?" Daisy offered, hoping her hunger wasn't apparent in how her stomach growled just then. She hadn't had breakfast, and she still didn't know where the servants ate their meals. "And a biscuit or two? I managed to steal a few before I left my last accommodation."

Jane's eyes widened as she took in the headmistress' parlor, wondering if Daisy was teasing or if she really had made off with a tin of biscuits. "I was thinking about finishing a painting for tomorrow's class on impressionism, but I do believe I have time for a dish or two of tea," she replied.

Daisy grinned. "Good. Because my next class isn't until two, and I have some questions I'm hoping you can help answer," she said as she made her way into the small kitchen, rather glad to see a servant had seen to putting the kettle on the stove. Her instructions to have hot water at the ready had been heeded, it seemed.

"Before I do that," Jane replied as she glanced around the parlor, nearly doing a complete turn as she took in the furnishings and artwork on the walls. "You have to tell me what you did with Miss Streater's apartment. I was sure this is where it used to be located."

Loading a silver salver with a teapot, cups, and saucers, Daisy continued to grin. "I had it replaced with this one."

Jane allowed an almost unladylike snort. "In one day's time? I hardly think so," she chided.

Moving to set the tea tray on the lower table in front of the velveteen settee, Daisy gave a nod. "My father said all the furnishings in my bedchamber were mine to do with as I pleased, so I had them moved here yesterday afternoon," she said, secretly wondering how long it would be before the Duke of Ariley learned she had taken nearly everything from her bedchamber and the adjacent sitting room. She had left a thank you note addressed to him with word of where the furnishings were located should he change his mind. "It sometimes amazes me what can be accomplished when one tips the labor." She paused and allowed a grimace at seeing the walls. "I still have to hang some silk, though. These walls are hideous."

Her hands clasped behind her back, Jane admired a small music box on a side table before turning her attention to an empty forest glass vase on another. Then her gaze went to one of the paintings on the wall, a landscape depicting an area in Derbyshire. "This is beautifully done," she remarked. "Do you know the artist?"

Daisy's gaze went to the painting, remembering the day her mother had set up an easel on the lawn of Cherrywood, the Burroughs' country estate in Derbyshire, and worked on the painting. Dotted with sheep and criss-crossed lines of rock walls, the green hills looked vibrant under a morning sun. "My mother. She didn't paint often, but when she did..." She allowed the sentence to trail off, a lump having formed in her throat.

"She did well," Jane remarked. "Her strokes are so tiny. So precise."

Daisy motioned for Jane to take a seat, and she took the chair opposite the settee. "Your father must live in town, then," Jane said, nodding to Daisy's query as to whether or not she wanted sugar in her tea.

"He does. Has for years. Same house as my grandfather and his father were born in, I think," Daisy said as she helped herself to a cup. "Now. I've gone over the roster of students and wish to know all I need to know about the girls."

Jane lifted her head from almost sipping her tea. "I'm not sure there's much to know," she hedged before returning her attention to the tea. "Daughters of the wealthy, mostly. A few who can claim barons for fathers. All very well behaved. Except for those jealousies I mentioned earlier."

Daisy blinked. A finishing school with this many girls in one place at the same time had the potential for disaster. Although she and Diana usually got along just fine when they were growing up, they had also had their share of fights. "Any... any other petty jealousies? Warring factions? Fighting?" she prompted.

Shaking her head in denial, Jane said, "None. Besides, Mrs. Streater wouldn't have allowed it. If the mothers found out..." She allowed the sentence to trail off, her eyes rolling when she considered how a bad word from any one aristocrat or wealthy patron might end additional enrollments. "We're a respected institution, and have been for a very long time. Some of the girls who attend here are daughters of women who attended when they were this age." She paused a moment. "Although, I can admit there is always a bit of a... chill... when the girls return from their holiday break at Christmastime."

Straightening on the settee, Daisy's eyes widened. "You're not referring to the houses being cold, I imagine. What happens when the young ladies are on holiday?"

Jane angled her head back and forth. "Some get engaged to marry. Some receive expensive gifts and brag a bit. Some don't come back. Some don't get to go anywhere at all."

Daisy furrowed a brow. The entire time she had been growing up, their father had made sure they had magical Christmastides. His respect for his German ancestry meant they always had a huge yule log burning for the entire holiday. An evergreen tree dressed with bows and candles. Wreaths on the doors. A sprig of mistletoe hanging in the vestibule, put there just so her father would have an excuse to kiss her mother whenever they returned from their trips to town or a horseback ride. "How unfortunate," she murmured. "Well, perhaps we can see to decorating one of the houses for the occasion," she suggested. "Give us all a place to congregate whilst everyone else is gone from town."

Jane merely nodded. "That sounds rather festive," she agreed.

Pulling the list of students from a pocket—she had copied the roster and kept it with her to review in the hopes of learning more about the families—Daisy unfolded it. "I am sure I recognize some of these names," she said. "Yet others have me curious."

Helping herself to a biscuit, Jane asked, "Such as?"

"Miss Hannah Simpson. I haven't yet met her, so I'm not sure which one she is."

"She's a twin, so her brother is off at Eton, of course," Jane replied. "Dark hair, just like yours, and a perfect English miss. She has an excellent disposition, perfect posture, an eye for good art, and can speak French fluently."

For a moment, Daisy thought Jane might be describing a Thoroughbred. In a way, she probably was. "Apparently she doesn't board here, but is always punctual, according to the records. Seems she hasn't missed a day, either."

Jane nodded. "That would be because her father drives her here," she said with a grin. "The Simpsons don't live very far away. Just over in Kingly Street, near Mrs. Pendergast's terrace. Mr. Simpson drove her here in a cabriolet this morning, and he will be waiting for her on his red phaeton when she finishes my class this afternoon," she added with an expression of amusement. "In the winter, it will be a town coach, and in the spring, it's sometimes a landau. The gentleman seems to own every kind of equipage ever made."

"A man of some means, and yet... *he* drives his daughter? Both ways?" Daisy questioned. Her eyes widened when she realized she might have paid witness to him pulling away from the curb that morning. "Is he that... older gentleman? Tall, rather dapper, gray at the temples?"

Jane gave a start before she nodded. "He's old enough to be her grandfather, to be sure, but he is her father. Her mother is older, too, but ever so elegant." Her brows suddenly furrowed, and she stared at Daisy a moment. "Pardon me, but just for a moment there, I thought perhaps you two could be related."

Daisy blinked. Perhaps they were. A memory of hearing about one of her great aunts—Sophia Burroughs Grandby—running away from Merriweather Manor to spend the rest of her life with the man she loved—a former butler for the estate—had her heart racing just then. And a grin coming to her face. "Perhaps we are," she replied, making a mental note to ask her father if Sophia was Hannah Simpson's mother. She looked at the list again. "What of Lady Lucida? Fletcher?" She leaned over and offered more tea, which Jane accepted.

"Father was a baron, but when he died, the barony went to his brother. Mother's name is Margaret. A very tall woman, I might add. She managed to remarry a count or some such over in Europe, which is why Lucida is now 'Lady Lucida'." She arched a brow, as if she was hinting the title wasn't the girl's birthright. "The mother is good friends with Lady Pettigrew, I think only because she likes to keep up on the gossip."

Daisy continued to grin, familiar with every name the art instructor mentioned. As for gossip, there was *The Tattler* for that. "And what about Lucida? Is she, too, a gossip?"

Jane allowed a shrug. "Truth be told, I believe she just wants to marry a nice gentleman and set up her own household."

"To escape from her mother, perhaps?" Daisy guessed.

"Indeed," Jane agreed with a nod.

"Hmm." Daisy looked at the list again. "Now here's a familiar name. Grandby. Ariel Grandby." She looked up. "But not 'Lady Ariel'."

The art instructor helped herself to another biscuit. "She's one of Gregory Grandby's daughters. The oldest, I believe. Her mother attended here back in the day," she offered, and then she gave a shrug. "Ariel is schooled in the natural sciences. All the Grandby children are, courtesy of their father. But Ariel also has talent. In fact, I haven't seen such skills in a painter since we hosted Lady Plymouth here."

Plymouth? Daisy nearly repeated, doing her best not to react to hearing the name of the marquess to whom she had been a mistress only a year ago. She had been undercover at the time, the position of mistress one she had accepted if only to prove her worth to the Home Office.

Marchioness of Plymouth. Lady Samantha had that name now. That title. Daisy had half a mind to ask if Jane knew anything about the marquess and his bride.

Not that I ever expected to marry the man.

"Spoiled rotten?" Daisy guessed about Ariel, managing to exhibit a pleasant disposition despite the reminder of the man she had fallen in love with. The man who had fathered what might have been her only child, if fate hadn't intervened and taken that babe away well before its time.

"With nine brothers and sisters?" Jane countered with a grin, referring to Miss Ariel Grandby. "The opposite, in fact. Sweet disposition. Makes friends with everyone. You would never know her father was rich as Croesus. From what I know of her mother, she gets it from her. She was a Wellingham, you see." Jane said this last as if Mrs. Grandby was no longer of the Wellingham line that included an earldom. "And if Lord Torrington's countess hadn't given birth to twins that included a boy, then it was likely Gregory Grandby would be the next Earl of Torrington."

Although Daisy knew all of this and a bit more, given the Grandbys and Burroughs went back many generations, she didn't offer the information. "Well, there are other names on the list, but I think I shall just learn what I must as I teach them arithmetic or dance," she said lightly.

Jane gave a nod as she accepted another refill of her tea. "Now, may I ask that you return the favor and answer a question for me?" she queried.

Daisy tried hard not to stiffen at hearing the art instructor's words. "Of course," she replied, keeping a pleasant expression on her face.

"How is it you know Mr. Streater? Enough so that you could land this position so soon after it was vacated?"

Feeling a bit of relief—she feared Jane might have known more about her than she had let on when they first met—Daisy allowed a shrug. "I know I didn't explain everything when I mention it earlier, but I was approached by Lady E, of 'Finding Work for the Wounded'," she admitted. "Apparently, Mr. Streater spoke with her after his mother died and requested she find a replacement for his mother as soon as possible. Lady E had my application—"

"You were wounded in the wars?" Jane asked, astonishment evident in her voice.

"I was... I was part of the... the effort to defeat Napoleon," Daisy managed to get out.

"And you lost your husband."

Daisy shook her head. "No. I've never been married," she replied. "But remember, Mr. Streater is hosting the tea on Saturday so he has a chance to meet everyone. He originally thought to discover if any current teachers wanted the opportunity to interview for the position."

Jane frowned. "None of us would want it," she said with a shake of her head, repeating what she had inferred earlier that day. "Especially now that all these workmen will be about, seeing to the repairs. I rather imagine it will be six months before everything is complete and the school is back to new."

An alarm bell went off in Daisy's head. "Six months?" she

repeated.

"Complete replacement of the roofs?" Jane countered. "Then all the work on the windows?" She allowed a sigh. "I rather doubt there is an instructor here who wants anything to do with managing all that... *chaos*," she whispered, as if the word were some sort of curse.

Well, it might be, Daisy thought just then.

"I see what you mean, of course," Daisy agreed. She allowed a sigh. "Well, I suppose I should be getting back to my desk," she hinted when she saw that Jane's cup was once again empty. "Perhaps we can do this every week? As an opportunity for you to share any concerns you might have," she suggested.

Jane blinked. "I would like that very much. Mrs. Streater never socialized with any of us."

Not a bit surprised to hear Jane's comment, Daisy allowed a nod. "Until we can find another dance and arithmetic instructor, I am simply another teacher here at Warwick's," she replied. "I don't wish to be seen in the same light as Mrs. Streater."

Jane moved to stand up. "Then I look forward to our next tea together," she replied. "For I never once had tea with the former headmistress."

And with that, Miss Jane Betterman took her leave of Daisy's apartment.

The headmistress helped herself to a biscuit and ate it in two bites, remembering how her collarbones showed in relief. When she ate another, she thought of what she would tell Mr. Streater when next she saw him. When she ate the last on the plate, she remembered the odd ledger she had found in the large mahogany desk and wondered if what Jane had just told her held the key to the entries in that ledger.

Repairs were about to begin at Warwick's. Repairs that would take a good deal of time. She could only hope Mr. Streater was well aware of what was about to transpire.

CHAPTER 17
LIFE AFTER A BABY

ater that Tuesday evening
George bent over his dozing wife's body and planted a kiss on the top of her head. Elizabeth stirred, giving a start when she realized she still held her daughter in one arm. The infant, long asleep after having had her fill, was still at her breast.

"I didn't mean to wake you, my love," George whispered.

"Is something wrong?" Elizabeth asked as she straightened in the overstuffed chair. With dusk having settled beyond the windows, their bedchamber was cast in near-darkness.

"Of course not. But I wanted to let you know I must go to the club tonight. It seems we're to vote on a new member," George explained softly. "Or I wouldn't bother going."

Rubbing an eye with the back of her knuckle as she struggled to wake up completely, Elizabeth gave a nod of understanding. "Are you planning to blackball him?" she asked, a look of worry replacing her sleepy expression. With membership in White's so limited these days—there simply wasn't room for all those who were recommended for membership—votes only happened when a current member died or resigned his membership.

And no one ever resigned.

George furrowed a brow. "I don't know. Truth be told, I'm not sure who we're voting on this evening." He hadn't been to his men's club since Christine's birth, and although he didn't miss the occasional evening outing, he decided it was time he return to his regular schedule lest his acquaintances forget he existed.

Elizabeth reached out and captured a few of his fingers in hers. "I could not have asked for a more attentive father for David and Christine," she said in a whisper. "Nor husband for me," she added, one elegant eyebrow arching in a suggestive tease.

George blinked. There was a time when a comment like that from Elizabeth Carlington might have earned her a trip to Bedlam, but in the three years since he had married her, Elizabeth had matured into a fine wife and a mother who was far more involved with raising their children than he would have expected when he first learned of her from his mistress.

They still engaged in a bit of frolic now and then. He would play the sword-wielding masked bandit to her negligée-clad maiden, chasing her about until he had her cornered. Then he would use the tip of his foil to snip away the cloth-covered buttons of her robe until the garment fell from her naked body. Dropping the foil, he would carry her off to his bed and pretend to have his way with her—rather difficult when she seemed to give as good as she got— although they did tend to fall asleep earlier these days.

"I love you," George stated. He moved his hands to the arms of the chair and lowered his head until he could capture his lips with hers. When he ended the kiss, he had half a mind to take the sleeping babe from her and do what he had just imagined.

But then he would be late. Very late.

"I won't be long. I promise," he whispered before giving her another kiss. "Perhaps I'll be in disguise, and my sword and I can pay you a visit before you retire?" he hinted.

Elizabeth's eyes widened with mischief. She watched him go, all the while wondering if her maid might have had time to reattach the buttons on her favorite negligée. If not, she might have to locate her sewing box and do it herself.

When she glanced down at her daughter, the baby was staring up at her with the oddest expression on her face.

"Oh, now. There will be none of that," Elizabeth scolded. "You might not exist if it wasn't for his swordplay," she added with a wink.

The babe's only response was a rather unladylike burp.

CHAPTER 18
A NEW MEMBER OF
THE CLUB

*L*ater *that Tuesday night at Teddy Streater's townhouse*

"You might have told me this was the night they were to vote on your membership in White's," George said in a scolding voice. "I almost didn't attend, and *I'm* the one who nominated you in the first place." That had been several years ago, a testament to just how long someone might wait for their membership to come up for a vote.

He almost hadn't nominated Teddy. Back then, Teddy had just regained his position at the bank after many months of living at the expense of his brother. Teddy wouldn't have had the income necessary to pay the dues in the club if he had been voted in any earlier than this evening. Either someone at the club knew he had been promoted, or they knew that he had inherited a good deal of blunt. George thought it was probably the former.

Teddy allowed a shrug as he moved to the sideboard in his townhouse's library. "How was I to know?" he replied. "It's not as if they informed me." He poured two glasses of brandy and offered one to George. "So... am I a member of White's now? Or...?"

The viscount bobbed his head back and forth as he took

the glass. "Well, there weren't any black balls in the voting box," he replied with a teasing grin. "So, yes, you're a member. If I recall, there's some paperwork you'll need to complete—"

"Dues to pay, no doubt," Teddy interrupted, rather relieved to know he had the funds readily available.

"That, too. I do hope this change in your good fortune won't cut into our fencing matches," George hinted. He worried that with his promotion and recent wealth from his inheritance, Teddy might look to make friends with a different class of gentlemen—one that didn't include George.

Teddy's eyes widened. "It will not," he replied. "I am still employed. And now that I have the responsibility of an entire institution and those who work there, I'm not about to live a life of leisure," he claimed in a huff.

"I'm glad to hear it," George said with a sigh. He took a seat on the library's long divan, ignoring the worn upholstery. "Speaking of your institution, any idea of how it's going with your new headmistress?"

Teddy joined him, setting his glass on a side table as he took an adjacent chair. "I haven't been there since yesterday. Not that I haven't wanted to just... show up and give my regards to Miss Albright," he murmured.

George gave him a curious glance. "You find her attractive, don't you?" he asked.

Practically sputtering on his latest sip of brandy, Teddy said, "I'd have to be a monk not to." He cleared his throat, about to mention he had spent the night before in a constant state of arousal just thinking about the comely Miss Albright.

"Did you learn much about her?"

Teddy wondered at his best friend's query. "She knows as much about arithmetic and dance as her sister did when she was hired, because they shared the same tutors and governesses," he replied, one brow arching up as if that was the best he could come up with in answer to George's query.

"And?" George prompted.

"She said the word 'administrative'."

George frowned. He was about to ask why that might be enough to secure a position when Teddy sighed. "I realize now I may have been a bit quick with my decision," he admitted. "But I just have this feeling that she has the best interests in mind for the school. That she'll do what's right."

Allowing a nod, George took a drink of brandy and settled back in the divan. "Could you... could you see yourself with her? In a... a relationship of sorts?" he prodded.

Teddy gave a start, wondering if George had paid witness to what was happening behind the placket of his breeches. Just speaking of the woman had an arousal starting. "I can imagine a good deal when it comes to Miss Albright," Teddy replied. "Probably none of it possible."

George struggled to hide a grin. "And why is that?"

Teddy sighed. "Besides the fact that she's a headmistress for a school I now own?" he countered. "Faith. When she showed up yesterday, I thought she was there to..." He allowed the sentence to trail off, too embarrassed to admit what had been going on in his head at the time.

Both of them.

Straightening on the divan, George stared at his friend. "You do like her," he accused.

"That's the least of it," Teddy replied.

"You wish to bed her."

"Don't you?" Teddy countered.

George leaned forward, nearly spilling his brandy. "No," he said, his gaze going off to one side as he considered his response. He hadn't thought of bedding another woman since his marriage. Before Elizabeth, he hadn't thought of bedding another woman besides his mistress of eight years.

For the entire eight years.

"No," he repeated for good measure. "Which is rather a relief," he murmured as he straightened and glanced at his chronometer. He still had every intention of arriving home in time to play a masked bandit in pursuit of his prey.

"Truth be told, when Miss Albright appeared yesterday morning, I thought perhaps a matchmaker had sent her," Teddy murmured. "And that she was there to consider being my wife."

George stared into his glass of brandy and wondered if Teddy had been drinking far more than just the glass he held. "I admit, my wife is quite expeditious when it comes to matters of... well, just about anything, but the shingle for her latest charity hasn't even been mounted above the office yet, nor has she hired a matchmaker," he explained. "She's interviewing two tomorrow, though."

Teddy sighed. "Will you help find me a mistress?"

Resisting the urge to agree, George instead said, "Elizabeth and I will be attending the theatre on Saturday night. Do join us, and bring Miss Albright along, won't you?"

His brows furrowing, Teddy asked, "Any particular reason why you think Miss Albright will agree to such an arrangement?"

George angled his head to one side. "She and my wife get along quite nicely. After a week in her new position, and after you two finish hosting that tea for your new employees, I'm of a mind to think Miss Albright will be ready for a night out."

Teddy blinked. "But I don't suppose Lady Bostwick will send the invitation to the theatre," he whispered.

Giving his head a shake, George said, "Probably not. Which means you should. If I don't see you before then, I'll see you at the theatre." He paused a moment. "Actually, we'll ride together in the coach," he amended. "Pick you up here at five, shall we say?"

"Oh... I could just leave with you from your house. Given the tea and all," Teddy suggested.

"Brilliant."

With that, George took his leave of Teddy's townhouse and returned to Bostwick Place.

When he found Elizabeth standing in front of the fireplace in his bedchamber, already dressed in her negligée, her hair down in mahogany waves about her face, he didn't bother with donning the mask or locating his foil. Instead, he carefully unbuttoned the sheer robe, kissed her senseless, and made love to her in front of the fire on a soft hide rug.

And they would have stayed on the rug the entire night, but at some point, a small boy appeared, tapped his father on the back, and asked when they might be joining him in their bed.

Never had George been so glad he hadn't brought his wife to their bed. "In a moment, son," he murmured. "Now get back to bed."

CHAPTER 19
LINING UP SOME DANCE PARTNERS

ednesday morning
About to take her leave of Omega House, Daisy dared a glance toward Alpha House to see several instructors take their leave of the boarding house. She gave a wave when Jane Betterman noticed her, and then set off to make her way in the direction of St. Martin's when she caught sight of a tall man just ahead. His gaze was aimed squarely at her instructors, although he walked slowly in the same direction she was headed.

Although she couldn't see all of his face, she was sure he was the same man who had been standing there on Tuesday.

Worried for her instructors, Daisy was prepared to do what she must to bring the man down should he make a move in their direction. A quick knee into the back of his knee would have him losing his balance, which she could exacerbate by punching him in the kidney. Once down, she might have to wrestle him until she had an elbow across his throat, but by then, surely someone would come to assist.

However, once the teachers were through the main doors of the classroom buildings, the tall man's step quickened, and he hailed a hackney.

Managing to secure the next hackney, she climbed in and watched as the conveyance in which the man was riding turned off to the right and finally headed east.

Daisy cursed for not having seen the man's entire face, but knew she would have to keep an eye out for him on the morrow. He might have just been curious, or perhaps he lived nearby and always secured a hackney at that particular spot, but Daisy had every intention of finding out just why he paid so much mind to her instructors.

When her own hackney came to a halt, she was jolted from her reverie. She stepped out of the equipage and paid the driver before her gaze darted up and down the street. Right in front of her stood the address she sought, but she still double-checked the address.

Daisy regarded the exterior of St. Martin's School for Boys and experienced a bit of the Green Monster.

However could a school for boys look as expensive as its tuition? The exterior stucco no doubt covered a brick building, but the white stucco was free of dirt and graffiti. Every window pane was clear and unbroken. The pavement in front had been recently swept. And the wrought iron fence in front had recently been painted a shade of green more commonly found in the expensive neighborhoods of Mayfair.

Making her way through the front door, she quickly found the main office. The headmaster wasn't seated behind the desk, however.

His receptionist was.

Receptionist? Daisy hadn't even considered employing a receptionist for Warwick's. She rather doubted Mrs. Streater had ever had one.

She introduced herself, asking if she might have five minutes of the headmaster's time. "It's about a dance class," she added, noting the boredom the young man displayed at hearing her name and position.

"The headmaster is with a student. It may be some

time..." His words were interrupted when a nattily dressed, balding gentleman emerged from the office directly to the right of the receptionist. That man's attention immediately went to Daisy.

"Miss Albright?" he said in disbelief.

Daisy blinked. "Mr. Lusk?" she responded, a brilliant smile appearing when she recognized the colleague from her past. Although Elias Lusk had rarely been on a mission outside of manning a desk at the Home Office, he possessed a number of skills and was highly educated.

She curtsied to his bow and offered a hand, adding, "It is still *Elias Lusk?*" she asked in a whisper. She wasn't sure if she knew him by his real name or by an alias.

The headmaster nodded. "It is," he acknowledged. "I know, this is probably the last place you would have expected to find me," he said as he waved her into his office. "But it was an opportunity I had to accept. Who told you I was here?"

Daisy took the proffered chair across from a desk that was even larger than the one at Warwick's. She noted the thick Turkish carpet beneath her feet and the row of bookshelves behind the desk, all filled with leather-bound books. The office smelled of vanilla and vellum and reminded her of her father's study. "Please don't take offense when I tell you this, but I was completely unaware you were employed here," she replied. "I came with the hope of speaking with the headmaster."

"Well, you're speaking with him," Elias replied as he straightened. "Which has me wondering what kind of assignment has you here at St. Martin's." His eyes widened. "Please tell me one of my charges isn't involved in some sort of international scandal. Or smuggling. Or an assassination attempt on Prinny."

Resisting the urge to grin at Elias Lusk's comment, Daisy

shook her head. Seeing a former operative in the position of headmaster had her deciding her employment wasn't so very unusual. "I haven't held a position with either office in over a year," she replied. "However, I am now the headmistress of Warwick's."

Mr. Lusk's eyes widened once again. "What are the odds?" he murmured, leaning forward so his elbows rested on the desk. "What, pray tell, happened to Mrs. Streater? I never thought she would give up her position there," he said.

Daisy inhaled and held her breath a moment. So word of Mrs. Streater's death hadn't reached the hallowed halls of St. Martin's. "She died. Her son inherited the school, and he hired me Monday last."

A brow furrowed, as if he didn't quite believe what he had just heard. "That's odd. I always thought that school was owned by a... a Worthington, wasn't it?" he asked, a look of confusion crossing his face.

"So did everyone else," Daisy agreed. "Tell me. Do your boys learn any dances as part of their curriculum here at St. Martin's?"

Elias allowed a nod. "Dance is part of the curriculum for the older boys, although it is not a favorite."

"Because they have to dance with one another?" she guessed.

He shrugged. "Probably," he agreed.

"Do you suppose they would be amenable to coming to Warwick's? For one or two days a week, so they might learn to dance with members of the other sex? I have four-and-twenty."

Elias blinked. He blinked again before taking a look at his chronometer. "What time?"

"Eleven o'clock."

His frown gave his answer. "Well, it cannot be today," he hedged.

"Oh, I wouldn't expect it to be," Daisy countered as she grinned. "What about Friday?"

"Done," he replied. "I should be able to line up some equipage to get them there and back."

"It is about a mile," Daisy agreed. "There's a makeshift ballroom in one of the classroom buildings, and the art instructor plays the piano-forté for the class."

Elias nodded. "I may have to come along as an escort and watch," he teased.

"You're welcome to, of course," Daisy said. She paused a moment. "I understand Miss Anders makes the walk here and back every day."

"Excellent French instructor," Elias stated with a nod. "Keeps order in her class, too."

"Oh?" Daisy replied, wondering what the woman did to keep the younger men in line. "Do you know how?" She might have to use similar methods to keep the boys in line during the dance class.

The headmaster allowed a slow grin. "Shame. A steely gaze. And she has a wicked ruler she raps on their knuckles should they pronounce a word incorrectly."

Daisy raised an eyebrow, wondering if Miss Anders employed the same technique on the girls at Warwick's. "Is she your only female instructor?"

"Indeed. But it's fine. She always has a companion with her."

"Very well, then. I shan't take any more of your time. Eleven o'clock on Friday, then?"

"We'll be there," Elias replied. He was about to stand up, but instead leaned over the desk. "Might you share just which dance you'll be teaching your charges on Friday?" he asked, one eyebrow arching in query.

"If they behave, they'll be learning the waltz," Daisy replied.

She rather liked how Elias' mouth dropped open just then. How he had ever managed as an operative, she didn't know. The man's face gave away his every thought! "Have a good day, Mr. Lusk."

And with that, Daisy hurried back to Warwick's.

CHAPTER 20
TEA WITH THE OWNER AND
A SIDE OF DRAMA

Later that afternoon

When Daisy dismissed her arithmetic class at half-past three o'clock, she allowed a sigh of relief as the last girl filed out the door. She couldn't help but feel frustration at how little the younger girls seemed to know about basic math. The older girls had a firm grasp of addition and subtraction, and some were even learning multiplication. How they had all ended up in a single class didn't seem to suit, though.

Daisy was about to take her leave of the classroom when she noticed Mrs. Fitzgerald tidying up her room next door. They had spoken the day before, but only in passing as they each had classes to teach. "Do you have time to join me for some tea?" Daisy asked when the theatre appreciation instructor lifted her head from her task.

"Time? Why, of course. There is always time for tea," the woman replied, her manner rather dramatic. "Whose kitchen, though?"

"My... parlor, actually," Daisy replied, grinning at Mrs. Fitzgerald's antics. "May I help with anything?"

Mrs. Fitzgerald shook her head. "I'm finished, I tell you. Done. And not a moment too soon."

"Oh?" Daisy wondered what might have happened to have the teacher make such a comment.

"It's nothing, really. It always takes me some time to leave the characters behind and return to my own skin."

Giving the older woman a knowing glance—she had played parts in her past that were sometimes hard to give up —Daisy clasped her hands behind her back as they made their way toward Omega House. "How long have you been teaching here?"

"Nearly twenty years now. I should have been an actress, I think, but society has such a low opinion of those who tread the boards."

"Unless they're men," Daisy commented, attempting to walk without the limp that threatened at any moment.

Mrs. Fitzgerald nodded. "Which reminds me. *The Brutus* is at the Drury Lane Theatre. I think I shall attend the rehearsal. Decide if it's appropriate for our girls to see."

Daisy agreed, but then remembered the tea on Saturday. "If you haven't already, please don't make plans for Saturday afternoon. Mr. Streater is hosting a tea for all the instructors, and he'd like all of us to be there. His hostess is seeing to the invitations," she explained.

"A *man*, hosting a *tea?*" Mrs. Fitzgerald replied, sounding ever so scandalized by the idea.

Daisy grinned. "Think of it as a *soirée* but with better food," she murmured. "It was Lady Bostwick's idea."

"Ah, the viscountess with that famous charity," the theatre instructor replied, one gloved hand lifting in front of them as if she was about to recite some lines from a play. "Are the rumors true? She and our illustrious owner are secret lovers?"

Nearly stopping in her tracks, Daisy wondered if the woman

was serious. "Doubtful," she replied, barely able to suppress a giggle. "No. They cannot be." After paying witness to the way in which Lord and Lady Bostwick behaved with one another, she couldn't imagine either of them carrying on *affaires* with others.

"Then perhaps the rumor is about you and him, then," Mrs. Fitzgerald said as they entered Omega House.

Not bothering to suppress her amusement, Daisy's laughter was abruptly halted when she realized the topic of their discussion was standing at her office door. "Mr. Streater," she said as she dipped a curtsy, hoping he hadn't overheard any of their conversation.

"Miss Albright," Teddy said, bowing as he held his beaver top hat in his only hand.

"Mrs. Fitzgerald, may I introduce you to Mr. Streater, the new owner of Warwick's?"

The instructor gave a deep curtsy, one more suited to the stage. "'Tis a true pleasure to make your most esteemed acquaintance," Mrs. Fitzgerald said, a gloved hand held out.

Teddy managed to tuck his hat beneath his arm and then intercept her hand with his before bestowing a kiss on the back of it. "And yours," he replied, giving Daisy a quick glance that proved he was a bit flummoxed as to how to respond to the exaggerated greeting.

"Mrs. Fitzgerald teaches the theatre appreciation class," Daisy said, deciding that would be explanation enough.

"Drama, too," the instructor added. "Even though these young ladies will only ever use the skills they learn to play charades or put on productions during house parties." From the comment, it was apparent she approved of neither pastime.

"We've just returned from our last class," Daisy said. "I hope you haven't been waiting long."

Teddy shook his head. "I've only just arrived." He didn't add that he had overhead something about a rumor that might have involved his headmistress and him. Several rather unsavory and rather scandalous thoughts came and went before he decided that, from his perspective, a rumor involving him and the headmistress couldn't be all bad.

If only it were true!

"Thought I should make myself available should you have questions or... concerns." His attention was squarely on Mrs. Fitzgerald when he finished this last.

"That's rather kind of you, given your position and all," Daisy replied. "Will you join us for tea? In my parlor?"

Teddy had been about to decline, but the additional comment about just where the tea would be served had him changing his mind. "I accept, of course," he said.

Daisy allowed a slight grin as she led the two to her apartment. "With any luck, the kettle will already be hot," she said as she opened the door to her apartment and waved them in. "Please excuse the walls. I still have two to finish," she added. She had stayed up far too late the night before, pinning peach silk to the walls in an effort to cover the old plaster.

Mrs. Fitzgerald breezed into the room and promptly took a seat, her gaze sweeping the parlor with a critical eye. "Such a wonderful color scheme," she said. "So restful."

Pausing at the threshold, Teddy took a step back, glanced both ways down the hallway, and then stared into the room. "I could have sworn this was my mother's apartment," he murmured, almost to himself. He glanced down at the Aubusson carpet covering most of the floor, then gazed at the walls, and finally studied each piece of furniture.

Daisy indicated the other upholstered chair and said, "I'll just be a moment." She hurried into the kitchen and repeated what she had done the day before, glad for the second tin of biscuits and the bit of milk left in the cold box. When she reappeared in the parlor with the tray, Teddy stood up and waited for her to be seated before settling himself again.

"This *was* Mrs. Streater's apartment, was it not?" he asked as Daisy handed a cup and saucer to Mrs. Fitzgerald.

Mrs. Fitzgerald answered before Daisy could. "It was, although I don't recall ever being invited in."

"Me, neither," Teddy claimed, a slight grin suggesting he might be teasing. His heart did an odd palpitation when he saw Daisy's dimple appear, just as she handed him a cup and saucer. She had already added the milk, bless her heart, and she had been generous with the sugar. "Thank you, Miss Albright."

"You're welcome, Mr. Streater," Daisy replied. "Mrs. Fitzgerald and I have only just met. I am on a mission to invite every instructor for tea in the afternoons in order to learn as much as I can about their classes and the students," she explained, hoping he didn't think she was shirking her responsibilities when it came to running Warwick's.

"What a capital idea," he replied. Suddenly nervous, Teddy remembered at least one of the reasons he was at the school. "I paid a call in the hopes you have received your invitations to Saturday's tea," he said. "Have you?"

Mrs. Fitzgerald straightened in her chair. "A tea party? Why, that sounds..." She turned to stare at him. "Just where are you hosting this tea, Mr. Streater?" she asked, a hint of alarm in voice.

"Bostwick Place," Teddy replied. "The viscountess is married to a friend of mine, and she is seeing to the particulars," he added, his gaze darting to see that Daisy was watching him with a most curious expression.

Oh, he really wished she didn't look at him so. As if she were imagining him with two arms.

If that was what she was really doing.

Perhaps she was merely gauging his reaction to the dramatic drama teacher.

Her eyes wide and her smile wide, Mrs. Fitzgerald fairly vibrated with excitement. "Oh, I shall look forward to it. I haven't paid a call in Mayfair in an age," she claimed.

"Me, as well," Daisy said, sure her white lie would go unnoticed. "I have been telling the other instructors in the hope they can free up their Saturday afternoon if they already have plans."

Teddy allowed a nod. "That's very kind of you. May I inquire as to how it goes here at Warwick's? I realize it's only been two days."

Daisy allowed a grin. "It's going quite well, I should think." She turned her attention to the other woman. "Mrs. Fitzgerald? Would you agree?"

Mrs. Fitzgerald's eyes widened at being singled out for her opinion. "Indeed. Nothing seems to have changed, so it's almost as if Mrs. Streater is still with us," she claimed with a shrug. She turned her attention to her tea as Daisy and Teddy exchanged startled glances.

"I do hope you find *The Brutus* an appropriate play for your students," Daisy remarked, not sure what else to say just then. She noted how Teddy jerked at the comment, and wondered if he knew something about the play that she did not. "Mrs. Fitzgerald is considering it for her theatre appreciation class," she explained.

"I have been invited to share a box at Saturday's performance," Teddy said, his gaze on Daisy. "I expect the tea will be concluded in time for us to make the curtain."

Daisy arched an elegant eyebrow. Was he inviting her to attend the play with him? If so, he was being quite bold in front of Mrs. Fitzgerald. "I should think a three o'clock tea would be concluded by four," she said. She tried to imagine changing clothes and being ready to leave by half-past five in order to ride in a conveyance and make it to the Drury Lane Theatre by six or so. There would be a crush in front of the theatre, of course. There always was. The plays started promptly, though, at half-past six!

"Well, that's a relief," Teddy replied, relief evident in his voice.

"Now where is it you reside, Mr. Streater?" Mrs. Fitzgerald asked, her attention having been on a biscuit.

Teddy angled his head and said, "I've a townhouse in Bruton Street."

From the way Mrs. Fitzgerald's eyes widened, Daisy could tell the woman was impressed. "And how is it at the bank, Mr. Streater?" she asked, knowing there could be no thread of conversation coming from where the bank clerk resided. "I understand you've recently accepted a promotion."

Teddy blinked, at first wondering how she might know. Then he remembered that Lady Bostwick would have told her. "I have," he stated, a hint of pride in his voice. "And all is well."

"Well, this is certainly a surprise," Mrs. Fitzgerald remarked. "I thought you were a baron."

Reining in his annoyance at being confused with his older brother, Teddy shook his head. "Not yet," he replied, a bit of spite sounding in the words. When he noted how Daisy seemed embarrassed on his behalf, he found he really wished the theatre instructor would make her excuses and take her leave. Although he would be uncomfortable in the company of Miss Albright, he knew he would prefer her—alone—to the current arrangement.

"I must be taking my leave," Mrs. Fitzgerald announced, as if she could read his mind. "I've a guest coming for dinner at Beta House this evening," she said as she stood up.

Teddy managed to stand, as did Daisy, and he said, "Good afternoon. It's been very good to meet you," before he watched Daisy escort her guest to the door.

"You will let me know about *The Brutus*, won't you?" Daisy asked of the drama teacher.

Mrs. Fitzgerald angled her head to one side. "You shall be the first to know," she replied. "Thank you for the tea." And with that, she made her way out of the apartment and then out of Omega House.

Daisy breathed a sigh of relief at the sound of the second door closing. She turned to find Teddy regarding her from where he stood. "Mrs. Fitzgerald is appropriate to her position," she remarked.

"Indeed," Teddy agreed. He was suddenly at a loss as to what to do. On the one hand, he knew he should take his leave—there wasn't another woman to act as chaperone—and on the other... well, he didn't have another, so he merely stood and regarded Daisy for a moment. "Lord Bostwick has asked that I escort you to Saturday night's performance of *The Brutus*," he said then, as if he was laying the blame for the invitation squarely at the feet of the viscount.

Daisy managed to maintain a passive expression. What else could she do? From the sound of his invitation, she wondered if he was annoyed by having to invite her. "Do you consider it an inconvenience?" she countered.

Teddy shook his head, his eyes widening at her query. "I do not. In fact, I rather look forward to spending the evening in their company, but not alone, if you catch my meaning."

Daisy wondered at his words. "You don't like to be their sole guest?" she clarified, wondering at his nervousness.

He shook his head. "They're rather affectionate with one another. I knew Lord Bostwick would like Lady Bostwick back before they met, but I did not know they would be a love match," he explained.

Remembering how affectionate her father had been with her mother, Daisy allowed a grin. "I am happy for them," she said in a quiet voice. She moved back to the settee. "I should look forward to an evening at the theatre." A thought as to how she might get ready in time—managing a hackney back to Warwick's and then another trip to make it to Drury Lane would allow her little time to dress—she added, "I'll be sure to bring a change of clothes with me to the Bostwick's so we aren't late. I'm sure Lady Bostwick would grant me a room in which to change."

Having a hard time controlling his arousal at imagining Daisy changing clothes after the tea, Teddy stared at her for a moment. "That is a capital idea. I think I shall do the same."

Perhaps Lady Bostwick would accidentally assign him to the same room as Daisy, so then they could help dress one other.

Then he remembered his lack of a right arm.

"Although, my townhouse is not so very far away as to make them late," he added with a sigh.

Daisy wondered at the disappointment she felt just then. What if Lady Bostwick had accidentally assigned Mr. Streater and her to the same room to change clothes? She could imagine him requiring a bit of help when it came to dressing. He could probably manage her buttons one-handed, though, judging from his long, tapered fingers. He could manage draping a shawl across her shoulders. Maybe even a mantle, if the butler didn't do it.

Why, Mr. Streater could probably manage quite a bit with that one hand. A frisson passed through her entire body at the thought of what it would be like to be stroked by the fingers on that one hand. To have her hand held by that hand. To be held by that one arm. To have her entire body pressed against his as they settled into the same bed for a night of passion. A night of satisfying sleep. A morning of quiet, slow lovemaking.

For the past year, she had only ever imagined such a night with Ethan Range, Marquess of Plymouth. Now, she couldn't even conjure an image of the marquess in her mind's eye.

Could time be credited with such a change in how she viewed the men with whom she had shared a bed? Or had Mr. Streater cast a spell that helped her forget both men to whom she had been assigned in the misguided mission to expose a smuggler, as well as the man to whom she had given her virtue?

She rather hoped it was the latter, for she was having difficulty remembering the first man she had bedded. At one point, she had thought they might remain lovers, off and on, for the rest of their lives.

Alex was married now, though. She would never again warm his bed, nor did she want to.

"I've not been to the theatre in a long time," Daisy murmured, waving Teddy to retake his seat. She settled herself onto the settee and leaned over to pour more tea. "I look forward to attending." She added milk and sugar to his cup. "Forgive me. You probably came to discuss the school, and I have kept you from your purpose," she said.

A bit concerned at being in the apartment—alone—with Miss Albright, Teddy realized Mrs. Fitzgerald was the only one who knew they were meeting. "I simply wished to discover how you were faring," he said as he lifted the teacup to his lips.

"Very well, thank you. I met with the headmaster of St. Martin's this morning. He will provide some young gentlemen to act as partners for the students in my dance classes. They are to be here Friday at eleven o'clock," she explained.

"Boys?"

From the sound of the word, Daisy wondered if she had been mistaken in her reasoning. The girls would only properly learn to dance if they danced with those of the opposite sex.

"Yes," she hedged. "They need to learn, too."

"But, they will be chaperoned?" Teddy half-asked.

Daisy allowed a grin. "Mr. Lusk will be with them. As headmaster, I expect he will be quite stern with his charges, as I will be with mine," she replied. Pausing a moment, Daisy wondered if she should bring up the pending repairs.

Before she could, Teddy asked, "Will they be here every day?"

Giving her head a shake, Daisy said, "No. Maybe once or twice a week."

Teddy nodded, apparently satisfied with the arrangement. "You've done wonders with this apartment," he said. "Made it look as if it belongs in Mayfair."

Daisy angled her head to one side. "The furnishings did come from a house in Mayfair," she admitted. "As did the silk on the walls. I just thought it would be appropriate to have a parlor in which to host the instructors on a regular basis. To get to know them and their concerns. Learn what I can from their experiences here."

Teddy regarded her for a moment before saying, "Then you have already succeeded. My mother never would have socialized with the instructors—"

"Do you think I should not?" Daisy interrupted, a look of worry creasing her brow.

Teddy held up his hand. "I think you should run this school as you see fit. Mrs. Streater's way was not the only one, I am sure," he replied.

Daisy couldn't help but notice how he referred to his mother. She wondered if they had been estranged. If Agnes Streater had sequestered herself at Warwick's whilst her sons lived without a mother at home most of the time. "I suppose you did not see her much in your youth," she murmured.

Teddy shook his head. "I did not. But I knew where I could find her if I needed her," he said. "We lived only a few houses down in Kingly Street."

The mention of Kingly Street had Daisy straightening. "Somewhere near the Simpsons?"

Recoiling, as if shocked by her query, he said, "They were our landlords in fact. We lived in a terrace at the very end of their properties." He angled his head. "How is it you're familiar with the Simpsons?"

Not yet sure she was actually related to his former landlords, Daisy allowed a shrug. "One of our students is Miss

Hannah Simpson," she explained. "Their daughter, I am quite sure."

Teddy frowned. "Granddaughter, more likely," he countered. "The Simpsons are rather long in the tooth."

Suppressing the urge to grin at his comment, Daisy gave a shake of her head. "They had their twins rather late in life," she explained. "Miss Simpson's mother, if I'm to believe the *on-dit*, is actually the daughter of a duke." She didn't add that the woman was also her great-aunt. A conversation with her father would clarify the situation. She just wasn't sure when she would next see the Duke of Ariley.

"We have a duke's granddaughter among our students?" Teddy asked in disbelief, his awe apparent.

Daisy wondered what he would think when he discovered she was a duke's daughter—from the same dukedom. "Mrs. Simpson married a commoner," she countered. "After she was left widowed by her first husband." She paused, but realized Mr. Streater was waiting for her to say more. "Her firstborn was Gregory Grandby, and his firstborn, Ariel, is a student here at Warwick's," she added, only because she wanted to see his reaction.

Teddy blinked. And blinked again. He swallowed. "I wasn't aware we had such young ladies of the first water," he murmured. "But doesn't that mean that... Miss Simpson is aunt to Miss Grandby?"

Daisy allowed a grin. "Indeed she is." At that point, she was nearly tempted to mention her relationship to the girls, but Mr. Streater straightened and glanced around.

"Forgive me, but I believe I should be taking my leave," he said, as if he were suddenly uncomfortable with the idea of being alone with the headmistress in her apartment. He could only imagine what Mrs. Fitzgerald might be saying since she had left Miss Albright and him without a chaperone.

"Oh, must you go?" Daisy asked in alarm. When she

noticed how he hesitated in getting up from his chair, she added, "There is the matter of some repairs that Mrs. Streater arranged some time ago. They are due to begin next week."

"Repairs?" Teddy repeated, a brow furrowing. "Oh, just maintenance issues, I suppose?"

"Yes," she hedged. "The roofer was here to confirm his schedule—"

"Very well. I shouldn't want any of our young ladies of the first water to be doused by it whilst they are in class," Teddy joked, a brilliant grin appearing to once again youthen his appearance.

Daisy grinned. "Of course not," she agreed. "Well, then, as long as you're in agreement, I shan't cancel any of her arrangements." Deciding he wouldn't object to the work on the windows, she didn't bother mentioning the schedule for those repairs.

"You can simply give me the invoice," he said, his face still displaying a pleasing expression.

"I admit to feeling a bit of relief knowing you're amenable. It will be such an improvement to remove all the buckets from the classroom buildings."

Teddy blinked. "Buckets?" he repeated, his expression changing to one of concern.

"To catch the rainwater when it comes through the roofs," Daisy clarified. "Mr. Jenkins sees to emptying them before the instructors start their classes."

Frowning at the thought of the school's only male employee hauling buckets of rainwater, Teddy felt a bit of relief knowing the roofs would soon be repaired. "That's very kind of him," Teddy remarked, wondering at the bit of alarm he experienced just then. "Does he... does he have to do that often?"

Allowing a one shouldered-shrug, Daisy replied, "Only when it rains, I suppose."

Feeling a bit off-kilter at the thought that the roofs

leaked enough to fill buckets with rainwater, Teddy was about to ask about other problems but decided he had spent too much time alone with her. If Mrs. Fitzgerald talked, there might be a scandal. "Well, I should be taking my leave. If I don't see you before Saturday, I shall see you at the Bostwick's for the tea."

Daisy stood up at the same time as he did, amazed at how easily he was able to get up from the chair without having to use even his one arm. "I look forward to it," she said as she escorted him to first the apartment's door and then to the front door of Omega House. She curtsied to his bow and watched as he made his way along the pavement until he could hail a hackney.

Closing the door, Daisy leaned against it and wondered at the sense of disappointment she felt just then. Despite barely knowing the man, she found him easy to converse with, and he seemed equally at ease in the company of women. Had he stayed, they might have discussed topics other than the school, such as his position at the bank or his time in the British Army. She might have learned how he lost his arm, and she might have explained why it was she limped.

She could just imagine the look on his face when she told him she'd been shot in the leg. One didn't speak of limbs in polite company, of course, but for some reason, she wanted him to know.

And she wanted to know more about him.

The thought had her inhaling a sharp breath. That "wanting to know more"—curiosity coupled with determination—had been the reason she had pursued a position with the Home Office in the first place. Unless she read the news sheets, a gently bred woman would never be privy to what was happening outside her home and her circle of friends. Of what was happening in other parts of England. Of what had happened on the Continent during the wars.

At least, not until someone informed them of the death of a son or brother or cousin or... an uncle.

Daisy squeezed her eyes shut at the thought of her mother's only brother, dead at the hands of armed forces when they attempted to press him into service. Possessed of a gentle character and the mind of a simpleton, he never would have been able to wield a weapon, much less understand the difference between friend and foe.

A year later, and her mother joined him in death.

Half a lifetime ago, she thought, wondering at the odd timing of her melancholy.

Blinking back the tears as she whispered a curse, Daisy used the back of one hand to wipe her cheek. She swallowed the lump in her throat and cursed again. Only a moment before, she had been so content in the company of Mr. Streater. Comfortable, even, despite the hint of crackle in the air, as if lightning from an impending thunderstorm was about to strike.

As if on cue, the boom of thunder rumbled in the distance, and Daisy gave a start. Her first thought was of the buckets strategically placed in the classroom buildings. Her second thought was of Mr. Streater. She hoped he would be inside a hackney, protected from the impending downpour.

When she remembered his invitation to attend the play, her mood lifted. They would have tea with the other instructors, then change clothes and leave for the theatre. Sit in a private box with the Bostwicks and enjoy the production. Afterwards...

Well, she decided it was better she not imagine what might happen afterwards. These days, her imagination was capable of conjuring images she best not study too closely.

Daisy returned to her apartment and set about hanging the rest of the peach silk on the remaining walls in the parlor.

Despite the rain outside, no water dripped from the ceiling.

CHAPTER 21
TEA WITH A REBEL

Thursday

When Daisy completed teaching her third day of dancing, arithmetic, and grammar, she sought out Miss Crofter in the hopes of inviting the sewing instructor for tea. She found the woman straightening spools of silk thread in the room in which the older woman taught her sewing classes. Lining the walls were examples of exquisite stitcheries, simple embroidery samplers, and needleworked chair cushions.

Daisy stared at one such cushion, recognizing the pattern from the dining chairs in the home in which she had grown up. A sampler was nearly the same as one that her mother had done long before Daisy had been born. She was admiring an elaborate embroidery when Charity Crofter finally took note of her presence.

"Miss Albright?" Miss Crofter said, one hand poised over a spool of thread.

"Yes. I wished to formally introduce myself," Daisy said as she turned her attention to the woman she thought might be a few years older. She gave a curtsy. Although, now that she saw the sewing instructor up-close, she realized Miss

Crofter couldn't be that much older. Five-and-thirty, perhaps? "And I wish to apologize for not having done so earlier this week. We always seemed to be passing one another on our way to somewhere else."

Miss Crofter blinked, as if she'd had a response all prepared and then had to rethink what she wanted to say. She curtsied. "It's very good to meet you," she managed. Glancing about the room as if to be sure everything was in order, her reading glasses perched on the end of her nose, Charity finally clasped her hands together and allowed a nod. "I rather imagine you were a bit... overwhelmed these first few days."

Overwhelmed wasn't exactly how Daisy would describe her first few days in the position of headmistress, but she figured it was a close approximation. "Only by the need to teach three classes," she replied. "I have developed a good deal of respect for my sister and what she had to do to prepare for her classes," she added.

"So the rumors are true? You are Miss Albright's older sister?" Charity asked, an eyebrow arching up in query.

Rumors? Daisy was quite sure she had been up-front about her relationship to the former instructor of the arithmetic and dancing classes. "I am," she admitted. "I was about to return to my office to work on some ledgers, but wondered if you might join me for tea instead?"

Charity regarded her with a good deal of suspicion. "To what end?"

Daisy blinked. "To enjoy a cup of tea. Eat a biscuit or two. Become better acquainted," she replied, deciding the rumors she had heard about Charity Crofter must be true. The woman was a bit prickly.

"It's true I don't hold a high opinion of most men," Charity stated.

The comment seemed to come out without forethought, and Daisy had to resist the urge to blink again. She gave her head a shake instead. "Oh? Did something... happen?" she asked in alarm, moving closer so she stood before the instructor.

The question caught Charity off-guard. "Nothing I'm willing to share," she replied, her chin rising in defiance. "Water under the bridge, after all," she added, not immediately aware that by answering as she did, she was admitting that something awful had indeed happened.

"Well, then we shall speak of other topics," Daisy stated as she made her way to the door. When Charity didn't follow, Daisy turned and regarded her with an expectant look. "You can join me?" she half-asked.

Charity's eyes widened before she dared another glance around the classroom. "I suppose," she hedged.

Daisy angled her head to one side. "If you weren't coming for tea, pray tell, what would you be doing instead?"

Her head dipping a bit, Charity took a deep breath and let it out slowly. "Having tea by myself in my rooms at Alpha House," she said in a quiet voice.

Daisy frowned. Apparently the instructor didn't socialize with the other teachers. "Do you prefer to drink tea by yourself?"

Charity lifted her head and regarded Daisy for a long time before saying, "No. Not on this fine day. I shall join you."

Allowing a nod, Daisy led the way out of the classroom and watched as Charity closed and locked the door using an iron key. Watched as the woman gripped the handle and jiggled it, as if she expected the lock to give way and the door to open.

"Once in a while it doesn't lock quite right," Charity said with a shrug. "One cannot be too careful these days," she added before she dropped the key into her needleworked reticule. The drawstring bag was covered in embroidery to the point it was impossible to distinguish what color fabric was hidden beneath the silk threads.

"You have the right of it," Daisy replied, moving in the direction of Omega House once Charity had stepped up alongside her. "Your reticule is beautiful. Did you make it?"

Charity dipped her head again. "I didn't make it, but I did the finishing on it. One of last year's classes was all about embellishing accessories," she explained. "Shawls, reticules, slippers and the like. This year we're spending more time on needlework for decoration. It is my belief that every gentle-woman must be responsible for decorating the walls of their homes, especially if paintings aren't in abundance," she went on. "Not everyone can afford paintings."

Daisy nearly flinched, hoping the instructor wouldn't find fault with her lack of stitcheries. She did have a few paintings to dress the silk-covered walls in the parlor. Having spent the night before seeing to covering the last wall with the peach watered silk she had brought with her from Ariley Place—she was sure it was leftover from when the walls of her bedchamber had been covered—Daisy had resisted the urge to go straight to bed in favor of rehanging the paintings she had taken down.

"I fear I haven't completed an embroidery in a very long time," Daisy said then, deciding it better she be honest with Charity. "I learned how to sew from my mother, of course, but I haven't practiced recently." She moved to unlock her apartment door.

"What then do you do with your idle time?" Charity asked, censure apparent in her voice.

Daisy allowed a chuckle. "Last evening, I hung silk on two walls in my parlor," she said as she pushed open the door and waved a hand to indicate Charity should go in.

She wasn't disappointed to hear the woman's inhalation of breath.

Charity turned and did a quick glance around the parlor,

her face giving away her confusion. She stepped backward and dared a glance down the hallway before she regarded her hostess with newfound respect. "It's lovely," she whispered. "Why, I cannot even..." She turned a bit and looked at the adjacent walls. "I cannot imagine this is the same apartment where Mrs. Streater lived," she said, before turning to say, "It's quite lovely."

"Why, thank you," Daisy said as she dipped her head. "I suppose I could have waited for the colorman who is to do the other painting here at the school, but it will be two months or more before he will get this far. I decided I didn't wish to wait that long."

"Colorman?" Charity repeated, just as she took a seat in one of the upholstered chairs. Given the small size of the parlor, Daisy had only brought the settee and two chairs along with a side table and the low table from her bedchamber at Ariley Place. A small secretary was the only other piece of furniture in the room, a leftover from Mrs. Streater's furnishings.

Daisy nodded. "It seems Warwick's is about to undergo a series of necessary renovations," she acknowledged as she made her way into the small kitchen. Having determined the third figure on Mrs. Streater's ledger was for the cost of painting the interiors of the buildings—and then only because she had spied two men measuring the buildings earlier that day—Daisy had confirmed a colorman had the school on his list of projects to complete during the summer months. "Roofs are first, of course. Then some windows. Then paint." She put together the tea set and pulled her last tin of biscuits from the room's only shelf, wondering which cook she might have to bribe to see to a refill.

Charity's eyes widened as she removed her spectacles. "You've made all these arrangements in three days?" she questioned.

Daisy allowed a chuckle. "As much as I need to, I am not

able to perform miracles," she replied as she set the tray on the low table. "Mrs. Streater acquired the quotes and set the schedule. I merely need to ensure her vision is carried out." She leaned over and poured the tea. "How do you take your tea?" She couldn't help but notice how Charity's eyes focused on the sugar-pot, as if the woman had never seen sugar before.

Charity glanced up. "Will you think me terribly selfish if I say milk and sugar?" she asked, her manner rather timid.

After a moment of forcing herself to display an impassive expression, Daisy shook her head. "Not at all. I take it Mrs. Streater didn't have sugar?" she queried, hoping to learn about the ancient woman who had run the school for over three decades.

Charity leaned forward. "No sugar, no milk. And rarely did she invite any of us for tea," she said in a whisper.

Daisy wondered how to respond. On the one hand, the sewing instructor might have been baiting her, to determine if she would be free with her gossip. On the other, she may have just shared an important tidbit about Mrs. Streater.

The former headmistress might have valued her privacy —she was in charge of a number of teachers as well as servants for the school, not to mention the two dozen young ladies who attended classes—and simply preferred to spend her time after classes alone in the tiny apartment.

Before Daisy could ask if Mrs. Streater usually spent her evenings alone, Charity said, "She didn't believe she should fraternize with the employees." She took the cup and saucer from Daisy, giving her a nod as she did so.

"But she did occasionally... meet with you? Discuss how your classes were progressing?" Daisy prompted as she offered a plate of biscuits.

Charity shook her head as she took a shortbread. "Never. Oh, she occasionally visited the classrooms, but I think it was more to count how many were in attendance than to actually check up on us. Why, I think I could have been teaching my charges how to... how to *gamble* and she wouldn't have been the wiser."

Until a young lady told her mother she was learning how to gamble at school, and then that would have been the end of that—and probably the school, too, Daisy thought. "But you're not," Daisy said, a huge grin forming to indicate she was teasing.

"I'm not, nor have I ever," Charity agreed, finally allowing a smile. "I did have to teach a mild curse word one might use when one sticks a needle in one's thumb by accident, though," she admitted then. "Darnal."

Daisy arched a brow. "I've not heard that one," she commented. She didn't dare admit the words she might have uttered when thoroughly frustrated. Or the one she said when she poked a needle into her thumb. "But it's a good one," she whispered.

"Rhymes with 'tarnal'," Charity said in a whisper.

The other word for 'damn' had Daisy nodding her understanding. The two drank their tea in companionable silence for a time before Daisy asked, "How long have you been teaching here?"

Charity seemed to think a moment. "It will be ten years come January. I remember because the former sewing instructor had to resign when she married."

Daisy blinked, rather stunned by the comment. "Because her husband wouldn't allow her to continue to teach?"

Frowning, Charity shook her head. "He would have preferred she continue—I believe he was counting on the income—but Mrs. Streater didn't allow instructors to be married unless they were men."

Remembering how she encouraged Jane Betterman and Mr. Jenkins to consider matrimony, Daisy realized they might not have pursued the arrangement thinking the draconian rule prohibited them from continuing their employment.

Or at least Jane's.

"I shall have to make it known that *that* particular rule is no longer in place," Daisy stated. "Should an instructor wish to wed but continue in their role at the school, they will be allowed to do so."

Charity looked as if she might faint. "Are you... are you quite certain Mr. Streater is in agreement?" she asked.

Daisy wasn't about to admit she didn't know one way or the other, but she couldn't imagine he would care one way or the other. He seemed determined to keep his distance as much as possible from Warwick's. Once she started giving him the invoices for the upcoming restoration efforts his mother had put into place, he might never want to set foot in the school again. "Quite sure," she replied with a nod.

Remembering Charity's initial reaction, Daisy leaned forward. "Have you a beau? Or someone you have put off because you thought you couldn't wed?" she queried.

Her eyes widening, Charity gave her head a shake. "Of course not. Remember, I do not hold the male sex in high regard."

Daisy decided to guess what might have turned the sewing instructor against men in general. "It can be hard to regard their sex with any favor when one has been left at the altar."

Charity sucked in a breath. "Who told you?" she asked in dismay, her face coloring up with embarrassment. She looked poised for a quick retreat from the small parlor.

Resisting the urge to express any form of victory at having sorted Charity's problem with men, Daisy gave a shake of her head. "No one, Miss Crofter. But with the number of men who went off to war in the past decade, it happened far more often than it should have."

This last was also a guess, but one based on something

she knew from her time with the Foreign Office. The widows of enlisted men didn't receive a pension when their husbands died on the battlefield. Only officers' wives did. Miss Crofter didn't strike her as one who had been betrothed to an officer. Perhaps her fiancé was concerned she wouldn't regain her position at the school after having to give it up to be married in the first place. Unable to break off the engagement without ruining her reputation, he might have simply left for the Continent, ensuring Charity could continue in her position at Warwick's. "Did he... did he come back to these shores after the war ended?" Daisy asked gently.

Charity looked as if she were about to cry. "I've absolutely no idea."

Daisy's eyes widened. The jilted woman's dismay had obviously turned to anger over the years, festering until she held the entire male sex in low regard for something a misguided young man might have done to see to her future. "Did you find his name on one of the lists?" she asked, worry evident in her voice.

Shaking her head at the same time a tear escaped, Charity managed to say, "I didn't think to look. I was still so..." She sighed a moment before a sob robbed her of breath.

Daisy held out an embroidered handkerchief. "Angry, no doubt," she murmured quietly. "Hurt."

Charity nodded. "I fear my pride suffered the most. I would have made an excellent wife."

"You still will," Daisy stated. "And a rather pretty one, too." Without her wire spectacles perched on the end of her nose, Miss Crofter appeared years younger, what with her smooth, pale skin and blue eyes the color of cornflowers. If the bun on the back of her head hadn't been so tightly wound and instead dressed into a softer one atop her head, she would look like any other eligible young lady, albeit a bit closer to being on the shelf. "Which begs the question. Why haven't you married someone else?"

Charity sniffled, the handkerchief held over her nose. Her eyes widened. "I haven't been courted by anyone. Not that I would have..." She allowed the sentence to trail off before she gave Daisy a beseeching look. "I've been a fool, haven't I?" she asked, setting her teacup onto the low table.

Daisy shook her head, noting how Charity's hands shook. "Not at all," she replied, refilling the woman's tea. "If you'd like..." She hesitated, using the pause to add the milk and sugar. She was about to offer to help discover what might have become of the woman's betrothed, but wondered if she might be giving away too much about her own background if she did.

I don't work for them any longer, she thought, deciding she could use what contacts she had to at least ask about the man. "I may know someone. Someone at the War Office. He might have access to records."

Blinking tears from her eyes, Charity sniffled and allowed a nod. "His name was Mr. Barnaby. Nicholas Barnaby."

Although the name seemed familiar, Daisy couldn't place just where she had heard it before. "Go on," she encouraged.

Charity angled her head. "Well, he's older than me—he was probably thirty at the time—but... he seemed so... *beholden* when we first met. He courted me for three weeks and then, one day in the park, he asked if I might become his wife. I was thrilled and agreed immediately. I didn't have to give it a second thought. It didn't matter I would have to give up my position here at Warwick's. We set a date. The banns were read, and on the day we were to be wed..."

New tears threatened, and Daisy sighed. "Do you have any idea where Mr. Barnaby worked? What he did for a living?"

Sniffling, Charity nodded. "He was a clerk. At a... at a warehouse down by the river."

Given the number of companies that had warehouses near the river, Daisy realized it would be like looking for a needle in a haystack if she started with that bit of information. "Had he been off to war before?" Daisy asked, thinking it would be easier to find information if he was on the Continent for one of the earlier wars against France.

"He mentioned he was in the army."

Well, that narrowed it down, although not a lot.

"I shall see what I can discover," Daisy promised as she helped herself to a biscuit. "And in the meantime, we shall finish our tea and look forward to a new Warwick's," she said lightly. "Oh, and should you decide to marry, know that you can keep your position here at Warwick's. I would really rather not have to line up yet another new teacher."

Charity allowed a nod. "It won't be an issue for me, of course, but it's good to know the new rule."

Her words had Daisy determined the new rule would apply to Charity Crofter, whether she believed it would or not.

Now, who could she bother at the War Office?

CHAPTER 22
QUOTES ARE DISCOVERED

A few minutes later

When Charity Crofter took her leave of Omega House, Daisy hurried back to her desk and opened the drawer containing the odd ledger. After her discussion with Charity about the impending repairs, and remembering the instructor's comment about the door lock, Daisy now guessed why there were so many more entries than just the three repairs she knew were imminent.

She removed everything from the drawer, piling the other leather-bound ledgers onto her desk in an effort to get to the bottom of the drawer. When she did, she found a sheet of pasteboard that had been folded in half. Lifting it by one edge—she had to use her fingernails to pry it out from its tight confines—she finally managed to extract it without bending it.

Pulling back the top, she found a sheaf of papers of various sizes within. The top sheet, a letter printed with the calling card for Thatcher and Sons at the top, contained the formal quote for the replacement of all the roofs at Warwick's. The next sheet, a parchment with the stamp of the British Cast Plate Glass Company and a date from six months ago, was a detailed accounting of every window needing replacement followed by the amount each one would cost to install.

The colorman's quote followed. Although not as detailed, it showed the addresses for all the buildings on the school grounds and the total for exterior and interior painting.

Relieved at finding the information—this was the documentation she sought to explain Mrs. Streater's entries in the odd ledger—Daisy now dreaded what she would find beneath. There were at least ten more sheets, all for companies that had apparently been hired to perform some sort of maintenance task at the school.

Comparing the numbers from the stack of quotes with the entries Mrs. Streater had made on a ledger sheet—numbers with some letters next to each entry—Daisy confirmed they matched the quotes for the maintenance work. The roofer's quote matched the first amount, as did his initials. The window quote matched the second amount. From there, she was able to match up most of the entries with the quotes for the work that was scheduled to be performed. Work that included new door locks, gas lighting in the classroom buildings, and carpets in the boarding houses.

When she totaled the amount, she cringed.

Would Mr. Streater have enough blunt to cover invoices that would total nearly ten-thousand pounds?

Returning the ledgers to their drawer but leaving the pasteboard folder with its contents on her desk, she was about to write a note seeking an audience with Mr. Streater. Then she caught sight of the time on the clock.

Daisy didn't have an opportunity to consider the matter further. She had to change clothes and be ready to leave soon.

CHAPTER 23
DINNER AT ARILEY PLACE

Thursday evening

The invitation wasn't unexpected. It arrived a day later than she thought it might, though, delivered by the handsome footman who stood just inside the doorway to her office, waiting for a reply.

Daisy lifted the dark wax embossed with her father's seal and quickly unfolded the parchment.

She scanned the masculine scrawl, not a bit surprised it was written in her father's hand.

My very dearest daughter,

I was given your note by one of the servants (the one who drew the short straw, no doubt).

You're welcome. The furnishings are truly yours to do with as you please, but know this: I have already given permission to my dear Helen to see to replacements (since she still holds hope you will spend another night or two or more under our roof).

Apparently, she was arranging an appointment with Chippendale when your employer arrived to place an order of his own. Having inherited a business and now that he is a member of White's, it seems Mr. Streater intends to furnish his house accordingly.

Make an old man happy and join us for dinner this evening. I promise family only—no balding, fat viscounts in need of a wife will be in attendance. At least, none by my invitation. I cannot vouch for what my duchess might do when she learns of this invitation (so I will not apprise her of it until five o'clock this evening). We may even allow the children in the dining room, if only so Helen can show off your siblings.

Please?

Your father

A pang in her chest had Daisy realizing she had no choice but to pay a call on Ariley Place and have dinner with her father and his new family. Although she had considered joining the young ladies in Delta House for dinner that evening, she knew another instructor would be a guest at their table.

"Let the duke know that I accept his invitation," she said to the footman.

He gave a bow. "Yes, my lady. I'm to inform you that a coach will arrive at half-past five to collect you."

Daisy resisted the urge to roll her eyes. Of course, her father would see to transportation. "Then I will be ready at half-past-five," she responded.

The ducal town coach pulled up in front of Omega House at precisely five o'clock. Daisy knew it because she had paid a street urchin a farthing to let her know when it did. The small boy, undernourished and covered with a year's worth of dirt, pounded on her apartment door. "The coach is here, m'lady," he called out from the hallway.

Dressed but not quite ready to leave—the coach was a half-hour early—Daisy opened the door, gave the boy another farthing and a biscuit, and told him to tell the driver she would be out in ten minutes. Then she watched as the boy took his leave of Omega House, a wan grin appearing when the door shook as he slammed it shut.

"He'll be back, miss," a maid said from where she was dusting at the end of the hall. "Now that he knows you have some blunt."

Daisy regarded the servant a moment. "Perhaps he will. But sometimes it's good to have a caddy," she replied, thinking the boy could deliver messages when necessary.

Maybe after he had a bath.

Dressed in a dark red dinner gown trimmed with tiny scallops and fabric rosettes at the hem and neckline, Daisy donned a black mantle and took her leave of Omega House. Pausing to lock the outer door, she was unaware of who watched her take her leave, although a familiar prickling sensation at her neck had her pausing before she stepped up into the ducal coach. Turning, she spotted the urchin watching from down the street and gave him a quick wave.

Had she turned in the other direction at the very same time, she might have paid witness to Mr. Streater duck in front of a parked barouche and then lean sideways a bit to watch her departure.

Perhaps she did.

*T*eddy Streater wasn't surprised to see Miss Albright leaving Omega House, apparently on her way to dinner. Given the hour, though, it was a bit early. Most of the boarding houses served the formal meal at seven o'clock.

He was surprised to see her stepping into a glossy black coach, however. With a driver, groomsman, and a tiger, it was evident the town coach was owned by someone of wealth. Someone of importance.

When her mantle splayed open as she climbed into the coach, he caught sight of the color of her gown. The deep red was a stunning color with her brunette hair. The coiffure was simple but elegant, probably a testament to her lack of a lady's maid.

As he watched the coach pull away from the curb, his heart sank at seeing a gold crest painted on the door. In an effort to keep from being seen by its passenger, he stepped onto the pavement and behind the barouche, so he couldn't make out the details of the crest.

But one thing he knew for certain.

Miss Albright was positively gorgeous!

Which, of course, he already knew. And so did his cock, which he was trying to keep under control lest a student take note from one of the five boarding houses lining Glasshouse Street.

Teddy tried to ignore how shabby the buildings appeared, each and every one of them in need of a new coat of paint. Several window panes appeared cracked in the afternoon sun, which only emphasized how much they needed cleaning. Only the landscaping kept the property from looking like a complete loss.

Teddy sighed in disgust, and then he remembered the conversation he'd had with Miss Albright over tea the afternoon prior. She had mentioned repairmen had been arranged. With that thought, he turned his mind back on Miss Albright for another reason.

If not with the students at Warwick's, then with whom was she having dinner that evening?

Or was she meeting someone for an assignation?

Was she a mistress for some fat, balding viscount? Hiding her true identity by playing at being a headmistress of a finishing school by day and warming some rich man's bed by night?

Teddy shook his head, deciding the idea was ridiculous. She had come seeking the position because she needed the employment. If she was a mistress, she wouldn't have need of a job, too.

Would she?

But seeing her dressed as she was this evening made him wonder if she would dress the same for the theatre on Saturday. *Exactly two days from now*, he thought as he gave his chronometer a glance. Perhaps she would tell him then with whom she had supped on this night. If not, maybe he could bring up the topic and she would admit she was available for such an arrangement. Perhaps then he could offer her *carte blanche*. A fleeting thought of marriage was just that.

No woman like her would never marry a man with only one arm, after all.

*D*aisy wasn't quite sure what had her glancing out the opposite window from where she was settled into the navy velvet squabs of her father's town coach. Perhaps it was the quick motion of the man who was leaning against the front of a barouche and then suddenly wasn't.

Is that Mr. Streater? she wondered as she slid over to the other side of the coach and dared a glance out the window. The man was now leaning on the side of the barouche, apparently believing he was out of sight from the town coach, when in fact she could clearly make out it was him once the coach made the right turn at the next intersection.

Whatever is he doing?

A thought that he had come for an appointment with her was quickly set aside. Their next engagement wouldn't be until Saturday's tea.

Deciding he was there to gauge the extent of the repairs that were to take place, Daisy once again settled into the squabs. She wondered instead what might be lying in wait at Ariley Place. Socializing with her father wasn't something she'd had a chance to do much of since she had left his protection. With his marriage, she didn't expect she would except under clandestine arrangements, made so because she was sure his duchess would abhor her very existence.

But Helen had been most welcoming this Sunday past. She seemed genuine in her insistence that Daisy become acquainted with her brother and sister.

The thought of the two siblings had her grinning just before the coach pulled up to the mansion in Park Lane.

She stepped down from the coach and was nearly bowled over when her brother, William, toddled into her. "Days-ee!" he said in his high-pitched voice, his gap-toothed grin broad. Dressed in short pants and a broad-collared pea coat, with a nautical-themed shirt beneath, he looked as if he could be any young boy in Mayfair.

"Lord William," she replied with a grin, bending down to greet the boy. She glanced up to find his nurse pushing a perambulator, the expression on her face one of horror. "How is my brother on this fine day?" she asked, giving the nurse a quick wave. "I've got him," she added.

The boy struggled a moment before bowing and saying, "I am well, m'lady."

Daisy stood up, managing to suppress a wince when her leg protested. She took his hand, secretly thrilled when he seemed so proud to be escorting her to the front door. "And what about your sister, Lady Rose?" she asked.

"She's 'sleep."

Wondering at her sudden disappointment, Daisy was about to lift the brass knocker when the door opened to reveal Jarvis. The butler's eyes widened at seeing the boy with her, but Jarvis soon regained his composure and stepped aside to allow her in, remembering her from her visit only this Sunday past.

"Good evening, Lady Daisy." He took her mantle and the boy's coat, once Daisy managed to get him out of it. She had knelt down in an effort to be at the boy's level. For a moment, she thought of what it would be like to arrive at her own home with a son. What it would be like to pull off his coat and straighten his clothes as she knelt before him. Smooth his hair into submission by first licking her gloved hand and running it over his head until all the fine strands of hair behaved.

She was about to imagine a little girl, too, but the hairs on the back of her neck prickled, and she glanced up to find her father watching her. "Hello, Father," she said. Her initial attempt to stand had her grimacing when her bad leg didn't allow it. The duke was suddenly there, his arms beneath hers, lifting her until she was standing. "Thank you," she managed, about to step away and give him a curtsy. Instead, she was suddenly in his embrace, nearly crushed by strong arms that held her for several seconds.

When he finally released her, James, Duke of Ariley, allowed a long sigh. "I was afraid you wouldn't come," he said in a whisper.

Daisy regarded him with a look of concern. "Why ever not? It's not as if I'm required to dine at Warwick's," she replied. "Besides, I'm in need of more biscuits," she added with a wink, just before her attention was drawn to her young brother down below. William had wrapped his arms around her legs and had the side of his face pressed against the silk fabric of her dinner gown. "Like father, like son?" she murmured, a teasing grin causing her dimple to appear.

James gave a chuckle. "No one will ever accuse him of being a cold-hearted Englishman," he said with a shake of his head, his pride in his only son evident.

"Just as no one would ever accuse *you* of having a cold heart," Helen said as she finished descending the stairs. When James stepped back and turned, giving his wife a short bow, Helen had a clear view of her son clinging to Daisy's legs. Her expression changed from delight to concern and then to embarrassment. "William," she started to chide the boy.

"It's quite all right," Daisy said as she dipped a curtsy, the maneuver made awkward with William still holding onto her leg. "He escorted me from the coach." She turned her attention back to the duke. "Thank you for sending it, by the way."

"It was the least I could do," James replied, bending down to pick up his son. "Will you two ladies join us warm-hearted gentlemen in the library for coffee and walnuts?"

Helen exchanged a glance with Daisy. "Of course." She then motioned to a footman and asked that the nurse be informed William was in his father's company. Daisy had thought the old nurse would have been behind her in the vestibule, but realized the servant would probably re-enter the house using the back door, even if she was pushing Lady Rose in a perambulator.

"Your father tells me you're the new headmistress of Warwick's," Helen said as they entered the library.

"I am," Daisy replied. "And teaching Diana's classes, too, at least until I can find a replacement." She settled into one of the chairs once Helen was seated on a divan. A footman saw to serving walnuts and coffee after her father had settled into one of the larger chairs. Still holding William, the boy's bottom resting on one arm and one chubby fist clutching his cravat, James arched an eyebrow.

"The arithmetic *and* the dance class?"

Daisy rolled her eyes. "Yes. I actually find the arithmetic easier to teach. Teaching the cotillion is proving problematic, although my students do fine with the waltz."

Helen allowed a brilliant smile. "Your father is a master at the waltz," she said. "But how do you find your charges? Do any of them give you trouble?"

Daisy shook her head, suppressing the urge to grin at how her father seemed surprised by his wife's assessment of his dance skills. "No trouble, really. They're all rather well behaved. Daughters of tradesmen, some rather wealthy. I am curious about a few of them, though."

"Oh?"

"Miss Batey, for instance. The new Viscount Lancaster's daughter. I wouldn't expect a viscount's daughter to attend a finishing school," Daisy explained. "She has a bodyguard, of course, but... why isn't she being taught at home? By a governess?"

Helen and James exchanged quick glances. "She was, by her mother," James finally said, readjusting William in his hold now that the boy was sound asleep. "When the viscountess died last year, Lancaster feared scandal should he hire a governess—he's only recently inherited the title from his late brother, you see—so he enrolled Analise at Warwick's."

Remembering Jane's explanation was nearly the same, Daisy felt a bit of relief. Nothing nefarious there, then. "Miss Hannah Simpson is one of my students," she said, watching her father for his reaction. She was surprised when he suddenly grinned. "What is it?"

"Aunt Sophia's daughter?" he replied. "My, but it's hard to believe that girl can already be old enough to attend Warwick's. She's... she's one of your aunts, actually."

Daisy dared a glance at Helen, wondering if the duchess knew anything about Sophia Simpson. "I thought so, but I haven't introduced myself as a relation. I thought it best—"

"You needn't hide your true identity from Hannah," Helen interrupted. "And Lady Sophia is well regarded, despite her odd choice of a husband. You would never know the man was a... a servant back in the day."

"It's been nearly forty years," James said then. "And he wasn't an odd choice. The two are hopelessly in love with one another. That they could manage to have twins when my aunt was nearly... well, I don't even know how old she was—"

"Six-and-forty," Daisy said quietly.

"—Is merely a testament to how devoted they are to one another," James went on. His eyes widened, though, at hearing how old Sophia was when the twins were born. He turned his attention to his wife.

"Don't even think about it," Helen said, her head shaking back and forth. "I cannot imagine having a baby at that age. It will be bad enough I have to wait so long to be a grandmother."

Daisy grinned as her father held up his free hand, as if he could stave off his wife's protests.

"I'm not expecting you to," he countered with a grin of his own. "But I must say, Aunt Sophia looks rather splendid for a woman of her age. Which is?"

"One-and-sixty," Daisy said. She knew he was testing her math skills, but she had already worked out the numbers in her head back when she first saw Hannah's name on the class register.

"But she doesn't look that old at all," Helen protested.

"The Burroughs women keep their youthful appearance. Just look at my youngest sister. Elise is..., what?"

"Six-and-thirty," Daisy offered.

"And Thorncastle is probably getting a child on her this very moment."

Daisy said, "Father!" at the same time Helen said, "James!", which had William giving a start in his father's arms. His eyes popped open, but upon seeing where he was and in whose arms he was resting, he allowed a grin and waved to his mother.

"They're in the Kingdom of Two Sicilys as we speak," James countered, as if that should be enough to defend his remark. "In Rome, if I remember their itinerary. Anyway, I know Elise wants a child, and Thorncastle is only..." He paused and turned his gaze on Daisy.

She blinked. "Five-and-thirty, perhaps? I'm not sure

about that," she hedged. She had never met the viscount who had married her Aunt Elise the same day Viscount Breckinridge married her sister, Diana.

"Close enough," James said. "Which brings us to you, my dearest Daisy."

Daisy blinked again. "You promised not to invite a fat, balding viscount to dinner tonight," she warned.

"And I did not," her father replied. "But, are you at least *considering* matrimony?"

Holding her breath at the same moment Helen said, "Now, James, you promised me you wouldn't bring it up," Daisy wondered how to respond.

Had he asked her only a week ago, she would have denied any desire to wed. Any desire to have children of her own. But much had happened in the past week.

Her attention fell on her brother, who was playing peek-a-boo by hiding his eyes with his hands. She covered her own eyes with her hands, which had William erupting in giggles. When she pulled them away, she finally responded. "I am, since I have every intention of being married when I have a child of my own."

Her father's expression faltered, his brows furrowing as he set William on the floor and dared a glance at Helen. The boy quickly toddled to Daisy and stood up next to her chair.

Daisy caught the odd looks. "What is it?"

James exchanged glances with his wife again. "So... you don't have one of your own already?" he asked, an odd inflection coloring his voice.

Her eyes widening in alarm, Daisy couldn't help the sound of disbelief she made just then. "Of course not!" She made the sound again before adding, "Why ever would you think such a thing?" She hadn't told anyone of her brief pregnancy. Hadn't told anyone of the miscarriage, either.

"Ever since that morning you recognized that I am expecting a child, your father thought perhaps you had... he thought that you had experienced morning sickness first-hand," Helen explained gently, well aware James was hoping the floor would open up and swallow him whole.

Well, she had experienced the nausea, but Daisy wasn't about to admit it. "Well, I do not, nor will I ever have an illegitimate child," she said quietly, turning to lift William onto her lap. "Besides, there's much to accomplish at Warwick's before I can be thinking of such things," she claimed.

"Oh?" her father replied, ignoring the sting he felt at hearing her words about not having an illegitimate child. He had acknowledged her as his daughter. Given her his name at birth. Raised her. Why was she so bitter about being illegitimate? "What's happened there?"

"It's what's about to happen," Daisy replied. "Renovations. Repairs. I've been able to determine Mrs. Streater arranged for new roofs, some work on the windows, and painting all the buildings. New locks, carpet, gas lighting—repairs she had scheduled before she died. Other than the total cost, her notes were rather cryptic on the matter until I discovered the estimates provided by all the companies that will do the work."

James angled his head and frowned. "Sounds awfully expensive," he replied. "Is Mr. Streater prepared to cover the invoices?"

Daisy nodded. "I think so. He inherited some money from his mother. He knows about the roofs, because a representative from the roofing company paid a call to confirm they would be starting the work. But I wasn't able to tell him what else I had discovered from his mother's ledger," she explained, frowning a bit when she realized this really wasn't an appropriate topic for pre-dinner conversation.

"Forgive me for asking," James said before giving a quick glance in Helen's direction. "But how much did Mrs. Streater think all these repairs were going to cost?"

Taking a deep breath, Daisy said, "About ten thousand

"pounds," in a quiet voice. She dared a glance at Helen, knowing they really shouldn't be speaking of money.

"It's all right," her stepmother said with a wave. "He does it all the time. 'A dukedom is a business and must be discussed as such'," she added, imitating her husband's comment on the topic.

"That's a good deal of blunt," James replied, ignoring Helen's comment. "Are you quite sure Mr. Streater can cover the expense?"

"Of course he can," Helen said, her response surprising Daisy. "He was at Chippendale's to place an order for a bedroom suite when I was there to order the furniture for your bedchamber," she added as she turned to regard Daisy. "Oh, I do hope you like what I've chosen."

But Daisy was staring at her father. His note had mentioned Mr. Streater joining White's. Mr. Streater had mentioned placing an order for a Tillbury. Furniture from Chippendale's was expensive.

If he was spending his inheritance on furniture, dues for an expensive men's club, and on equipage, there might not be enough to cover the repairs his mother had lined up.

"Are you thinking what I'm thinking?" Daisy asked, her worried gaze directed on her father.

"That a bank clerk will not have enough blunt to cover the repairs his mother arranged?" he countered.

Daisy nodded. "He has an inheritance. But I believe it was exactly the amount that will be needed to cover the repairs. I haven't yet done the numbers to determine how profitable the school can be, though. Perhaps there will be enough from tuition."

"Surely enrollment will increase once the repairs are complete," Helen offered. "There are some who have said it's just a bit on the shabby side, but the school has such a fine reputation."

"Reputation will do it no good if Mr. Streater can't pay for the repairs," James said with a shake of his head.

"In which case, Mr. Streater will simply have to sell it," Helen said, her features suggesting she was proud to have come to such a simple solution. She was about to suggest her husband buy it, but James held up a staying hand.

"I am not about to become the owner of a finishing school, my dearest. I've quite enough properties to oversee as it is," he said gently. After a moment, he added, "You mustn't tell anyone what we've discussed here tonight. Not any of your friends," he warned.

Helen gave him a quelling glance. "I would never," she replied.

Holding up the hand that wasn't wrapped around her little brother's waist, Daisy said, "It's too soon to panic," she said. "I'll review the ledgers from the past year and see how profitable the school can be with the number of students we have right now."

"Which is exactly what you should do," her father agreed. The dinner bell chimed, which had William straightening in Daisy's lap.

"Dinner," he called out happily.

"Indeed, little brother," Daisy replied with a grin. She pulled him from her lap and held him until his feet took purchase on the Turkish carpet below. "Will you escort me?"

William beamed as he looked up at her. He held out a chubby arm. Daisy took his hand, and they followed the duke and duchess to the dining room.

CHAPTER 24
A CONFESSION OVER BRANDY

few hours later
When it was apparent Daisy wouldn't be allowed to return to Warwick's until the morning, she agreed to stay the night in her sister's bedchamber.

Expecting to spend the rest of her waking hours working on notes for her classes and thinking about Mr. Streater, she was startled when a knock sounded at the door.

"Yes?"

The door opened to reveal her father. He held a decanter in one hand, and the stems of two glasses were threaded between the long fingers of his other hand. "Join me for a drink?"

Daisy's eyes widened. "Is that brandy?" she asked in a whisper. He had never offered her anything stronger than claret in the past.

"The very best," he replied in a quiet voice. James moved to the sitting area at one end of the bedchamber and went about pouring brandy for the two of them.

Thinking he planned to lecture her on how she had chosen to live her life, Daisy was prepared to be defensive. She took the glass he offered and held it up in a salute before she took a sip. "Are you doing this because... you have some fat, balding viscount in mind for me?" she asked, a wan grin appearing.

James shook his head and indicated she should be seated. "I do not. Nor would I bother to even try."

Daisy's eyes widened once again. "Oh," she managed as she sat in an overstuffed chair. If he wasn't going to persuade her to marry, then perhaps this was just a social call.

"I just wish to know. I wish to understand you," he said after taking a sip of the brandy. "Why it is you seem so bitter about being illegitimate when you have my name." He took the chair opposite and settled into it, although his back remained ramrod straight.

Sighing, Daisy closed her eyes and thought of her mother. Thought of all the times Lily Albright had lectured her daughters about the ways of the world. About what they might have to do should the duke ever decide he would no longer provide protection.

Until James had hired her as his mistress, Lily had never had the benefit of a protector longer than a Season. Her father, Sir Ronald Twickham, had never acknowledged her as his daughter, nor had he allowed the courtesan who bore her the use of his name. Despite spending the rest of her life with the future Duke of Ariley, Lily never believed they would stay together. Her experience as a courtesan wouldn't allow it.

"I am my mother's daughter," Daisy finally said, her voice quiet. "Diana is, too, but she is not as... not as jaded as I am, I suppose." She looked up to find her father's eyes closed, as if he might be staving off tears. "You gave her a home and children and everything a woman could ever want—even offered marriage—but she was *her* mother's daughter. Raised to believe she had to rely on her wits and on her body."

"Is that what Lily taught you?" James asked, the words strangled. "That you couldn't rely on me?"

The expression of pain on his face had Daisy dipping her

head in shame before she shook it. "She knew you would have to marry a peer. She knew you would have to sire an heir and a spare, and she knew that when that happened, Diana and I would have to give you up."

His breathing quickening with her words, James shook his head. "Never," he replied. "I would *never* give *you* up. I would never disavow you—"

"I know that now," Daisy said gently. "Diana does, as well. But we also know you happened to have married the only woman in the entire *ton* who would ever welcome us with open arms as your Helen does."

James lifted his gaze to hers, his furrowed brows relaxing a bit. "It was not an accident," he said, thinking back to the two years he had spent in pursuit of a wife. He was well past the age where he should have been seeing to his nursery when he finally proposed to Helen Harrington. She was well past the age he should have been considering in a suitable wife, but there were more important considerations.

Such as two young women he had acknowledged as his daughters.

"Nevertheless, you have managed to do what Mother claimed could never happen," Daisy replied. "So I find myself having to... *unlearn* so much of what Mother insisted I know to survive. I didn't go to work in Whitehall because I was trying to spite you, or because I didn't love you, or because I didn't trust you to provide protection. I do love you. I adore you. But I had to know that I could survive on my own."

"And now?" he asked. "You don't have to work. You don't have to be a headmistress."

"No, I don't," Daisy agreed, a grin slowly turning into a smile. "But I like it. I wish to do it. But that's not to say that I don't want the other things you want for me. Someday... I might have those, too."

Her father nodded, a grin finally lifting his eyes so they

no longer appeared as if tears would escape. "But it won't be with a fat, balding viscount," he guessed before he took another sip of brandy.

A dimple appeared in Daisy's cheek as she considered what had happened to her in only a few days. A fat, balding viscount would never have her heart, it was true. But a rather short, blond-haired boy had certainly opened hers to possibilities.

She drained her brandy and reveled in the warmth that spread through her body. Then she stood up, gave her father a kiss on the cheek, and bade him good-night.

CHAPTER 25

A MAN IN NEED OF A
MISTRESS—OR A BACKBONE

eanwhile, at Bostwick Place
George Bennett-Jones rushed into his study, expecting to find his friend in an agitated state, or, at the very least, pacing the floor in front of the desk. Instead, he found Teddy sprawled in one of the room's two upholstered chairs, a glass of brandy dangling from one hand.

"From what Elkins just told me, I feared I would find you wearing a hole in the carpet," George said as he moved to the liquor salver behind desk. Although he rarely drank at home—he reserved the treat for his visits to White's—he poured a finger's worth into a glass and joined his friend by taking the other chair. "You look..." He paused, not sure how to describe the bereft man who was staring into space, as if he hadn't even noticed George's presence. "Like you've lost your best friend."

Teddy slowly turned his gaze onto George. "She's someone's mistress," he whispered.

George blinked. "She... being...?"

Giving him a quelling glance, Teddy straightened in the chair while seeing to it the last dregs of the brandy didn't splash from his glass. "Miss Albright, of course," he replied, his manner most impatient.

His eyes widening at hearing Daisy Albright was someone's mistress, George gave the comment a moment of thought before he shook his head. "I rather doubt that," he hedged. "Whatever led you to believe such a thing?"

Teddy drained the glass and allowed his head to drop back in the chair. "I saw her. Expensive dinner gown the color of a fine Burgundy, covered with a black mantle, stepping into a town coach—an expensive town coach—"

"They're all expensive," George murmured.

"—with a crest painted on the door."

George angled his head, knowing immediately to whom the coach belonged.

Ariley. She was probably going to the duke's home for dinner.

"Did you make out the crest?" George asked.

Teddy closed his eyes. "I did not. I was trying to hide at the time," he groused.

On the one hand, George thought his friend was awfully grumpy over the situation, while on the other... well, he wondered if Teddy wasn't just a bit too enamored with the headmistress of Warwick's. "Tell me, my friend. When you interviewed Miss Albright for the position, did you happen to ask her any questions?"

Teddy turned to stare at his best friend. "Of course. Mostly having to do with her past work experience. She used to..." He almost mentioned her work to protect the country from traitors, but thought he best keep that to himself. He still wasn't sure which office in Whitehall—if she worked in Whitehall—could have employed her.

"Used to...?" George prompted, curious as to how much Daisy Albright might have admitted during her interview.

"Perform administrative duties," Teddy stated.

George's eyebrows both arched up. Not exactly what he

was expecting his friend to say, it was a perfect response given that administrative duties probably made up the majority of what Miss Albright had to do at Warwick's. "Did you have her complete some sort of form with her personal information?"

Teddy blinked and then shook his head. "No, but... but I thought your wife's charity had already done that."

Giving Teddy a frown, George leaned forward, his elbows supported on his knees. "May I suggest you speak with Miss Albright?"

"What? And ask if she's someone's mistress?" Teddy countered, his impatience turning to anger.

Sighing, George was about to tell Teddy what he knew about the woman when he realized it wasn't his information to tell. If Daisy Albright wanted Teddy to know she was Ariley's illegitimate daughter, then she would have to be the one to tell him. "That might have been an appropriate question given you hired her to be the headmistress of a finishing school," he chided. "Look. Do you really think she would have applied for your position if she was someone's mistress?" he asked in a gentle voice. "When she could be earning ten times her hundred-pound salary—"

"Two-hundred pounds," Teddy interrupted.

George blinked, rather stunned at hearing the amount. "Five times her two-hundred pound salary—or more—as some aristocrat's mistress?"

Teddy slumped in his chair. "I suppose not," he reluctantly agreed. He was quiet for a moment before he asked, "Then where in the world was she going all dressed to the nines?"

"Probably for dinner with her family," George replied, deciding he wasn't giving away any private information with his response. "But why don't you ask her?"

Getting up from his chair, his wooden arm banging against his thigh as he did so, Teddy said, "I will. In the morning. And I swear, if she isn't there, then I'll *know* she spent the night—"

"Careful," George said in a patient voice. "If she's having dinner with her family, she may also spend the night at their house," he warned. "In which case, you'll have spent the night fighting the Green Monster over nothing."

For a moment, Teddy looked as if he was satisfied with George's explanation. Then his expression changed to one of pain. "What's wrong with me, George?" He rolled his eyes. "Besides the fact that I'm missing an arm?"

The viscount gave a slow shake of his head. "You, I fear, are probably in love. Definitely in lust."

"Lust. It's true. Yes," Teddy agreed. "I like her. She's... she's smart, and she's beautiful, and you should see what she's done to my mother's old apartment."

George did a double-take. "You've been in her apartment?"

Teddy held up his hand, immediately regretting having made the comment. "She invited me for tea with the theatre instructor. Mrs. Fitzgerald. Strange woman, that one, but it was all very proper."

Giving his friend a dubious gaze, George asked, "Did you invite Miss Albright to attend the theatre with us?"

"I did," Teddy replied with a nod. "And she's going to bring her evening clothes with her so she can change here. She said she didn't want to make us late, what with the tea Lady Bostwick is hosting and all."

George's expression proved his appreciation for Miss Albright's foresight. "That's very good of her. If you play your cards right, I believe I can see to it you two will be left alone for a bit of time. That is, if you want to be left alone with her," he teased.

Teddy blinked. "You would do that? I would be forever grateful."

George gave a shrug. "Prepare to be grateful."

"You're a sport. I may even let you win our next match," Teddy claimed, his manner no longer so morose. With that, the bank clerk took his leave of Bostwick Place. Although he wasn't completely convinced of Miss Albright's innocence, he decided to give her the benefit of the doubt.

This one time.

CHAPTER 26
A PIRATE FROM THE PAST

Friday morning

Daisy regarded the white exterior of Horse Guards from across the street, still a bit unsure as to whom she might meet with regarding the whereabouts of Nicholas Barnaby.

Poor Miss Crofter. She deserved to know what had become of her betrothed. Especially before she could disabuse any more young women of the value of men in general.

Nicholas Barnaby.

The name niggled at her brain. She was sure she had heard of him before, but she couldn't place just where. Perhaps she had seen the name in print, in a report, or on a list, or... she shook her head and crossed the street, determined to keep from limping as she did so. Despite the early hour, traffic was heavy in Whitehall.

The duke's coach had delivered her to Omega House at half-past seven. She might have arrived a bit earlier, but she had paid a call to the nursery just before seven. Both her half siblings were wide awake, dressed, and in the middle of their breakfasts. Lady Rose smelled of wool and milk and a hint of rosewater. Lord William beamed at her appearance, his twin dimples denting chubby cheeks. *Days-ee*, he had said. He struggled to get up from his small chair so that he could afford her a bow that nearly had him toppling over. Before he was upright, she had him held in her arms.

Look after our sister, and I shall see you again soon, she had promised.

For a moment, she had considered staying in the nursery the rest of the day. But reminded it was Friday by the nurse, she thought of the boys from St. Martin's who would be coming for dance class at eleven.

She also thought about Miss Crofter and Nicholas Barnaby.

Once she was back at Warwick's, she shed her dinner gown in favor of a printed muslin day gown. At eight o'clock, she left a note on her office door that explained she would be back before eleven and then hailed a hackney.

Now she wondered if she might be on a fool's errand.

Having reported to one of the other nearby buildings a number of times—Lord Chamberlain's office was located in a smaller structure in the corner of the complex—Daisy didn't feel the least bit nervous. But she had to admit to experiencing a bit of impatience. She had to be back in time to teach the dance class, and she feared she might use up two hours merely looking for the correct office in which to make her query.

Daisy paused just inside one of the entrances until her eyes adjusted to the dimmer interior. Hoping to locate a receptionist or at least a list of offices, she was halfway down the hall when the hairs on the back of her neck prickled. Slowing down a bit, she studied the faces of those who passed her in the hall. Few paid her any mind, but one had stopped in his tracks and was staring at her.

"Alex," she whispered. Her heart hammered as she approached her former colleague. Intending to stop and curtsy before offering a hand, Daisy was instead pulled into a hug by the man who had been her first lover.

"Daisy!" the man exclaimed before he suddenly let go, stepped back, and bowed. "Forgive me," he managed in a quieter voice. "You... you've caught me completely by surprise. Quite a feat, you must know."

A brilliant smile appeared on Daisy's face as she took in the sight of Alex Bradley. A dozen memories flashed before her eyes, and from the expression on his face, she could tell Alex was reliving some of the very same ones. "There's nothing to forgive. In fact, I am the one who must beg forgiveness. I should have sought you out when I first returned to London," she said. "Are you well?"

Alex sighed and offered an arm. "I am. My office is down the hall. We can speak freely there," he said.

"Office?" she repeated. In the years she had known the operative, she had never known him to have an office. He had a desk near Lord Chamberlain's office, although he was rarely there.

He opened a door and waved her in. "It's not much, but it's what was available for my current assignment," he said as he shut the door. "I'm not at liberty to say what that is, exactly," he added with a shrug.

"Nor would I expect you to," Daisy replied as she glanced around the small room. Besides a desk, two chairs, and a few filing cabinets, there was only a hook by the door for a coat. The walls hadn't seen a new coat of paint in probably fifty years. She took a deep breath. "I understand congratulations are in order. I do hope you're enjoying life as a married man," she said as she took one of the chairs.

Truth be told, she couldn't imagine the operative married. His assignments usually required he take on the persona of a sea captain—a pirate named Jack Crawley— charged with finding the sources for smuggled goods, or boarding ships that carried contraband to England and then stealing it.

Alex regarded her a moment before allowing a nod. He sat at his desk. "I am," he finally admitted. "She's Mykonian. Most unexpected thing that has ever happened to me. I met her while I was on a mission to locate a missing duke," he explained. "She's brave and beautiful. Loves living in London, especially since she is best friends with Lord Everly's countess."

That tidbit explained why Nike Xenakis would agree to leave her home island in the Cyclades and live in London.

And what about her best friend? "The Countess Everly is Westhaven's daughter, is she not?" Daisy asked, remembering the notice in *The Times* about the wedding of the Earl of Everly to the only daughter of Alexander Jones, Duke of Westhaven. Lady Estelle had attended Warwick's the year of her come-out. With a Mykonian mother and an English duke for a father, Estelle didn't quite fit as a daughter of the *ton*. Daisy could certainly empathize, given her own situation.

At least Lady Estelle was legitimate.

Alex seemed to struggle a moment. "I must say, though, I..." He sighed, as if he decided it better he not put voice to any sort of confession.

"If you were under some sort of impression that I expected an offer of marriage, please know that I did not. At some point in the future, I might have been amenable, of course, but—"

"I've worried about you, Daisy. About what happened in York," Alex interrupted, leaning forward so his elbows rested on his messy desk. "Not so much about... Lord Plymouth, of course. But the other one. Did Longburn... did he hurt you?"

Daisy's eyes widened, realizing Alex had imagined the worst when it came to what she might be expected to do in her role as a mistress to the smuggler. "He did not," she said with a shake of her head. "And I didn't have to play Myles Longborn's mistress for long before I learned he was the one paying for all that smuggled liquor," she added. "I admit, it was a relief when I was able to get word to the authorities. He was arrested whilst caught in the act, so to speak."

"You disappeared, though," he argued.

A bit taken aback by his accusation, Daisy shook her head. "I came back to London by stagecoach and reported to Lord Chamberlain. Told him I wanted a few weeks off to clean off the stench of the assignment, and then I left," she explained, giving a dismissive wave with one hand. She didn't add that she had been told there wouldn't be any more assignments. Not with the way her limp made her easy to identify.

"But, where did you go?" he asked in dismay.

From the way he asked the question, Daisy wondered if he had searched for her. "My childhood home. In Kent. My father lives in London most of the year now, so the country estate seemed the perfect place to stay. And it was," she claimed, hoping he couldn't see through her white lie.

The problem with her childhood home was that it held too many memories of her mother. At that point in her life, she wanted her mother. Needed her mother's shoulder to cry on and to hear assurances that she hadn't made a mistake in playing mistress as part of her undercover work for King and country.

Every day she was there, she relived the pleasant memories of her time with Ethan Range, Marquess of Plymouth. For the last week she was there, she was sure she would be thinking of him every time she held his babe in her arms.

But then that tiny life had been taken from her womb before it was even four months along.

Alex sighed. "I really wish you hadn't taken that assignment," he whispered. "I've always felt ever so guilty—"

"Alex!" she scolded, her voice gentle. "I cannot tell you

how much I appreciate what you did to prepare me for that mission."

"By taking your virtue?" he countered in a hoarse whisper. "And *then* finding out you were Ariley's daughter? I thought for certain I would be drawn and quart—"

"You weren't supposed to ever learn that about me," she argued. Alex hadn't asked as to her background, trusting she had been hired much like any operative—for a specific set of skills. Disguises and dialects had been Daisy's specialty. "How did you find out?"

His eyes darting to one side, he gave a shrug. "I asked to see your file."

Diana's eyes widened. "It was in my *file?*" she asked in disbelief. No wonder her father eventually found out she worked as an operative.

Alex nodded. "Probably put there by Chamberlain. The man knows far too much about everyone," he murmured. He allowed a sigh. "Still, had I known then—"

"You did nothing I didn't want you to do," she argued. "As I recall, I begged you to share your bed so you could teach me what I needed to know." She didn't add that curiosity had more to do with it than an impending mission. From the moment she met Alex, she had been intrigued by him. Attracted to him. *Do not fear it,* her mother had said on one occasion. *That desire for a man, for the power you have over him, for that is all the power you will ever possess.*

"Besides..." She sighed and rolled her eyes. "It's not as if I would ever need those skills for a husband." An odd twinge had her wondering where those words had come from. Should she ever end up married, those skills would likely keep a husband in her bed and less likely to employ a mistress.

Finally allowing a nod, Alex frowned. "So, you're still not married?"

Daisy grinned. "No. In fact, I am headmistress of

Warwick's Grammar and Finishing School," she stated, and then watched carefully as Alex's face screwed up into a most comical look of disbelief.

"You?" he countered in disbelief. "Undercover?"

"No," she said with a grimace. "My limp got me fired, so I sought employment elsewhere."

"But, Warwick's?" he countered, allowing a chuckle.

"Indeed. I'm teaching, too. Grammar, of course. And my sister's classes, at least until I can find a suitable replacement. She's married now, you must know."

"She managed to snag Breckinridge, although no one is actually sure just how," Alex said then, referring to Viscount Breckinridge. "There are witnesses who claim he kissed her on the corner of Jermyn and St. James in broad daylight—"

"Diana wrote of the details," Daisy said by way of confirmation. "It was all his doing, of course. In the meantime, I've taken her place at Warwick's." She paused a moment. "Any chance you know of someone who can teach dance and arithmetic?" she asked rhetorically.

Alex shook his head. "I'd heard about Mrs. Streater, of course, but I wasn't aware arrangements for her replacement had already been made," he admitted.

"Do you know her son? Mr. Streater?" Daisy asked.

Alex shook his head. "Only that his brother is a baron and that he's a bank clerk." He paused a moment. "And didn't he lose an arm in the war?"

Daisy nodded, realizing she had the perfect opportunity to ask about Miss Crofter's betrothed. "Would you know how I might determine the fate of another soldier?" she asked then, thinking perhaps Alex would know which office she should visit next. "It's why I've come today. One of my instructors was betrothed, but the groom disappeared just before the wedding, and I think it was because he left for the Continent. He had been a soldier, before, you see, but was a clerk when he proposed marriage."

Allowing a shrug, Alex said. "Do you have a name?"

"Barnaby. Nicholas Barnaby. He would have been in the army—"

"Mr. Barnaby?" Alex repeated, straightening in his chair. "Why, if it's the same Nicholas Barnaby, then of course I know *of* him," he replied. "He's off helping old fogeys find employment from that charity in Oxford Street. Doing a damn fine job of it, too."

Daisy blinked. And blinked again. "Of course. *That's* why I've heard his name before," she murmured. Her head fell back as she silently berated herself. "Lady E's 'Finding Work for the Wounded'," she whispered, before allowing a chuckle. When she noted how Alex stared at her, his expression betraying his puzzlement, she added, "It's how I landed my position at Warwick's."

Alex frowned. "*You* were a client of Lady Bostwick's?" he asked in disbelief.

Nodding, Daisy reminded him she had been shot in the past. "My employer, Mr. Streater, was her very first client," she said in a quiet voice, wondering at how her insides seemed to do a little flip at the thought of the one-armed man. Reminded of the school, though, she inhaled sharply and looked about for a clock. "Pray tell, what time is it? I must be back to teach dance class at eleven o'clock."

Allowing a grin of amusement, Alex pulled a chronometer from his waistcoat pocket. "Half-past nine. May I... escort you back to Warwick's?" he offered.

Daisy shook her head. "I've taken up entirely too much of your time already," she said.

"Nonsense," he argued.

"I'll take a hackney and have the driver go by way of Oxford Street," she continued, ignoring his comment.

Alex stood up. "I worry about you," he whispered. "Please, Daisy, do keep in touch," he begged. "At least I know where to find you now."

Daisy sighed. "You and my father," she said quietly.

"Now don't be berating the men who love you," Alex warned as he reached for her hand. He kissed the back of it.

Rather touched by his words, Daisy curtsied. "I look forward to meeting Nike," she said.

Alex allowed a smirk, knowing he hadn't mentioned his wife's name during their conversation. "I think you'll like her," he said.

"She took a bullet for you, so I expect I will." With that, Daisy took her leave of his office, noted its location in the building, and made her way to Whitehall Street to hail a hackney.

She intended to find a missing groom.

CHAPTER 27
INTERVIEW WITH A
RUNAWAY GROOM

ifteen minutes later

Stepping down from the hackney, Daisy regarded the shingle above the door at No. 30 Oxford Street and grinned. Lady Bostwick had already begun her latest venture, it seemed, for a second sign announcing 'Finding Wives for the Wounded' hung from short chains attached to the main sign, 'Finding Work for the Wounded.'

Daisy briefly wondered who might have secured the position of matchmaker, hoping she might spot the woman once she was inside.

Augustus Overby rose from his chair and limped around his desk. "Good morning. Miss Albright, isn't it?"

Rather impressed the clerk remembered her name, Daisy gave a nod. "I am, Mr. Overby." She suddenly paused, her brows furrowing when she remembered the list of students who had attended Warwick's last year. "By any chance, do you have a relation by the name of Katie Overby?"

"I've a niece by that name," he acknowledged. "Nineteen, she is, with a half-dozen suitors."

Daisy grinned. "I only asked because I'm the new headmistress of Warwick's now."

His eyes widened. "Congratulations," he replied, a grin appearing. "So... if you've been hired, what brings you back here?"

"I wondered if Mr. Barnaby might be in?" Daisy asked, just before her gaze settled on a rather tall gentleman who was reading a newspaper in one corner of the office. He seemed oblivious to her presence.

Displaying his disappointment she wasn't there to see him, Mr. Overby held up a finger before he limped over and tapped his colleague on the arm. He whispered something, and Daisy found she was the object of scrutiny when Mr. Barnaby pinned her with a look of curiosity. Then he stood up and made his way in her direction.

That's when Daisy realized he was the tall man she had seen standing across the street from Warwick's. He never stayed long, but a few of the students claimed they thought he might be planning something nefarious.

"I am Mr. Barnaby," the tall man said with some concern. "You asked for me, Miss Albright?"

Daisy nodded. "It's good to make your acquaintance, Mr. Barnaby. I wondered if I might ask you a couple of questions?" When it was apparent he was nervous, she added, "It's about Miss Crofter."

Nicholas Barnaby inhaled and glanced in the direction of the other clerk before he leaned in and whispered, "I only did what I thought was best."

Arching an eyebrow, Daisy thought it odd he didn't pretend ignorance or at least claim she had the wrong man. "You thought leaving her at the *altar* was best?" Daisy countered, wondering if he would explain himself.

"I didn't know I was going to be forced to go back to fight the French until the night before the wedding," he said in a quiet voice, his manner most defensive. "I was out with some mates having an ale—night before the wedding and all—and the next thing I knew, I was on a ship bound for

Calais before daybreak and on a battlefield the following day. Did... did she send you?"

Daisy furrowed a brow. She had heard similar stories, of course, but usually when a ship needed a crew. "Miss Crofter has no idea I'm here. As headmistress at Warwick's, I hosted her for tea and wondered how it was she had such a poor opinion of men. She's not said a word to anyone else, preferring instead to despise all men for what you did," she accused. She gave a shake of her head. "Or rather, what you didn't do."

The tall man seemed to deflate before her eyes, his eyelids covering most of his eyes until they were almost closed. "Honestly, I didn't mean to leave her like that," he said as he shook his head. "I thought to write her a letter when I could —explain what happened—but we engaged the enemy the day after we hit landfall and..." He allowed the sentence to trail off, glancing over to be sure his colleague wasn't eavesdropping on their conversation. "Then I was wounded—twice—by bayonets. Wondered what a pretty English miss like Miss Crofter would want with a man who was as cut up as I was, and so I never did send the letter."

Wincing at this last bit, Daisy allowed a sigh. "Perhaps you should have allowed *her* to make that choice, Mr. Barnaby," she murmured.

Nicholas regarded her for a moment before his gaze darted about the office again. "Are you... are you saying... Charity doesn't hate me?" he whispered.

Daisy sighed, not exactly sure how the sewing instructor would feel once she learned the truth about what had happened to her betrothed. "I am saying you should find out for yourself. And know this, Mr. Barnaby. Now that I am headmistress, some of the rules that used to apply to our teachers are no longer in place."

"Rules?" he repeated.

"Should Miss Crofter agree to a marriage—to anyone—she will not lose her position if she needs to keep it."

Frowning, Nicholas said, "I wouldn't want a wife of mine to have to... to have to *work*," he claimed.

Struggling to keep her impatience with the man at bay, Daisy said, "So you would prefer to live a life of quiet desperation—all alone—knowing there is a woman here in London who would be happy to be your wife? She could continue to teach sewing classes—in a safe classroom—when you are here at your work."

A flash of anger seemed to pass in Nicholas' eyes as he regarded her. "But, she deserves better than me," he stated.

"Yes. Yes, she does," Daisy agreed. "But she's in love with *you*, Mr. Barnaby. And I rather imagine you still hold a candle for her since you've been spied watching her from across the street."

Nicholas' eyes widened. "I only do that to be sure she's... well," he replied defensively. "To be sure she makes it to her classroom without being set upon by thieves." He sighed then, realizing he'd been caught. "Does she know it's me? Watching?"

Daisy didn't know one way or the other, but Charity had implied she hadn't seen her betrothed since before the wedding. "I don't think so, but there are students who have spotted you. They think you are plotting something dastardly. Such as a kidnapping. You could be arrested."

He gasped. "I wouldn't do such a thing," he countered, his voice rising so that Mr. Overby looked up from his desk. "You have to believe me. I'm only out there to see that Miss Crofter makes it to her classroom without some... without some *bounder* making off with her."

Nearly forced to take a step back at the forcefulness of his words, Daisy stared at Nicholas Barnaby for a full ten seconds before she said, "I believe you. I think she will, too.

Now, I must take my leave, or I will be late to teach a class. Good day, Mr. Barnaby."

With that, Daisy gave a quick curtsy and turned to make her way out of the office.

Before the door had shut behind her, she took a deep breath, murmured the words, "Stupid men," and hurried off to find a hackney.

CHAPTER 28
DANCING CAN BE A
DISASTER—OR NOT

Friday at eleven o'clock in the morning

True to his word, the headmaster of St. Martin's School for Boys appeared at the door to the ballroom at Warwick's with four-and-twenty young men lined up behind him. None appeared as old as the girls who attended the finishing school, but Daisy knew appearances could be deceiving at their age.

It was after Daisy completed a count of their guests when she realized the ballroom might not accommodate what she had in mind. "Oh, dear," she murmured to Jane as the art instructor set her music on the piano-forté. "Do we have room for six sets of eight?" she asked.

"Doubtful. At least they are dressed appropriately," the art teacher said, giving the line of young men a quick glance as they filed into the room and lined up along one of the walls. They all wore the same clothes—black knee breeches, red stockings, red waistcoats, and navy blue topcoats.

She dared a glance at the line of young ladies adjacent to where the piano-forté was located, noting how several simply ignored their visitors while others whispered behind raised hands.

Daisy stepped to the middle of the room. "Welcome to Warwick's," she said. "My name is Miss Albright."

The entire line of boys bowed in unison, as did their instructor. Daisy curtsied, as did the line of young ladies behind her. "Today, we'll be doing the waltz." She wasn't surprised at hearing gasps from both sides of the ballroom. She had told the girls they would start with the cotillion, but given the limited space and forty-eight students, she decided to start with a dance that wouldn't take up as much of the floor space. "This is a bit different from other dances you might do at a district ball or at your parent's rout as you count to three instead of four," she explained. "How many of you know the steps?" she asked, her attention still on the young men.

A few raised their hands, while the younger ones seemed as if they wanted to disappear into the wall behind them.

"Pair up. Oh, and do try to find someone of a similar height," she called out. "We'll forgo formal introductions, but do greet one another with a bow or curtsy. First, you'll learn how to do the steps in the shape of a square, and if you're especially good, we'll see how you do in a large circle."

Although she expected some hesitance, Daisy wasn't expecting everyone to remain standing exactly where they were. Allowing a sigh, she waved the tallest girl, Ariel Grandby, forward and indicated she should be paired with the tallest boy.

When the boy rolled his eyes, apparently in disgust, Daisy regarded him with an arched brow. "Do you have an objection to dancing with Miss Grandby?" she asked in a hoarse whisper, reining in the annoyance she felt on behalf of her second cousin.

"She's my sister, Miss Albright," he replied in a similar whisper. He gave a bow. "I'm Roger Grandby. We're always partners when we dance at home."

Daisy studied the boy—he was probably fourteen—and

realized the two students shared similar features. Same eyes, same hair color, similar noses. Definitely Grandbys, the both of them. It was then Daisy noticed how Ariel could have been mistaken for her own sister. The heart-shaped face and dusting of freckles on her nose were the same as Diana's. "Oh," she said then. "Well, Mr. Grandby, we shall spare you from having to waltz with your sister just this once." She glanced over at Ariel. "You shall dance with the next tallest," she said before she turned her attention back to the line of boys. Her brows furrowed when she noted the next taller seemed an almost exact match for Roger. "I suppose he's your brother, too?" she asked as she dared a glance back at Ariel.

"Yes, he is, Miss Albright. That's Thomas, and William is at the end."

"How many brothers do you have?"

Ariel dipped her head. "Five, but only three are in school at St. Martin's," she whispered.

Daisy blinked. *How many second cousins do I have?* she almost asked. "Do you have sisters, as well?"

"Four of them. All younger, though," Ariel replied with a nod.

One of the young men stepped forward and gave a bow. "If I may be allowed, I should like to dance with Miss Grandby."

Aware the attention of the entire room was on the four of them, Daisy gave a nod when she noticed Ariel seemed pleased by the request. "And you are?"

Before he could even respond, Daisy realized who he was. The family resemblance was remarkable. "Mr. Simpson, perhaps?" she ventured, daring a glance over at Hannah Simpson.

"I am, Miss Albright. Henry Simpson, at your service."

Another young man of perhaps thirteen stepped forward and gave a leg. "If I may be allowed, I should like to dance with Miss Simpson." He stood proudly, his query loud enough for the entire ballroom to hear.

Hannah Simpson dimpled as she stepped forward.

"And whom might you be?" Daisy asked in a quiet voice.

"Graham Wellingham, at your service, miss."

Wellingham? No doubt a cousin of the Earl of Trenton, Daisy thought as she gave a nod. Then she remembered what Jane has said about Ariel having inherited her sweet disposition from her mother, a Wellingham.

Ariel leaned in her direction and whispered, "He's my cousin."

Daisy continued to nod, deciding she would have to sort the relationships later. Right now, she had another two-and-twenty girls to match up with boys who were now stepping away from the wall and hesitantly making their way to the girls. A bit of shuffling, a few red faces, and several minutes later, four-and-twenty couples stood staring at her expectantly.

Mr. Lusk was suddenly in front of her. "May I have this dance, my lady?" he asked as he bowed.

Daisy grinned. "Indeed," she replied as she curtsied. She held out her arms as Elias did the same. "Gentlemen," she called out. "Right hand at your partner's waist, left hand in the air. Ladies place your right in your partner's hand and your left on the sleeve of their upper arm. Be sure to leave a space between you. A sort of box," she explained as one of her hands waved the shape of a square between her and Elias. She indicated he should turn sideways so the rest of the class could see her do it again.

Since her girls knew the dance, Daisy was heartened to see them already positioned correctly, even though some barely touched the sleeves of their partners. She turned her attention to Elias. "Have any of your charges learned this dance?" she asked in a whisper.

Elias allowed a teasing grin. "I may have seen to a bit of

early instruction," he admitted with a quirked brow. At her arched eyebrow, he added, "Come now. I couldn't have my boys looking like idiots. Some of these boys may end up married to some of these girls." He glanced around the ball-room then and added, "At least two, I should think."

Daisy dimpled before turning to Jane, not sure if he was teasing or not. "Music, please," she called out. Although there were a few stutter-steps and the tell-tale sounds of impatience throughout the room—Daisy was sure she heard a feminine curse—every couple seemed to grasp the basic steps.

"Shall we show them how it's really done?" Elias asked after they had performed the basic box four times. "I think we can still manage even if the floor isn't properly finished."

Daisy managed to hide her initial reaction to his comment. She had been so concerned about her charges being ready for class, she hadn't considered the condition of the floor. Elias was right, though. The wood floors needed a new coat of varnish. "Do you think they're ready?" she asked then, hoping he didn't notice her hesitation.

Before she had a chance to call out the change, Elias had them waltzing in an arc between the students. A quick look around, and she saw that the pairs that included Grandbys and Simpsons were following suit. Indeed, it was evident the eight of them had all done the dance, apparently with one another. Soon, some of the younger couples dared break out of their boxes, the boys leading their partners into tentative arcs while trying not to bump into their neighbors.

Attempting to watch her students while Elias guided them across the ballroom, Daisy noted how uneven ovals had formed, one inside the other, with Elias leading the inner oval and Graham Wellingham leading the outer oval. "Everyone seems to be doing fine," Daisy murmured in awe.

"Shall we add the underarm turn?" Elias asked, his head held up as he stared at the space beyond her shoulder.

Daisy was about to protest—she hadn't yet taught her students the move—but he dropped his right hand as he stepped back while at the same time he raised his left arm. Daisy was forced to step forward, remove her hand from his sleeve, and step under his raised arm, all before turning around to face him again. They resumed the dance for another complete box before he repeated the maneuver.

Although a few of the couples around them attempted the move—with varying degrees of success—not all had paid witness to what they had done. One couple near the corner had begun to giggle when the boy, who was considerably shorter than the girl with whom he was dancing, couldn't begin to lift his arm high enough for his partner to pass under.

When the music came to an end more than a half-hour later, the girls all curtsied to the boys' bows and returned to the walls along which they had been lined up earlier.

"Very good, everyone." Daisy turned to the headmaster. "Do we have time for the cotillion?"

He dared a glance at his chronometer. "Doubtful. However, I promise my boys shall be ready for it. Say... Friday next?"

Daisy nodded. "We shall be ready." She turned and dismissed the class.

The boys waited until all the girls had taken their leave before they filed out the door. Elias gave a deep bow, and Daisy responded with a curtsy. "Thank you, Mr. Lusk." He followed his charges out the door while Daisy hurried over to Jane.

"Did you see any of it?"

Jane grinned. "As much as I could. They all did so well," she gushed. "You do realize you may cause a scandal if you do this again, though."

"Whatever do you mean?" Daisy asked, her good humor quickly disappearing.

"The waltz, I mean," Jane replied. "I rather imagine there are some parents who would rather not have their daughters dancing it with boys just yet." She gathered up the sheets of music into one of her arms. "But there are others who are probably relieved they're learning it here rather than at Almack's."

Although she had never been to Almack's, Daisy had heard about the business that hosted subscription dances on Wednesday nights. With four patronesses deciding whom among the young ladies could be permitted to dance a waltz, it seemed rather arrogant to her. "I shall be on my guard then," Daisy replied. "Mr. Lusk says they will be back next Friday. For the cotillion."

Jane gave a nod. "I shall be ready with appropriate music," she replied.

"I wish the floor could be refinished by then," Daisy murmured. "Mr. Lusk mentioned its poor condition."

"Oh, I'm sure it's on Mrs. Streater's list," Jane countered. "There was a man here about it a few weeks ago. Taking measurements."

Daisy inhaled and wondered which entry in the odd ledger had to do with refinishing the ballroom floor. "Do you know who it was? Or the company he was with?"

"I'm afraid I don't. He left just as I arrived to play for Diana's class."

The headmistress allowed a nod. "I'll see if I can't sort it," Daisy murmured. "Can you come have tea?"

Jane looked as if she were tempted, but she shook her head. "I've a table I need to finish painting for this afternoon's class. By the way, how are you getting to Bostwick Place for the tea?" she asked. "My invitation arrived via a rather handsome footman Wednesday afternoon."

"As did mine," Daisy said as she walked out of the ballroom with the art teacher. "Share a hackney with me? I've already made arrangements for after the tea, though."

Jane arched a brow. "Ooh. An assignation, perhaps?" she teased.

Daisy gave her a quelling glance. "More like the theatre," she replied. "Lady Bostwick invited me."

"Ah," Jane murmured. "Then I shall see you on the morrow." She hurried off to her classroom while Daisy made her way back to Omega House.

She had a ledger to study.

CHAPTER 29
A VISIT FROM THE OWNER

ater that afternoon
Teddy Streater entered Omega House and paused a moment before making his way to the door directly across from the vestibule—the door that would take him into Miss Albright's office. A door that was wide open, apparently because she was in the office.

Despite having paid a visit on Wednesday—he had managed to time his arrival at teatime—and learning she was getting on just fine, Teddy had thought to wait until Saturday's tea before seeing her again.

Then he had spent the last four nights imagining her at the very moment he closed his eyes. Sleep eluded him as visions of her formed in his mind's eye. Visions of her wearing next to nothing. Visions of her lying in his bed, beckoning him to join her. Visions of her beneath him as he made mad, passionate love to her.

And this morning?

A vision of waking up to find her nestled against the side of his body, her head resting in the small of his shoulder. A vision of him holding her in his arms—both of them—as they kissed one another.

That last thought had him sitting up in bed, cursing under his breath when he remembered he had spent the entire night with a cockstand tenting his bed linens.

Unfortunately, his valet was in his bedchamber, about to open the drapes. "Sir? Is something amiss?" Perkins had asked.

Of course it is. My arm is missing, he had nearly replied. Instead, he simply shook his head and said he had just awoken from a bad dream.

Liar!

Even now, on such a fine afternoon as this, without a cloud in the sky and all in readiness for tomorrow's tea, the thought of waking up next to the rather prim Miss Albright had him a bit aroused. He paused before he stepped over the threshold, his attention at first on the door. At his request, a sign painter had lettered "Miss Albright" on a placard and mounted it on the white painted door just the day before. Then he turned his attention to the woman who had haunted his dreams for the past four nights.

Well, *haunted* wasn't quite the right word. *Blessed* was probably more appropriate. Haunted would have been if his valet had been featured in his dreams instead of the lovely brunette who sat at the oversized desk gazing at a ledger. She held a quill in one hand as she studied the page before her, her concentration so utterly complete, she didn't seem to be aware of him.

Such devotion to her work! Such single-minded focus! Such attention to detail!

Or perhaps she was treating him like a recalcitrant student, ignoring him until he made his presence known by knocking on the door and requesting a moment of her time.

Teddy was about to do just that when Daisy inhaled sharply.

"Oh!" she said, just before she quickly rose to her feet.

"Why, good afternoon, Mr. Streater," she said, sounding a bit startled. "To what do I owe this honor?"

*D*aisy hoped she hadn't been displaying the expression of a love-sick school girl just then. Her thoughts had been on the very man who stood before her. The rather dapper gentleman who was wearing an obviously new suit of clothes, the topcoat and his wooden arm making it appear as if he hadn't lost an arm at all.

But she hadn't been imagining him dressed. She had been thinking of what he might look like wearing nothing at all, his fencer's body lean and muscled. His torso displaying the ridges of abdominal muscles evident in men who exercised regularly. His upper left arm bulging when he bent his elbow to lift her onto his bed. The nest of curls at the top of his thick thighs and the turgid manhood he was about to plunge into her warm and welcoming body.

Sure her hardening nipples might make themselves apparent through her stays and the muslin of her round gown, Daisy dipped a deep curtsy and concentrated on why the owner of Warwick's would be paying her a call today.

*S*orry he had interrupted her studious perusal of a ledger, Teddy quickly bowed and said, "Please, accept my apology. I didn't mean to—"

"Oh, no apologies are necessary, Mr. Streater," Daisy said with a shake of her head. "Actually, your arrival is most welcome."

Teddy's heart soared, and his cock would have, too, but he forced himself to think of his mother just then. She had been the author of that bedeviling ledger that seemed to possess Miss Albright's complete and total attention only a moment ago. "It is?" he replied, surprise evident in his voice.

Daisy waved him over to the desk. "After I spoke with Miss Betterman—"

"Which one is she again?"

"The art teacher. Mr. Jenkins' future wife, if things go well over the next few days," Daisy added with an arched eyebrow.

Teddy blinked. "Why, Miss Albright, are you... are you playing *matchmaker?*" he asked, wondering if perhaps Lady Bostwick had considered Miss Albright for the position of matchmaker at the charity she had mentioned wishing to start. Apparently there was already a shingle above the door announcing the new enterprise.

Daisy frowned. "Not exactly. Mr. Jenkins has been sweet on her for a long time, and he just needed to be told she was of the same mind about him," she explained. "She and Miss Anders—"

"The French instructor?" Teddy interrupted, one brow cocked in query.

"The very same. With last Sunday's rains, the ceilings in all the classrooms were leaking—"

"All of them?" Teddy asked in alarm.

"Indeed. But it's been going on long enough that there are buckets in place all the time to collect the water. Mr. Jenkins sees to emptying the buckets—"

"Why hasn't a... a maintenance man seen to the roof?" he asked, mostly to himself. Certainly his mother would have been aware of the problem, especially if the buckets seemed to be a permanent fixture in the classrooms.

Daisy took a deep breath and held it a moment. When Teddy noticed, he gave a shake of his head. "Please, continue. I shall wait until you are completely finished before I say another word," he promised, feeling just then like a recalcitrant student.

"There is no maintenance man on the payroll," Daisy stated, one finger tapping on the ledger containing the payroll figures. "However..." She paused a moment, sure he was about to ask a question. When Teddy merely gave her an expectant look, she continued. "Miss Betterman informed me before classes on Tuesday that Mrs. Streater had promised all the roofs would be repaired. That she had already hired a Mr. Thatcher to see to it. He provided a quote for the work several months ago, and he and his crew of workman are scheduled to begin the repairs on the morrow."

Teddy blinked. "You hired him?" He was about to admonish her for not consulting with him first. The repairs might cost hundreds of pounds!

Daisy furrowed a brow. "Of course not, Mr. Streater. I wouldn't have done such a thing without your approval," she insisted. "Mrs. Streater did. Several months ago, it seems. Mr. Thatcher's schedule is just now allowing him to do the work here at Warwick's. He paid a call Tuesday afternoon to confirm he would be replacing the roofs over the next month or so."

Replacing the roofs? Not just repairing them? *Why this might cost me more than a few hundred pounds!*

His breathing suddenly difficult, Teddy stared at Daisy. On the one hand, he wanted to kiss her because she was doing the very job he had no desire to do, and on the other —well, there was no other, but if he had another hand, he would use it to close the damned door and kiss her just because he was so overcome with desire for her.

What the hell is wrong with me?

Then he remembered what she had said and frowned. "I don't suppose Mrs. Streater has already *paid* Mr. Thatcher?" he asked with too much hope in his voice.

Daisy shook her head. "He expects payment at the end of the month," she replied. "He said that Mrs. Streater had his estimate along with several others—"

"Others?" Teddy repeated, once again suffering from a lack of air.

Nodding, Daisy used a forefinger to point to the series of entries in the ledger on her desk. "I believe I have sorted the ledger you mentioned having trouble understanding." She beckoned him to stand next to her with one crooked finger.

At first thrilled at the thought she was inviting him to stand next to her behind the desk, Teddy stood up. Why, he would go wherever she wanted him to go. He would probably walk off one of the cliffs of Dover if she bade him to do so.

Then he winced, remembering he hadn't been able to decipher the ledger the first day he had looked over his mother's books.

When he was standing next to her, Daisy began her explanation. "The 'T and S' refers to Thatcher and Sons, and the amount written here is how much it will cost to replace the roofs," she said as she made sure her fingertip was next to the entry. "According to Mr. Thatcher, the roofs are beyond repair and must be completely replaced."

Hesitant to look, Teddy took a deep breath before he finally dared a glance down. His hiss was barely audible, but Daisy caught the sound as well as noticed how taut he held his body. A most pleasant scent—a cologne perfectly suited to him—wafted past her nose, and Daisy inhaled deeply.

Teddy watched as her eyes closed for a moment, as if she appreciated the scent of his new cologne. Seeing her like had him tempted once again to kiss her.

Could there be another woman in all of London who had this effect on him? She smelled of lemons and honeysuckle and other scents of spring. She looked like a siren, calling him to do her bidding.

Including walking off one of the cliffs of Dover.

But, at the moment, she was beckoning him to look down. To look at the damned numbers.

So he did. Her finger had moved to the next line down.

The amount wasn't nearly as large, but it was still significant. "What might this one be?" he asked, rather hesitantly.

"Windows," Daisy replied. "There are a number of broken panes that need replacing throughout the school, and two of the boarding houses need all their windows replaced. Apparently, those two houses required as much coal to heat them last winter as all the other buildings combined. The rest are in need of some glazing to help keep the cold out in the winter." She indicated a pasteboard folder that was opened to reveal a short stack of sheets covered in writing and figures.

Teddy nodded his understanding. "I suppose someone is coming to do that work, too?"

Daisy nodded. "Week after next. Mrs. Streater arranged for someone from the British Cast Plate Glass Company to follow the roofers." She pulled that estimate from the stack in the folder and showed it to him.

Alarms bells started going off in Teddy's head. The British Cast Plate Glass Company made plate glass panes for the homes of the very wealthy.

His mother had saved an enormous amount of money prior to her death.

Money he had thought she had in her account because she was a miser.

What if his mother hadn't been a miser at all, but a responsible business owner who merely saved what she needed to pay for the repairs to Warwick's? To pay for the replacement of old crown glass windows in favor of new glass panes? To pay for new roofs and who knew what else?

There were those who talked of the finishing school being a bit on the shabby side, what with the broken windows and sagging roofs, chipped paint and banged up front doors. Only the landscaping looked in good shape, so that those who passed in their carriages and town coaches would probably miss the worst of Warwick's less noticeable troubles.

"Your mother wasn't a miser, was she?" Daisy asked in a

whisper, noting how Teddy seemed deep in thought, his expression one of contrition.

He lifted his gaze to meet hers. "Apparently not," he agreed, managing to keep his voice from displaying too much despair.

"You mentioned you had inherited a sum from her. I don't mean to pry, Mr. Streater, but is it enough to cover all these costs?" Daisy pointed at the column of numbers. At the bottom, she had added the total in her own hand.

Nine-thousand, nine-hundred, and eighty-two pounds.

"I finally confirmed just who these vendors at the bottom are." She pointed to the pasteboard folder. "Gas lighting, carpet, locks—"

"Locks?"

"Door locks, yes. Apparently they don't always do their job," Daisy explained. "There's also the refinishing of the ballroom floor. Given the colorman will be coming after the windows are complete, and Miss Betterman mentioned the ballroom floor was to be refinished, once classes are done for the summer season, I have to believe your mother has already arranged for these other repairs to be done as well," Daisy said with a sigh.

His heart hammering in his chest, Teddy thought of the new furniture that had been delivered to his bedchamber that morning. Thought of the tailor and the additional suits of clothing he had ordered. The boots. The shoes and cologne. But most of all, he thought of the glossy black Tillbury that would be built to his specifications over the course of the next few months. "It was," he hedged. He glanced over at her.

Daisy lowered her eyes back down to the ledger and nearly fell into her chair. "Does this mean you have to let me go?" she asked in a quiet voice.

Teddy shook his head, rather stunned by the question. "No. Not at all. I can pay for all of it," he promised, thinking that he worked at a bank. Surely he could arrange some sort of loan if necessary. "Besides, we'll have tuition money coming in."

Daisy brightened. "With the repairs, Warwick's will be more appealing. Perhaps more cits will be encouraged to enroll their daughters," she offered, remembering that Ariel Grandby had four younger sisters. The middle class and wealthy traders in London were always in search of ways to elevate their stations in life. Arranging for their daughters to attend an elite finishing school could only help their cause.

Then she remembered her dowry.

Her inheritance.

So far, she had only withdrawn the interest from the account her father had set up in her name. He always intended for her future husband to claim the funds.

But what if she used some of it to help with the repairs?

"Mr. Streater," she murmured, noting how sad and broken the man appeared just then. His right arm—or rather his wooden one—wasn't even evident, either, as he stood with his left side aimed in her direction. "Would you consider a partnership of sorts?" she asked as she looked up from the ledger.

Teddy regarded her with furrowed brows. "Partnership?" he repeated, his eyes widening as he grasped her meaning. "With whom?" he asked then, suddenly suspicious.

Daisy thinned her lips. "Me," she finally said. "I have... I have some funds my father left me. For a dowry. But since I haven't married, and I'm well past my majority, I can use the money for whatever I wish."

His eyes widening, Teddy stared at her. "Is that how you can afford such beautiful furnishings in your apartment?" he asked.

It was Daisy's turn to blink. "I... I didn't actually buy those," she admitted, a bit sheepishly. "I... I helped myself to those furnishings. Some were from my bedchamber in Kent and the rest were from here in London," she explained. "But father said they were mine to do with as I wished, so... I took them when I moved out of his house Monday last."

Teddy regarded her with an expression of amusement. "It's a bit of a relief to hear you say that. I was afraid you might have borrowed against your future earnings here at the school and owed a money lender a huge deal of blunt. With interest," he said with a sigh of relief.

Her eyes rounding in shock, Daisy was about to admonish him for thinking such a thing. Instead, she said, "I would never!" Remembering he was a clerk at a bank, she supposed he would assume the worst when it came to such displays of wealth.

Teddy shrugged. "Well, I know that now," he replied before he sighed. He indicated she should sit, and then he moved to the other side of the desk and took the chair opposite of hers. "What kind of partnership are you proposing?" he asked. The word had him thinking he should simply propose to her. Marrying her would gain him the dowry, but he was sure she would never agree to such an arrangement. He was missing an arm. No gently bred woman would wish to marry an old fogey like him.

"Certainly not equal, of course," Daisy replied. "A small percentage of Warwick's. Do you have any idea of the school's total worth?" she asked, mentally adding up the possible sale prices of the boarding houses and the two classroom buildings, given their location in Glasshouse Street. As for how much the school was worth—future tuition receipts and the value of the classes offered—she couldn't begin to determine that particular number.

Or could she?

Embarrassed to admit he did not know the worth of the finishing school, Teddy allowed a shrug. "I can sort it, of course. Have an agent work out the particulars as far as the value of the buildings are concerned," he replied. "Add up the annual tuition receipts and subtract the expenses. Determine the annual profit."

But Daisy was already adding all those figures in her head. In the past few days, she had studied every ledger—income and expenses. Having to teach arithmetic had reminded her how to quickly add and subtract. How to multiply and divide. How to determine percentages. "I will invest five-thousand pounds in exchange for fifteen percent of the school," she stated, deciding to err on the side of caution. That would leave forty-five thousand pounds in her inheritance account. If Mr. Streater made a counter-proposal, she decided she would offer no more than another five-thousand, perhaps for a larger share of the school.

Teddy blinked. And blinked again. "You have that kind of blunt?" he asked in alarm.

Daisy almost admitted her father was a duke just then. How else would she have a dowry of fifty-thousand pounds? An investment of five-thousand pounds in the school wouldn't make much of a dent in her account, but she knew Ariley would be well aware of the expenditure after it was removed. His banker would no doubt send him a letter advising him of the transaction.

"I do," Daisy replied carefully. "Since I don't expect to marry, the funds are mine to do with as I wish," she reminded him.

Teddy sighed, and then shook his head. "I cannot accept," he replied. At her widened eyes, he added, "What if all the repairs are made and no one enrolls next Season?" he asked rhetorically. "Your investment would be forfeit. Lost."

Daisy frowned. "We've already discussed how enrollment will increase as a result of the repairs, and besides, the buildings are worth the majority of the value, Mr. Streater," she replied, as if lecturing a failing math student. "At least eighty-percent. Mayhap closer to ninety-percent once the repairs are complete," she argued.

A marriage proposal was on the tip of his tongue just then. Did the woman have any idea just how erotic such talk of percentages and value was to him? How exciting it was to learn she knew of such things? That she could add and subtract? Multiply and divide? Why, she could probably compute fractions! Maybe even to three decimal places!

His cock was thoroughly engorged and throbbing with the thought.

But more important, did she have any idea just how positively gorgeous she looked sitting at the huge, mahogany desk? Despite her petite stature, she managed to appear seven feet tall sitting behind it. Perhaps she was perched atop a stack of books, for how else could it be he was gazing at her from below her eye level?

Unless his chair was considerably lower?

That was it, of course. His mother had chosen this particular chair for that very purpose! To make any visitor to her office feel small.

Teddy closed his eyes a moment in an effort to concentrate on her offer. Her rather generous offer. An offer that would allow him to pay for all the repairs and still leave him with enough to cover his recent expenditures on the luxury items that were on order. For the furniture that had just been delivered to his townhouse earlier that morning.

"I accept your offer," he said, rather relieved when his voice didn't come out sounding like a croaking frog.

A slow smile spread over Daisy's face. "We should have a solicitor draw up the papers, of course," she said. "Unless you have one of your own, there is one I know of in Oxford Street," she hedged.

"Mr. Barton, perhaps?" he countered. "Next door to 'Finding Work for the Wounded'?"

Daisy continued to smile. "Indeed."

"I shall see to it first thing Monday morning," Teddy

said, feeling as if a huge weight had been lifted from his shoulders.

Remembering George's invitation to share the Bostwick box for Saturday evening's performance, he asked, "In the meantime, I do hope you are still amenable to attending the theatre tomorrow night? The Bostwicks are counting on it. I expect the tea will be done by four o'clock, which should give us enough time to change and be at the theatre by half-past six," he reasoned.

Daring a glance at the invitation she had received Wednesday last from Lady Bostwick, Daisy had a thought the viscountess was playing at matchmaker. Surely she would have known her husband had extended the same invitation to Teddy. "I am delighted, of course," she replied, thinking she had at least one appropriate gown for the theatre. "As we discussed this past Wednesday, I will bring my gown with me to the tea, and shall change clothes at Bostwick Place," she explained.

"As will I," Teddy said then, wondering why a grin suddenly lit her face and caused a dimple to appear. Then he remembered she had mentioned a gown, and he gave a shake of his head. "I'll be bringing my formal clothes, of course," he amended.

Daisy gazed at him for a long time. "I have looked forward to it these past two days," she said quietly. She inhaled then, and asked, "What of tomorrow afternoon, though? Do I need to have anything prepared to say to our teachers? Or will you see to their welcome and words about their continued employment? I know at least two are concerned for their futures."

Teddy watched her lips as she said the words he knew he should have said. He was the host of the tea scheduled for the following day, after all. "Will you help? I fear I am terrible at such things," he said in a quiet voice.

A shiver ran down Daisy's spine. However was she going

to sit next to this man for an entire afternoon and then again for several hours in the evening whilst they attended the theatre? Sit next to him and not reach out to touch the back of his hand? Not turn it over so that she could draw circles with her fingertip in his palm. Grasp his fingers with her own so they might eventually intertwine?

She could imagine him grasping her hand and holding it well above her head whilst she writhed on his bed, his lips suckling her flattened breast just before he plunged his throbbing manhood into her wet, warm cocoon, her womanhood having been sweetly tortured with his tongue and lips.

The moment before she imagined an intense wave of pleasure crashing through her body, Daisy realized Teddy was staring at her, his gaze suggesting he might be thinking something similar.

"I'll help, of course," she managed to get out, her breaths far too quick. If she wasn't careful, she would faint.

"I'd like that," Teddy replied. He finally tore his gaze from hers and dared a glance in the direction of the door that led to her bedchamber. He almost—almost—suggested they move their discussion to the elegant room, but reason and sanity returned.

Miss Albright was the headmistress of his school. She was about to become his partner in the school. The very last thing he should be doing is imagining her playing the role of his mistress.

"I should take my leave. See if I can't prepare a few words," he said, his breaths coming far too quickly. If he wasn't careful, he would faint. He stood up, his top hat moving to cover the evidence of his erection. "I will see you tomorrow, Miss Albright. Good day." He managed a bow to Daisy's curtsy and then took his leave of Omega House.

Daisy settled back into her chair and allowed a long sigh. At least she hadn't been alone in her state of arousal, for she knew Mr. Streater had been in a similar state. She had seen the evidence of it whilst he stood next to her at the desk, his manhood pushing out the placket of his breeches. His arousal continued even after he took the chair opposite the desk, although it was hidden from her once he sat down. When he stood up, he held his top hat directly in front of his crotch, a clear indication he was still hard.

The thought had her breasts tingling once again.

Which had her wondering if perhaps she needed to do something with regard to their partnership.

Change the terms, perhaps?

CHAPTER 30
A VISIT FROM A VERY
SORRY MAN

*L*ater that night

When the knock came at the door of Alpha House, Charity Crofter was the only teacher in residence. Jane Betterman and Annabelle Anders had left for dinner at one of the other boarding houses, and Mrs. Fitzgerald had just departed in a hackney for her trip to the Drury Lane Theatre for that night's rehearsal of *The Brutus*.

The man who stood on the other side of the door knew all this, of course. He had been watching the house for the past half-hour, waiting for an opportunity to speak with Charity—alone.

When she opened the door, Charity expected one of the other teachers to claim she had left behind a shawl or pelisse. The last person she expected to see was Nicholas Barnaby, top hat in hand, looking as if he had lost his best friend.

Perhaps he had.

Charity's first inclination was to slam the door shut. And she would have, but her visitor was quick with his words. "I came to apologize," he said, before adding, "I don't expect forgiveness, but I do need to explain what happened."

Frowning, Charity took a step back. Nicholas angled his head, as if he wasn't sure what else to say.

"You look... different," Charity said, taking another step back. There was a white scar along one side of his face that hadn't been there when they were betrothed. And he looked as if he had lost some weight. She indicated with a wave that he could come in—she certainly didn't want him standing out on the stoop where anyone passing by could see him.

"You look more beautiful than I remember," he countered, stepping into the vestibule but stopping just inside the door. Charity had made it clear they wouldn't be moving to the parlor given the way she stood before him. "I've missed you terribly, Miss Crofter."

Not about to be swayed by his words, Charity angled her head and crossed her arms. "You said you were here to explain," she replied in a voice that warned she had no patience for him.

Nicholas dipped his head. "The night before we were to wed, I was pressed into service. The army. Again," he said with a roll of his eyes. "I thought I was all done with soldiering, but they found me, and the next thing I knew, I was on a ship bound for France at daybreak. I was on a battlefield the following day." He allowed a long sigh. "I was going to write—"

"Then why didn't you?" Charity interrupted, her eyes wide. From her expression, Nicholas couldn't tell if she was angry or sorry for what had happened to him.

"I was wounded. By a... by a bayonet," he stuttered as he indicated the facial scar with a wave of a finger. His hand continued to wave down the front of his body as his face screwed into a wince. He cleared his throat. "I was cut up bad, and, well, I didn't think you'd want me," he whispered. "The field doctor... he stitched me up where I'd been stabbed, but he didn't do nearly as fine a job of it as you would have."

Charity stared up at Nicholas, her mouth slowly dropping open in shock. She blinked. "You should have written," she whispered. "You should have allowed *me* to decide if I wanted you or not," she added just before tears filled her eyes.

"Oh, don't cry," Nicholas said as he struggled to fish a handkerchief from his waistcoat pocket. "I'm hardly worth it," he added as pressed the linen to her face.

Giving her head a shake, Charity covered his hand with one of her own. "No, you're not, you big dolt," she agreed, before she sniffled.

"Anyway, I've been keeping watch in the mornings. Across the street. To be sure you make it to your classroom safely," he went on. "I don't know what I would do should something happen to you."

Charity gasped. "That's you?" she replied, her shock apparent as her teary eyes widened. "They think you're plotting to kidnap one of the girls," she claimed.

"So I've been told," he said with a sigh.

Frowning, Charity asked, "By whom?" Had someone from the school crossed the street and confronted him with their suspicions?

Nicholas dipped his head again. "Your headmistress. Miss Albright paid me a visit where I work," he explained in a soft voice. "She's the one who... well, let's just say she's the reason I decided to pay a call on you. Truly, Miss Crofter. I am so sorry about what happened."

Ignoring his apology, Charity displayed a number of emotions all at once before she asked, "Where do you work?"

"At 'Finding Work for the Wounded'," he replied. "For Lady Bostwick. I was her first hire when she opened the charity a couple of years ago," he continued, a hint of pride sounding in his voice. "We're also 'Finding Wives for the Wounded' now, although our matchmaker has yet to be hired."

Charity gave a start. "Matchmaker?" she repeated.

He nodded. "Those of us who were wounded in the wars aren't likely to find wives willing to marry us, given... given how ugly we are," he stammered. "But according to Lady Bostwick, there are women out there who can overlook a missing limb or... or some bayonet wounds."

Angling her head to one side, Charity dared a glance into the main hall of the house before turning her attention back to Nicholas. "I wish to see these wounds of yours."

Nicholas gave a start. "Oh, I cannot, my lady. A gently bred woman such as yourself should never have to pay witness to such a horror. They're all over my..." He waved his arm down the front of his torso. "They're hideous."

Charity stared up at him for several seconds, her eyes darkening. "I think you should allow *me* to be the judge of that, Mr. Barnaby." She reached up and pulled on the bow that secured his cravat, the linen unraveling with her quick tug.

"What?" he managed, rather startled when she began to pull on the ends.

"You're going to show me your scars, Mr. Barnaby," she stated, an arched eyebrow punctuating her demand.

"But..." His protest was cut off when the cravat tightened around his neck.

She headed into the hallway and to her bedchamber while pulling him by his cravat. When he was inside, she pushed the door shut, turned the lock, and went about undoing the length of muslin from around his neck.

One of his fingers had managed to work its way between the fabric and his neck, pulling on it in an effort to keep from being strangled. He let out a gasp when it finally loosened. By then, her deft fingers were undoing the buttons of his top coat and then his waistcoat.

"My lady—"

"Quiet, Mr. Barnaby," she ordered, her manner at odds with the prim and proper sewing instructor she was by day.

Her hands pushed the garments from his body before they moved to tug his shirt from his breeches.

"Charity?" He used her given name in an effort to gain her attention, but she seemed determined to undress him. "Whatever are you...?"

But the palms of her hands were already traveling over his torso, her fingertips sending a series of frissons beneath his skin that had him breathless. Those fingertips followed the trails of his scars, the long, winding ones as well as the short lines from several stabs. Where the skin was raised, her fingertips circled his flesh, sending an entirely different sensation to his brain.

She had never done anything like this before with him. Their courtship had been rather chaste, their most scandalous act having been a stolen kiss behind a hedgerow in the park.

"Off. Take this off," she ordered, her small hands attempting to push the shirt from his body, the front of her body pressing against him. "I wish to see your scars."

His brows furrowing, Nicholas wondered at Charity's behavior. She had turned into a wanton right before his eyes! "Please, remember, my sweet. I warned you," he said before stripping the shirt from his body. It landed in the heap already begun with his topcoat and waistcoat. Charity still held the ends of his cravat between two fingers.

The expanse of Nicholas Barnaby's chest was suddenly before her eyes. Charity inhaled and held her breath a moment as one of her fingers traced first one scar and then another down the front of his torso, through the dark, crisp curls that covered his chest. The thin, white welts wound this way and that, as if someone had taken a sharp quill and drawn on him with white ink. Both uneven lines were punctuated with scars from stabs lined on either side with stitch marks, and both ended somewhere below the top edge of his breeches.

She went to work undoing the buttons of his breeches.

Nicholas couldn't help his sudden arousal. Her fingertips had set off any number of pleasant frissons beneath his skin. Her feminine touch had him craving her, craving what her body might offer should he do her bidding. He hadn't been with a woman—not even a prostitute—since before he had left for France.

He covered her hands with his own, forcing her to look up at him. "If you continue, Miss Crofter, I warn you, your virtue will be at risk," he warned, his eyes darkening to match hers.

He watched as the edge of one of her lips curled up at the same time an eyebrow arched. "Then so be it," she whispered.

Although one of his eyebrows furrowed—he would have admitted to a bit of confusion just then—he captured her lips with his own and kissed her quite thoroughly. When he came up for air, it was because she had his member grasped in one hand.

"I want this," she hissed.

Nicholas blinked. And blinked again. "It's yours," he replied, which he just then realized was probably not the correct response, for she led him—by his cock—to her bed, and pushed him onto it.

She went about removing his boots and stockings and then stood with her hands on her hips. "Off with the breeches right now," she ordered.

"Yes, ma'am," he murmured. He had the offending garment down to his knees when he realized she had begun undressing herself. After untying her round gown, she slipped it from her shoulders. Down it went, her stays following close behind. When she was left with just her chemise and stockings, she turned back to him and gave him a quelling glance. "Off, I told you. Were you one of my students, I would be forced to dock you a grade for your inability to follow simple directions."

Nicholas swallowed, but quickly did her bidding.

Completely naked, his scars were visible despite the dim light in the bedchamber. He stood to his full six-foot, two-inch height and watched as she divested herself of her chemise.

Naked, her skin pale and perfect, Charity looked as if she could have been some naughty woodland nymph. Her tiny upturned breasts were tipped with tightened nipples he wanted desperately to suckle.

When her attention was back on him—on his erect member—she stepped forward and finished drawing the lines of his scars with a fingertip, her lips curling up when she heard as well as felt his sharp inhalations of breath. Then she used two fingers to lift and caress his sac before tracing the throbbing vein on the back of his manhood to its tip. "Lie down," she whispered at the same time she gave him a push with the palm of her hand.

Nicholas did her bidding, wondering when his prim and proper seamstress had been replaced with an immodest and adventurous seductress.

Or had she always been this way, and he just never knew it?

Charity didn't bother removing her stockings, but Nicolas didn't mind as she climbed onto the bed and strad-dled him

He stared up at her engorged breasts. "God, you're beau-tiful," he murmured.

The words seemed to bring her back to reality. She sat atop him, her hands resting on her thighs as she regarded him. "Am I?" she asked in a quiet voice.

Nicholas nodded. "More beautiful than the night I proposed," he answered. He reached for one of her hands and brought it to his lips. He kissed the knuckles before turning it over to kiss the palm. "How is it a beautiful woman such as yourself is not... appalled at the sight of me?" he asked as he indicated the scars.

Her gaze swept his body, even down to where her quim

covered the end of his scars. "I never saw what you looked like before the scars," she murmured with a shrug. "Other than your face, of course. But I find them rather intriguing. Much like an interesting stitchery." Her fingertips once again traced the scars, one after the other as he inhaled sharply and reveled in the sensations they set off throughout his body. "Do you still want me?" she asked in a hoarse whisper.

"More than you could ever know," he replied, his voice sounding more strangled than it had been when his cravat had been wrapped around it with her pulling on the ends.

"Then I am yours. But know this, Mr. Barnaby. Should you *ever* disappear again, I shall find you and bestow you with a matching set of scars using my sewing scissors," she warned. "And I may or may not stitch you up."

Nicholas nodded. "I understand," he replied, wondering why the thought of her scissor blades against his flesh had him so aroused. "How long do we have? Before your housemates return?" he asked.

Charity blinked. "At least an hour, I should think," she replied, sounding ever so reasonable. "Maybe more."

Giving a nod in the pillow, Nicholas said, "That won't be enough. I'll require the rest of your lifetime." With that, he flipped her over onto her back and saw to it she was pleasured to within an inch of her life before he plunged his turgid manhood into her welcoming body. "You're mine, now, my lady," he whispered as he reveled in how she held him with her splayed fingers. "And we shall marry on the morrow."

Charity blinked beneath him. "We will?" she countered, breathless.

He nodded as he thrust into her over and over. "I still have our marriage license," he said betwixt labored breaths, just before his release took him into oblivion.

Arching into his body, Charity allowed a long, satisfied

sigh. "Well, as long as we're finished by two o'clock. I have a tea to attend at three."

Although he was prepared to argue, Nicholas thought it better he keep quiet.

No need to have her threatening him with the scissors the night before their wedding.

CHAPTER 31
TEA TIME AT BOSTWICK PLACE

The following day

At two o'clock in the afternoon, Daisy and Jane joined Annabelle and Mrs. Fitzgerald at the curb as they waited for a hackney to take them to Bostwick Place. "Where's Miss Crofter?" Daisy asked, her gaze going to the front door of Alpha House. She hoped the fact that she carried a small valise instead of a reticule wouldn't seem suspicious to the teachers. She had rolled up her evening attire, jewelry, and a pair of slippers and stuffed them into the bag.

Annabelle and Jane exchanged quick glances. "She said she would meet us there," Jane replied. "Just before she left with a rather tall gentleman." Her eyebrows waggled as a grin split her face.

"A rather dangerous looking man, if you ask me," Annabelle said in a lowered voice. "He had the most vicious scar running down the side of his face."

"I don't think I've ever seen Charity dressed so fine," Mrs. Fitzgerald added. "Primrose silk with furbelows and the tiniest embroidered flowers scattered all over it. Why, you would think she was off to get married."

Blinking, Daisy managed to keep her mouth from dropping open. "Probably because she was," she murmured in awe.

The other three teachers turned to look at her in surprise. "What?"

Daisy gave a shake of her head. "That man was Mr. Barnaby. Her betrothed," she explained, remembering her encounter with the clerk at 'Finding Work for the Wounded'.

"Betrothed?" Jane repeated. "But... she despises men."

"Hates them," Annabelle agreed.

"Well, hate is a bit strong, but she would probably castrate every last one of them with her finest scissors if given the chance," Mrs. Fitzgerald said in her rather theatrical manner.

Allowing a slight wince at this last, Daisy decided she could share what she knew of the sewing teacher. "Her opinion was formed solely on the basis of what occurred the day she was supposed to get married," she explained. "She was left at the altar, although her betrothed, Mr. Barnaby, was not at fault. Now that she knows he was conscripted back into the army and had no way to inform her of what had happened to him, she's no doubt forgiven the man." Just seeing the scar on his face would be enough proof he had been wounded in the war. If Charity needed more proof, Daisy was fairly sure Mr. Barnaby could provide more, although it would require he remove his clothes.

She couldn't imagine Charity making such a demand, though.

"Oh, and Mr. Barnaby is the tall man you've no doubt spotted watching you as you make your way to your morning classes," Daisy added. "He likes to ensure Charity makes it to her classroom safely."

The other three women exchanged glances of confusion, but Daisy's attention was on the street as she searched the midday traffic for a hackney.

Before one appeared, though, a glossy black coach pulled up and stopped in front of them.

Daisy was about to curse her father, even though she couldn't remember having mentioned the tea to him. Then she realized the gold painted crest on the door wasn't his, but rather that of Viscount Bostwick. "It seems our host has sent us transportation," she remarked as a tiger stepped off the back of the town coach and hurried to open the door. He set down the steps and gave a bow. "Good afternoon, ladies," he said as he helped each one of them into the equipage.

"Well, this is a treat," Mrs. Fitzgerald remarked as she settled into the squabs. "So new. So elegant," she added as her gloves slid over the butter soft leather.

The others agreed, happily taking their seats.

"Has Mr. Streater shared any news with you?" Jane asked once Daisy was seated. "I cannot help but think he plans some changes at the school, and we all know that cannot be good."

Daisy furrowed a brow. "No changes, other than the repairs that have already been scheduled," she replied. "He wants Warwick's in tip-top condition for next year's class of young ladies. So there's no need to be concerned."

Their expressions conveying doubt, Daisy decided she wouldn't be able to assuage their concerns. They would have to hear of the plans from Mr. Streater.

Once they reached Bostwick Place, a groom had the door open just as the town coach came to a halt. The teachers stepped down to find Mr. Barnaby and Miss Crofter walking from the direction of the park. Both looked as if they were dressed in their finest.

Daisy hurried over to greet them before they joined the others. "Are best wishes in order?" she asked in a quiet voice.

The two exchanged glances before they both nodded. "We've just come from St. Paul's," Charity said, her face displaying a pink blush beneath a stylish hat adorned with silk flowers.

"Best wishes to you both," Daisy said with a grin. She suddenly sobered. "I do hope you'll still continue to teach at Warwick's. I can't imagine having to take on the sewing classes in addition to the three I already teach."

Once again, the newlyweds exchanged glances.

"She will," Mr. Barnaby assured her. "I'd rather her be in the company of the teachers and students at Warwick's than have her home alone whilst I'm away at work all day."

Relieved to hear it, Daisy was about to make her way to the front door when Mr. Jenkins appeared from the other direction. Mrs. Pendergast was not far behind, her perfect posture and measured steps managing to make her appear as if she ruled Park Lane.

Rather surprised at Mr. Jenkins' arrival, Daisy wondered if any of the other servants had been invited, but the gardener was quick to explain his presence. "Seems Mr. Streater doesn't wish to be the only one of his sex at tea today," he said as he waved his invitation. He immediately offered an arm to Jane, who colored up a bit before she placed a gloved hand on it. Before they were at the front door, Elkins, the butler, had it open and was waving them in.

They filed in, Charity holding back until everyone else was through the door. "I'll be right here," Nicholas said before he lifted her hand to his lips and kissed the back of it.

"Mr. Barnaby?"

Nicholas looked up to find Elizabeth Bennett-Jones regarding him from the door. "Good afternoon, m'lady," he said as he bowed and Charity curtsied. "I was just escorting my wife to the tea," he added.

Elizabeth nodded and angled her head. "Why, I had no idea you were married," she replied, her expression reinforcing her words.

"Just this morning, m'lady. Miss Crofter..." He gave his head a shake. "I mean, Mrs. Barnaby, teaches at Warwick's."

Beaming, Elizabeth beckoned them both into the vestibule. "Well, we can't have you waiting outside for your bride whilst she's having tea," she replied. With Elkins still seeing to the wraps and pelisses of the others, Elizabeth took Nicholas' hat. "I'm quite sure Mr. Streater won't mind another man in the parlor."

"Indeed I won't," Teddy called out from the great hall, struggling with the introductions Daisy was making on his behalf. "So good to see a familiar face," he added with a nod to Nicholas. "Even if it is as ugly as yours," he teased.

"Mr. Streater," Charity said in a scolding voice. "I'll not have you speaking ill of my husband."

Teddy did a double-take. "I apologize, Miss Crofter. I mean... Mrs. Barnaby?" he half-asked as he gave his head a quick shake. He glanced up at Nicholas, but found the man gazing down at his wife in a most peculiar manner. Like he was besotted. "I wasn't aware Mr. Barnaby was married."

But before Nicholas could answer, Elizabeth was leading the teachers up the stairs and into a spacious parlor on the first floor. Daisy watched as Elkins saw to taking her valise as well as another to bedchambers somewhere on the second floor.

Murmurs of compliments and appreciation could be heard as the ladies took to the chairs and settee while the gentlemen formed a group next to the fireplace mantle. Once it was clear there was plenty of seating, Nicholas moved to sit next to his wife while Mr. Jenkins took a chair adjacent to the settee where Jane was perched. Daisy surreptitiously slipped a bank draft into Teddy's hand before taking a seat in one of the upholstered chairs.

Trays of cakes and biscuits covered the low table in front of the settee where Lady Bostwick did the honor of pouring tea and adding milk and sugar for those that wanted it. Quiet conversation soon increased in volume as Charity's colleagues learned of her wedding.

Before Teddy could put voice to his welcoming comments, Mr. Jenkins cleared his throat and announced he and Jane would be marrying when the school closed for six weeks in the summer. "Miss Betterman has agreed to be my wife and to be a mother for my Emily," he said proudly.

"But you won't be seeing the last of me," Jane said. "I intend to continue teaching music and drawing."

Expecting the announcement but not this soon, Daisy felt relief at hearing this last bit. The others murmured their best wishes as smiles replaced the uncertain expressions they had worn coming into the parlor.

Recognizing the slight lull after the murmurs died down, Teddy cleared his throat. "I believe I've met all of you. I feel a bit sheepish it's taken me so long given you all knew my mother for so long. But you see, I was not the best son. I didn't pay regular calls on Mrs. Streater whilst she toiled away at Warwick's every day. Instead, I joined her for an occasional luncheon or dinner away from the school," he explained. "We didn't speak of Warwick's but rather of my position at the bank and sometimes about my brother, Baron Streater. All that time, she was running what has become a rather fine school. A well-regarded school. Made so because of you and your classes."

Daisy blinked a few times as she listened to his words. Despite his comments the day before suggesting he would be unable to address the instructors, he was doing a damn fine job of it. So she could barely hide her annoyance when Mrs. Fitzgerald sat shaking her head, as if she expected there was a 'but' coming in his speech.

Teddy seemed oblivious to her, though, when he continued. "I wish to thank Lady Bostwick for hosting us on this fine day. From what I learned yesterday afternoon, it might not have been."

This last was met with expressions of worry and an exaggerated gasp from Mrs. Fitzgerald. "I just knew it," she whispered.

Teddy took a deep breath and continued. "I'm sure you all thought of my mother as a... a dragon. She was strict for a reason, of course—Warwick's is a finishing school with students from some of the finest families in London—but she was also a woman of foresight and self-discipline," he said, his voice sounding with pride. "She died having saved enough money to have Warwick's restored to its former glory. She also saw to hiring those that will do that restoration. While classes are out for the summer season, Warwick's will undergo many changes—all good—so that when you resume teaching classes, you shall do so in buildings that do not leak and in classrooms with new paint, windows, gas lighting, refinished floors, and door locks."

Soft inhalations of breath could be heard throughout the parlor, and Daisy allowed a grin when she caught Teddy looking in her direction.

"Now that I have secured the necessary funds to complete my mother's vision, I can assure you all the work will be done. I ask only that you agree to continue in your roles at the school. Miss Albright and I will see to it another instructor is hired to cover at least one of her three classes," he explained. He took a breath then, holding it a moment as if he was trying to remember more of his speech. "Are there any questions?"

Mrs. Fitzgerald glanced around the room before raising a hand. "Does this mean... no one is being let go?" she asked. "Even those who are to be *married?*"

His eyes darting sideways, Teddy said, "No. No one is being let go. Should you decide to remarry, Mrs. Fitzgerald, you, too, shall be allowed to continue in your position."

The theatre appreciation teacher's eyes widened. "Well, then," she replied. "Perhaps I shall have to make myself known to the actor who is portraying Brutus at the Drury Lane Theatre," she said as she fanned her face with a hand.

A series of titters made their way through the parlor before Teddy dipped his head. "May I ask that you refrain from doing so until after tonight's performance? Our hosts are attending this evening, and I shouldn't want the actor playing Brutus to be missing when it's time for the curtain call."

When everyone simply stared at Teddy, he gave a quick shake of his head. "I meant that as a joke, of course," he said in a quiet voice.

Daisy couldn't help the giggle that erupted just then, which had Jane joining in at the same time Mrs. Prendergast allowed a grin. But it was Mrs. Fitzgerald who laughed the loudest. "Oh, if I must, then I shall wait until *after* the curtain falls a final time," she assured him, which had everyone laughing.

And so the level of the conversation increased as more tea was poured and trays of biscuits and cakes were offered. At precisely four o'clock, several made their excuses and took their leave of the parlor. By ten past the hour, only Daisy remained as Teddy and Elizabeth saw to the departing guests at the bottom of the stairs.

"Pardon me, Miss Albright," a young woman said from the threshold. "Name's Christiansen. I'm to be your lady's maid for the evening. Whenever you are ready, I'll escort you to your room."

Daisy regarded the servant with a look of surprise. She had just been imagining Teddy helping with her fastenings. "Very well, Christiansen," she said as she stood and joined the maid. "Lead the way."

CHAPTER 32
A NIGHT AT THE THEATRE

Just over an hour later

When the Bostwick town coach pulled up to the front of Bostwick Place, Daisy was already on her way down the steps from the guest bedchamber Lady Bostwick had insisted she use. The young woman assigned as her lady's maid had spent nearly an hour dressing Daisy's hair.

Daisy had allowed Christiansen to take down her simple top knot. The young woman brushed out her hair and took time deciding on a style before weaving most of it into an elegant chignon. Then she went about securing the leftover curls of brunette hair with dozens of pins around her creation. "It's beautiful," Daisy breathed, turning first one way and then the other to regard the styling. "Can you add these?" Daisy asked as she fished a set of jeweled combs from the valise. Christiansen regarded the combs and then the chignon for a moment before carefully setting them in place.

"It's perfect," Daisy murmured.

"Thank you, my lady. Do you need me to do anything else?"

"Two fastenings," Daisy replied, turning her back to the maid after she stood up from the dressing table.

Christiansen made quick work of the tiny hooks and then walked around Daisy before giving her a nod. "You'll have him speechless, my lady," she said with a nod.

Daisy almost repeated, "Him?" but managed to grin instead. "I know I'm not supposed to thank servants, but please accept my gratitude. It's a rather auspicious day."

She was officially a part owner of Warwick's. And she was about to attend the theatre with her new partner in business.

"You're welcome, my lady." Christiansen curtsied and took her leave. A few minutes later, Daisy stepped out into the hallway and almost collided with a young boy.

"Well, hello," she said as she regarded David Bennett-Jones. Except for his auburn hair, and chubbier cheeks, he might have been her brother, William.

The boy giggled and then bowed, nearly toppling over as he did so. "Is very good to meet you, Lady Flower," he replied. When he returned to standing, he reached for her gloved hand.

Not expecting the courtesy and wondering at how he addressed her, Daisy thought he meant for her to lift him into her arms. So she did, just as a harried nurse hurried in her direction.

"Oh, I apologize, my lady," Mrs. Foster said, nearly breathless. She curtsied once she was in front of Daisy. "Master David has mastered door handles," she said as she reached out to take the toddler from Daisy.

Settling the boy onto a hip, Daisy turned her attention to the boy and gave him a grin. "Have you now?" She glanced up at the nurse. "May I see his sister?" she asked in a whisper, suddenly desperate to hold a baby.

Mrs. Foster blinked. "I... I suppose."

"Lead the way, while I discover more about this handsome young gentleman."

"But, my lady. He's crushing your gown," Mrs. Foster warned in a worried voice.

"Nonsense," she replied, turning her attention back to the boy who was staring at her with wide eyes. "Now, Mister Bennett-Jones, what did you call me?"

David hid his face against her shoulder and giggled.

"Did you call me Lady Flower?"

Straightening in her hold, David finally made eye contact and nodded. "I can't remember," he whispered.

"You're a flirt," she accused.

David's eyes widened. "Mama calls me that."

"Oh, of that I'm sure. Now, can you say, 'Daisy'?" she asked, well aware of the nurse's occasional worried glances in her direction as they made their way up a flight of stairs and to the nursery.

David hit his forehead with his hand. "Daisy," he repeated. "Lady Daisy." And then he giggled again. "Flower."

"He's learning the flowers in the garden, my lady," Mrs. Foster said then, as if she thought that was the reason he had referred to her as Lady Flower. They entered the nursery, where a large bassinet held a fussing baby.

"Oh, is this your sister?" Daisy asked as she moved to stand next to the bassinet. She gazed down onto the small baby, its cries ceasing when it realized it was no longer alone. "May I hold her, do you think?"

The boy nodded. "Lady Christina," he said as he indicated he wanted down. "She's my lil sister. Dada says he go broke 'cuz her dow-ree." He giggled then when Daisy rolled her eyes.

"I rather doubt that," Daisy said as she lowered him to the floor and then reached for Christina. "Oh, such a pretty little darling," she murmured as she lifted the babe into the crook of her arm. "You look just like my little sister." She simply stared at the bundle for a time before she was suddenly aware of someone at her side.

"I'd offer to let you borrow her for a day, but my husband would probably punish me, and not in a manner I would enjoy," Elizabeth said with a wink.

Daisy suppressed the urge to giggle. "I suppose you would like to say good-bye," she said as she passed the blanket-wrapped baby to its mother.

"Mr. Streater is downstairs. George and I will be at least a few minutes," Elizabeth said, one of her eyebrows arching suggestively.

"Oh," Daisy replied. "I'll... I'll go keep him company," she said as she curtsied. She tousled David's hair and gave him a wink before hurrying out of the nursery. She was down the two flights of stairs and into the main hall only a moment later. When there was no sign of Mr. Streater, she allowed the butler to place her mantle on her shoulders before she made her way into the vestibule.

She would have made her way to the coach on her own, but Teddy was there, standing near the front door. Dressed in black satin breeches, a new topcoat, and a silver waistcoat, he looked as if he was headed to a ball.

"I hope you haven't been waiting long," she said as she approached and curtsied to his deep bow.

"Only a moment." Although she didn't offer her hand, Teddy reached for it and bestowed a kiss on the back of her satin glove. "Your gown is lovely," Teddy remarked as he offered his arm. "No one would ever believe you're a headmistress."

Daisy angled her head. "They will if they know their fashions. I do believe this gown is three Seasons out of date," she claimed. "Thank you again for the invitation."

Teddy was about to step out the door, but he paused. "I cannot take all the credit. Viscount Bostwick insisted I invite someone, and when I told him I didn't know whom that would be, he mentioned you."

Her disappointment was hard to mask, but Daisy

managed to say, "How very kind of him," at the same time Lord and Lady Bostwick hurried past them and out the front door.

"We should be going," Teddy said.

"Of course," Daisy replied, placing her hand on his arm. They made their way to the Bostwick town coach, the door held open by the same groom who had held it for the teachers when they had arrived for that afternoon's tea.

Lady Bostwick grinned and patted the leather squabs next to her. She was sitting so she faced the direction of traffic. "Do join me, Miss Albright. The men will just have us for a view this evening."

"A rather gorgeous view, if you were to ask me," George Bennett-Jones said as Teddy settled next to him.

"And me," Teddy added, allowing a sigh when he found he was directly across from Daisy.

Daisy couldn't help but blush. "Thank you for including me this evening. I haven't been to a play in an age," she said. "Mrs. Fitzgerald attended the rehearsal last night, but I've yet to hear her review. Well, except for assessment of the actor who portrays Brutus," she said in a quieter voice, which had Elizabeth chuckling.

"It's been a long time since we've attended," George said. "Since well before Christina was born."

"We had considered going that one evening, but it's a good thing we didn't," Elizabeth said. "Or Christina would have been experiencing her first play *and* her first ride in a coach."

Daisy widened her eyes as she looked to Elizabeth for an explanation. "Quick labor?" she guessed.

"Indeed," the viscountess replied. "Not quite as quick as her brother. Poor George had to play midwife for David," she said in a hoarse whisper. "He arrived early, too."

"Is a crowd expected this evening?" Teddy asked, his question directed to George.

"Opening night always fills the house," George replied. "But I have a box with room for eight and a bottle of champagne, so we'll be comfortable."

Room for eight meant they might all sit in the front row, Daisy considered. She had expected to sit way in the back—in the shadows—and would have been happy to do so. Opening night meant most of the *ton* would be in attendance. The Duke and Duchess of Ariley, too.

She dared a glance at Teddy, who she caught staring at her. He quickly averted his eyes, and she allowed a grin even as she wondered how she would handle a situation where she and her father might cross paths.

How would she explain how she knew the duke? Would Ariley make it apparent she was related to him? Or behave as if they were mere acquaintances?

Was she ready to tell Teddy she was the illegitimate daughter of a duke?

Her reverie was interrupted when the coach halted.

"I won't mind if we have to walk a bit," Elizabeth said, parting the curtains to reveal the crowds heading toward the theatre. The coaches were three-deep, making it difficult for the drivers to negotiate the limited space. "It's not raining."

"Me, neither," Daisy agreed, realizing the men were waiting for the women's permission to take their leave of the coach.

George used his cane to tap on the trap door. His driver opened the door, his face appearing after a moment. "We'll get out here," George called up.

"Vera good, guv'nor," the driver replied.

A tiger had the door open and the steps down even before George could do so. Teddy followed him, and then the ladies stepped out, each taking their escort's proffered arm. A linkboy led the way until they reached the entry, and George tossed him a coin before he and Elizabeth passed through the front doors into the lobby.

Daisy scanned the room with a practiced eye, her gaze taking in the crowd as well as the individual faces she recognized. Lord and Lady Chamberlain were engaged in conversation with Lord Sommers and his baroness, Evangeline. The Earl and Countess of Torrington were holding court with a number of younger aristocrats, most probably his godsons. The Cunninghams and the Sewards were already making their way up the steps, the "second sons" deep in conversation as their wives grinned at one another in shared understanding.

At the top of the stairs, her father and stepmother were just about to turn and look out over the crowd when another couple caught their attention.

Daisy sighed in relief.

"You needn't be worried about your gown," Teddy said in a whisper, his head leaning in her direction.

Blinking, Daisy was about to claim she wasn't when she realized he had misunderstood her perusal of the crush. "Thank you for saying so. It's not as if I've had a moment to go shopping," she said, giving him a wink when he regarded her in shock.

"Should you need some time off, you only need..."

"I am teasing, Mr. Streater," she replied, patting the top of his gloved hand with the hand that rested on his left arm. "I have no need of such gowns or frippery."

Teddy tried to imagine her in the gown that Elizabeth was wearing and found he could not. Daisy was stunning in the peach confection she was wearing now, her brunette hair piled high atop her head and held in place with decorative combs. The jewels that lined each one were probably paste, but they looked real enough. As did the ones that dangled from her plump earlobes.

He imagined nibbling on one of those lobes, imagined kissing the space just under her ear, down the long column of her neck to the tops of her shoulders. Imagined pulling her sleeves down to her elbows so that he might kiss the tops of her breasts and maybe even nibble on a nipple, should one escape the confines of her gown. He was about to imagine what he might do even lower on her body when he realized she was staring at him.

"Are we going with Lord Bostwick?" Daisy asked, her head angling toward the stairs.

Teddy blinked and followed her gaze. "Oh, of course," he replied, before leading her to the base of the stairs. "I'm a bit awed," he said by way of an explanation. "I haven't been here since before it burned down and was rebuilt."

Daisy frowned. "That was ages ago," she said, just as she was forced to walk closer to him when several couples joined them on the stairs. Their bodies brushed against one another, but rather than slow their pace so that the other couples could pass, Teddy kept her close until they had reached the top of the stairs.

"I'm afraid the theatre wasn't a welcome pastime back then," Teddy murmured. He gave a nod to George, who stood waiting for them at the end of a long gallery.

"Did something happen?" Daisy asked, hoping he wasn't predisposed to having a bad night. She kept her eyes moving over the crowd around them. In the unlikely event someone might recognize her, she didn't want to be caught by surprise. She was also on the lookout for her father, sure he and his duchess hadn't yet gone to their private box.

"At the time, I could not afford a box, so we sat with the riff-raff down below," he replied. "Couldn't hear a word from the stage, what with all the talking, and I think I held my breath lest I pass out from the odor."

Daisy gave him a sympathetic glance. She had never been forced to sit with the unwashed masses, and rather doubted she would ever attend a play should she have to.

George held out his arm to indicate the entrance to his box, and Daisy stepped in. Elizabeth had already moved to a seat in the front row and was surveying the crowd below and those who sat across from them. She turned and motioned for Daisy to join her.

"Come sit next to me," Elizabeth implored as she indicated the seat to her right. "At least until the intermission. The men can sit behind us," she added with a wink directed to her husband.

With an apologetic glance in Teddy's direction and with George's help, Daisy removed her mantle and took the seat next to Elizabeth. A moment later, Teddy leaned over and offered her a set of opera glasses. She turned slightly and said, "Thank you," shivering when his gloved hand barely brushed her arm. She caught how his gaze, which was directed over her shoulder and down the front of her gown, was suddenly aimed at the stage.

"Can you see from your vantage?" Teddy asked, hoping she hadn't noticed him noticing the gown she wore. Or rather, how it displayed her rising moons. He wished he was sitting on the opposite side of the theatre, armed with opera glasses, so that he might spend the entire evening staring at her.

"Oh, yes. I've an excellent view of the stage," Daisy assured him. She was about to lift the opera glasses to her eyes when she was aware she was being watched. Pretending to look in one direction with the glasses, she was instead concentrating on the occupants of the box opposite and just above the one in which they sat.

The box occupied by the Duke and Duchess of Ariley.

"I think the Duchess of Ariley just waved at me," Elizabeth said in awe. Then she frowned. "Or you."

Daisy dared a glance at Elizabeth before she lifted a gloved hand and gave a quick wave in her stepmother's direction. "It is rather difficult to tell from this distance," she whispered. Her father seemed to be in conversation with someone else in the box. By the intermission, he would no doubt know she was in attendance.

Elizabeth arched an elegant brow. "Does Mr. Streater know?" she asked in a matching whisper, her fan held up to hide her face from the men who sat behind them.

Daisy immediately understood the query and shook her head. "He does not."

Blinking, the viscountess allowed a sigh. "Were you planning to tell him?"

Allowing a sigh, Daisy nodded. "I think I shall have to at some point. Now that my father knows I am here, he will no doubt pay a call during the intermission."

Elizabeth considered her words and angled her head. "May I inquire as to why you haven't told him?" She gave her head a quick shake. "Forgive me. It's none of my—"

"Very few in London know of my relationship to Ariley," Daisy interrupted. "I am well past my majority. I suppose since I have never required my father's permission, I have become a bit too independent," she explained. She took the glass of champagne George offered her, giving him a nod of thanks.

Acknowledging her comment with a wink, Elizabeth leaned back and turned to regard her husband with a brilliant smile. "Thank you for agreeing to this night out," she said, making sure he had a clear view down the front of her gown when he half-rose from his chair to better hear her remark. "It's been an age since we attended the theatre."

George gave her a glass of champagne and then reached for her other gloved hand and kissed the back of it. "Of course, my sweeting. But if you should grow tired, do let me know so that I may escort you home. There will be no shortage of hackneys at intermission," he hinted. "We can leave the coach for our guests." One of his eyebrows arched up as if to emphasize his point.

Elizabeth was about to claim she could easily make it

through the entire production when she sorted what he was about. "You're a darling to suggest it," she said as she gave him a wink.

A chime sounded from somewhere near the stage, and George took his seat, his glance in Teddy's direction proving the clerk hadn't come for the performance on the stage as much for the woman who sat in front of him. He leaned over and whispered, "Will you propose marriage?"

Teddy's eyes widened even before he could redirect them on his best friend. "George!" he admonished in a hoarse whisper. Then he gave an exaggerated shrug.

George allowed a grin and turned so his attention was on the stage, just as the play started.

Although Daisy hadn't expected to enjoy the performance, she watched most of it through the opera glasses and found she was completely absorbed in the story. When the second act ended for the intermission, she turned to say something to Elizabeth, only to discover the viscountess was no longer sitting next to her. Alarmed, she turned around to find Teddy getting up from his seat, an empty champagne glass dangled from his one hand. He moved to stand next to her chair. "Did they... leave?" she asked.

"About ten minutes ago," he replied with a grin, amused she hadn't even noticed the other two leave the box. "I think her ladyship was quite tired. Anyway, George was kind enough to leave us the coach."

"That was very considerate of him," Daisy replied as she stood up and shook out her skirts. "You should have moved into Lady Bostwick's chair," she added. "The view is much better."

Teddy felt a jolt of desire at hearing her words. The view would have been better indeed, but only if he looked in her direction. "Would you like a drink?"

Daisy shook her head and indicated she still had champagne. "No, but do get one for yourself," she encouraged. "I'll just stay here and stretch my legs."

Hesitating, as if he was trying to decide if she would be safe while he made his way to the bar, Teddy finally gave a nod and took his leave of the box, leaving the door ajar.

Counting the seconds in her head, Daisy moved to stand near the door and wasn't the least bit surprised when James, Duke of Ariley, poked his head through the opening and grinned. "I thought Helen mad when she said you were here with the Bostwicks," he said as he dipped his head.

"Hello, Father," Daisy said as she dropped a curtsy and allowed a grin.

"It appears your hosts have left you all alone for the evening," he replied as he regarded her from the threshold, his gaze having taken in the interior of the box to discover she was alone.

"The Bostwicks have taken their leave, it's true, but Mr. Streater is my escort this evening. He will be seeing me home," she replied.

Her father frowned. "Streater?" he repeated. "Your employer?"

"Indeed."

"Ah, yes. The bank clerk."

The words weren't said with any kind of derision, but Daisy couldn't help but think he disapproved. "He pays me quite well to be headmistress of the school." She was still counting the seconds in her head, knowing Teddy would be returning from the bar shortly.

"Not to be his mistress, I hope," James said in a whisper.

Anger flashed across her face, but before Daisy could give him a suitable rebuke, the duke held up a gloved hand and gave his head a shake. "I... I apologize. That was uncalled for," he said. "I don't even know why I—"

"I think you should leave," she said, her words clipped. How could he think such a thing? Say such a thing? She had never engaged in more than the one *affaire* with Alex, and then only to learn what she must to carry out her mission.

"Daisy—"

"Please, Your Grace?" Her voice filled with more pleading than rebuke, Daisy made sure her expression showed worry instead of annoyance.

Sighing, the duke took a step back and gave a bow. "Please, do come to the house when you can. At least come to see Helen and the children. I promise I won't be such an..." He was about to say, "ass", but simply gave a shake of his head before turning to head down the hallway behind the box.

"I will, Father. I promise," she said, hurrying to the door to watch him depart. When he paused and angled his head to one side, she knew he had heard her. Allowing a sigh of relief, she stepped back into the box and waited for Mr. Streater's return.

*H*olding his drink in his only hand, Teddy watched the immaculately dressed visitor to the Bostwick's box stalk toward him, the man's attention on the carpet below. He didn't even seem to notice Teddy—or any others in the crowded hallway—as he passed, but Teddy overheard him muttering something about stubborn women.

He followed the man's retreating back through the mass of theatre goers, noting that a fellow fencer from Angelo's Academy, Lord Barrings, seemed to watch alongside him. "Who was that?" Teddy asked of the gentleman sporting a gold metallic waistcoat and a glass of gin.

"Ariley," Barrings responded, a brow furrowing as he, too, watched the retreating back of the aristocrat.

Teddy frowned. "The duke?"

"Aye. And he didn't appear to be very happy at all."

Redirecting his gaze back down the hallway, Teddy saw

Daisy standing outside the box, looking to her left and right as if in search of someone. From this distance, she looked resplendent in the peach and sarcenet over-skirted gown that left little to the imagination when it came to her figure. Teddy would never have guessed she was the headmistress of a finishing school.

His school.

He would guess she was someone's mistress, though.

Sure the duke had come from the same box where Daisy was standing, Teddy wondered if the duke had stopped to speak with George or if he had paid her a visit.

Had he arranged an assignation?

Was she his mistress?

A jolt of jealousy had Teddy's brow furrowing. He had half a mind to follow Ariley and confront the man, but a chime sounded, and those around him quickly made their way back to their seats.

"Did you see any of your friends?" Daisy asked as she dipped a curtsy upon his return to the Bostwick box.

"Just Lord Barrings," Teddy replied, his manner rather terse. "And you?"

Daisy frowned, wondering at his sour expression. "No, but then I didn't expect to," she said with a shake of her head. She was about to make her way to her seat when she noted how he continued to stare at her. "The Duke of Ariley stopped briefly," she offered then, watching Teddy's reaction to determine if the duke's visit had something to do with the change in his demeanor.

"Are you his mistress?" Teddy squeezed his forgotten glass of brandy so hard, he thought perhaps the glass would shatter. At seeing Daisy's widened eyes and look of offense, he gave a quick shake of his head before she could respond. "I apologize," he said in a whisper, aware the noise in the theatre had died down so the actors on stage could be heard. "It's none of my—"

"I assure you, Mr. Streater, I am not *anyone's* mistress," Daisy replied in a hoarse whisper, her words terse.

Despite the manner in which they were delivered, her words were more welcome than Teddy thought imaginable. "You're not?" he replied, not intending to make it sound as if he didn't believe her.

Aware they would be noticed if they didn't at least sit down, Daisy dropped into a chair at the back of the box and waved for Teddy to sit down. She leaned in his direction and lifted a hand to the side of her face to hide her lips from whomever might have had a pair of opera glasses aimed in their direction. "I am headmistress of a finishing school. I cannot be engaged in... *improprieties*," she hissed.

Although her words should have had Teddy feeling relieved—or at least assured he hadn't made a mistake in hiring her—he found he felt a profound sense of disappointment. "And if you weren't?" he asked, his face so close to hers he thought he might be able to kiss her. "A headmistress, I mean?"

Daisy's eyes widened in alarm before she pulled away from him a bit. "What are you suggesting?" A tingle of excitement shot through her when she imagined him propositioning her. Asking if she might join him in his bed so that they might finally discover what it was that had them so frustrated with one another. He needed a woman, she was sure. As to whether a mistress would be enough, she didn't yet know.

He would do better with a wife.

Teddy blinked, realizing he had asked the question—out loud—about what she might be if she wasn't a headmistress. "I apologize. I don't know what's come over me," he whispered as he gave his head a shake again. Dammit, but his cock had hardened at the thought of Daisy in the role of his mistress. His personal headmistress, demanding he serve her whenever she desired him.

The thought of paying a visit to her bedchamber on the other side of the office door in Omega House came to mind. A visit that would find her wearing nearly nothing and ready for him. The thought of bedding her—of bringing her exquisite pleasure before experiencing his own blessed release—had him nearly groaning in dismay. "Tell me what to do," he croaked, grimacing when he realized he sounded like a love-sick frog just then.

Daisy blinked, not quite sure she understood his meaning. One thing had become clear, though. Teddy Streater wanted her, and at that moment, several years of loneliness could end with a few gentle words. "Take me to your townhouse. We shall do what we must," she murmured.

Teddy didn't give her response a second thought. He was up and offering her a hand, nearly forgetting his great coat and her mantle. They were down the stairs and out to the Bostwick's coach a moment later, the driver and tiger scurrying to take their places after Teddy reminded them of his address.

Once they were in the town coach, Daisy regarded Teddy with a serious expression as he settled into the squabs next to her. "I do hope you're not about to change your mind," she whispered. The coach jerked into motion, its speed increasing as they traveled farther from the theatre.

Teddy blinked. If he changed his mind, his cock would disown him. He would disown himself. Disavow all knowledge of a man who was too stupid to realize just what it was they were about to do. "Of course not," he replied, his one gloved hand holding onto hers.

"You won't... dismiss me over this?"

Dismiss you from what? Teddy nearly put voice to the question before his addled brain formed a coherent response.

Her position, of course. She was the headmistress of a finishing school. *His* finishing school.

Given what they were about to do, he really should

consider what might happen should someone discover them. The reputation of Warwick's would suffer. Might be forever tainted.

But Teddy couldn't imagine dismissing her. After today's tea, it was evident she was perfect for Warwick's. The instructors seemed content now that repairs were about to be made. The gardener would have more time to see to the landscaping, so the exterior would look immaculate. The painting in the classrooms as well as the boarding houses would be completed before the new term started. The brighter rooms would make for happier students. And best yet, no servants had threatened to leave the school's employ on account of Daisy's hiring.

He rather doubted there was anyone else who could run the school with the kind of passion she displayed in the week she had been in the position.

So the idea of dismissing her was ludicrous. "No, of course not," he managed to say without sounding too much like a frog.

"How long has it been?"

His breathing having quickened, Teddy wondered why he was feeling a bit light-headed. "Since when?" he replied, now unable to form a coherent thought, other than the one his other head seemed to have formed since they left the theatre box.

Daisy swallowed. "Since you were last with a woman?"

Teddy sighed. If her query hadn't been made in such a soft voice, he might have refused to answer. But there was something about her manner—genuine concern coupled with empathy—that had him responding. "Since I... since I lost my arm," he whispered before he allowed a groan. "Too long. I may have forgotten what to do," he added, not intending for her to hear that last.

"Nonsense," she whispered. "I'm counting on you to know."

Turning his body to better see her, Teddy leaned over and wrapped his arm around the back of her shoulders and pulled her to his chest. He was heartened when she didn't resist his hold but settled against him with a soft sigh. "Don't even think about falling asleep on me," he murmured, a hint of humor in his words.

Daisy grinned and sighed. "Not even when we're on your bed?"

Imagining her slumbering warm, soft body atop his, Teddy allowed another groan of frustration. "Only then," he replied, just as the coach came to a stuttering halt.

A quick glance out the coach window confirmed they were in front of his townhouse in Bruton Street. A few moments later, they were in the townhouse.

CHAPTER 33
A BEST FRIEND
CONTEMPLATES A COUPLE

A bit earlier, in front of the theatre

"However did you know to have the barouche brought to the theatre?" Elizabeth asked as George assisted her into the equipage.

George followed her in and settled into the squabs. "I've been plotting, my sweet."

Elizabeth's eyes widened. "Oh, do tell," she replied, one of her arms wrapped about his as she leaned against him.

Despite the dark, George allowed a grin as the horse pulled the barouche into the Drury Lane traffic. "Teddy is most taken with Miss Albright. I'm merely seeing to it they spend some time together," he explained.

"Do you think he'll do what's necessary to make her his wife?" she queried.

Frowning, George regarded his wife's coiffure for a moment—her face was pressed into the small of his shoulder—before responding. "Necessary?" he repeated. "And what might that be?"

Elizabeth lifted her head from his shoulder and gave him a quelling glance. "Why, he has to seduce her, of course," she replied.

George seemed to deflate at hearing her words. "I rather doubt Teddy will do such a thing."

"Why ever not?"

Inhaling slowly, George wondered how something so obvious to him could be invisible to her. "He has one arm, my sweet, and he's rather—"

"Full of nonsense. I can assure you, it matters not to Miss Albright."

George stared at his wife. "What do you know?"

Elizabeth angled her head back into the small of his shoulder and shrugged her own. "I watched her at tea today. I watched him, too. It will take little in the way of encouragement to get those two together. So either he has to seduce her, or she'll have to seduce him."

Allowing a chuckle, George sighed. "Then my money is on her, because Teddy will not make it known he wishes to court her."

He had almost said, "Bed her," but thought better of it. He hadn't mentioned his conversation with Teddy about the man's desire to take a mistress. That he wanted Miss Albright in the role.

"Oh, come now. You don't think Teddy will use tonight as an opportunity to... to make his wishes known?"

George winced. "I don't think he's as brave as he used to be," he murmured. Indeed, Teddy's last foray into battle had him losing far more than just a limb. At least his confidence on the pisté had been restored. His confidence in his skills as a clerk restored.

Now if his confidence as a man could be restored, Teddy might prove the perfect mate for Miss Albright.

"Well, at least they're in business together. Or rather, will be, once the papers are drawn up," Elizabeth said.

George straightened in the squabs, his arm tightening around Elizabeth. "What are you talking about?"

Secretly pleased she knew something her husband did

not, Elizabeth grinned. "It seems Mrs. Streater wasn't a miser. Teddy's inheritance is really the money necessary to cover a number of renovations she arranged prior to her death. Since he's already spent some of it—"

"Most of it," George interrupted, a hint of alarm in his voice as he considered the items Teddy had claimed to have purchased since last Sunday.

"—And there's no longer enough, Miss Albright offered to invest in the school in exchange for a percentage of the ownership. She told me about it after the tea. After everyone else had taken their leave."

"And Teddy agreed?" he asked in disbelief.

Elizabeth blinked. "Of course. What else could he do?"

George gave a sound of derision. "He could have come to me. I would have loaned him the blunt."

Allowing a loud sigh, Elizabeth straightened and shook her head. "Oh, George. Don't you see? If they're to end up together, they need to *be* together. In every way."

George blinked. "I thought I was the one playing matchmaker here," he murmured.

Angling her head with new-found appreciation for her husband's efforts, Elizabeth gave him grin. "Leaving them the town coach was a brilliant idea," she said as she kissed him on the cheek. "And if what you claim is true about poor Mr. Streater, then I suppose Miss Albright will have to be the one doing the seducing." She sighed. "Oh, if only I could be there when she informs him she's going to seduce him."

George furrowed a brow. "It doesn't really work like that, my sweet," he said patiently.

"It's what you did with me," she countered.

Well, she had him there. "You had never been with a man before. I wanted to make it clear what I intended to do to you. Give you an 'out' should you come to your senses and realize just how ludicrous my plan was," he explained.

"I'm so glad I didn't," she replied with a happy sigh.

"Didn't what?"

"Come to my senses, of course."

George grinned as he leaned over and kissed her quite thoroughly. "Going on three years now," he teased. Before she could put voice to a protest, he kissed her again and continued to do so until the barouche pulled up to Bostwick Place.

Now that he had her thoroughly aroused, he had plans to keep her that way the rest of the night.

CHAPTER 34
A NIGHT OF WONDER

*M*eanwhile, at Teddy's townhouse

Despite his assurances he wasn't going to fire her, Daisy couldn't help but believe Teddy Streater would be forced to replace her if he gave a second thought to what they were about to do.

If that happened, she supposed she could see Lady Bostwick about the matchmaking position. Given her background—and her understanding of men and what they wanted versus what they needed in a wife—she thought she could do a better job than most in selecting their mates. She could even cite her success with Nicolas Barnaby and Charity Crofter.

The thought of having to walk away from Warwick's, just when she was sure everything was progressing smoothly, had her feeling a twinge of regret, though. She liked teaching. She liked her students. She liked her office and her small apartment.

Daisy glanced over at Teddy, wondering if he, too, was having second thoughts about what they were about to do. She hoped he wasn't. He couldn't.

Did he have any idea how her pulse increased whenever

he entered the office? How her breasts swelled a bit? How her nipples tightened into buds and her breathing quickened?

Just what was it about him that had her reacting so?

Attraction?

He was handsome in a rather rough-around-the-edges sort of way. How a dashing highwayman might look if he didn't wear the ridiculous mask so many were described as sporting.

Or was it lust?

She couldn't help how her body responded, nor could she pretend it didn't. She couldn't remember this kind of desire, not with the marquess, and certainly not for Alex.

Or was it need?

She had held four children in her arms this past week, and every time, she felt a yearning to have a baby. Even when she was expecting, she didn't *feel* the sort of need she felt now.

Well, no matter the reason, Daisy had decided she could at least help Mr. Streater in one regard.

It had been too long since she had shared a bed with a man. And far too long since she had done so with a man to whom she felt any sort of attraction. Despite his lack of a right arm, Theodore Streater had her aroused in a manner she hadn't experienced since the nights she had warmed the bed of the Marquess of Plymouth.

She wondered for a moment if it was because Mr. Streater was fair and blond-haired, like her father, or if it was because he was pretending no woman on the earth would have him due to his missing limb.

Or maybe because he believed that last bit.

"Has it really been that long since you were with a woman?"

"Isn't that question a bit... personal?" Teddy countered, as if he hadn't just answered it a few minutes ago.

"It is," she agreed with a nod. "But how am I to know what to do if you don't remember how?"

Teddy blinked. "If I don't remember how?" he repeated, straightening so his arousal was suddenly apparent. "What are you talking about?"

Daisy turned and placed her arm on his, making sure they were headed to his upstairs bedchamber rather than to the ground floor study. "Making love, of course."

He seemed to waver a bit. "I don't think it's something you can forget how to do," he argued, just as the two reached the landing. "But I suppose... I suppose it's possible to forget all the rest of it." When he didn't make a move in any particular direction—two staircases went in opposite directions—Daisy studied the Aubusson carpeting at their feet and followed the path of most wear.

His response surprised her, but it also confirmed he was a bit addled. As a result, she wondered if she should pretend she was a virgin or if she should play the seductress.

Daisy was still sorting what to do when he asked, "You are going to stay at Warwick's, aren't you?"

She nodded. "Of course. I would be honored to continue as your headmistress. But if for some reason—" *like what we're about to do*—"You *had* to let me go, I would probably apply for the position of matchmaker for Lady Bostwick's new charity, but I'd really rather not," she said, unable to hide the quaver in her voice. Damn, but she would miss Warwick's if he let her go. She hadn't considered just how much.

"I'll do no such thing," he argued with a shake of his head. "I am the owner. I set the rules. And besides, we're partners in the business now, remember."

Daisy gave a sigh of relief. *Partners.* She had given him the bank draft for her investment in the school when they were at Bostwick Place for the tea. She was part owner of the school now. A school she hoped would one day appeal to more than just the wealthy.

"Can you abide a headmistress who would flaunt convention in favor of new ideas?" Daisy asked softly, climbing the steps slowly in favor of delaying their arrival at the top of the stairs.

"New ideas?" he repeated.

"Maybe encourage more of the middle class to send their girls instead of just wealthy cits?"

Teddy considered the query. "I certainly don't expect Warwick's to remain the same as when my mother was in charge," he replied, an eyebrow arching. "Mrs. Streater was always after daughters of the aristocracy to attend, thinking they provided some kind of cachet for the school. But aristocrats don't send their daughters to finishing schools," he murmured. "They educate them at home."

"When they can," Daisy agreed. "But sometimes, like in the case of Lady Annalise, they cannot, and so they send them to Warwick's. I don't intend to turn them away, of course, but I also wish more girls could be educated. The less fortunate."

Although he despised the country that had caused him to lose so many comrades-in-arms—as well as his own arm—Teddy had no argument with those who sought to overthrow the arrogant rich. He dealt with them every day at the bank.

Despite his recent inheritance, which would certainly rank him among the almost-rich, it was hard to think of himself as one of the wealthy. And he wouldn't be for long if he wasn't more careful about how he spent his money.

Sudden wealth was a heady experience.

Teddy took a deep breath. "There are those who believe if more are educated, they will realize how poorly run the country is, and they will revolt, much like the French did."

Daisy considered the comment, recognizing the theory of those who wanted only the elite to be educated. "I rather doubt the poor are going to attempt to overthrow the king," Daisy said when she reached the top of the stairs.

But Teddy was thinking about the young ladies who made up the current crop of students at Warwick's. "Most of the girls are daughters of tradesmen," he said, remembering the list of names on the register Daisy had provided him earlier that week. "Some are wealthy, of course, but most cannot claim a single duke, marquess, or earl as even a relative. Some will be lucky to land husbands who can afford to buy them a new wardrobe every season, let alone house them in splendor."

Daisy hid her astonishment at hearing his words. The majority of the students were daughters of wealthy cits— young ladies whose fathers were engaged in lucrative businesses or banking. Surely they wouldn't have trouble in the marriage mart. Their dowries would be large enough to attract any number of suitors. They might even keep the couple living in more than modest means for the rest of their lives.

But what if they didn't land wealthy husbands upon their completion of finishing school?

"If they cannot find husbands, what do you suppose they'll do instead, Mr. Streater?" Daisy asked, again using a soft voice in an attempt to calm him.

Teddy shook his head. "They can be governesses, or run an office much like Lady Bostwick does, or..." He allowed the sentence to trail off before he gave her a worried glance. "Become operatives for the Home Office or—"

"Become mistresses?" she offered in a whisper, leading him down the hall in a slow stroll.

Swallowing, Teddy shook his head. "I didn't mean to imply their choices were so limited."

"Ah, but they are," Daisy replied with a sigh. "Now, how can I expect you'll continue to employ me given what we're about to do, Mr. Streater?"

Frowning, Teddy dared a glance around, realizing they were in front of his bedchamber door. "And what might that be?" he asked, his words sounding a bit strangled.

"Why, we're about to make love," Daisy replied as she reached out for the door handle and pushed it down. "We do have the right bedchamber, do we not?" she asked as the door slowly opened.

Teddy glanced down at her gloved hand, the one that had just opened the door to his bedchamber. "How did you know?" he asked, returning his attention to her face.

"I merely followed the path in the carpet," she replied with an arched brow. She made her way into the dark room. A single candle lamp was lit on a nightstand, and the remains of a fire lit long ago gave off a soft, golden glow from the fireplace. But the odors of freshly cut wood and varnish as well as wool made it apparent the bedchamber contained new furnishings and carpet.

Teddy resisted the urge to say he would have to see to the hallway carpet when he found himself following her into his bedchamber. Damn his new valet, but the man had already seen to turning down the counterpane and the bed linens. A rather large expanse of white made it look as if he had been expecting company of a carnal sort. "I was not expecting this," he said as he waved at the bed.

"The bed?" Daisy asked, a hint of confusion crossing her face.

"Well, the bed, yes," Teddy said, giving his head a shake. "But not... not like this."

Angling her head as she surveyed his room—a rather richly decorated men's bedchamber in dark blues with gold accents—Daisy gave an approving nod. "Your valet is to be commended. New to the position, isn't he?"

Frowning, Teddy asked, "How did you know?"

Daisy gave a shrug. "There's not a thing out of place. Not a stitch of clothing anywhere. Nor a shoe."

"I do have a dressing room," he said, sounding a bit offended.

"Which is also probably in perfect order, as well," she countered. She dared another glance around the bedchamber, noting how new everything appeared. About to say something about new-found wealth, Daisy had to suppress the comment when Teddy held up a staying hand.

"I admit. I... splurged a bit. Having lived the past two years well within my means and the year before that at the expense of my brother, I decided to replace the old furnishings," he explained. He didn't add that he had purchased the townhouse from his brother.

"In the whole house?" Daisy asked in alarm.

"Just in here," Teddy said.

Daisy furrowed a brow. "Because you were... expecting me?" she guessed, her voice tinged with a tease. "I am honored."

He furrowed a brow. "Truth be told, I'm not even sure why I did it," Teddy countered. "I never thought... I never really thought anyone other than me would see it. Or my valet, I suppose."

He had hoped a particular someone would see it, though. Eventually. That she happened to be standing next to him just a day after the new furnishings had been delivered struck him more as a coincidence than a deliberate attempt at seduction. He felt a good deal of satisfaction when he noted how she openly admired the pieces.

Daisy wondered at his words. "But you had hoped?" she asked in a quiet voice. To have replaced all the furnishings in the room—the carpet, too—suggested he was trying to impress someone.

That thought led her thoughts in an entirely different direction, and the sense of disappointment—nay, jealousy— she felt, had her struggling to breathe. *How could I have been such a fool?* she wondered as she realized there could be only one reason he would do such a thing. "Does your mistress approve?" she asked quietly.

Teddy frowned and shook his head. "I've not had the pleasure of such an arrangement," he replied, closing his eyes tightly when he realized exactly what he had said.

Daisy felt a combination of relief—for herself—and sorrow for him. Apparently what he claimed in the coach was true—he hadn't been with a woman since the war.

"What about your wife?" It was possible he had remarried, she considered.

"*Late* wife," he countered quickly. "I think she would have approved, although..." He sighed. "It's been some time."

No mistress. No wife. There was nothing to stop her from completing her mission that night.

Unless he did.

Daisy placed her valise next to the nightstand nearest to where she stood and then faced him. "Was she the last woman you were with?" she asked, her words gentle.

Teddy closed his eyes again and finally allowed a nod. "I got back from the Continent just after Gertrude died. I thought about turning around and heading back. Find another war. Thought perhaps I could join her quicker that way, I suppose."

Daisy gave a thought to taking her leave. The widower obviously still held Gertrude in high esteem if he wanted to hasten his own death. "And now?" she asked in a whisper.

Teddy swallowed. "I'm having second thoughts?" The way he ended the comment with a question had Daisy allowing a slight grin.

"As I said earlier, I would like to make love to you," she whispered.

His heart pounding so hard he was sure Daisy could hear it, Teddy regarded her for a moment more before giving her a slight nod. "Does that include... kissing?" he managed to ask, rather surprised his voice didn't crack or squeak or otherwise sound like a frog in heat.

Kissing.

The word had Daisy blushing, and she was thankful the room wasn't better lit. Other than pecks on the cheek, she had never kissed a man in her entire life. *It's far too intimate*, her mother had warned her and her sister. *Give a man your body, you still have your body. Give a man a kiss, and you give up your heart.* She supposed her mother knew to what she referred. Lily Albright had been hopelessly in love with James Burroughs after just such a kiss. But then, he had fallen in love with her, too.

"If you would like it to include kissing, I suppose I am not opposed. But, I must warn you. I haven't any experience with kissing," she said, a bit breathless. "I think I would enjoy it very much, though. But if you're having second thoughts..."

Teddy blinked at this bit of news. *No kissing?* Daisy Albright had the most kissable lips in all of London. He could hardly believe that if he kissed her, he would be her first. "No. No, I'm not. I am..." He sighed, his eyes closing in an attempt to prevent her gaze from having its hypnotic way with him. *Honored. Horny. Aroused, and amazed.* This beautiful, worldly woman wanted to make love to him, and he was hesitating.

He knew why, of course. On the one hand, he hoped she knew it, too. On the other... well, he didn't have an 'other,' so it probably didn't matter that it might not matter.

Even if it did.

But of course it did! He was missing an arm. An arm that could otherwise hold him up, or wrap around her, or provide an anchor of support.

Before he could say another word, he was aware she had moved closer. He didn't have a chance to step back, or to open his eyes before her lips were suddenly within inches of his.

"Teach me how to kiss you," she whispered.

Every contrary thought flew from his head in an instant. Teddy lowered his lips to hers. He could have described what he was about to do, or given her instructions on what she should do, but dammit, actions spoke louder than words.

Soft and sweet, open and welcoming, her lips responded to his in only a moment. When her hand moved to the side of his head, her fingers spearing his short hair, a shiver shot through him. His arm wrapped around the back of her waist, he spread his fingers wide, and then he pulled her hard against his chest.

Teddy wasn't sure if she moaned or if he did. Perhaps they both did. She had said she was going to make love to him. Did she really intend to share his bed with him? Engage in sexual congress? Sleep next to him?

He reluctantly pulled his lips from hers, leaving his forehead barely touching hers. "If I don't stop this right now—"

"I'll have my way with you," Daisy warned with an arched brow. She was already seeing to his cravat's knot, her slender fingers easily freeing the fabric ends.

His own brows furrowing in confusion, Teddy was at a loss as to how to reply. Instead, his attention went to the cravat. The length of silk passed in front of his face three times as she unwound it from around his neck. Deft fingers were already undoing his topcoat and waistcoat buttons, her small hands pushing open the garments so they slid from his shoulders. The button at the top of his shirt was undone even before he realized she was working on the fastenings of his breeches.

If he didn't do something to stop her right then, she was going to have him completely undressed before he would get a single article of clothing removed from her body.

Except, how would he manage with just one hand?

"May I help with your boots?"

Teddy gave a start. "Boots?" he repeated.

Daisy had to stifle the grin that threatened just then. "If you sit on the edge of the bed, I can remove them for you," she offered. How else would they come off? She couldn't imagine it would be very easy for him to get them off with only one hand.

Hence, the reason for a valet, she supposed.

When he made no move to move, Daisy placed the flat of her hand on his lawn-covered chest and gave a gentle push. "Sit down before you fall down, darling," she whispered.

Darling? No one had ever called him "darling" before. Not even his mother.

Blinking, Teddy did as he was told, watching in wonder as she knelt before him and removed each boot with a practiced tug. "You've done this before," he accused quietly.

Lifting her eyes to meet his, Daisy gave a shrug. "Removed boots? I don't know that I have," she said, before turning her attention to his stockings. "Other than my own, of course." She wasn't about to add that she had removed just about every possible article of clothing from a man at one time or another.

"Seduced a man, I meant," he countered in a whisper.

Daisy's gaze met his again as she settled onto her thighs. "Am I seducing you?" she asked as she angled her head. "Here I thought *you* were the one who was doing all the seduction." Knowing she had to get up before her injured leg protested too much, she straightened from her knees and leaned forward, her hands pressed against the bed to provide support as she lifted herself until her face was directly in front of his. Grabbing the sides of his shirt, she was about to lift it over his head when his hand covered one of hers.

"No," he said with a shake of his head. "If we do this, it stays on."

If we do this?

Daisy wasn't about to stop now. Besides, she couldn't imagine taking her leave of his house this time of the night.

Straightening to her full five-foot, one-inch height, she crossed her arms. "If you don't show me yours, then I won't show you mine," she warned.

The look of confusion crossed his face again before she once again gave his chest a push. He fell back onto the bed, and she went about pulling his breeches from his body. His manhood, already engorged, made the removal difficult at first. "You're *what?*" he asked, lifting his head and watching as she made quick work of the breeches and his smalls. At least his shirt was long enough to cover the evidence of his arousal.

Once the garments were free of his body, Daisy pretended not to notice his lean legs, muscled from fencing and horseback riding. "My leg," she said, using one hand to pull up the satin and chiffon of her skirts to just above the knee—just above where her silk stocking ended. Enough to show the puckered skin where a bullet had penetrated her leg. Although the projectile had passed completely through her leg, it had nicked the bone and destroyed the muscle tissue in its path.

A look of shock appeared on Teddy's face. "Damn! What happened?" he asked as he sat up on the edge of the bed. "Oh. Pardon the curse," he whispered, rather surprised she didn't seem the least bit scandalized by his language.

Daisy let go of her skirts and turned to sit next to him. "I was shot," she said, turning slightly so her back was angled in his direction. "Could you undo the two hooks, please?"

Without thinking, Teddy reached up and used his thumb and forefinger to unfasten the hooks. Then he watched as she removed her slippers and lifted a calf to roll down a stocking.

He sighed at the perfectly formed limb. Despite its obvious scar from the bullet wound, it was still a beautiful leg. He had half a mind to lean over and kiss the spot where the skin was puckered.

Daisy turned her attention back to Teddy. "It's why I limp on occasion," she murmured as she waved to the scar. She removed the stocking before rolling down the other stocking, suppressing a grin when she noted he was watching her every move with bated breath.

Teddy blinked. "I hadn't noticed," he replied.

Well, truth be told, he *had* noticed her distinctive sway when she walked. A sway that accentuated her hips. And everything else about her.

Getting to her feet, Daisy turned and regarded Teddy for a moment. The one piece of clothing still on his body—his shirt—not only covered the evidence of his erection but also the fact that he was missing most of his right arm. "Liar," she teased.

She pushed down the sleeves of her peach and apricot gown and allowed it to fall from her shoulders and onto the floor. Then she went about undoing the tapes of her petticoats, well aware that Teddy's gaze followed her hands. "I don't suppose you can help with my stays?" she half-asked as she allowed the petticoats to drop from her hips.

Daisy turned around and presented her back to him, well aware of his barely audible gulp. The slight pressure of a thumb and forefinger undoing the fastenings had her pushing back a bit, the heat from his fingers permeating the thin fabric of her chemise. "Not bad for a one-handed man," she said as she rested her chin on her shoulder and watched as his expression of concentration aged his face. "But then, I never doubted your skills."

Teddy cleared his throat. "And what skills might you be referring to?" he asked when he had the last fastening undone.

Since he hadn't been in the company of a woman—like this—since before he had lost his arm, he wasn't sure if he had the ability to make love to a woman. *How am I supposed to hold myself up?* he had wondered on occasion.

Fencing had helped to keep his one good arm strong as well as the shoulder of the other, but what if he lost his balance? Fell on top of her? Or went tumbling over to one side? Or worse, fell entirely off the bed?

Embarrassed didn't begin to describe how he would feel. *Humiliated* might be a better word.

"Since you're a clerk at a bank, I should think you can write numbers and words," Daisy replied in answer to his query about skills. "Left-handed, no less." One of her eyebrows arched up as she turned around, the stays loosening of their own accord until their sleeves fell from her shoulders and dropped down her arms. "The Devil's hand?"

Inhaling sharply, Teddy watched as the garment fell to the floor, and then he returned his gaze to her face, trying with all his might not to stare at her now that her translucent chemise barely hid her breasts from view. The dark triangle at the apex of her thighs was even evident. "Usually, I would attempt to disabuse someone of such an idea, but at the moment, I'm inclined to let you think that," he managed to get out between labored breaths. Although he desperately wished to have his right hand again, he was rather glad to be left-handed just then.

He was fairly sure he could still perform miracles with his left hand.

Daisy allowed a wan smile as she sat on the bed next to him, resting an arm on her thigh so her chemise was pulled taut over the front of her body. The silhouettes of her nipples appeared through her chemise, and although Teddy's eyes never left hers, Daisy knew he was aware of them from the way his Adam's apple bobbed against his throat. "Would you be inclined to make me believe it?" she asked in a whisper as one of her fingers drew a line along the back of his hand where it rested on his thigh.

"Depends on how much convincing you require."

Her eyes darting to the side, Daisy allowed a grin. "I'm quite sure it won't take much," she whispered as she lay back on the bed. She used a bare foot pressed into the mattress to push herself farther into the middle, the move forcing the chemise to reveal one of her shoulders and the shape of her breasts in relief.

Sucking in a breath, Teddy regarded her for only a moment before he allowed his body to simply take over and do her bidding. Supporting himself on his stump, he discovered how easy it was to use his hand to smooth over her entire body, to cup her breasts and hold and mold them before lowering his lips to suckle the nipple that poked into the chemise. He lifted his head and was about to lean over to capture the other one when he realized he couldn't quite reach it. "Could you... turn?" he asked between labored breaths.

Daisy angled her body in his direction, one of her hands moving to the back of his head to draw it down. Inhaling as first his lips and then his tongue worried the nipple through the fine silk, she found she was impressed. The man seemed to know what to do and where to touch. Indeed, with his hand smoothing down the front of her body, his finger tips barely grazing over her mons, she felt a thrill when he gripped the bottom edge of the chemise and slowly pulled it up.

"And here I thought I would be making love to you," she whispered just as his hand moved between her thighs, two fingers sliding along her honeyed folds. Gasping when he barely touched her womanhood, she arched her back and spread her legs a bit.

"I won't object when you do," he murmured, before his lips returned to their worship of her nipples.

Grinning at his comment, Daisy was about to respond when his hand did *something* down there. She let out a yelp of surprise as a frisson of pure pleasure shot through her lower body. "Oh!" she breathed before he did it again. Sensations she hadn't experienced in a very long time had her writhing beneath him, had her mewling and moaning and speaking in Italian. "Come into me," she begged.

Teddy lifted his head to regard her before giving it a shake. "I don't think—"

"Get off the bed," Daisy ordered. She was using her hands to push herself to the edge. "Hurry," she pleaded when he didn't do her bidding.

Teddy managed to work his way off the bed, not sure what he was supposed to do until he saw how she pushed herself until she was almost sitting up. She used one hand to guide him between her bent knees, her other sliding along the back of his rigid manhood and down to his sac, cupping it as the length of him slid along her wetness.

He allowed a growl as her hands moved to his buttocks, grasping them until his manhood was firmly pressed against her quim. He watched as her back arched and her head fell back, jerked when he was aware of her legs wrapping around his hips. And then her fingers gripped his manhood, and she guided him into her wet, warm haven.

He allowed a curse when his first attempt at a thrust required he hold onto something. Despite standing on both feet, he feared he might fall over. Given the position of her legs, he wrapped his hand beneath one thigh and tried again.

Pleasure he hadn't felt in a very long time consumed him. He steadied himself to try it again. He found he didn't have to try hard—Daisy had both of her hands wrapped around his hips, her fingers pressed into his buttocks. Despite knowing what she was about to do, he still had to suppress a growl when she pulled hard at the same time her own hips thrust forward.

Teddy wished he could understand Italian. Wished he could speak it, for her murmurs sounded as erotic as she appeared just then. Wanton. Sensual. Having barely recovered conscious thought, he was lost again when she repeated her movements.

"Harder," she murmured, the word clearly spoken in English. Or perhaps he had managed to learn some Italian.

Having established a rhythm, Teddy found he could do her bidding, and so he did, pushing into her as hard as he could manage.

"Faster," she begged, the whispered word sounding as desperate as he felt just then. The added, "Please," only gave him more incentive to please her. To see to her pleasure so that she might beg him to do this again.

For he had every intention of doing this with her again.

He couldn't give the thought more than a moment's consideration when he realized how tightly she held onto him. How she had dropped her head back and arched her chest up, how she exposed her neck and the hint of her collarbones above the edge of her chemise. Another thrust, and then another, and he watched as she seemed to break apart beneath him.

Which was just as well, for his own release had him groaning with pure pleasure. That is, when he could breathe.

Had he ever felt this intense pleasure with Gertrude?

As he fell forward, his legs giving out on him so he could no longer stand, Teddy chastised himself for the odd thought and instead concentrated on just where he would end up—leaning over the bed and pressed onto Daisy, still firmly buried inside her.

Her hands moved to his back, her fingers gripping him as she mewled and struggled to breathe. Her bent legs hitched higher about his hips, her thighs gripping his.

For just a moment—or perhaps it was five—the two lay wrapped around one another, Teddy's face pressed into the space above one of her shoulders, his one hand wrapped behind the other shoulder in an effort to simply hold on while his body put itself back together.

"I must be crushing you," he whispered in dismay. But Daisy's hands only increased their hold on him.

"You're not. Truly," she said in a hoarse whisper, her lips taking purchase on one of his eyelids to leave a kiss there.

"I won't let you leave this bed," he said then, finally lifting his head to regard her from above.

"Then I shan't leave it," she replied, giving her head a shake to reinforce her words. "But I do think we'll be more comfortable if you are actually *on* the bed instead of halfway off of it."

Teddy sighed. "But then I would have to give up my hold on you," he argued, sounding ever so disappointed.

Daisy allowed a wan grin. "But only for a moment."

They would be more comfortable on the bed. Under the covers. Their heads on the pillows. "You promise you won't leave the bed?" he asked in a whisper.

Spearing her fingers into his dark blond hair, Daisy asked, "Where would I go?" She had briefly wondered what might happen if her ruse didn't work. If she hadn't been able to convince Teddy to bring her to his home. She couldn't very well seduce him in her quarters. Given the servants who lived above and the instructors who lived in the house next door, Teddy's presence would be noticed. The scandal would have her losing her position.

If this night didn't.

The thought had her wondering once again just what Teddy Streater might be thinking about her right this very moment. She was about to ask when he finally said, "Out the window—"

"What?"

"Or out the door and into a hackney."

Daisy raised herself onto her elbows, a rather difficult task given most of his body rested atop hers. "I would never," she said in a hoarse whisper. "How could you ever think such a thing?"

"You have before, have you not?" he countered.

Daisy gave a start, her brows furrowing. "Never. Why would you...?" She sat up straighter, pulling herself farther onto the bed while Teddy seemed determined to hang onto her.

"Weren't you a spy?"

The question was punctuated by how his index finger found the divot just above her knee, the place where the puckered flesh proved she'd been shot. The finger circled the wound, barely touching her skin and sending a shiver up her thigh. "How... *why* would you even ask me that?" She was sure she hadn't done or said anything specific as to what she had done for the Home Office.

Teddy gave up his hold on her and moved to settle himself in the bed. He would have pulled the downturned linens over his legs, but they were still trapped beneath Daisy's body. "How else does a woman get shot on a battlefield?" he asked as he watched her turn over and reposition herself so she was on her front, her bent legs crossed at the ankles and her breasts pressed into the mattress. Although she still wore the silk chemise, it didn't cover her naked bottom. The pale globes formed a perfect heart shape where they tapered to her waist. He briefly thought of what it might be like to have that bottom tucked against his manhood.

For an entire night.

He managed to squelch a sound not unlike a frog in heat before it left his throat.

"Three other women were shot and killed that day," she countered. "Camp followers." She hadn't known about the deaths at the time, but learned of them later whilst she recovered in a hospital in Belgium.

"But you weren't a camp follower." Teddy said the words

more in the hope she wasn't, for he feared if she was, she would have been one of those who provided sexual favors to the soldiers. He couldn't imagine her as a laundress or seamstress, a sulter or a cook. The thought of how many she might have bedded before the Battle of Ligny, or worse, Quatre Bas, had him nearly sick to his stomach.

"I was not," she agreed, realizing just then that he was imagining the worst. "It's true. I was an operative," she finally admitted. "I was one of at least four who carried messages to Wellingham."

Teddy straightened, his one arm supporting his torso as he leaned toward her. "Ligny?"

"How... how did you know?"

"I was at Quatre Bas."

Daisy hissed. "You have my deepest sympathies," she whispered, his words confirming what she had thought for a long time—that he had lost his arm in one of the last decisive battles involving Napoleon. She lifted herself onto all fours and scrambled to join him at the head of the bed, pulling on the downturned linens until they were both covered to the waist.

"You must have made it to Wellingham," Teddy whispered, rather dismayed she had positioned herself to his right rather than on his left. He wanted desperately to wrap his arm around her back and pull her close.

"I didn't," she replied. "At least, not right away. I was on my way. I could see the tents of his men off in the distance," she murmured, recalling the incident as if it had happened only a moment ago. "And then I spotted another one of our operatives. At least, I was fairly sure it was another operative. I hadn't seen him in months, but..." She sighed and dropped her face into her hands. Disbelief at the time had her discounting her initial identification of the man. But later, in hospital, she was sure there had been a traitor in their midst. Another operative with the same assignment—at least from the Foreign Office—but whose loyalties lay with the French.

"What?" Teddy asked gently. "What happened?"

"He shot me."

"By accident?"

Daisy shook her head, lifting it from her hands to regard him directly. "Oh, no. He took aim with a pistol and shot me," she whispered. "Quite deliberately. I thought I could at least make it to Lord Barrymore. He and his men weren't yet engaged," she whispered, referring to Viscount Jasper Barrymore. Another operative—Donald Truscott—had been assigned to deliver a message to him, and Daisy was quite sure Truscott had made it to Barrymore's camp. She later learned Truscott had survived despite a horrific injury to his leg, although he wasn't well enough to return to the Foreign Office when the war was over. "But I had to wait until the traitor was convinced I wasn't going anywhere—"

"Was he caught?" Teddy asked then, his sleeve-clad stump pressed behind her shoulder blade in an effort to make her understand he wanted to hold her.

Daisy understood the prompt and turned and moved her body down along his torso so her head rested into the small of his shoulder. "He was, but not then. Not until a year later, in fact. Barrymore's widow caught him trying to pinch one of the late viscount's rings from his bedchamber," she whispered.

Teddy considered the information and frowned. "Because its gemstone was particularly valuable, or because...?" he paused, realizing the ring must have held a secret. Something the traitor needed.

"It held the proof the man was a traitor. And you did not learn that from me," she warned.

Teddy wrapped his arm around her waist and pulled her closer. He knew of Viscount Barrymore, of course, but he also knew the man had died at Ligny. He had never considered the officer might have died at the hands of a traitor to the Crown. "How did you survive?"

Remembering that afternoon of excruciating pain wasn't a welcome thought just then. Daisy had learned the bullet had passed completely through her leg when she wrapped the wound with a length of fabric ripped from her petticoats. It was nearly an hour before she was sure the bleeding had stopped enough that she could move, and then she did so gingerly. "Once the shooter disappeared, I managed to crawl to a nearby road. One of the camp followers found me. Scolded me for having been in the line of fire. I was sure there wasn't a French soldier within a half-mile, but by that time, I didn't have the strength to argue."

Teddy's hold on her tightened. "You could have died," he whispered.

Daisy gave his comment a moment's thought. At the time, she hadn't considered death an option. Her mission was to deliver a sealed missive to Wellingham. Although she didn't hand it to him directly, she made sure to give it to a trusted aide. "*You* could have died," she countered.

Teddy jerked beneath her arm. "I was ready. I had nothing to live for. Nothing to come home to."

Daisy lifted her head and regarded him with a frown. "Your mother? Your wife?"

"Remember, Gertrude died while I was there," he replied. "As for Mother, well..." He sighed. "She was doing quite well for herself, it seems."

Continuing to regard him with a worried expression, Daisy sighed. "Surely there was someone you wished to see again?" she prompted. "A friend? Lord Bostwick, perhaps?"

Teddy allowed a wan grin. "Yes. Him, I suppose. He beat me in our last match on the pisté before I took my leave of England. I thought of that when my arm was blown off. Wondered how I was ever going to be able to fence well enough to get my revenge."

Daisy was aware of how the stump next to her elbow jerked in reflex to his comment. "How many times have you bested him since your return?" she asked, a slight smirk causing a dimple to appear in one cheek.

Teddy seemed to consider her question a moment before he grinned. "We're even, I believe," he replied, his expression indicating pride.

Her gaze leaving his eyes to travel down the counterpane that covered most of their bodies, Daisy allowed a sigh. "I should like to see you fence someday," she murmured, deciding it better she not admit she had watched him best the viscount just this past Monday. "I already know how well you wield a sword," she added as her hand moved to cover the growing mound at the base of his torso.

Teddy shifted beneath the covers, a growl sounding as he grinned at her. "For that, I believe you deserve a kiss, my lady," he said in a soft voice.

Daisy blinked. "I do?" His lips were nearly on hers when she placed a hand on the side of his face. "Remember. I don't know how to do this."

It was Teddy's turned to blink. "Don't know how?" he repeated, his brows furrowing. "Even though I demonstrated it quite thoroughly only a half-hour ago, you still don't know how to kiss?"

"No," she replied, although her denial wasn't the least bit convincing. "We were standing before, and now we're not. It will be different."

Teddy regarded her in disbelief. "I am not the first man you have bedded," he said, his voice betraying his jealousy. Even before this evening, he had the feeling she was quite educated in the art of making love.

"You are not, it's true. But I never allowed the men I was assigned to as a mistress to... to kiss me," she argued. "It would have been far too...too intimate."

Frowning, Teddy considered her words. "How many?" he asked, his voice so quiet she could barely hear it.

Daisy sighed. She had known that at some point, the question would be asked. She was always sure it would be her father who would put voice to the query. For some reason, telling him the truth seemed far easier than telling Theodore Streater. "Three," she managed to get out, deciding to include Alex Bradley in the count.

She watched as Teddy blinked and seemed relieved. "Is that all?" he asked, his question not sounding the least bit sarcastic.

"What were you imagining?" Daisy countered, lifting her torso so she rested on an elbow.

Despite his prone position, Teddy seemed to shrug. "Ten? Twenty? You're rather... skilled, if I may be so bold."

"Oh!" Daisy sat up and stared at him. "I'm not old enough to have been on that many missions," she said in a hoarse whisper.

"The man who first..." Teddy paused, knowing he shouldn't ask her about her former lovers. Curiosity and worry would nag him until he learned more about her, though. His heart was in danger. If he couldn't abide what she had been—who she had been with—he needed to know right then.

"The man who took my virtue?" Daisy asked in a whisper.

"I know it's none of my business—"

"He was a friend. A... a colleague. I knew my next assignment was going to require me to... to act as a mistress, and I couldn't exactly do the job if I were a virgin, so I asked him to... to help." The words came in fits and starts, partly because Daisy knew they were hard for him to hear. He almost seemed ready to silence her before she finished.

Teddy winced. "Do you still—?"

"No," Daisy replied with a shake of her head. "Truth be

told, I've only seen him once since that assignment, and I didn't even recognize him at first. He's a married man now. Married a young Greek woman while he was on a mission in the Aegean Sea."

Considering her words for a time, Teddy thought to ask more about her assignment as a mistress when Daisy said, "He taught me how to pleasure a man. Told me how a mistress would behave. He never took advantage. He could have, of course," she said in a whisper. "But I think he held me in high regard."

"Because he loved you?" Teddy asked, his voice gentle. *How could he not?* The petite brunette was beautiful and clever in ways most women would avoid. Refreshing and yet challenging, too.

Daisy blinked, the question completely unexpected. "I don't think in the way you mean," she murmured, remembering how concerned Alex Bradley had been when he learned she would be playing mistress to a marquess who wasn't well known to those at Whitehall—part of the reason he was suspected of illegal activities.

How wrong they had been!

"But… but if at some point in the future we discovered neither of us had someone in our lives, we might have settled with one another. A cottage by the sea." Daisy rolled her eyes at the image the words brought forth, blinking to stave off the tears that threatened.

The very last place she could imagine living at this point in her life was in a cottage by the sea! Alex, on the other hand, would do well living next to the water—his alter ego, a pirate by the name of Captain Crawley—spent most months on the Mediterranean and in the Channel pursuing smugglers and spies, pirates and missing persons.

"And the man for whom you were a mistress?"

Daisy sighed. "A lonely marquess who lived in the moors of Yorkshire," she said sadly. "Turned out, he was not at all involved in the smuggling that was happening on one of his beaches."

"But you... caught the guilty party?"

Regarding Teddy for a few seconds before responding, she decided he didn't need to know the particulars about that poor excuse for a man. "Yes. Finally. He was... he was hanged, along with several of his cohorts," she said.

She remembered the relief she had felt at knowing she would never run into Myles Longborn again. She never again wanted to experience the sensation of being followed. Of being watched. And not just because Myles found her attractive. She had often wondered if he suspected she was still seeing the marquess on the side. He would have killed her if she had, and he would have thought nothing of it. "And now I have left that life behind," she added.

Teddy arched an eyebrow. "Yet, you're in my bed."

Daisy started to respond and then closed her mouth. She didn't consider this time with Teddy anything like what she had done in her work as an operative. "It's not like that," she finally replied. "I'm not being paid to bed..."

"Then, why?"

Allowing a sigh, Daisy was tempted to simply roll off the bed, wrap herself in her mantle, and take her leave of his townhouse. But she knew if she did so, she would never see him again. She would have to return to her father's house. Decide to live the life of a spinster, or marry someone who had managed to avoid the marriage mart and was desperate for a wife. For someone to bear him an heir and a spare.

Probably some fat, balding viscount.

So why was she here at Teddy's house? In his bed? Telling him things she hadn't told anyone else? Not even her sister, and certainly not her father.

"I don't wish to sleep alone tonight." Or any nights.

Teddy sobered at hearing the simple explanation. He

pulled her down so her face was within an inch of his. "If I kiss you again, do you promise never to kiss another?"

Daisy stared at him, stunned by his question. "You'll have to teach me how to kiss again," she whispered.

In the next moment, Daisy wondered how it was possible a one-armed man could have her flat on her back and his body atop hers so quickly. "You're going to kiss me again, aren't you?" she whispered in awe.

"Promise me, Daisy. Promise me I'll be the only man you ever kiss."

"I cannot," she replied, her head shaking against the bed. "My father always expects a kiss on his cheek when I greet him."

"Kisses on the cheek don't count," he replied, just then wondering who her father might be.

Daisy gave a slight nod, aware her pulse had increased to the point where she could hear it in her ears. Feel it in her chest as his pressed onto it. She had never thought she would look forward to a kiss so much. Anticipation had her agreeing before she considered the ramifications. "I promise."

Teddy regarded her for only a moment more before he lowered his lips to hers. He used the tip of his tongue to separate her lips, coaxing the soft pillows apart so his could take purchase with his own.

When he finally had her lips locked with his, he touched her teeth with the tip of his tongue. Then he barely pulled away so that he could nip her lower lip and then start all over again.

When Teddy finally pulled his lips away from hers, he felt a bit of a thrill at seeing the expression of awe on her face. Her blue eyes, wide and rimmed by dark lashes, seemed unfocused for a moment or two before they cleared. "Well?" he whispered.

Daisy blinked. "It's different whilst lying down. It's not at all what I expected," she murmured.

Frowning, Teddy pushed himself up as far as he could on his stump. "What did you expect?"

Her eyes darting to the side, as if she was trying to decide how much to admit, Daisy sighed. "Wet, slobbery, mush mixed with halitosis and a fair bit of moaning, I suppose. Instead, it was rather... lovely, with just a hint of champagne. Would you think me greedy if I asked you to do it again?"

It was Teddy's turn to blink. Then he grinned. Rolled his eyes and allowed a slight chuckle. "Never greedy," he replied before he lowered his lips back down to hers.

This time, Daisy knew what to expect. Knew what to do with her lips. Her hands moved to either side of his head, her fingers spearing his dark blond hair. A moan from his throat was followed by a quick end to the kiss.

"I apologize," he said as he fell back onto the bed. "I cannot hold myself up like that for very long."

Daisy lifted herself onto one elbow, her gaze going to where his right arm ended beneath the sleeve of his shirt. She regarded the fabric-covered stump, realizing it had been shoved into the mattress to hold him up as he kissed her. She lowered her lips to it, and was about to bestow a kiss when Teddy pulled it away from her.

"Does it still hurt?" she asked, moving her lips to his shoulder. She kissed the space where a collarbone and the edge of his shirt ended.

"Not usually," he managed, rather stunned at the sensation her lips created where they touched him. "Sometimes it... tingles, though," he replied. "As if the rest of my arm and hand are still there." He gave a start when her kisses moved down the side of his chest. Despite the layer of fabric that separated her lips from his flesh, her kisses were still effective at arousing him.

"Could you see to removing your shirt, please?" she asked in a quiet voice. "It's become quite inconvenient."

Swallowing hard, Teddy moved to sit up. "Close your eyes," he said.

Daisy sighed but did his bidding. From the way the mattress moved, she knew when he lay back down. "Can I open them now?" she asked, just before she moved her face closer to his torso. Reaching out with her lips, she kissed him between two ribs, grinning when he gave a start and inhaled sharply.

"If you must," he replied on a sigh.

By the light of the room's only lit candle lamp, Daisy studied his chest as she placed a hand atop it. Crisp curls, nearly translucent, formed a thin carpet that tapered over his flat stomach. Beyond that, his manhood stood erect from its nest of dark curls.

A frisson passed through her body at the reminder of what he had done to her earlier that night. Desire swelled her breasts and hardened her nipples. Despite the fine fabric of her chemise, it felt rough as it slid over her heated skin.

When she returned her gaze to his face, she was aware of how he had kept his stump in the shirt, hiding it in the bunched up lawn. While she watched him, she pushed her body up and over his, her bent legs straddling his hips. The tips of her fingers caressed the skin just above his manhood, the frissons they created eliciting a growl from deep in his throat.

Although she considered asking permission, she instead simply impaled herself on his tumescence, earning a, "Bless you," from Teddy as his one hand moved to cup her bottom. She pulled her chemise from her body, her movements slow and deliberate. She knew he watched, and wondered if he was comparing her body to that of his late wife's. Wondered if her breasts were fuller or flatter, her belly more rounded or pronounced, her shoulders softer or more angled.

Leaning forward until her nipples touched his chest, she regarded him for a moment before kissing him on the lips.

When she finally ended the kiss, she murmured, "I think I shall never tire of doing that."

His whispered, "Neither shall I," was barely audible.

Then she lifted her bottom until his manhood was nearly free of her body. She slowly lowered it, clenching on him when his hold on her bottom tightened.

"Neither shall I," he repeated, his voice sounding strained. He hissed when the edge of a fingernail scraped over a nipple.

With her hands pressed into the mattress on either side of his chest, Daisy once again lifted her bottom, this time pushing down without a pause. From there, she established a familiar rhythm punctuated by his groans and her pulse.

When his breathing grew ragged and his hips thrust up to meet hers, she opened herself completely to him, accepting the entire length of him. He filled her near to bursting, the velvet-soft rod setting off a riot of sensations deep within her body.

Once ecstasy took her in wave after wave of pleasure, his entire body seized, his head tipped back into the pillows, and he allowed a low growl of satisfaction. A moment later, and Daisy collapsed atop him, her head burrowing into the small of his shoulder as she straightened her legs a bit. Her breathing and soft mewls matched his as she clung to his torso.

Within moments, they were both sound asleep.

*T*eddy awoke with a start, aware that bed linens had been pulled atop his body to replace the warm, feminine bundle that was now lying along his side. From the sound of her even breathing, Teddy figured Daisy was asleep. He took a deep breath, reveling in the scent of her hair where it tickled his stump. At some point, his shirt had come loose, exposing the remnant of his right arm.

Apparently Daisy hadn't seen it, for she was nestled quite tightly to that side of his body.

The thought of her sleeping in that very spot every night brought a sigh to his lips at the same time his heart clenched a bit. Given what she had been doing to him just before ecstasy took him from the here and now, he understood why he had wanted her as his mistress that day she had first appeared at the office. Why he now wanted her to be his wife.

Would she agree to such an arrangement, though?

There would be decisions to make either way. He couldn't very well keep her on as headmistress of Warwick's if she was his wife. And yet, earlier that night, he had promised he wouldn't fire her given what they were about to do.

For a moment back then, he had thought just one quick tumble would satisfy his needs for a time.

Maybe for the rest of his life.

Then she had employed her feminine wiles on him—seducing him—until he was suddenly standing before her, experiencing a style of sexual congress in which he had never before engaged.

He would have been satisfied for a time. Would have gladly returned to his life as a clerk, toiling away at a position he was well suited to hold until it was time to either die or be pensioned.

And then she had climbed atop him and possessed him in a way that had him wanting to be possessed. Wanting to do her every bidding. Wanting to satisfy her in every way possible.

At what point had his heart decided it wanted in on the action?

Teddy blinked as he stared at the ceiling.

He wanted her as a wife, but not just because she was a perfect bedmate.

I think I love her.

He swallowed and dared a glance at Daisy, a slight grin coming to his face when he remembered how she had reacted to his kiss. He may not have been her first when it came to sexual congress, but he was her first when it came to kissing.

Kissing is too intimate, she had said.

Until tonight, he wouldn't have believed such a sentiment. Now he knew better.

Sliding his body sideways until he could step off the bed, Teddy made sure Daisy was still asleep as he crept to the other side of his bedchamber. Opening the jewel box atop his dresser, he searched for the garnet ring he had found among his mother's possessions. The square cut gemstone was surrounded by diamonds, a design usually done with a sapphire. By the dim light from the candle lamp, he read the inscription on the inside of the gold band, deciding it probably meant something far different when it was bestowed on his grandmother's finger the century before.

A circle of stars, a beating heart, come what may, we'll never part.

His grandfather, an astronomer of some note, had been near death at the time he had the ring made in Chichester. He was sure his grandmother hadn't much chance to wear it. She had died within a month of her husband's death.

Palming the ring, Teddy climbed back into bed and sighed when Daisy moved an arm to rest on his chest. He carefully slid the ring onto her fourth finger and regarded the bauble for a few minutes before finally settling back into the pillows.

He fell asleep imagining how he might propose.

CHAPTER 35
AN ATTEMPT AT
RECONCILIATION

Sunday morning
Dawn cast a grayish light over the bed in which Daisy found herself nestled against Teddy. She had a thought to simply dress quickly and take her leave of his house before he awoke. Find a hackney and return to Warwick's. Act as if she had spent the night in her quarters.

Then she remembered it was Sunday.

A combination of relief and dread followed that thought. She didn't have to rush off, slink away as if she were ashamed of what they had done the night before. But she would have to face Teddy. He deserved to know the truth about her before he discovered it on his own.

"I cannot recall ever waking up to find something so beautiful in bed with me before."

Daisy inhaled, startled to see that Teddy was awake. "Where? What is it?" she asked, lifting herself onto an elbow and glancing about the bedchamber.

Teddy grinned and bestowed a kiss on her cheek. "Minx," he accused.

Sure she was blushing, Daisy sighed and dropped back down to the mattress. "Bounder," she countered.

He took one of her hands in his hand and kissed the back of it. "We need to talk," he said, deciding he would propose right then and there. After their night of wonder, he knew he wanted her as his wife. She had said she wasn't bothered by his lack of a right arm, and then she had proven it with how she had made love to him. He didn't dare allow her to leave his house until they had arrangements in place for their life together. "I've given this a good deal of thought..."

Her eyes widening in alarm, Daisy sat up and regarded him for a moment, a blanket pulled up to hide her nakedness. "You promised," she said in a hoarse whisper, her head shaking back and forth. "You promised, damn you!"

Before he understood what had her so upset, Teddy felt the sting of a slap across his cheek and saw stars before his eyes. "But..." he started to say before he realized Daisy was already out of the bed, the counterpane following her until she had it wrapped about her body. He could hear her footfalls in the carpet, hear her muttering something about broken promises. Then he heard the door to the bathing chamber slam shut at the same time he felt a thud deep in his chest.

*D*aisy stared at her reflection in a shaving mirror. For a moment, she was appalled at how wanton she appeared. Her dark hair was tousled, most of the curls having escaped their pins and the jewel-lined combs that held up her hair. Her lips were a bit swollen. But at least the slight flush on her cheeks had her looking five years younger.

A good tumble is always good for the complexion, her mother had said. Well, she'd had two of them with Theodore Streater. She wouldn't have the benefit of any others, it seemed.

The tears had already collected in the corners of her eyes, and one spilled over to slide down her cheek. Despite his promise he wouldn't fire her for what they had been about to do, his serious words—*we need to talk*—merely proved he had lied to her. He had changed his mind. He would probably require she move out of her quarters within the next day or two. She would be forced to return to Ariley Place.

A sob escaped as she wondered how she would face her father. She knew he wouldn't gloat, at least. But he would be ever so pleased she was under his roof again. He would probably have a suitor or two lined up by the end of the week. In a month, she would probably be married to some old fart of a viscount with a protruding belly and a bald pate.

Letting go of the counterpane that barely covered her body, Daisy dropped her face into her hands. Then she split her fingers to regard her reflection in the mirror again.

She blinked away another round of tears and then stepped closer to the mirror, a flash of red catching her eye.

And not the red from her teary eyes.

"What?" She held out one hand before her and regarded it as if it wasn't attached to the end of her wrist. Or, rather, regarded the ring on her fourth finger.

She stared at the huge garnet. The image wavered a moment until she could blink away another tear. Then she noticed the circle of diamonds around the blood-red gemstone. "Oh!" she cried out.

Whirling around, her attention went to the door. Or where the door would have been if it had still been closed.

Teddy stood there, in all his Greek god glory. Naked, with his right arm sliced off halfway down to what would have been an elbow, he looked as if he could have been any of a number of the marble statues in the British Museum. A perfect body in shape and form, muscle and sinew, broken by the ravages of war.

Before she could put voice to a question, he took the four steps to get to her and wrapped his one arm around her shoulders, using his hand on the back of her head to bring it to his chest.

"I think there's been a misunderstanding," he murmured. "At least, I... I hope that's all it is."

Daisy sniffled. "Me, too," she whispered.

"What did you think I meant when I said we needed to talk?" he asked, his words gentle.

"That you had decided to fire me," she replied, the words broken by a couple of sobs. She felt his chest expand beneath her cheek as he inhaled a slow breath.

"I decided no such thing," he replied. "I did decide it was time I make an honest woman of you, though. I can't very well be tumbling the headmistress of Warwick's if she's not my wife, now can I?"

Daisy gasped and pushed her head from his chest. "You wish to marry me?" she asked in awe.

"Well, you needn't act so surprised," he chided. He released his hold on her and moved to take her hand in his. "I meant for you to see this when you first woke up this morning," he murmured, referring to the ring. His thumb brushed over the backs of her fingers. "It was my grandmother's."

"It's beautiful," Daisy said before she sniffled. "And rather... large."

"That's so everyone will know you are betrothed from across a room," he teased gently. "Even if *you* didn't notice it right away."

"They'd have to be blind to not see it," she agreed, swallowing a sob. "I don't know how I missed it."

"You weren't wearing your spectacles," he countered, just before he kissed her temple.

Daisy's eyes widened before she allowed a sigh. "I don't really need to wear them. I just use them to play the part," she admitted. "At least, I didn't think I needed them." They did help when she was writing numbers in the ledgers.

"I can get you something smaller, if you prefer," he offered, referring to the ring. At first, he wasn't sure how he would pay for such an extravagance. Then he remembered he might have some of his inheritance left now that Daisy had given him the bank draft to help cover the cost of the repairs to Warwick's. "A sapphire, perhaps. Or a diamond—"

"No. It's perfect," Daisy interrupted. "Why, if it was a sapphire, it would look like everyone else's," she murmured, remembering the diamond-rimmed blue stone on her step-mother's ring. Her father had always preferred sapphires for his women.

"Does that mean... you'll marry me?"

Daisy inhaled slowly and regarded Teddy for a moment before finally giving him a nod. "I will," she replied. "But does that mean—?"

"Given my... altered circumstances, I regret to inform you that you really must continue in your position as head-mistress," he whispered. "At least until—"

"I will, you bounder," she said before kissing him. Her attempt awkward at first, she soon had her lips perfectly placed to kiss him quite thoroughly. "But I do hope you don't expect me to do needlework at night whilst you're at your men's club," she said when she came up for air.

Teddy frowned. "I don't plan to go to White's at night," he replied. "I'll merely meet George there after our fencing matches. Maybe go when I get done at the bank on occasion."

"I will see to the household ledgers, of course," she said.

"Be my guest," Teddy replied.

"It will take me some time to learn how to do menus—"

"My cook has always just seen to putting a meal on the table," he countered. "And I eat it."

Daisy blinked. "As for the servants—"

"There is a housekeeper, a cook, a scullery maid who sometimes is the laundress, and my valet," he said with a sigh. "We'll just need to find you a lady's maid. Maybe a housemaid," he offered, deciding his salary would be enough to cover the added expenses.

Allowing a nod, Daisy realized he had already considered the expenses involved in taking a wife.

Or had he meant to take a mistress?

"Tell me, Mr. Streater. Before last night, did you really intend to take a wife?"

"First, I should like you to call me Teddy. Or Theodore, if you must. And second..." He paused and took a breath. "I never believed there was a woman who would deign to marry me." He lifted his stump as if to drive home his point, the ruined arm no longer covered by a wound-up shirt sleeve. "So, yes, I thought I was in the market for a mistress."

Despite expecting the admission, Daisy still winced. "Did you... offer a contract to anyone?" she asked as she attempted to take a step backwards. She had no intention of marrying the man if he intended to employ a mistress on the side.

"No," Teddy assured her, not allowing her out of his hold. "Although I admit I asked George to help in that regard, he seemed ever so hesitant." His eyes suddenly darted sideways. "And now I think I know why," he said with an arched brow, his gaze returning to her.

"Pray tell, why?" Daisy asked.

Teddy regarded her with a wan smile. "I do believe the man is filling the role of matchmaker until his wife can find one for her new enterprise," he said with a hint of wonder.

Daisy remembered her visit to 'Finding Work for the Wounded' on Thursday. Although the shingle was above the door, there hadn't been a new employee in the office.

"And he's doing a fine job," she whispered, grinning when she remembered the viscount's words at the theatre the night before.

"Damn fine," Teddy agreed. "Excuse the curse." He pulled Daisy hard against the front of his body. "Come back to bed, won't you?" he whispered. "It's Sunday, and I do believe I have a deity I wish to worship. One I find I love with all my heart."

A frisson shot through Daisy as she considered his words. "This from a man who is the epitome of a Greek god?" she teased. "At least, the statue of one I find I'm rather in love with?"

Teddy thrilled at hearing her whispered words. "Your flattery has been noted and will earn you extra rewards, my lady," he replied with a grin. He kissed her then, slowly, until his manhood pressed hard into her belly.

"The statue has come to life," Daisy whispered, one of her brows arching as she pulled away.

"Will you come back to bed with me?" he asked.

"May we stay there all day?" she countered, hope in her voice.

Teddy chuckled. "For the rest of our lives, if you'd like," he whispered. "Or, at least until tomorrow morning. I have to be at the bank at eight o'clock."

"I have to be at Warwick's then, too," Daisy replied, her manner all business.

"Then there's no time to waste," he said as he led her back to the bed.

Or the altar, really, for he spent the rest of the day worshipping his betrothed. And she spent the rest of the day allowing him to do so.

CHAPTER 36
CLEARING UP A MISUNDERSTANDING

Monday afternoon

Having completed his work early, Teddy took his leave of the Bank of England with the intent of paying a visit at Warwick's. Although he had seen to it Daisy was safely back in her apartment just the evening prior—he had ridden with her in a hackney and then remained in the conveyance until she had disappeared into the building—he had spent the day thinking of her far more than the columns of numbers he should have been auditing.

Although she had agreed to be his wife, they hadn't set a date for a wedding. He supposed he should see about obtaining a marriage license.

A costermonger selling cut flowers caught his attention. Just about to hail a hackney, Teddy instead stopped and purchased a bouquet of daisies from the young woman. Armed with the white and yellows blooms, he made his way to the finishing school and thought to surprise Daisy with the namesake flowers.

He was the one who was surprised, though, when he discovered Daisy wasn't alone in her office.

James, Duke of Ariley, bearing a pasteboard box and a few roses, stood in front of her desk.

*A*lthough she had spent the night in her own bed, Daisy still felt a thrum throughout her body. She had forgotten how the sensations of a newly awakened body felt. How it buzzed with excitement. How it yearned for more.

She had spent most of the night and day before in Teddy's bed, sure the man had touched every inch of her body. She had probably done the same with him, although he still wasn't comfortable with her insistence at exploring his injured arm. *I never knew you with it*, she reminded him, just before her lips traced the skin from under his arm to where it ended abruptly. Despite his initial protests, Teddy gave in and simply allowed her to do with him as she pleased. It was as if they had been two parched souls finally discovering water and then nearly drowning in it.

When they came up for air, they simply held one another. While a light drizzle fell from gray skies, they made slow, quiet love. Sometimes they dozed, and sometimes they spoke of anything and everything in quiet murmurs.

The valet brought up a late breakfast, which they fed one another as they discussed their favorite flavors of ices at Gunther's and what kind of biscuits to have on hand for tea.

At five o'clock, the rain finally ceased, and so they dressed. Wearing the gown she had with her from the tea the day before, Daisy joined Teddy on a long walk to the park. Behind a hedgerow, he kissed her and formally proposed marriage. She accepted, but on the proviso she not have to give up her position.

At least until she was with child and about to give birth.

"I wish to tell Bostwick when I next meet him for a match," Teddy said as they made their way back to his townhouse. "If that's acceptable with you. And then I plan to best him quite thoroughly."

"Of course," she replied with a chuckle, retrieving her valise before joining him in a hackney for the trip to Warwick's.

$\mathcal{A}$s she reviewed the pages of estimates of the work to be done at Warwick's, Daisy transferred the numbers into a new ledger sheet. She was considering how she might use the figures in her arithmetic class when she was suddenly aware she wasn't alone.

Daisy looked up with a start to discover her father standing just inside her office door, roses in one hand and a pasteboard box in the other. "How long have you been standing there?" she asked as she quickly stood and dipped a curtsy.

"Long enough to realize I should employ you to do my books instead of the clerk who does them now," James, Duke of Ariley, stated before he stepped completely into the office. "Should you ever wish to oversee one of my properties..."

Daisy allowed a grin and gave a shake of her head. "I'm afraid I wouldn't have the time to give it the attention it deserves," she murmured with a grin.

"Forgive the interruption. I just—"

"Oh, you're forgiven, of course," Daisy said as she walked around from behind the desk and stood before him. Standing up on tiptoes, she kissed her father on his cheek and was about to take the proffered roses when Teddy appeared behind the duke. Stunned at how her body reacted—a frisson skittered through her abdomen—she allowed a brilliant smile and said, "Mr. Streater!"

But the bank clerk wasn't looking in her direction, but rather in the duke's, and his expression suggested he was not at all pleased to see the aristocrat. "Miss Albright," Teddy acknowledged with a curt nod. With another glance in the duke's direction and then a glance at the flowers he held in his gloved hand, he said, "It seems I've come at an inconvenient time." He gave a short bow, tossed the flowers in the nearby waste container, and disappeared.

Daisy furrowed a brow, rather startled Teddy would take his leave so quickly. She ran over to the waste container and fished the bouquet of daisies from it, rather heartened Teddy would bring her flowers. She turned her attention back to her father. "Well, that was rather odd," she said, her gaze going to the roses her father held. Her eyes widened when it dawned on her what Teddy had seen just then.

She had been kissing her father on his cheek.

What he must have thought!

Oh, no.

He had paid witness to the duke leaving the Bostwick's box the night before last. She had been able to explain his presence easily enough then, telling him that Ariley expected to find Viscount Bostwick.

But now? No wonder he seemed so sure she was someone's mistress!

James glanced back at the office door and angled his head as he watched Daisy's growing worry age her features—and noticed the only ring she wore on the hand that clutched the daisies.

"Isn't he your... employer?" he asked carefully, his head nodding toward her hand.

Daisy sighed. "And my betrothed," she admitted. "As of yesterday," she added, wanting to avoid the scolding he would give her for not having informed him of the fact earlier. "I was about to tell you..."

The duke arched a brow. "Then I believe there's been a misunderstanding," he offered.

"Oh!" Daisy replied, her eyes widening. She headed

toward the door, intending to go after Teddy, but her father stopped her with an outstretched arm.

"Here. These are for you," he said as he pressed the roses into her free hand. She was forced to take the box between both hands. "I'll see to this."

"Father, he doesn't know—"

"For once, Daisy, please *trust* me," James said with a sigh. "Something very similar to this happened only a month ago," he interrupted, referring to the morning his other illegitimate daughter, Diana, was to be married to Adam Comber, Viscount Breckinridge. Diana hadn't told Adam she was the daughter of a duke, either, which made for a rather awkward discussion with his son-in-law-to-be at the church. "I took care of it then, and I shall see to it now." Without waiting for a reply, he hurried out the door.

Daisy followed, the roses and box still clutched in her hands. Teddy had obviously left the building, and so had her father, given there was no one else in the hallway leading to the front door.

She hurried to that door, managing to get it open by using her elbow against the handle. But she paused when she saw that the duke and Teddy were facing one another at the edge of the pavement. There was no sign of the ducal coach, which meant Ariley had his driver park it farther down the street or around the corner. There was also no sign of a hackney or other conveyance for Teddy, which was probably the only reason he was still in front of Omega House.

Deciding to trust her father to make things right, Daisy sighed and simply stood and watched the two gentlemen as they engaged in their discussion.

"Sir, a moment of your time, please," James said as he chased after Teddy.

Allowing an exaggerated sigh, Teddy finally slowed his

steps and turned to regard the Duke of Ariley. He managed a bow before saying, "I cannot begin to compete against a duke, so I shall simply step aside and allow you—"

"Nonsense, Streater. I've seen you on the pisté. You would beat me every time," James interrupted, moving to face Teddy.

"I meant for her affections, of course," Teddy stated, not feeling the least bit of pride at hearing Ariley's assessment of his skills as a fencer. "I saw the way you looked at her. You obviously... *love* her," he managed to get out, despite the lump in his throat. Despite how his heart clenched in his chest. Despite how he just wanted to die at that moment.

James straightened, as if he'd been slapped in the face. "Indeed. I do love her. I suppose I looked like that the very first time I laid eyes on her," he agreed.

Teddy struggled to swallow, and couldn't manage a response before the duke added, "A few minutes after she was *born*. When the midwife put her into my arms, in fact."

Furrowing his brows, Teddy was about to say something about robbing the cradle, but instead simply stared at the duke, his confusion apparent.

"She's my daughter," James said quietly. "Illegitimate, yes, but I love her just as much or more as I would if she were legitimate. Her sister, too," he added with an arched eyebrow. "Her late mother was the love of my life."

Teddy blinked. "Wh... what?"

James was about to repeat himself, but instead said, "Sir, I find I must commend you, for you have managed to do what no other man on this planet has managed to do."

Still a bit confused—the duke was claiming he was Daisy's father!—Teddy gave a shake of his head. "And what might that be?"

"Get my daughter to agree to matrimony," the duke replied with a huge grin. "I saw that ring. Rather impressive bauble, I might add," he said with some awe. "It's obviously not paste."

Teddy shook his head. "It is not."

"Truth be told, I never thought I'd see the day my Daisy would agree to be a man's wife. She's been far too independent. Won't use her dowry, even though I saw to it she could have it when she was five-and-twenty."

"Dowry?" Teddy repeated, still a bit discombobulated over learning Daisy's father was the Duke of Ariley. A second later, and he remembered the bank draft she had given him after the tea. She had the funds because of her inheritance. He had just deposited the bank draft into the school's account before paying a call on Andrew S. Barton, Esquire, to draw up the papers for their partnership.

James allowed a chuckle. "Not that you need it, given you're the owner of this fine school, but I should like it very much if you lay claim to it on your wedding day."

Suddenly aware they were being watched, Teddy turned his attention to the open door where Daisy stood holding handfuls of flowers and a box, tears streaming down her face. "Oh, damn it, I think I've made her cry," he murmured.

James dared a glance in her direction before saying, "You're probably the first one to manage that, too."

Giving him a quelling glance, Teddy regarded the duke for a moment. "I would like to request permission to marry your daughter, Your Grace."

A rather indecorous guffaw sounded from the duke. "You don't need it. And trust me when I tell you this. She will respect you far more if you don't mention you asked," James responded as he turned his gaze on his oldest daughter. "It's very good to meet you," he said as he gave a nod. He was about to offer his right hand when he seemed to think better of it, and then reached out with his left instead.

Teddy shook it with his left hand, his gaze going from the duke's hand to his face. "You as well, Your Grace."

"I will leave you to it," James said with a wink before he gave Teddy a nod, turned to wave at Daisy, and then headed off down the street.

Teddy stood and stared at his betrothed for several seconds before he finally made his way to her. He thought to simply gather her into his arm and pull her close, but with her hands full, he knew it would be awkward. Instead, he gave a bow. "My apologies, my lady," he said as he approached her. "It seems I've been a jealous fool for no reason."

Daisy sniffled. "I should have t...t...told you. I almost did that night at the th...theatre. But I didn't want to lose..." Her words were stopped when Teddy's lips came down onto hers, his kiss short but sweet. He seemed oblivious to passersby who stared in alarm, or to the group of young ladies about to go into one of the classroom buildings. Just the moment before, their attention had been on the departing duke, their hands moving up to their mouths to hide them as they whispered to one another.

When he ended the kiss, Teddy regarded Daisy with a sigh. "I'll never tire of doing that, my lady," he murmured. "And I don't care who knows it."

Daisy blinked, her eyes darting left and right. She had half a mind to slap him, for there were witnesses to what he had done. When she noticed the students, eyes agog and some with their hands over their mouths, she managed a nod, not sure what else to do. Her hands were full, tears stained her cheeks, and she desperately wanted to fish her hanky from her pocket. "You might when you discover what I've done," she replied between sniffles.

Angling his head to one side, Teddy wondered at her words. He pulled a handkerchief from his topcoat pocket and dabbed at her cheeks. "Now, now. There's no need to cry. Let's go inside," he suggested. "May I help with something?"

he added, as if he just then noticed her hands were full. He held up his gloved hand.

"Could you take the box?"

Teddy extracted the small box from her tenuous grip between her fists of flowers and offered his arm. A moment later, they were back in the office regarding one another.

"I'll just find a vase for these," she said as she moved to her bedchamber door. Although she expected Teddy to stay in the office, he followed her into her apartment.

"On the one hand, I rather wish you had mentioned your relationship to Ariley," Teddy said as he made his way past her beautiful four-poster bed and the japanned dressing table and into her parlor.

When he didn't continue, Daisy turned. "And on the other?" she prompted.

Teddy shook his head. "I don't have one, you see." His words were said in such a deadpan voice, Daisy gave a start. Then, when she noticed his slight grin, she gave a sigh of relief.

"If I had told you—and I'm not sure when it would have been appropriate to even mention it, would it have made a difference? To your offering me the position of headmistress, I mean?" Daisy clarified as she placed the three roses into a small vase on a side table.

"Not then, of course," Teddy said as he once again surveyed the room that looked entirely different from when his mother had occupied the apartment. Despite the position of the doors to the building's main hallway, the bedchamber, and the small kitchen not having changed, he could hardly recognize anything else given the elegance of the furnishings and walls.

He watched as she took a seat and arranged the daisies he had brought into a glass vase on the low table in front of the settee. When she finished, she lowered her face to the blooms and inhaled, a smile forcing a dimple in one cheek before she finally turned to regard him. "And now?" she prompted, one of her hands patting the space next to her on the settee.

Teddy moved to sit with her, rather heartened at the invitation. He settled next to her, finally wrapping his left arm around her shoulders when she rested her head in the small of his shoulder. The pasteboard box still dangled from his fingers. "Perhaps it's best I didn't know, for I would have been honor-bound to ask his grace if I had his blessing to ask for your hand before I did so," he explained, remembering the duke's words of warning. When Daisy stiffened in his hold, he added, "And I have since learned I would have lost your respect had I done so."

Daisy gave her head a shake. "That's not exactly true," she hedged, about to claim her age exempted her from such consideration.

"How long have you been estranged from him?"

The question, completely unexpected, had Daisy straightening on the settee. "Estranged is a bit strong. But if you're asking how long it's been since I've lived under his roof, then, yes, it's been a long time. Eight years. I've since made my peace with him, though," she replied.

"But, why? As the daughter of a duke—"

"Illegitimate daughter," Daisy interrupted. "I was born to his mistress. Long before he ever married Helen Harrington, of course."

"Still, you could have lived a life of privilege."

"I did," she countered. "Until I was two-and-twenty." She didn't add that she was now thirty.

"You could have an aristocrat for a husband—"

"The very *last* kind of man I wish to marry," she claimed. At Teddy's look of disbelief, she added, "To have to welcome a man into my bed knowing he employs a mistress? Despite his wedding vows?"

Teddy was about to defend George Bennett-Jones, for he knew the viscount hadn't employed a mistress since his marriage to Lady Bostwick, but Daisy continued her tirade before he had a chance.

"To know he has no comprehension of what it is like for those who must work for a living? No knowledge of how the laws he passes affect those who must abide by them, since he won't be expected to follow them? To know that to him, I am merely property? A womb from which his heir and spare are to be birthed, probably while he's with his mistress?"

Frowning at her, Teddy gave a shake of his head. "Is that what Ariley did?"

Daisy blinked, realizing just then how her words might have Teddy coming to that conclusion. "No," she replied with a shake of her head. "He doesn't employ a mistress now. He... he hasn't since my mother died," she acknowledged. "He mourned her for years before he even looked at another woman." She allowed a watery grin. "He loves his duchess."

"And he wasn't married when he employed your mother?"

"No," Daisy acknowledged.

"So your poor opinion of aristocrats isn't based on your father's behavior?"

Shaking her head, Daisy said, "No. Merely on the actions of others, I suppose." She didn't add that her mother had helped to shape those opinions. Her father wasn't Lily Albright's first protector. There had been two others before a pre-university Lord James, still two decades from inheriting the Ariley dukedom, had decided he wished for Lily to be his one and only mistress. They were together for nearly nineteen years before Lily died.

"I promised you, and I say it again, I shan't take a mistress," Teddy said in a whisper. He knew Daisy was about to remark that he had better not when he added, "I think I shall have my hand full with just you. That is, if you're still of a mind to marry me."

Daisy nodded, a sob interrupting her watery smile. "I am," she agreed.

"You're sure? You seem to have an awfully poor opinion of marriage—"

"I didn't wish to marry—before now, of course," she said as she gave him a wan smile.

"Why now then?" he asked, a bit suspicious of her motives. Ever since that night—just two nights ago—when she had seduced him, he wondered at her motives.

"Hmm," she murmured as her head moved back to the small of his shoulder. "It has little to do with marriage and more to do with the man, I suppose," she said.

"The man?" Teddy repeated, his heart skipping a beat just then.

"Yes. The first man to kiss me. Other than my father, and he only ever kisses me on the cheek," she said with a grin.

"I shall remember that first kiss for the rest of our days," Teddy whispered.

"The only man besides my father to say that he loves me," she went on.

"That I do."

"The only man besides my father to whom I've ever said those words."

"The most welcome words I've heard in my entire life," Teddy said, just before he kissed the top of her head.

"The man who is going to be the father of my children."

Children? he nearly repeated, not having given a thought to that particular issue. "I'll do my best," he managed.

"Since I don't intend those children to be illegitimate, then it means we must be married."

Teddy frowned. "I was just about to say you could just be my mistress, but it would have to be a contract for life, and then we couldn't have children if they had to be legitimate," he said, a hint of sadness creeping into his voice.

"Oh, no. I'm not about to take up my mother's profession," she replied with a shake of her head.

"Thank the gods," Teddy said as he tightened his hold on her. "Besides, I don't think I could afford you."

The pasteboard box bumped against her shoulder, and Teddy was reminded he still held onto it. "By the way, you've a box to open." From the weight of it, he couldn't imagine it holding very much. Jewelry, he imagined, if only because of the flat shape of the box.

Daisy pulled it from his fingers and regarded it for a moment. "I'm always very surprised by my father's gifts," she said as she regarded the box.

"What do you think it is?"

"As an operative, I knew these to be jewelry boxes from Ludgate Hill," she replied. "Usually containing a bracelet."

"Why not a necklace?" Teddy asked.

"Too small. The necklace box would be larger by at least two inches. Heavier, too. This..." She gave the box a shake. "Doesn't feel as if it contains anything more than paper."

"Perhaps that's what it is," he replied, trying to imagine what might be hidden beneath the white lid. "Open it, my sweet, or I shall," he warned with a grin.

Daisy pulled the lid from the box, not surprised to find a folded piece of paper fitted perfectly into the square bottom. "Paper. See? I told you," she said. She plucked the parchment from the box bottom, allowing the box to drop into her lap. Unfolding the paper, her eyes widened at seeing a bank cheque made out to her name in the amount of ten-thousand pounds. "Oh!" she breathed, her brows furrowing.

Why ever would her father give her ten-thousand pounds? He had already given her an inheritance—her dowry —in a separate account at the Bank of England.

"There's another paper in the box," Teddy said, a combination of shock and uncertainty making it hard for him to breathe just then. With this kind of money, Daisy didn't have to continue in her position. With this kind of money, she might not wish to marry, either.

Daisy unfolded the square sheet and held up the note, her father's familiar script filling the small paper almost all the way to the edges.

My Dearest Daisy,

Please forgive my interference—just this once. After our discussion about the maintenance issues at your school, I wish to see to it repairs are made immediately. I shouldn't want you losing pupils because, as Lord Lancaster complained in my hearing, "A drop of water fell upon my daughter's head as she was learning to make a French knot."

Now, I've no idea what a French knot is, but it sounds rather important to a young woman's education. I shouldn't want any others to be plopped on the head by an errant raindrop and thus prevented from learning what they must.

Knowing of your attention to such details, I rather imagine you have already lined up a suitable roofer to see to the repair, but may I suggest an entire replacement? And not just for this one classroom's roof, but for all of those on the premises? I've some experience with such matters, you see, and know 'tis better to simply replace a roof. While you're at it, why not simply see to all the necessary repairs?

Remember, you promised you would visit.
Your loving father,
Ariley

*D*aisy let out a sound indicating disbelief coupled with a snort. "Did you read it?" she asked as she turned her attention back to Teddy.

He swallowed as he glanced in her direction. "I admit, I did. It's not his responsibility to pay for the repairs, though. And with your investment, we have the funds to cover all the invoices..."

His words were stopped when Daisy placed a finger on his lips. "Let him do this. Just this once," she said in a whisper. "He has tried for years to get me to take my inheritance—"

"Have you?" Teddy asked, despite her fingers still resting on his lips.

Daisy held her breath a moment. "I admit that in addition to the five-thousand pounds I gave you for my investment, I withdrew the interest. About fifty pounds, but only because I had no other income, and my account from when I was an operative was depleted," she explained, sounding almost as if she had stolen the money. "If we're careful, we'll never want for money," she whispered.

Teddy furrowed a brow. "The *interest* was fifty pounds?" he repeated. He sat back and attempted to figure how much was in her account. "You've been a wealthy woman this entire time, but instead of simply living on your inheritance, you've been... *working?*" He straightened, though, when he recalled her earlier words. Living the life of a privileged daughter of the *ton* wasn't her choice. "You're probably never going to spend your inheritance, are you?" he asked then. He could think of a dozen ways in which his townhouse could be improved, or how they might have a second Tilbury and a matched pair to pull it, or how he might have suits of clothes for six days a week and she could have a wardrobe full of beautiful gowns and all the fripperies to go with them.

Daisy regarded him with a wan smile. "I suppose we could order a Tilbury," she suggested. "Bid on a matched pair of greys at Tattersall's. Maybe modernize your townhouse a bit. But I do think we need to keep some for the children. For their inheritance."

Teddy blinked. "Children?" he repeated again.

Wondering at the odd way in which he said the word, Daisy moved a hand to her belly. "I could already be with child," she whispered.

A slow smile spread over Teddy's face as he thought about what it would be like to have a tot like David greeting him in the morning. What it would be like to toss him into the air as George did. Swing him through the air in a circle.

Then he remembered he couldn't do such a thing.

He only had one arm.

He was about to suggest they forego children when Daisy said, "I shouldn't want you tossing our babes into the air, though. Or swinging them about so their arms almost come out of their sockets."

Teddy blinked. Could she read his mind? "Did your father do that to you?"

Grinning, Daisy gave a nod. "As I recall, my sister vomited on him every time he did it to her. I've no idea how I reacted, but suffice it to say, he doesn't do it with my stepbrother or my stepsister. I don't think his duchess would allow it."

"I love you," Teddy said, just before he captured her lips in a kiss. "I've a mind to give you the rest of the day off just so I might have my way with you."

Giggling, Daisy replied, "I've a mind to let you." She suddenly sobered. "But I've a class to teach, and there are roofers—"

"Later, then," Teddy said. "I must be getting to Angelo's. I've a match with George, and I intend to skewer him."

"But, why?" she asked in alarm. "You do realize he's responsible for seeing to it we ended up together at the theatre?" she half-asked. "And all the rest."

Teddy inhaled and held his breath a moment. "True," he acknowledged. "Perhaps... perhaps I'll go easy on him."

With that, he gave her another kiss before taking his leave of Warwick's.

CHAPTER 37
INATTENTIVE WITNESSES TO
A WEDDING

Four weeks later

James, Duke of Ariley, held onto his duchess' hand as he watched his oldest daughter exchange marriage vows with the head of clerks from the Bank of England. Their witnesses, Lord and Lady Bostwick, stood off to the side, their gazes not on the bride and groom, but on each other, as if they were reliving their own marriage vows all over again.

And happily so.

He could just imagine what they would be doing when they returned to Bostwick House later that day.

As for his daughter, Daisy looked every inch the daughter-of-a-duke she was, dressed in a gown he had insisted she allow him to have made for the occasion. *Just this once*, she finally agreed, but only after he presented her with the ivory silk confection. Adorned with embroidered daisies made with pearls and row after row of satin ruches at the hem and neck, the gown was probably more appropriate for a younger bride. Once she was in the gown, she seemed to transform into the daughter she had been those few years after her mother's death.

If the front of the gown appeared crushed, it was because he had hugged her so tightly just before she joined her betrothed at the altar.

Try as he might to remain stone-faced through the ceremony, James found he couldn't when he noticed how tears streamed from Helen's eyes. "What ever is wrong?" he whispered in alarm.

Helen sniffled into a lacy handkerchief. "I always cry at weddings," she replied in a whisper interrupted by a sob.

"You didn't cry at ours," James countered in a hoarse whisper.

"That's because I was frightened out of my wits," she whispered back.

James frowned and turned to stare at his wife of over eight years. "Pray tell, why would you be frightened?" As he remembered it, she was rather willing in the marriage bed that night, but then, it hadn't been their first time together. As her betrothed, he had deflowered her well before the ceremony.

Given his age, he was determined to get a child on her as soon as possible. That it took four years was probably because he was trying too hard.

Helen allowed a shrug. "We were married in front of a huge crowd of aristocrats, if you recall. The queen was there. The prince was there. And I left Harrington House knowing the wedding cake had fallen at some time in the middle of the night. The cook was frantically trying to repair it with sugar frosting when I left for St. George's."

Blinking, James remembered the cake he had been served at the wedding breakfast. He always wondered if the person who had cut his piece did so knowing he had a sweet tooth. "Best cake I ever ate," he murmured, just as Teddy and Daisy were about to say their vows.

"As I recall, your piece was all frosting," Helen said, her breath catching in a quiet sob.

James grinned. "It was," he agreed, just before he surreptitiously kissed her. "Best cake ever."

Helen gave him a look of disbelief. "We're in church!" she whispered in a scold.

Managing a look of contrition, James turned his attention back to his daughter. "Will today's cake be just as good?" he asked.

"Better," Helen whispered, sniffling into a lace hanky. "I have assurances from the cook that it turned out perfectly."

"Hmm," the duke replied with a hint of disappointment, his gaze going to his almost son-in-law. "He's a fierce competitor on the pisté."

Helen's watery eyes widened. "I thought he was missing an arm," she argued.

"He is, but don't let that fool you, my sweeting. I've seen him skewer Bostwick on more than one occasion."

Giving him a quelling glance, Helen sniffled again. "William wanted to come today," she whispered. "He's quite taken with his older sister."

James sighed, a wan smile appearing just as his daughter completed her vows. "Smart boy, he is. Do let him come to the wedding breakfast, won't you?"

"Of course. I rather doubt he could be kept away. He's learned how to manage door handles." This last was said as one of her eyebrows arched up in warning.

Blinking, James regarded his wife for a moment—the very moment his daughter was being declared Theodore Streater's wife—with a hint of alarm.

"When was this?"

Helen allowed a teasing grin. "Sometime in the middle of the night," she replied in a whisper. "About the time you were attempting to get another child on me despite the fact that you already have," she added as her eyebrows waggled suggestively. "You didn't lock the door."

The Duke of Ariley allowed a groan before he gamely

stood up and watched Daisy and Teddy take their leave of the altar.

"Well, I suppose that means I'll have some explaining to do during the wedding breakfast," he replied. He was about to suggest they send their daughter to a nunnery, but thought better of it.

He was sure he would be as proud of Rose as he was of his other two daughters.

EPILOGUE

Four months later, on a Saturday afternoon

"What are your thoughts?" Teddy asked as he angled his head to one side.

Daisy regarded her husband with a wan smile. "My gowns are all too small, my ankles are swollen, and two of my students are most vexing," Daisy replied from where she stood to his right.

Teddy frowned, hoping he appeared appropriately sympathetic.

George had warned him this would happen.

"The modiste will deliver your new gowns on the morrow, and I shall see to massaging your feet as best I'm able when we get home," Teddy replied, rather glad he could support her ankles with his wooden arm while he massaged her feet with his hand. "I'm not sure what to do about your vexing students, though, other than to say they will no longer be your vexing students when Miss Easterly and Miss Weston take on your classes Monday."

The two new instructors had just that day moved into Alpha House, Miss Easterly having been hired from her position as a governess for an earl, and Miss Weston from an agency promising she could teach even the most left-footed young boy how to dance.

Teddy took a breath. "Now. What do you think?"

Daisy dimpled as she regarded her husband with a widening smile. "It's beautiful. They're all beautiful," she said, referring to the buildings lined up across the street from where they stood. "They look like they were built with marble. However did the colorman manage it?"

Teddy grinned, rather glad he had arranged for the brick buildings to be encased in a layer of white stucco the week before the colormen arrived to do the painting. "It is rather amazing what can be done to stucco," he agreed with a sigh. "It's paint. Merely paint made to look like marble."

Daisy's eyes widened. "I suppose it cost a fortune," she said in awe.

Teddy wasn't about to argue, but marrying a duke's daughter meant having to accept a gift of ten-thousand-pounds to help renovate an aging finishing school. That didn't mean he had to spend it all in one place, though. "Half a fortune," he replied.

Daisy rolled her eyes. "So, we have Father to thank for that," she replied, all too familiar with the expenses associated with the renovations.

She was seeing to the books, after all.

"The windows are splendid," she added with a sigh.

"Indeed," Teddy replied. "But then, they should be. They cost enough." Instead of just a few replacements here and there, the entire school had new plate glass windows.

"When will the locksmith be done?"

"He finished this morning." Teddy pulled a few keys from his waistcoat pocket and held them up. "These, my sweeting, are the keys to your apartment, your office, and Omega House," he said, not adding that he had copies for himself in his other waistcoat pocket. Although he didn't expect to have to use them, he thought they might come in handy should he wish to join his wife for tea some afternoon.

Daisy dimpled as she took the set of keys. "Did you give Mrs. Barnaby a key to her classroom?" she asked.

"Mr. Barnaby has it," Teddy replied. "He insisted on watching the entire installation." Although Charity no longer lived at Warwick's, Nicholas Barnaby saw to delivering his wife to her classroom every morning as well to escorting her home from it every afternoon. "Apparently she's bemoaning having moved out of Alpha House, though. She learned of the new carpets, and now Mr. Barnaby is having to arrange new carpets in their townhouse."

Daisy allowed a gasp. "I wonder if Mr. Jenkins will have to do the same?" she asked in dismay. Jane had married the gardener the week after regular classes ended in June, although she had returned to teach the music and art classes once school resumed.

"No doubt he will," Teddy commented.

"I never realized just how important carpets were to the comfort of a house," Daisy said with a sigh.

All the carpets in the Warwick boarding houses had been replaced during the school's closure for the summer recess. Gas lighting had been installed in all the buildings, too, including the classrooms. Some carpentry work was still scheduled in the boarding houses, but for the most part, the renovations were complete.

"What's your favorite, do you suppose?" Teddy asked.

Daisy regarded him as if he'd sprouted a second head. "Why our bedchamber, of course," she replied with a grin. "And if you don't get me there right this very minute and have your way with me—"

Teddy didn't give her a chance to finish the thought as he opened the door to their new Tillbury and helped her into it. "Home, and quickly," he called out to the driver.

Although he hadn't thought he would look forward to having children, he was certainly enjoying the time until one was born.

After that, he would be locking the doors.

George had warned him about that, too.

ABOUT THE AUTHOR

A self-described nerd and lover of science, Linda Rae spent many years as a published technical writer specializing in 3D graphics workstations, software and 3D animation (her movie credits include SHREK and SHREK 2). An interest in genealogy led to years of research on the Regency era and a desire to write fiction based in that time.

A fan of action-adventure movies, she can frequently be found at the local cinema. Although she no longer has any tropical fish, she does follow the San Jose Sharks. She makes her home in Cody, Wyoming.

For more information:
www.lindaraesande.com
Sign up for Linda Rae's newsletter:
Regency Romance with a Twist

www.ingramcontent.com/pod-product-compliance
Lightning Source LLC
Chambersburg PA
CBHW030554170726
48283CB00002B/315